DAVENPORT MACHINERY

Using Intelligence, Grit, and Hard Work to
Build an Empire

by Arthur C. Eastly

4TH
FLOOR
PRESS

www.4thfloorpress.com

ISBN 978-1-988993-38-6
eISBN 978-1-988993-39-3

Published by 4th Floor Press, Inc.
www.4thfloorpress.com
1st Printing 2020
Cover Image: iStock Photo

AND NOW:

DAVENPORT MACHINERY

**Using Intelligence, Grit, and Hard Work to
Build an Empire**

Chapter 1

Mary Blakerly walked along the farms driveway until she reached the county road where she stood to wait. It was the first day for Casper to attend the two story school which they had driven past in the town of DeWitt, Iowa, in far eastern Iowa along the Mississippi River. DeWitt was just under five miles north of the farm where all children in the Blakerly family had gone to school for three generations. She had worried off and on all day about Casper, a quiet, almost shy boy, but smart and very good with mechanical things. The boy loved to work in the farm shop with his dad Jeff and had started by toddling around getting tools needed for repair jobs when he was barely walking and not very steady on his feet. Now, Casper was six years old and had bravely climbed aboard the school bus at seven in the morning. Jeff and Mary Blakerly were standing on the side of the road when the school bus pulled to a stop and the door opened. Jeff waved to Paul Johansguard, the school bus driver, and called, "Good morning, Paul, another nice day." Paul smiled and waved back. Both parents waved goodbye to their son as the bus began to move and Casper's little head was visible in the bottom of a window. His parents had explained to Casper what the bus would be like and what he would find when he arrived at the school. The biggest problem for Casper would probably be the large herd of other children, most of whom would be older and bigger and stronger than he was. DeWitt had a population of some five thousand people plus all the farm kids from the surrounding area.

Jeff Blakerly was a quiet, hardworking man who loved the farm, produced very good crops, raised a herd of cattle, and was content doing that; he seldom showed much interest in socializing with people off the farm. When visitors came, he was always friendly and courteous and chatted with them but Mary had always recognized his silent sigh of relief when the company left. He liked to be left alone, except of course for Casper. For six years now, he had spent uncounted hours with his son, reading books to him, talking, walking around the farm, leaning on corral rails to watch any cattle that were in from the pasture and best of all working in the farm shop where all the equipment was repaired and kept in top shape. Each year, Casper had grown more helpful and this past summer, he had been allowed to paint a cultivator for his dad. A job he worked at carefully for several days while Jeff was out in the fields baling hay for the coming winter. Sounds of a bus coming along the road alerted Mary and she stood up straight to wait for her son.

Mr. Johansguard stopped the bus with the entry way right in front of Mary and opened the door. Mary was looking up over the steps at the driver. She raised one hand, smiled at him, and was about to speak when Casper walked onto the steps carrying his lunch pail and started down. Mary strained to stop herself from rushing forward. Casper jumped off the bottom step and ran to his mother. She went down on one knee so he could hug her. They were still hugging when the bus drove away.

Casper held her hand as they walked to the house. "Was the lunch I made for you okay at noon break?"

"Yes, Mother, except there was too much for me to eat all of it. I am still a little boy, not big like my dad."

"I didn't want you to go hungry; tomorrow you will get a smaller lunch."

"A smaller lunch will be better." After a few more steps, he asked, "What is Dad doing?"

"He is hauling in hay bales and stacking them in the hay shed. At noon, he told me it will be full sometime tomorrow."

Casper looked up at her. "All those hay bales are in the shed with no rain falling on them. Dad will be happy. Did Dad say how many will have to be stacked out in the open?"

"He didn't say anything about that, Casper. Why don't you ask him when we eat dinner?"

Casper held the mudroom door open for his mother to enter and then followed, stating, "Got to get my clothes changed so I can walk over to the hay shed." From the kitchen, Mary watched him disappear up the stairs to his bedroom. The boy when he came down the stairs was dressed the way she was used to seeing him as he hurried past to the mudroom to put on his leather boots. Mary watched Casper stick his head into a wide-brimmed straw hat, pick up a pair of gloves, and head off across the farmyard to where the hay shed was located alongside the corrals. Mary smiled to herself. *'Calling it a hay shed is very misleading, it is a tall pole building with a dark green metal roof and bright red metal siding on three sides to keep out wind, rain, and snow and provide high quality feed hay to the cattle.'*

Over the next few days, Mary recognized that Casper wasn't happy going to school and wasting his time when there were so many things to do on the farm. He hadn't said anything, at least not to her, and she wondered if he was talking to his father. Two weeks later, she started to notice a change in him. The first sign was when Casper told his mother she didn't need to waste her time walking out to meet the bus. For three days, she watched through a bedroom window as Casper stepped off the bus and walked at a good pace to the house.

Dinner was almost over when Casper asked his father, "Dad, do you know a farmer by the name of Simpson from over east a couple of miles?"

Jeff's eyes twinkled as he looked at his son. "Expect so, son. Sold James Simpson six yearling heifers back about two years ago.

Why are you asking about James?"

Casper smiled. "He has a son in my grade at school and we ride the same bus. Lockley said his dad was farming same as you. We sit side by side on the bus."

"Sounds good to me. Do you think this Lockley will make a good school friend for you?"

"We are both farm boys. When I told him you were hauling hay bales and had filled the shed right to the roof, he told me his dad was doing the same. We have things we can talk about."

"Having things to talk about is important, sounds to me like you have made a friend who is much like you and knows many of the same things from living on a farm. A man doesn't make many good friends during his life. You get to know a lot of different people, but they are acquaintances. A friend is someone special that comes along rarely and sometimes helps you with a problem and at other times needs your help. It would be nice if you and Lockley stayed friends for a long time."

"Only met Lockley last week, guess we will find out as time passes."

"Good observation, son, as time passes you will find out. Of course, I need your help here on the farm and can't be having you running off visiting."

Casper laughed. "Lockley lives too darn far away for me to go visiting. Besides, I like working with my dad."

Mary had listened closely to the men talking and now decided to interrupt. "While you men were lying in the shade this morning, I was busy baking a pie. Do you fellas want a slice?"

Casper grinned. "Expect so, Mom. Dad will want a quarter of the pie and give me half as much." They watched as Mary brought the pie to the table and went to the cupboard for plates and a large knife. She cut the deep-dish apple pie in quarters and placed a large piece on a plate which she handed to Jeff. It looked moist and full of apple slices and there was brown cinnamon spread on the top of the crust. Casper licked his lips as his mother cut one quarter in half and scooped a piece onto a plate and held it out to him. "Thanks, Mom! Sure does look good." Neither man picked up a fork until Mary had her slice of pie in front of her, then they dug in.

Half of Casper's pie was eaten when he looked over at his mother. "This is good pie, why I do declare it is the best pie you have ever made. It has lots of flavor, is juicy, and those apples we grew are in top form." Everyone laughed and continued to enjoy the pie. When dinner was over Jeff sat down with the latest edition of the DeWitt Observer to see what was going on in the area while Casper helped his mother clean up the kitchen.

*　*　*

Winter was drawing near with fewer hours of daylight bringing lower temperatures, and today it was windy and spitting rain. Saturdays were when Mary Blakerly went to town to buy groceries and other needed supplies for the coming week and she was happy to have gone early in the day. Now, she had dinner ready and her husband was in the house washed up to eat. It was six o'clock and Mary decided to go and look around the yard for Casper. He would probably be busy doing some project, unaware of the time of day. Starting across the yard, Mary found the wind annoying and decided to go to the farm shop first. It wasn't likely Casper would be out of doors on a day like this. She opened the shop door and the wind blew it closed behind her with a loud bang. She saw Casper's head come up from what he was working on. Mary walked over and stood looking at Casper's metal wagon which he used to haul tools and other items around the farmyard. The wagon was upside down and all four wheels were off. "What in the world happened to your wagon, Casper?"

"Winter is coming close, so I figured to grease the axles so the wagon will work well in cold weather. Don't want it to be frozen up when I need it."

Mary smiled. "Very smart, Casper. Can you stop now and come to the house for dinner?"

"Oh sure, Mom. I can finish greasing the wheels tomorrow." Casper grabbed a cotton rag and wiped his hands to remove the grease and dirt. "Where's Dad?"

"Your father is in the house all washed up and waiting for his dinner. Please hurry so we don't delay him too long." Casper picked up his jacket and stuck his arms into the sleeves. He was zipping up the front as they walked to the door. "It has been a nasty day out there, son."

"It has been a great day to be inside the workshop." Casper smiled and opened the porch door for his mother. He had to hold the door tight until they were both inside and then the wind slammed it shut. "Whew, that wind is sure blowing; may not be a good night."

Mary listened as the two men ate dinner and discussed the weather. Casper told his dad what he was doing to his wagon and his dad congratulated him for thinking about keeping the wagon in top shape. Mary loved to sit and listen as the two men discussed many things and marveled that Jeff always treated Casper as though he was full grown, not a young son.

The years went by and Casper did well at school and found many things to do on the farm. Mary had been called to the school several times because of fights Casper got into, always with larger or older town boys. The principal told her as near as the teachers could tell, Casper hadn't started any of the fights but he was stubborn and wouldn't back down from the larger boys. When a fight started, Casper used his muscle strength and work-hardened hands to hit the opponents hard, always going for the nose. Bleeding noses had a way of ending fights, although Casper often walked away with bruises and cuts. He had never mentioned the fights to his mother, and she was told he never complained or blamed the other boys. He seemed to want to be left alone but wouldn't back down for anyone. Mary discussed these fights with her husband, and Jeff advised her to leave things alone until Casper spoke of his troubles. He never did.

At ten years of age, he was learning to weld with the acetylene torch, running beads to join two pieces of steel, and practicing cutting off bars and pipes. After much practice, he became very good. Using the torch, the first project he tackled was his father's old bicycle. He hauled it out of a storage shed and started taking it apart to make sure everything worked properly. Jeff went to the shop to have a look and was surprised to find Casper had the bike in good shape. They turned the pedals to drive the rear wheel into rotation and the steering seemed to be working smoothly. Jeff pointed at the tires. "Both of these tires seem to be in poor condition, they look cracked on the sides and there are places where the rubber has rotted. We best drive into town and buy new tires and tubes for this machine and while we are at it should replace the drive chain. When I was a young fella, I put a lot of miles on this bike."

The two men walked to the house and asked Mary if she wanted to ride to DeWitt with them. The farm was on the north side of Wapsipinicon Creek which flowed into the Mississippi River. The drive to the small town of DeWitt was just over four miles. Jeff drove the pickup out of the farmyard with Mary sitting in the middle and Casper sitting beside the passenger door. When they arrived at the bicycle store, Jeff carried the drive chain and Casper carried the two wheels while Mary held the door open. The store owner saw them coming and walked around the end of his counter. "Good morning, folks. Is there something I can help you with?"

Casper was leaning on both wheels and answered. "Yes, sir, we need new balloon tires and tubes for these two wheels."

The store owner got down on one knee and inspected the wheels. "From the looks of these tires, it has been some time since these wheels have made any miles."

"Yes, sir, these wheels are off my dad's old bicycle." Casper grinned. "I have been restoring the bike and with new tires, it will be ready to go."

The owner ran his hands over the spokes of one wheel. "Well, son, we can put new tires and tubes on your wheels and there are some of these spokes that need to be adjusted. We will do that for you also. I best write up a work order so no mistakes are made." He looked at a tire and found the size numbers. Back behind the counter, he pulled out a work order and started writing down the tire size and mentioned the spoke adjustment. Jeff put the chain on the counter. The store owner asked, "Need a new drive chain for the bike?"

Casper answered, "Yes, sir."

"Take a couple of hours for us to do the work. Ten o'clock now so around noon the wheels will be ready."

Casper smiled. "Thank you, sir. We will come back to pick up our wheels."

Walking back to the truck, Jeff asked his wife, "You got any shopping you need to do while we're in town?"

"There are a few things we can use if you men will drive me over to the grocery store." They climbed into the truck and Jeff started the motor. When they arrived at Mary's favorite store, he pulled into a parking space.

"Are you guys coming with me?"

Jeff grinned at her. "There's a comfortable-looking bench over there in the shade. You go ahead and get the items you need, and we will be sitting there catching up on our rest." The two men stood by the truck and watched Mary enter the store before they walked over to the bench and sat down. Jeff commented, "A fella can feel how much cooler the air is when you get in the shade."

"Why is that, Dad?"

"Good question, Casper." There was a pause as his father thought about it. "In my mind, it seems it's because when you are in the sunlight all those rays hitting you heat up your clothes and body. Here in the shade, there are no sun rays shining on us, so we don't get heated up the same way. Besides, sitting here a fella can relax and slow down and as a consequence, our bodies aren't generating heat like they do when we are working." There was silence for a few minutes and Jeff knew Casper would be thinking about what he had heard. A blue Chevrolet car parked two spaces away from the Ford half-ton and Jeff recognized Mrs. Simpson as the driver. As she exited the car, he stood up and smiled at her. From the passenger door, her son Lockley appeared, and Jeff used his left foot to touch Casper's leg. Casper's head turned to look up at his dad and then his eyes went to where Jeff was looking. He saw Lockley and jumped to his feet. "Hi Lockley! What are you doing in town the same time as me?" Lockley ran over to the bench and the two boys began talking excitedly.

Jeff walked over to the car. "How are you today, Andrea?"

"Everything is fine with the Simpsons; we are all busy with the farm work and before long it will be haying season once again."

"Yes, it will be. How's James keeping?"

"He's doing well and went out to check on the cattle this morning. Is Mary in the store?"

"Yes, she is. There were items she wanted to purchase and has only been in the store for a few minutes."

"Sounds good, Jeff. I'll look for her and we can catch up on all the gossip before she leaves. Nice to see you again. Are you okay with Lockley staying here with your son?" Jeff nodded and Andrea hurried away to do her shopping. The boys were talking and laughing, and Jeff sat down on the bench again, his mind now on haying. The hay was growing thick and tall and the first cut would be ready to start very soon. He expected this summer he would be able to put up two cuttings of hay. If he did, the second cut would be stacked out in the pasture where it could be fed to the cattle starting in the fall and hay from the first cut kept over. With luck he would have hay to sell to neighbors before the winter was over.

The squeal of shopping cart wheels caused him to look and there was Mary coming with her groceries. He hurried to the half-ton and lifted the shopping bags into the truck box for her. Jeff leaned on a fender as Mary returned the cart. She came out of the store walking beside Andrea who was carrying two bags of groceries. They were laughing about something. Andrea put the bags in her backseat, closed the car door, said something to Mary and put two fingers in her mouth. A loud shrill whistle came out which could most likely be heard for several blocks. Jeff's head turned to look at the boys. They stopped what they were doing and had startled looks on their faces. Lockley laughed and told Casper, "Mom is ready to go. Hope we can get together again this summer." Both boys hurried to their parents.

When they were seated in the truck, Jeff looked at his watch. "Will be another hour before the wheels are ready, what do you think of going someplace for lunch while we wait?" Mary nodded. Jeff looked at Casper. "What would you like for lunch son?"

Casper grinned. "It has been some time since I've had a cheeseburger."

"Cheeseburger it is. Where do you suppose the nearest place to get burgers would be?"

10

Mary smiled. "I remember seeing a burger shop just this side of the bicycle store, why don't we drive over there?"

"Good idea, Mary, and it will put us close to the wheels we have to pick up." Jeff started the truck and backed out. He drove to the burger shop and parked again.

Casper led the way and held the door open for his parents. Once inside, he looked up at his mother and asked, "Mom, can you eat half of my cheeseburger?" Mary smiled at him and nodded. There were two people lined up in front of them, so they waited in the line. When their turn came, Casper told the clerk he wanted a well-done cheeseburger and a root beer. Jeff ordered the same cheeseburger and two cups of black coffee. Mary gathered up napkins, knives and forks, packets of ketchup, and asked for an empty paper plate. When they were seated, Mary used a knife to cut Casper's cheeseburger in half while he opened a packet of ketchup and squeezed the contents into a pile beside the fries. Jeff kept an eye on his son as he tackled the food with gusto and looked at his mother whose eyes were sparkling with pleasure. He smiled at her and took his first bite of burger. A few minutes later, when Jeff had finished his food, the other two were still working on theirs. The thick burgers were hard to fit into their smaller mouths. He sipped coffee from his cup and waited. When the food was gone, there were only fries left so Mary asked, "You want to take these fries home with us?" Casper nodded. "While I clean off this table, you go to the bathroom and wash your face and hands." Mary gathered the fries into a container and handed it to Jeff before she picked up the papers and plastic silverware and deposited them in the trash barrel. They stood by the exit door and waited for their son.

The wheels were ready, and the owner came from behind his counter and showed Casper the oil tube sticking out of the back-wheel hub. "We oiled your drive axle for you but remember to put in a drop of oil from time to time. All your spokes were checked and several of them tightened. It is important to have them at the same tension to keep the wheel rim from warping. When you're riding, have a look at the wheels once in a while to check for any wobble and make sure you correct it." Jeff went to the counter to pay the bill while Casper made three trips to the truck, taking out the bike parts, a few minutes later they were into the drive home.

Mary was in the midst of a major house cleaning and returned to it. Jeff drove away in the pickup to check on the growth progress of his grain crops. Casper went to the shop and started putting the wheels on the bike. Late in the afternoon, he was installing the drive chain and wrestling to get the rear wheel in the correct place to keep the chain tight but not over tight. Finally, he had the bike ready for riding and wheeled it outside. He quickly found his legs were too short to reach the pedals while straddling the crossbar. Casper studied the bike and walked around it several times, finally deciding he would have to put one leg under the bar and lean the bike at an angle to be able to pedal it. He fell several times before he succeeded in riding in a circle in front of the shop. He felt happy to be riding the bike, but it wasn't very comfortable. Sitting on the bench outside the shop door, he studied the bike and decided he would cut the crossbar off. Then, the thought hit him. If I cut the tube off at the back-end and bend it down and then weld in a piece of tube, it will still give strength to the bike. In a hurry, Casper wheeled the bike into the shop and removed the leather seat. He measured out two inches from the upright to leave a stub of pipe under the seat. He went to the tool drawers and found the pipe-cutter which he was lugging over to the bike when the dinner gong rang out several times. Casper put the pipe-cutter on the cement floor alongside the bike, turned out the lights, and went out the door. His stomach felt ready for dinner.

The next morning, Casper hit the shop early, right after having finished his breakfast, and sized up the bike once again. The pipe-cutter had a handle too long to go over the pedal hub so

Casper had to use the ratchet feature of the cutter and slowly worked the cutting knife deeper into the steel tube. When the tube parted, he removed the pipe-cutter and had a look at the cut. A little rough, still he felt it was not a bad job. In his head, he had a picture of how the tube should be bent down and then back to be rejoined with the upright that had the seat on top of it. He went out to the pile of old parts and came back with a foot-long chunk of heavy-walled four-inch diameter pipe to use for a bending die. Casper didn't want to bend the main bike frame so he spent almost two hours rigging up and bracing everything to avoid that. Now, he was ready and stood back to look at the setup. The four-inch diameter pipe was on a two-inch pipe firmly held in the bench vice and the bottom of the frame where the pedals were located was sitting on a sturdy chuck of oak firewood so the rest of the bike was not going to feel the bending when it took place. With welders chalk, he had marked where straight up was on the bar so when he heated it he had a guide. He was ready so he pulled out the hoses from the acetylene tank and put a heating nozzle on in place of the cutting head. Instead of the welding goggles, Casper decided to wear the welding helmet for more protection. His dad always told him to be careful. With his gloves on, he lit the torch and adjusted the flame for maximum heat. He watched the tube closely as he carefully heated it from the chalk mark out away from the four-inch mold pipe. When the pipe was glowing red, he turned off the torch and grabbed hold of the two-inch pipe he had for leverage and slid it along the tubing almost up to where he had heated it. As he leaned on the pipe, he watched it slowly bend down and kept going until it was pointing at his mark on the bike frame. He continued to hold it in place as the tubing cooled and lost its red color. A few minutes later, he removed his bending pipe and looked closely at the bend. It seemed to be okay, but he would have to give it time to cool off. He took off his gloves, helmet, and the old well-worn welding jacket he always used when welding. Suddenly, he felt hot and realized his body had generated heat that was trapped in the jacket. It was time for a rest to cool off and get a drink, so he checked everything to avoid a fire and walked to the house.

Later in the afternoon, Mary saw Casper trying to ride the bike. He fell down twice while she watched through the kitchen window. She put on her garden hat and a pair of gloves and went out to help. With Mary holding the bicycle up, Casper concentrated on learning to balance, pedal, and steer the bike and Mary kept him from falling over. In less than a half-hour, he was on his own, riding in circles between the house and the shop. Mary stood in the center of the circle and watched him steadily improve. Finally, she waved at him and walked back to the house. She felt pride in her son for restoring the bike and remodeling it so he could ride with his short legs and wondered what if anything Jeff would say to their son. He would approve but often he was reluctant to say much in terms of words.

At dinner that evening Jeff announced, "Time to pay the land taxes and in the morning I am going to drive over to Clinton, the County Seat, to pay them. Would you two care to go with me?"

Casper replied, "I have never been to Clinton. Yes I will go with you."

Mary smiled at her husband and nodded her head.

In Clinton, the County Courthouse was built of brick and stone and reminded Casper of Gothic buildings he had seen in books. Jeff paid his taxes and took the time to drive his family around to look at the town. Clinton has some twenty-six thousand citizens, a high percentage of the people living in the county because the rest of the county was mostly occupied by farmers.

Chapter 2

Mary sat on a bench in the shop watching her son as he wrestled with his latest project. He was fifteen years old now and as tall as his mother and soon he would catch up and pass his father. She watched Casper pick up a heavy welder and place it on a workbench displaying his strong physical strength which for some reason caused her mind to flashback to a phone call from the high school principal during Casper's first month at the school. He was young in years but already growing, physically strong, and very well coordinated from the many hours he spent working with tools.

The principal of the high school started by explaining why he was calling and Mary stood holding the phone in semi-shock as she listened. "Every school has a variety of students, although most are basically average. Your son is far above average in intelligence so we will be keeping a close watch on him. We also have two second-year football players who are big and strong and frankly not very academically inclined. They have been bullying other students. As near as we can determine, they were trying to convince Casper to join the football team and he had several times told them no, he wasn't interested. This noon hour, they decided to give him a beating, no doubt to demonstrate how strong they are. One student grabbed your son from behind and the second was preparing to punch Casper when he reacted. We have heard several versions but, basically, your son kicked the puncher in the groin which of course caused him to collapse on the floor. Next, he threw the other bully over his head and as he rushed in to hit that one, his knee solidly thumped the first bully under the chin and knocked him unconscious. The bully who held him from behind received a solid right-hand fist on his nose and he bled all over the cafeteria floor. In fact, his nose had been broken."

Mary stammered into the phone, "Is Casper okay, was he hurt?"

"He is fine, Mrs. Blakerly. After we got the two bullies off to the school doctor, I sat with your son and asked him what had happened. He told me it was just a little roughhousing among the students and they were upset because he didn't want to play football. He didn't suggest any complaints to me and ate his lunch while we were talking. May I suggest if you learn anything more from your son, please phone me with the details." Mary smiled at the memory. The principal had told her about the football coach. "Our coach of football has already been in to see me and asked if there is any way to persuade your son to come out for the team. The way he handled the two bullies impressed him and I predict there will be more attempts to lure Casper out to play football."

"My son has never shown any interest in sports and it is unlikely he would join the team."

"We know the school has a very special student in Casper and will see that no one becomes unreasonable with him. Sorry to have bothered you but I wanted you to know what happened. Goodbye, Mrs. Blakerly."

Mary put on a jacket and rushed out to the Ford half-ton and drove to the field to talk to Jeff. He listened to her silently as she related the story before she asked, "What should we do when our son comes home from school?"

Jeff smiled at her. "When he tells us what happened, we might tell him to be careful and not cause problems for other students." At dinner that evening, Casper didn't say a word about the altercation at school. His parents waited but he gave them nothing to respond to and often since then she had thought that might have been deliberate on his part. As far as Casper knew, they had never heard a word about the fight.

Mary refocused on what Casper was doing. He had taken his Dad with him and gone to a farm auction sale and came home with two old electric welders. One was still working and the second wasn't but Casper had been happy. He had acquired the parts needed to build an electric welder for the farm shop. He had studied electric welders in the public library and even gone to a welder dealer and brought home technical literature put out by one of the large manufacturers. Over the years, he had built so many toys, tools, and done restorations that she had no reason to doubt his welder would work well and improve the repair jobs the men were often doing.

Casper had skipped two grades in the public-school system and would graduate from high school next spring. He had his mind set on going to university to study mechanical engineering and was already working his way through many of the first and second-year texts. His grades had always been superb, especially in math and science, but saying that wasn't meant to take away from his performance in English and social science. If he had an academic weakness, it had to be his lack of any interest in athletics. He tended to be like his father, remaining silent and seeming hesitant about speaking up when in a social setting. She had tried to loosen Casper up but finally realized he wasn't interested. The same seemed to be the case when it came to girls. For a while, she had blamed it on his being in grades with students two years older than he was but she had noted he joined the conversations when it was about a subject that interested him. When it was just social chit chat, he clammed up and she often wondered what his mind was working on during those intervals. He had gone to a few birthday parties but soon started making excuses, he wasn't interested. The exception was for Lockley Simpson's birthday; he always had time for that day, even though Lockley was two grades behind now. Lockley was a good solid normal student; the exception was Casper who was very intelligent and quickly mastered whatever a class was about. Mary smiled. *'Must be hell having a student as smart as Casper in your classroom. Many of his teachers must have had fits over the years.'*

It was time for her to prepare dinner, so she stood up and walked to the door where she paused to check on Casper. He hadn't even noticed she was leaving. Mary went out and closed the door softly before she walked to the house.

Three days later, the electric welder was up and running and Casper had built a sturdy metal cabinet to house it in. The cabinet had wheels to allow movement around the shop or even into the back of a pickup. Mary came to the shop to have a look at it and found Casper spray-painting the cabinet with black machinery paint. As she sat in a chair watching, it seemed to her that what Casper had built was as presentable as the commercial welders on sale in retail outlets. He could build and sell welders if he wanted to. When he finished painting, Casper cleaned up and put every-thing away. The paint would need to dry overnight before he could put it all together. The cabinet had round and oblong holes that Casper had cut where the gauges and switches would be mounted and there were bins to store welding rods and a place to hang the welding cables. He had even put on a pipe handle to grab hold of when wheeling the welder around. His construction of tools and equipment had steadily improved over the years. During the com-ing winter, he would fill out the application forms to attend univer-sity. She was proud of her son being a top-notch student but knew it would be lonely for her when he was away studying to become a mechanical engineer. Well, he would come home on the week-ends, probably with a sack full of dirty clothes to be washed. Mary would be happy to wash his clothes as long as he came home.

Senior year in high school went by quickly and Casper was happy. He was driving tractor and helping his dad with the farm work, fixing broken-down machines, and all his spare time was spent out in the shop. When a letter arrived from the high school with a list of the graduating students, Mary talked to Casper about attending graduation. She wondered if he was going to invite a girl to go with him. Casper had looked at her with amazement and announced, "Not going to the graduation; it doesn't interest me. I expect they will send my marks and diploma." Mary fretted over this statement for several days and then decided to phone the high school and talk to the secretary. She dialed the phone and waited for three rings before the secretary answered. "Hello, Mrs. Mc-Clung, this is Mary Blakerly calling, Casper Blakerly is my son."

"Thank you for calling, Mrs. Blakerly. There are several items on my list that I need to talk to you about. Casper is the most brilliant student we have ever had and we want to honor him at the graduation." Mary was shocked at what she was hearing and didn't know what to say. "Mrs. Blakerly, are you still there?" She listened for a moment then asked again, "Mrs. Blakerly?"

"I am standing here and shocked. Do you have time for me to drive to the school and talk to you?"

"Of course, Mrs. Blakerly, when do you want to come in?"

"I will leave the farm in a few minutes and probably be at the school in about an hour."

"Very well Mrs. Blakerly. I will be waiting for you."

Mary stood there holding the phone for a minute before she hung up. What kind of mess was she in now? The school wanted to honor her son and he wasn't interested in going to the graduation. *'How in heaven's sake was she going to solve this dilemma?'* Mary hurried to the bathroom and brushed her hair into shape. In the bedroom she applied makeup and lipstick before looking in the closet for one of her better dresses. When her dress shoes came down the stairs to the ground floor, she was dressed as well as any of the city woman and had her purse hanging from her left shoulder. Mary stopped to look in a hall mirror and smiled. Not often she got out of her jeans, not many of her friends would recognize her today. Then, the thought hit her. *'Oh, I hope Casper doesn't see me coming to his school.'*

Mary crossed the kitchen and went out the back door on her way to the garage to get the car. Jeff drove into the yard and got out of the truck. He looked at her in amazement. "You are all dressed up, Mary. Where in the world are you going?"

She marched up to him and spun around. "How do I look?"

"Why now, if I wasn't already married, I do believe you'd be my first choice."

"Thank you, Mr. Blakerly. I am on my way to the high school to talk to the lady about the graduation. Your son says he doesn't plan to attend the ceremony. This evening, I will be lecturing you two men on the proper way to behave and I fully expect my husband to support me no matter what he thinks on the issue. Now, you go and open the garage door for me."

Jeff opened the garage door and stood back out of the way. Mary backed out, waved at him, and drove away. She drove into the staff parking lot and found a shady spot under a large elm tree, locked up her car, and walked to the school building. The receptionist showed Mrs. Blakerly to Mrs. McClung's office who looked up and smiled. "Please come in and have a seat, Mrs. Blakerly."

"Thank you and please call me Mary. My son, Caspar, told me he isn't interested in attending the graduation ceremony. I find it disappointing and wanted to find out what will be going on. Really, I am looking for things that might catch his interest. You mentioned on the phone that you had a list of items to talk to me about."

"You are correct, Mary. First, let me tell you that you have raised an exceptional student, the brightest to ever attend this high school. You must be very proud of your son."

"Yes, we are. His father and I discovered when he was very young that he was smart as a whip. As time went by, we just got out of the way and let him go. We watched and made suggestions and helped when we could. If I sat here and told you all the things he has done building toys, rebuilding bikes, and creating welders, helping to repair and improve farm machinery, you wouldn't believe me. He started to read long before he started school and is busy now reading second-year mechanical engineering textbooks. To be honest with you, we have never gone on holiday. All our spare money goes to support Casper, buy books, and materials for him to use on his projects, and whatever he becomes interested in."

"My goodness Mary none of us here at the school have ever heard about such things. We all recognized his high level of intelligence but now you are saying he is very practical and capable of building and repairing items in the real world."

"Casper is much like his father. They both prefer to live quietly and rarely talk in social situations. When someone wants to talk about farming, repairing equipment, and such things, they will talk freely, and both are very good at helping our neighbors. Could you tell me what you have on your list?"

"Certainly, your son has achieved exceptional grades all through school and the graduation committee suggested he be asked to give the valedictorian speech, which he has shown no interest in. He is going to go to university and has qualified for several scholarships, and several universities have inquired about him registering at their school. Casper has shown no interest in athletics so is not recommended for recognition in that area, but the students want him to be recognized as the most congenial and helpful student in the class. Frankly, he has helped and advised almost all the students when they were having trouble with a course. If Casper doesn't come to graduation, there are going to be many graduates who will be disappointed and many teachers will be sad.

You must understand that having a student that often knows more about a subject than the teacher does puts enormous pressure on the teacher, although many admitted having him in the classroom has improved their knowledge."

Mary and Mrs. McClung discussed the graduation for almost an hour and when Mary left, her head was full of information on the proceedings and possible honors her son might receive. Arriving back at the farm, she put her car away and changed back into her everyday farm clothes and proceeded to clean her kitchen, not that it really needed to be cleaned, but she wanted time to think and while cleaning was the best time for her to think. When Casper arrived home from school, she had two loaves of bread in the oven baking. She made him a sandwich while he went to change his clothes. While he ate, she explained that Jeff had taken a few fence posts out to the cattle pasture and was driving them into the ground with a post maul. Casper knew this meant his dad would be standing in the back of the pickup to swing the maul and hit the post square on the top. It was heavy work and suddenly he had an idea. When Casper left to go to the shop, Mary turned to preparing dinner and rehearsed the remarks she had been thinking about.

A large cast-iron frying pan went on the stove and she filled it with bacon. The men liked their bacon dry, not covered in grease, so Mary laid paper towels in a long platter as she kept an eye on the bacon. With a fork, she removed each piece as it became well done and laid it on the paper towels to dry. She decided to cook some extra bacon to make sure the men got all they wanted. Removing the loaves of bread from the oven, she covered them with a clean dish towel so they would cool down slowly. Next, she cracked eggs into a large bowl and whipped them in preparation for making scrambled eggs for dinner. With the bowl covered, she set the table with three large dinner plates, put salt and pepper, butter, and salsa on the table. Two coffee cups for herself and Jeff went on the table along with a water glass for Casper. Mary sliced raw potatoes and started dropping them into the frying pan where she continuously turned them to cook both sides. The bacon went in the oven which was still warm and as the potatoes browned and were cooked through she put them alongside the bacon to stay warm. When the two men walked in and went to the bathroom to wash up, Mary began cooking the scrambled eggs. She was pouring hot black coffee into the cups when the men returned. Casper took his glass to the sink to fill it with cold water and Mary put food on the table. As the men sat down, the toaster popped and Mary brought four slices of homemade bread browned by the toaster and put the plate on the table. She set all the food on the table and sat down. It was a happy meal and Jeff told them about repairing fences.

When dinner was finished, Mary removed the plates, refilled Jeff's coffee cup and stood behind her chair looking at the men. "I have something to say to you two men and don't interrupt me. This is very important to me and if you argue I will be terribly angry." She had their attention. "On the second Friday of June, the high school will be holding a graduation for the senior students and this family is going to be there. Casper has always been a good student and made good marks and his mother wants to see him stand up and receive his diploma. Even better, I want to see him walk onto the stage with a young lady holding his arm. If anyone, teacher or student has something to say about my son, I will clap loudly. We are going and there will be no argument about it." Mary stopped talking and watched the men.

Jeff sipped his coffee, shrugged, and smiled at his son. "Makes all kinds of sense to me." Mary switched her eyes to Casper. Finally, he grinned and nodded agreement.

"The issue is settled then. Next Saturday, we are going shopping to purchase a sports coat, dress pants, and black shoes for Casper to wear to graduation and have for next fall when he begins attending university." Mary wiped her forehead with her apron and both men recognized how tough it had been for her.

* * *

Over the next month, Casper drew sketches and plans for a new project he was determined to build and spent all his spare time in the shop. Mary often went to watch him work and didn't ask what he was building. In a little over three months, her son would be leaving home to study mechanical engineering and already she was missing him.

June 9th, Jeff and Mary Blakerly were seated on the aisle end of the second row from the front in the school gymnasium waiting for their son to enter. Jeff was wearing his only suit and Mary sat beside him in her best dress, her hand playing with a tissue even though she had promised herself she wouldn't be crying or making any kind of fuss to upset her son. There was a high school band playing background music as they waited. Finally, the high school principal walked onto the stage and pickup up the microphone. He waited for the band to finish the current musical number before starting. "Welcome, everyone, to our annual graduation, all the parents, relatives, and friends of students. My name is Thurstand and I am the principal of the school. Officially, my job is to run the school and for many years that is what I have done, but with this ceremony, I found the Graduation Planning Committee had taken over and bypassed me." The crowd clapped and cheered. "There is a very good reason for them to do that. Our school has just finished three years of very special events. In this group of graduates, we have an outstanding student who has excelled at every class and the committee insisted on honoring him. He doesn't know what they are planning so we expect him to be surprised and while he is a quiet, talented, modest individual, we hope he will be happy. This said, it is not intended to detract from each of the graduating students, all of whom have worked hard, and we are very proud of. The graduation class contains forty-eight students, of whom twenty-eight are ladies and twenty are men. Now, we are going to open the doors and invite the graduates to come forth and sit on the stage."

Two students opened the double doors and the parade started. The crowd stood up so everyone could turn and see the students. All the girls wore long dresses in various colors, their hair well prepared and they attracted most of the eyes so the boys were not particularly noticed. Mary was only looking at the boys and spotted Casper and the girl he was escorting placed fifth in the lineup. She nervously grabbed Jeff's arm and hung on. Casper winked at his dad as he went by. When all the graduates were seated, Casper was in the middle of the front row beside the extremely good looking girl he had escorted into the gym.

Thurstand came back to the microphone. "Do you agree they are a fine looking group of students?" The clapping and yells went on for several minutes. "The first changes you are going to see start now. Firstly, there will not be a student emceeing the graduation as we have done for years. That duty will be handled by our teachers. From this point on, my only participation will be to hand out diplomas to the students." Mr. Thurstand glanced down at the program. "Please welcome Mrs. Argyle who will start the program."

She shook the principal's hand and waited until he was seated with the teachers before stepping up to the dais. "Good afternoon everyone, we are pleased to see so many of you in attendance. The first item on the agenda is a musical dance written by our music class and will be presented by them. Pay particular attention because up to now only the musical group has been allowed to hear it. On the piano accompanying the group is our music teacher, Mrs. Young." The music group filed onto the stage and Mrs. Young sat at the piano. When all was ready, she hit the keys and right from the start it was a lively, swinging rhythm. The crowd began to clap in time with the piano. There were eight girls lined up to sing and three couples dancing. Mary's eyes kept switching from the musicians to her son where he was seated, back and forth. She was pleased to see that Casper seemed to be enjoying himself. When the music ended, the crowd gave them a rousing ovation.

Mrs. Argyle came back to the dais. "The school has three teachers, by the way all male teachers, who will be retiring at the end of June. We will now honor and thank them." Mary watched but her mind wandered. She watched her son who was an honor student, who had been all through school, and he was a fighter when provoked. Never had he mentioned the fighting but she heard it from the teachers and some of her friends. It was hard to believe looking at her well-dressed son sitting with all the graduates.

"Now, I will turn the dais over to Mr. Sullivan to emcee the presentation of awards and bursaries." Sullivan came forward and explained the sequence of events. They started with sports and called a tall, rather skinny young lady forward for winning two backstroke races. A boy from the back row got an award for winning a diving competition. Two boys received awards for their performance on the football field. Sullivan returned to the dais. "There are other awards to be given out. Today we are concentrating on the graduation students, the others students will receive theirs when the student body gathers next week. Now, we are going to give out bursaries won by a graduating student."

Without looking, Sullivan pointed with his right hand. "You will see nine teachers lining up. Each one has a presentation to make as we call up the graduating students. First on our list is Miss Anajoy von Stagile. Please come forward, Anajoy." The first teacher in the line stepped up beside the dais and presented the grad with a bursary for two hundred and fifty dollars for being the top student in the home economics course. Ed Twilling got the bursary for woodworking and so it went until five bursaries had been handed out. After each presentation, the teacher went back to a seat with the other teachers. Sullivan stepped up to the microphone and announced, "As you can see, there are four more awards to be presented and by coincidence they are all going to one student. Casper Edward Blakerly, please come to the dais and stand beside me." Casper stood up and came to shake hands with Sullivan. The four remaining teachers all came forward and number six shook Casper's hand. She turned to look at the crowd and announced, "This is a bursary for five hundred dollars as the top-performing student in the school. It is coming from the school staff." She turned back and handed Casper the check and then kissed his cheek. Everyone saw him turn red. The next teacher stepped up and shook Casper's hand before announcing in a loud voice, "This bursary is an annual award to the top mathematics student from the School Board for five hundred dollars. Congratulations, Casper." The third bursary was for five hundred dollars as the top student in physics. The last teacher in the line stepped forward and shook Casper's hand before turning to look at the crowd. "We have had Casper in our school for three years and all that time he told us he was going to be a mechanical engineer. Our high school has been approached by four universities, telling us he would be welcome on their campus. Casper always told us he wanted to stay here and go to university where he would be close to his parents. It is my pleasure to present to Casper a check for two thousand dollars from our great university, St. Ambrose." He handed the check to Casper and went to sit down.

Sullivan stepped close and asked, "Would you please say something to the crowd?"

Casper looked at him and thought about it before stepping up to the microphone. "Mr. Sullivan has asked me to say a few words. First, I would like to thank the planning committee and all the other students for planning this graduation." The crowd clapped and yelled. "Secondly, my thanks to the sponsors of the four bursaries I was awarded which are greatly appreciated. For three years, I have attended the high school and it has been a great experience and all the staff and students have treated me well; my thanks to them— each and every one of them. My biggest thanks must go to my parents who over the years have let me go my own way but were always there when I needed advice. They are sitting right down there in front of me." The crowd started calling *'stand up.'* After a moment, Jeff and Mary stood and waved to the crowd. Jeff could feel Mary's hand shaking. Casper stepped away from the dais and Sullivan thought he was going back to his seat. Instead, Casper went down the stairs to the aisle and handed his mother the bursaries. She hugged him and he shook his dad's hand before going back up the stairs.

Sullivan laughed into the PA system. "Well done, Casper, for a moment there I thought you were going to leave us and go home." The crowd laughed and cheered once again. Casper shook Sullivan's hand as he went by to sit with the graduating class. Sullivan smiled at the crowd. "The presentation of diplomas is the main reason for holding this event but before we do our school choir is planning to sing for us once again. You will understand when you hear what is going on. While the choir gets on stage, I wish to ask Miss Stacie Locksmith to join me here at the dais."

Stacie stood up and reached for Casper's hand to pull him to his feet. She held his hand as she led the way to Mr. Sullivan. She whispered to him, *'You stand beside Mr. Sullivan where everyone can see you.'* Stacie stepped up to the dais and announced, "Casper has shown many strong traits the last three years but the one the students rank the highest is his always being willing to help other students who were having problems in their courses. Over three years, he has helped a high percentage of the students. The planning committee didn't have money to give him a bursary so we attempted to write a song to sing to him. Many hours went into the project and we never created anything we thought would be appropriate. Therefore the choir is going to sing an old, old song all of you will have heard many times. Please clap along and sing if you wish." Stacie stepped back and looked at Mrs. Young.

The piano started up with a familiar tune and beat and she played through it once before the choir started singing. "For he is a happy go lucky fella, a happy go lucky fella..." They went through three verses of the song with the crowd singing louder and louder. All the students stood and clapped to the music. Casper wasn't sure what he was expected to do until Stacie whispered to him, "Let's go back to our seats."

Mr. Sullivan walked to the microphone and announced, "Thank you, Casper, for all you have done. Thanks to the graduating class, the school choir, and to all of you in the crowd for joining in. Now we are going to present the graduation certificates. Please note that the presentations will be in alphabetical order using last names. Mrs. McClung, our school secretary, will call out the names and Mr. Thurstand will present the diplomas. Please note that the grads are not sitting in order by their names so if there is a bit of confusion, you have been warned." Sullivan looked around, "Oh, where is Mrs. McClung?"

"I am right behind you, Mr. Sullivan." Mrs. McClung was smiling and the room reacted with amusement. Sullivan turned the other way and grinned. She stepped up to the microphone and told the crowd, "Mr. Sullivan is always accusing me of sneaking around and spying on the staff, which is not true." As the crowd laughed, she looked at Mr. Thurstand and asked, "Are we ready?" He nodded. "For your information, Mr. Sullivan, who is our assistant principal is standing some twenty feet to my right. We have asked the grads to walk to Mr. Sullivan and stand beside him while the student ahead is being presented with a diploma. We want all of you to see our grads. Now the first grad is Marcie Adams." She stood up and walked to Sullivan who stopped her, shook her hand, and told her. "Just take your time and enjoy the moment." When Marcie started to move, Mrs. McClung called the second name. Each grad walked slowly across the stage passing in front of the dais and over to Principal Thurstand, who shook their hands, held out the diploma for the grad picture, and congratulated each grad. Casper Blakerly's name was called fifth in the order and so it went.

When the ceremonies were over, Casper drove his parents' home and told them Stacie had asked him to take her to the graduation dinner. As he drove out of the yard, Mary told her husband, "I do believe this will be the first date he has ever gone on and the girl had to ask him." They walked to the house and sat in the kitchen to look at all the bursaries and awards Casper had received. Jeff mentioned to Mary the money their son had been given would certainly ease the financial burden of his first year at university.

Chapter 3

On Saturday morning, Casper came to the kitchen at his usual time and ate breakfast with his parents. They discussed the graduation, how nice it had been, and told Casper how proud they were of him. Casper responded by telling them, "Sure am glad I went to the graduation and you deserve credit for me being there, Mom."

"Thank you, son, your father and I enjoyed every moment of it, and seeing our wonderful son up there in front of all the people in the crowd pleased us greatly. Many people came to congratulate us and we only knew a few of them."

Casper and Jeff walked out of the house together. Jeff went to check the cattle herd and Casper went into the shop to continue his work on the fencepost pounder he was building. Neither of his parents had asked what he was building, they had been putting up with his projects for many years, so it didn't surprise him. He had a single axle running gear with two inflated tires he had pieced together. Today, he planned to build a V-shaped frame to put on the front of the pounder so it could be hauled behind the tractor or his dad's Ford half-ton. There were patches of rough ground in some of the fields so the hitch had to be heavy-duty to last. Casper hummed to himself as he cut out the pieces for the hitch. He laid them out on the floor in front of the running gear and stood back to look everything over. Everything looked right to him. After propping the running gear the way he wanted, he positioned the central beam of the hitch in place and started welding. In this case, he ran a weld across the top and the bottom, leaving the sides open temporarily. With the central beam attached, he put a wooden box under the hitch end so the 'V' was level and measured how high it was off the floor. With the tape measure in his hand, he walked out to the tractor and checked the height of the hitch. The heights were within an inch of each other so that would work. Back in the shop, he trimmed the outside arms of the hitch and put them in place. It only took a few minutes to weld them securely. The inside edges were not welded because he planned to put steel wedges in to strengthen the hitch. It was close to noon and everything was hot from the welding so he walked to the house for lunch.

A week later, the fencepost pounder was wearing a coat of yellow paint. Together, Casper and his dad went out to the pasture to drive posts and see how it worked. When they finished, they had a difference of opinion although neither told the other. Jeff considered the pounder to be a massive improvement over driving posts with a handheld maul. Casper was already planning the next model which would be far better than the first. He was learning by experience. Back in the shop, Casper sketched out a new model that would be several strides better. When his drawings were complete, he wrote out a list of the items he would have to buy. Steel bars for the frame, two single-wheeled axles, a hydraulic cylinder, a heavy square of steel for a hammer, various sizes of angle iron, and a high horsepower gasoline engine and hydraulic pump. As an afterthought, he added hydraulic hoses and a hydraulic controller to operate the pounder. Looking the list of items over, Casper sheepishly added a gallon each of rust undercoating and yellow metal paint. Unless he could find some of these items in good used shape, it was going to be expensive. Casper looked in the catalogues they had and estimated the costs of the items. He put the papers together, planning to talk with his parents at dinner. In two weeks, he would be starting university and would have much less time to work in the shop, probably only on the weekends.

As they ate dinner, Casper told his parents what he wanted to build, his plans on the table beside him. Casper helped his mother clear the table and then spread out his plans and catalogues. At first, Casper did all the talking. When Jeff made a suggestion, it was a good one. "Why don't you build it for PTO drive on the hydraulics which should save you several thousand dollars?" The silence extended as Casper ran the idea through his head. "You can always convert it to independent hydraulics down the road a ways."

Casper grinned. "A great idea, Dad, and it will reduce the costs right up front."

"Son, you will have to buy the hydraulic cylinder new, there is nothing that large on the farm." For another hour, they went over the plans, arguing, and finally decided on a game plan.

Casper asked, "At the graduation, I received several thousand dollars in bursaries. Would it be proper for me to use some of that money to buy these parts?"

Mary looked at Jeff as he shook his head no. "May be best to let the farm buy the first things you are going to need. As time goes by, we will work out a plan that will get the job done. If money is scarce, you may have to use a little of the bursary money, but always remember that getting through university is the most important thing." On that point, they all agreed.

Jeff and Casper went shopping for heavy-duty running gear and the structural steel for forming the basic frame, which would keep Casper busy for several weekends. They made three trips to neighboring towns searching for good deals and just before Ambrose University in Davenport, Iowa, scheduled opening, they purchased the items he would work with to get the basic machine framework put together.

Jeff drove Mary and Casper to Davenport to get a look at the university's campus and the buildings so he would know where to go. They found the dorm building he had been assigned to and figured it would be best if Casper came in the afternoon before registration.

Casper found university was taking a good deal of time as he figured out the routine and learned his way around. After a month, he was finding the courses easy and soon the professors began to notice. A faculty meeting in November decided he could be given "A" grades in all his courses and moved into second-year courses. Now, all the professors were focused on Casper and kept each other informed. Over previous years, the university had experienced several far above average students and now they had another. The university president set up a special three-man committee to monitor Casper's progress because if he became bored sitting in courses he had already mastered, it might lead him to quit and the university didn't want that to happen. He was a friendly student who got along with everyone despite his young age, except for three occasions when students found out how strong and tough he was. They learned and the news spread through the students that Casper was a student to leave alone and certainly not to start a fight with.

Casper felt like he was in heaven when the university put him in structural courses; strength of materials, stress analysis, advanced algebra, analytic geometry, and differential equations. It was a heavy workload that he sailed straight through and looked forward to more advanced courses still ahead. He studied hard and often stayed after class to discuss the subject with the professor. He was unaware that a three-professor committee was keeping track of him and receiving regular reports from each course he took.

He became so engrossed in the courses that building his post-pounder slipped to the side as he poured over the textbooks. In most of the courses, there were regular snap quizzes to test how well the students were learning. With Casper, they noticed that often he wasn't writing much down, just the question and the answer. Occasionally, there would be simple conversions or notes and soon they realized he was solving the questions in his head. One professor reported to the committee that in a quiz with an hour allocated to answer the questions, he finished in less than fifteen minutes, set the quiz book aside, and picked up a textbook on mechanical vibrations to study. They all laughed and noted in the history they were recording that Casper Blakerly had an advanced analytical mind and a fabulous memory. Gradually, Casper became entertainment for the professors who, when they stopped to talk to each other, loved to relate his extraordinary talents.

During the Christmas break, Casper went back to the farm shop and welded the framework on which he would build his improved fencepost driver design. After New Year's was over, he happily went back to the university. Many weekends he didn't come home because of something new he was engrossed in figuring out and his parents missed him. Mary wandered around the farm just waiting for her son to visit and it being wintertime, Jeff had spare time after feeding the cattle herd each morning. They talked, drank coffee, and worried. Finally, in February, Jeff told Mary to write to the university and ask for a meeting so they could receive an update on how Casper was doing. Mary wrote to the dean of mechanical engineering. Two days later, the dean's secretary phoned the farm. Mary and Jeff were invited to lunch with the dean and professors at eleven-thirty a.m. on the coming Thursday.

It was a cold snowy day and Jeff drove Mary to the university in his Ford half-ton. Mrs. Rourke, the dean's secretary, had told Mary to come to Ambrose Hall on Locust Street between Ripley and Caines Streets. Jeff dug up an old street map of Davenport which they had visited only a few times and before taking Casper to see the university. When they got to the university, it took a few minutes to find the correct parking lot. When they entered the building, they didn't realize they stood out like two elephants in an ant colony. Jeff was wearing his Stetson and a sheepskin-lined denim coat and his western boots. Mary was bundled up in a long winter coat with a scarf over her hair. Everyone in the hallway knew immediately who they were because news of the requested meeting had spread through the faculty. People watched Jeff as he looked around trying to figure out where they should go. A professor stuck his head into the office and told the secretary, "I believe your lunch guests are standing in the hallway."

Mrs. Rourke hurried out and marched down the hallway. As she neared the Blakerly's, she put her hand out. "Welcome to the university, Mary and Jeff. I am Mrs. Rourke, secretary to the faculty."

After shaking hands, Mary asked, "We are here for lunch. Can you tell us where to go?"

Mrs. Rourke smiled. "Please come with me and I will take you to the dean's private meeting room." As they walked along the hall, she asked, "How were the roads for driving?"

"Somewhat slippery and it is cold out today." Jeff was walking along behind the two women. "Traffic is moving slowly today."

They stopped beside a door and Mrs. Rourke told them, "The dean and several professors are waiting for you inside." She opened the door and led the Blakerly's in and stood between them. "Gentlemen, your guests have arrived. On this side is Mary and on the other Jeff Blakerly, they are the parents of Casper."

The dean came out of his chair and hurried toward them. All the other men stood up. "Jeff Blakerly, I am so pleased to meet you. I am Christian Sprague, Dean of Mechanical Engineering." They shook hands and the dean moved on to Mary to welcome her. "Please, may I hang up your coats for you?" Mrs. Rourke helped and quickly the Blakerly's were seated at the table. Dean Sprague leaned forward in his chair and commented, "First, I want to tell you how very pleased we are to have you visit us. These three gentlemen are senior professors in this faculty and are a special committee we formed to follow Casper on his progress. Please understand that Casper does not know this committee exists, at least we do not think he does, but your son is extraordinarily talented in digging out facts."

Mary gasped and her eyes grew large. "Mr. Dean, why is there a special committee watching our son? He is a fine boy and has never been in trouble, we are very proud of him."

Dean Sprague sat back in his chair. "I must offer you an apology, Mrs. Blakerly, obviously my explanation was inadequate. Your son is a very rare student who is far ahead of any other we have seen in several years. This committee is not watching Casper for trouble; it is keeping track of his academic progress so the university can discuss with him the best courses for him to take. We do not want him to become bored and decide to leave because of a lack of challenge." The Dean noticed Mary was holding Jeff's hand.

Mary sighed. "Oh, you gave me such a scare. Our son is the most important part of our lives and he doesn't come home as often anymore, and we have been worried."

Jeff spoke up. "We aren't a wealthy family and we have given up many things in order to pay for what Casper needs. Mary hasn't been on a holiday for many years to save money and we live as cheaply as we can. Do you know if he is eating proper meals and has a decent room to live in? Those types of things are important to his mother."

The Dean turned and spoke to one of the men. "Oscar, would you care to answer those questions?"

"I would be proud to answer Dean. I am Casper's faculty advisor and chairman of the special committee. First, let me talk about his room. Under university rules, first-year students are required to live in one of the dorms with other freshmen. In Casper's case, we were forewarned about his academic achievements and also his young age. He is at least two years younger than other first-year students. As a result of these factors, the university decided to diverge from the rules and Casper was assigned a two-room apartment with a small kitchen and its own bathroom. He can cook for himself or walk across the street to the cafeteria which is open from six a.m. until eleven p.m. I have been told by the staff that Casper keeps his apartment very clean and neat. We do not want to pry into his private affairs, for example, we do not know if he has a girlfriend. Certainly, nothing has been reported to the committee. Your son is a brilliant student and causes problems for his professors who are trying to keep him challenged. We and his professors have had many a good laugh at the surprises we get from him. On tests, the students struggle to get done in the time allotted and fill pages with formulas and numbers. Casper most often writes the answers down because he solves the problems in his head. Be assured there are very few students who can do the same. By the way, I must tell you that some of his professors become upset because they can't check on what happens in his brain and have watched him closely. They have all been told to keep an eye on him but not to interfere."

"Your committee is keeping notes on our son and he does not know of this practice. There could be notes in the files that are negative to our son."

The committee head opened his briefcase and removed a three-ring binder and slid it across the table. "This binder contains everything we have accumulated so far. Feel free to go through and raise any concerns you may have."

Jeff opened the binder and he and Mary started reading as the staff came in with a platter of sandwiches and asked each person what they wanted to drink. The Blakerly's both asked for ice water. The Blakerly's ate their lunch and read the pages in the binder while the other men at the table chatted about several events going on at the university. Jeff listened to them with half an ear as he read. When they finished, Mary leaned in and whispered in Jeff's ear for several minutes and he replied before laying the binder on the table. "Dean, my wife and I wish to thank you for allowing us to come here today to meet with you and for you allowing us to read the notes you are keeping. We will not take any more of your time and will return to our farm. Our son does not know we are here today. Would it be possible for us to speak to him before we leave? We have raised him to be independent and make his own decisions. On occasion, he comes to us to discuss what he wants to do and we tell him what we think. He has done many things and only on rare occasions has he made a mistake. We are very proud of him and want him to learn and go on to do whatever he wishes and be very successful."

"Mr. Blakerly, we are very happy you have come here today to check on your son. Just give me a moment and I will ask Mrs. Rourke to find Casper for us." The Dean pushed a button on the phone and carried on a discussion with the Secretary. When he finished he told them, "Mrs. Rourke said she knows where Casper is and will have him here in a few minutes."

"You said Casper has done *'many things,'* would you mind relating to us what those things were?"

Jeff smiled. "You are asking me to tell you his life history which would take too long. He started helping me as soon as he could walk, running to fetch tools and went on to learn to weld, fixing toys, and rebuilt a metal wagon. When he was eight, he repaired and modified my old bicycle, and then he began to help repair equipment. There were many other things but skipping ahead to when he was fifteen, he went to a farm auction sale and came home with two old electric welders from which he built us a 2500 watt, 20 amp welder which can handle all the farm welding. That same summer, he built a fence post pounder to ease his father's workload. He built the pounder from plans he had in his head. There have been many other things, but I don't want to bore you. Not only is our son smart, he is also very mechanical, and he totally focuses on what he is doing."

The door opened and Mrs. Rourke came in followed by Casper. Casper looked around and spotted his parents and his face lit up with a wide smile. "Mom, Dad, what are you doing here on the campus? It is so good to see you," He rushed over and hugged both of them. Mary started to cry with happiness. "Mom please don't cry, I am so happy to see you."

"I am sorry son, you haven't been home for a long time and I was worried."

"It is my fault Mom; I get so involved I forget about other things. Next weekend I will drive home and visit with you and Dad."

Jeff spoke up, "We would be happy to have you home for the weekend. Could you show us where you live before we leave?"

"Sure thing Dad, we can go and have a look at the place right now." Casper went for his moms coat and waited for her to finish talking.

The Dean was shaking her hand and told her. "Thank you for coming to talk to us today. May I suggest you both come anytime you have concerns and please, come at least once a year?" The men all stood up and Dean Sprague helped Mary on with her coat, shook hands with Jeff and Casper and held the door open for them to leave. Sprague reseated himself and looked at the professors. "Well, gentlemen what do you have to say about Casper and his parents?"

Professor Hildebrandt spoke first. "I was impressed by their straightforward approach and how they are working hard to do everything they can for their son. We must look into a scholarship for Casper to ease the burden on them. A student like Casper is often taken as being an academic but that is not a proper category for Casper. He is exceedingly intelligent and now we know he is also very mechanical and can work well with machinery. It seems to me his parents have set a very strong example for us to follow and not interfere with where his interests take him."

"Very good, Oscar, anyone else have a suggestion?"

"Yes, sir. It did seem to me that Casper has been raised in a very orderly home by parents who may not be rich but certainly are astute. They very early figured out their son was intelligent and willing to work and have given him mostly a free hand to tackle any project he comes on. We should consider pulling some of the side courses which I don't think he needs and offering him a couple of machine shop courses to advance his metal lathe and milling machine experience and introduce him to the electronics that are becoming more widespread."

"Great suggestions, thank you all for picking up on them. The special committee should consider each one and make recommendations. Is there anything else?" After a pause, he added, "Thank you for coming and let's make sure we give Casper the best possible education this university can provide. Good day gentlemen."

* * *

Casper proudly showed them his living accommodations. It wasn't overly large but was spotlessly clean and everywhere they looked they saw Casper just like when he was home. He wanted them to stay for dinner with him but Jeff declined, it was winter, and the weather wasn't the best so he wanted to get home.

Mary was happy on the drive home and that pleased Jeff. They discussed everything they had been told and were pleased with the notes about Casper that the professors were making. Their son was just turning seventeen years old and was already doing very well at university. Mary stated, "It was wonderful to have a visit and see where our son is living."

Jeff considered for a minute before suggesting, "When Casper comes home for a weekend, why don't we tell him we are lonesome, and ask if we can come to visit him?"

"Oh, Jeff, such a good idea, I'd be very surprised if Casper said he didn't want us to come to the university."

"He is probably keeping himself occupied with his studies. I must admit, it would be nice to see his textbooks and find out what subjects he is studying and find out how he is fitting in and getting along with the other students. We shouldn't stay overnight; we must be very careful not to intrude on his study time."

Chapter 4

Casper Blakerly put his shoes up on the old oaken desk he used in his office and leaned back in the office chair to relax after a morning of meetings to review financials, inventory, and numbers of units being shipped. His eyes wandered around the overly large office he used which was full of drafting tables, four-drawer file cabinets, a chesterfield, and numerous chairs. There were a few old pictures on the walls along with his engineering diplomas, a Bachelor of Science in Mechanical Engineering, a Master's Degree, and a PHD from St. Ambrose University in Davenport, which he had received before he was twenty years old. That had been a long time ago; he was now thirty-two years old. The company he formed after his first year of university was now fourteen years old. What made it seem like a long time was the fact he couldn't remember being a child. He had grown up spending all his spare time in the farm workshop building machines he designed, knowing he wanted to be an engineer. His projects started small and at fifteen he built an electric welder to expand his welding to exceed the acetylene gas welder his father owned. His first really useful machine was the fencepost pounder his father immediately started to use as Casper went to work building a better, larger, and more refined version. Out of university for the summer after his first year of studying, he had been in the shop welding up the second model of his fencepost pounder when a neighbor had walked into the shop and stood watching him work. When he finished the weld he was applying and laid the welding gun down, the man spoke to him. "Good afternoon, Casper."

Casper took off his helmet and stood up before turning to look. He stuck out his hand to shake as he said, "Nice to see you, Mr.

Anderson."

"Good to see you Casper. What are you building?"

"Well now, Mr. Anderson, I built a fencepost pounder which Dad is using and this is a much-improved version which will do a faster and better job for him."

"Just came from talking to your dad. Saw him out in the pasture pounding posts and stopped to have a look. He even let me try it out and told me you were building a much better machine. He said if I came and talked to you and liked the machine, it might be possible to buy it from you."

Casper stared at Anderson in amazement. After a moment of thinking, he replied. "Don't see any reason we can't do that. I will have to sit down and figure out a price."

"You do that and I will come back in a day or two to see if we can deal." Anderson left and Casper sat on the machine and thought. When his dad came in from the pasture, Casper was still working on the numbers. Together, they went through the notes and discussed the cost of the machine. "You can't work for nothing," Jeff said. "So, figure out what it would cost if you used all new steel, hydraulic cylinders, running gear, and your hours building it, and don't forget paint. Then double the costs to make a profit."

When Anderson came back, Casper had two sets of numbers. The first for the machine he was building using some parts from the farm and the second using all new materials and parts. Anderson didn't quibble and they made a deal for him to buy the current machine which had been built using some farm material for parts. The sale gave Casper the cash to buy materials for two fencepost pounders with money left over. His dad took him to the lawyer who handled business for the farm and Black & Black incorporated his company as Davenport Machinery Inc. The lawyer doing their work was Wilford Black. By the time he went back to school for his third year, he had sold four yellow fencepost pounders and along the way had added a decal that read, DAVENPORT, which he had decided would be the logo for his company using the first part of the name.

When he graduated from St. Ambrose University, he immediately began building fencepost pounders and electric welders to sell to anyone who wanted to buy and he kept in touch with the buyers to learn what needed to be improved and why they liked certain features. His products evolved, becoming more refined and improved until he was producing the top line of machines on the market and business was growing rapidly just through word of mouth praise from buyers who liked Davenports machines. Every machine was built to last, to stand up to steady use, and he began giving four-year guarantees on every machine he sold. Two years after university, his business had far outgrown the capacity of the farm facilities. The company needed a bigger and better workspace. Casper had been very careful with the money coming into the company and was thankful that he had built up a sizable bank account. Money would be needed to buy a building and get the company moved to a new location.

Davenport Machinery got lucky when a Realtor came to Casper and explained there was a large metal building sitting on a large block of land along the railroad. It had been for sale for three years and the asking price reduced several times by the owner. The Realtor took him to look at the buildings which contained several lathes, vertical and horizontal mills, drill presses, and miscellaneous carts, hand tools, and many other assorted items. When the Realtor told him the current asking price was seventy-five thousand dollars, Casper managed to put a dismayed look on his face. The Realtor knew Casper was only twenty-one years old and most likely didn't have much in the way of capital. Casper said he would have to think about the possible purchase and the Realtor left to talk to his client. Casper went to talk to his banker. Not only would he need money to buy the property but also to make the move and purchase tools, milling machines, and other items. He showed the banker the budget he had made, and they went over the numbers. The bank was well aware of Davenport's fast growth. Casper was told to come back at eleven a.m. the next day and the banker went to talk to the president of the bank.

Davenport got the financial backing it needed and Casper waited on the Realtor to return. When he did, Casper told him he could only afford to spend fifty-thousand dollars on the property. He was hoping the owner would bring his price down to sixty-five thousand. They stood in the farmyard and the Realtor watched all the employees working for Davenport and the machinery they had built and the stacks of steel in various forms cluttering up the farm. There were trucks loading and unloading and he wondered how Casper kept track of everything. When he was asked about this, Casper didn't mention Mrs. Sparks who had been with him for six months and worked long hours keeping everything sorted out and on schedule.

The Realtor went to talk to his client again and Casper waited. All the lights in the farmyard, both permanent and temporary, were on when the Realtor returned at ten p.m. He was impressed by how hard everyone was working. It took a while for him to find Casper who was helping with the welding to get another post-pounder ready for delivery. Casper was bundled up in a welding jacket, reversed baseball cap, mask and gloves and an employee had to point him out to the Realtor. When Casper put down the electric welder and tipped up his mask, the Realtor called, "Is that you, Casper?"

Casper's head turned and the Realtor was shocked by how tired he looked. "Yeah, this is me."

The Realtor held out the offer sheet. "We talked about the deal for several hours and the owner finally signed your offer sheet. You have purchased the property for fifty-thousand dollars."

After looking at the Realtor for several minutes, Casper replied, "We best go to the house and do the paperwork." Together, they walked to the house and Casper shed his welding gear on the porch. At the kitchen table, he looked over the offer sheet. "The description we put on this sheet says the purchase includes buildings, tools, supplies, and everything else inside the fence including fifteen acres of land. In the sales agreement, do we need to expand the wording to make sure there is no argument?"

"We can do that, Casper, although it probably isn't necessary."

"Put in such things as descriptions of the lathes, mills, other tools, buildings etc. and change the padlocks on the gates. The only keys to those locks are to be in my possession in the morning." Casper went to a drawer and came back with a business card. "This is my lawyer's name and address, talk to him in the morning so he can put together the sales agreement. Now, is it time for me to write you a check?"

"Yes, it is, Casper. We should have put a down payment with the offer sheet."

The Davenport checkbook was on the side of the table. Casper opened it and picked up a pen. "This check should be to your realty company?" The Realtor nodded. Casper wrote out the check and handed it over. "I want an agreement approving Davenport putting security guards inside the fence tomorrow."

"I will talk to the seller in the morning. After that, I will talk to Wilford Black, your lawyer, and we will attempt to close this deal as quickly as is possible."

Casper rubbed his tired eyes and replied. "Thank you, come and see me whenever you need something." The Realtor stuck out his hand to shake and walked through the door. Casper just sat there resting. Finally, he got up and put his welding equipment back on and went out to the farmyard.

Immediately after the sales agreement was finalized and the

seller received his money, Casper started moving Davenport's operations to the newly purchased property. Now they had adequate space to spread out the building operations and to organize all parts of the company. Davenport had office space for more people than they would require for several years and Casper selected a second-story office for himself, mainly because it had ample room for him to run the company and work on his projects.

It was a happy and sad year for Casper. His mother died after her feet slipped on a spot of ice and the fall caused her head to hit the frozen ground. She had spent two days in the hospital with Jeff and Casper taking turns sitting beside her bed. She never did regain consciousness, just passed away. After the church service, they had buried Mary in the family cemetery plot with all the other Blakerly's.

After a few months, he slowly got over the sadness of losing his mother. He noticed his dad was losing interest in life and starting to neglect the farm work. Jeff was so lonesome with his wife gone that Casper recognized his father didn't care to live without her. Casper hired a man to help with the farm work and his dad never made any comment. Ten months after he lost his mother, the hired man walked into Casper's office at the plant with the news his father had died. The autopsy found he had suffered a heart attack. Casper was the only Blakerly left.

* * *

In late winter, the spring after his father died, Casper was in the farm shop playing with a new idea when he heard the door open and looked around. Old Joe who had worked for the Blakerly's when Casper was still a youngster was closing the door. Casper smiled happily and greeted his guest. "Joe, it is good to see you again, how have you been keeping?"

Joe smiled back. "Pretty good Casper; spent the winter sitting around the house reading books and hauling firewood for the cook stove. It has been one of the coldest winters I can recall in all my years."

"How old are you now, Joe?"

"Fact is I had my seventy-second birthday back in January. Now the doctor tells me to quit farming because my heart is growing weaker. That's why I came to see you; drove over to ask if you might be interested in purchasing our half section of farmland."

In the back of his mind, Casper was still thinking about his new project and Joe's words grabbed his focus. He had never thought about enlarging the farm operation but now he could afford it and hell, why not? He owned one full section so another half would be a significant increase in size. Casper smiled and asked, "Got a pot of coffee on the stove, you want a cup?"

"Sure thing Casper. The doctor told me to cut down on the coffee and not to drink any after lunchtime. Probably be wise for me to only drink half a cup with a touch of cream in it."

"Will do Joe, you sit down here by the stove and I'll get the coffee." A few minutes later, Casper came back with two cups and set one beside Joe's chair. "Best let that coffee cool a mite." Casper hadn't been on Joe's farm since he was a young lad. "To refresh my memory, Joe, please tell me about your farm."

Joe sipped carefully from his cup and began. "The home quarter where we live has the buildings, about forty acres of hay to put up for feeding cattle and horses, and the rest of it is pasture although a fair bit of it could be cultivated and grow grain. The other quarter has about one hundred and fifty acres in crop and about ten acres in trees and water. Have a good flowing spring of sweat water out in the pasture so there are no worries about water for the cattle. On the building site, we have two wells, one in the house and one out close to the corral and barn with a windmill on it. You'd be best to come over and look at things and see for yourself."

Casper nodded. "Would it work for you if I came over around one o'clock?" Joe nodded. "Joe, if I buy the farm, what are you and your wife going to do?"

Joe laughed and replied, "We don't really know. My wife figures we should go down south somewhere where the winters are warm. Should have gone south this last winter but I didn't really want to. If you buy the farm and aren't going to be using the house, it would be good if you let us live there for maybe a year and next winter we will drive down south and look around."

"Sounds fine to me, Joe, wouldn't want to see you rush into something and then be feeling bad about it. Let's plan on driving around this afternoon and discuss all these things." Joe nodded and sipped the coffee. Finally, he stood up and walked to the shop door, raised one hand in farewell, and went out. Casper smiled, thinking, *'Still doing the same as when he worked for Dad.'*

Casper drove his pickup into Joe's yard just after one p.m. and Joe got in. After driving around the yard and looking at the buildings and corrals they went out to look at the land and cattle. It was three hours by the time they came back and stopped in the yard. Casper looked Joe directly in the eye and asked, "How much do you want for the farm?"

Joe replied immediately, "For the grain quarter, I figured on one hundred and forty thousand dollars. This here home quarter, where the buildings are getting old and there are more trees, I figure around one hundred and twenty thousand."

Casper looked out through the windshield for a few minutes before turning back to Joe. "Seems to me you have your prices in the range of the current market so on Monday I'll talk to my lawyer, Wilford Black, and tell him you and your wife will have the right to live in the house for one year. That sound okay to you?"

"Reckon so, Casper. Haven't used a lawyer for many years, so likely I will be fretting about understanding what they put into the words."

"We will read the agreement over together and if we don't know what something is all about, we will go back to the lawyer. The other thing would be for you to hire a lawyer to represent you."

"Don't know any lawyers so let's try it your way, we can always go looking for a lawyer if need be."

"Sounds like a good idea, Joe." Casper held out his hand and they shook. "Expect it will take a few days for the lawyer to obtain copies of the land titles and whatever else he may need. You want to come with me to talk to the lawyer?"

"Thank you, Casper, that may be a good idea, and probably make me feel better."

"When I have an appointment made, I'll phone and tell you the timing. Enjoy your weekend and say hello to your wife for me." Joe got out of the truck and Casper drove away. On the drive home his mind started wondering how they would farm the additional acres.

*　*　*

Monday morning, Casper phoned Wilford Black and made an appointment for two p.m. He hung up and dialed Joe's number and gave him the news.

At five minutes to two, they were sitting in the waiting room. It took an hour to explain the deal to Wilford. Casper wrote out a check for the total sales price and gave it to the lawyer. He told them to come back on Thursday.

Thursday afternoon, the lawyer was waiting for them and took them straight to his office. "This is a very straight forward deal," he explained. "The only thing that complicates it is the right for the current owner to live there for one calendar year. You two gentlemen seem to both understand the arrangement so it should be fine.

I have a check for the total amount. After the sales agreement is executed and registered, Joe will receive his money in the amount of two hundred and sixty thousand dollars and I will send Casper an invoice for my time."

* * *

Nine years later, it was still the same. The demand for the company's machines grew steadily and there was continuing pressure to expand. As the owner, he was caught between the demands of his employees for more space, more facilities, more products, and the financial requirements to provide those things and debt was something he disliked. So, he was always trying to balance the act, finding ways to increase the number of machines being produced and finding the money to pay for facilities, tools, and the operating costs of the company. Four years before, he had clamped down and refused any and all expansions until the bank loans were paid off; he increased his own salary and paid substantial dividends on the shares. He had never told anyone that he owned Mid-West Holdings, the holding company that was the only shareholder in Davenport. Now, he personally, the holding company, and Davenport all had large bank accounts and he was in a position to expand the company's facilities and introduce some of the new products the staff were developing.

Casper stretched and extended his arms as high as they would go above his head before settling back in his chair. Fencing companies and large landowners were asking for a bigger and faster fencepost pounder and Davenport had the design ready. It would be the company's third model and this one would have a laser system for guiding the machine along a set-out line ensuring the posts are put in the ground in an arrow straight row. Requests for a larger capacity welder were coming from construction companies and Davenport had built and tested a larger model that produced 3500 watts of 24 continuous amps and would run for up to fourteen hours due to an enlarged diesel fuel tank and it had an electric starter. It could also serve as a generator. Casper considered the data on both projects for the last time. He had decided the previous evening to go ahead and was having a last consideration of the idea. Now he felt certain. Picking up the phone, he called the secretary and asked her to arrange for the three managers to come to his office for a meeting at one p.m.

The meeting took an hour and the managers went away happy to put the projects into operation. Casper went to his drafting table to continue the work he was doing on designing log splitters. He had wrestled for some time with what size the company should offer. There were a lot of small, fragile-looking splitters on the market and he didn't want to waste time in a market flooded with small machines. He had settled on two sizes of machines; a twenty-ton and a thirty-ton. The twenty-ton would be capable of both horizontal and vertical splitting, mobile on a two-wheel mounting and the customer could choose gas motor driven hydraulics or attachment to a farm tractor for hydraulic power. He was at the stage of drawing hand sketches of the twenty-ton machine and trying out different configurations until he was satisfied he had an outline of a good product. Most firewood was used at twenty-four inches long or shorter, he settled on thirty inches to start and planned to make a four-foot option available.

First things first, Casper switched his mind to focus on the hydraulic cylinder and splitting action of the machine. He sketched what he felt would work. Walking to the wall cabinet, he dug out the hydraulic technical manual supplied by the company they bought hydraulic parts and controls from. He searched for a cylinder suitable for a twenty-ton splitter and found two he thought would be ideal. He chose one four inches in diameter with a thirty-inch stroke by a two and one quarter inch diameter shaft. He listed the two that seemed best suited to the job and went on to list a hands-free controller, the volume and pressure of hydraulic fluid required, and all the other parts needed to build a test model. Late in the afternoon, he took the list and went to the fabrication section of the plant and walked around until he found Ralph.

Ralph Shaw saw him coming and smiled. Almost quitting time and here comes Casper with one of his projects all written down. He was scheduled to bowl with his wife in the evening and hoped the boss wouldn't keep him until midnight. Such delays had happened too many times and his wife understood but still didn't like it. "Hi Casper, how are you doing today?"

The boss's head nodded as he came to a stop. "Got a new project and want to discuss with you building a working model so we can test the idea. Let's go to your desk and I'll show you the rough sketches I've got laid out."

Ralph's face didn't change. He walked to the old table along the wall and took off his leather gloves. They sat side by side at the table and Casper showed Ralph what he was hoping to start manufacturing. "Need you to build this test model so we can put it through its paces and make all the changes required? While you are building it, I will figure out the rest of the machine."

Ralph looked at the sketches and read down the list of controllers and parts Casper had written out. He looked at his boss. "You figure to start building log splitters?"

"Right you are, Ralph, and this is the main part of the machine. We need to play with it until we have everything working the way we like. You got time to put together a test model we can try out?"

Ralph nodded. "You want me to do it here or out in your farm shop?"

Casper smiled. "Are you looking for a way to get away from all the hustle and noise around here?"

"Expect so, gets hard to concentrate when everyone around is asking questions and wanting to change things." They both looked around as the plant was beginning to shut down for the night. People were hurrying about and gradually the noise was dropping in volume. They watched people gather their belongings and start leaving through the nearest door.

"If you want to work at the farm do so and I will tell your manager I've stolen you."

Ralph grinned. "I will drive out to the farm shop in the morning." He folded the papers and stuck them in his soft-sided leather briefcase. "May need to take some of the steel, etc. from here?"

"Do what you need to; just make sure you tell the parts people what you are running off with." Casper stood up and started away. "See you tomorrow. Thanks, Ralph." Ralph watched him go and sighed in relief. Now he could go home and take his wife out to bowl. Wasn't often they got to do things together.

* * *

The Ford half-ton drove into the yard and Ralph climbed out. When he came through the kitchen door, Margret was standing there with a smile on her face. "You get your clothes changed, then come back here to eat dinner with your family."

As he crossed the kitchen he asked, "Who do you have lined up to fill in for me?"

"Barb said she would bowl with me. Now I've got to cancel her out, you no good lout."

Ralph smiled at her and kept going. Twenty minutes later, he was back all showered and wearing his bowling pants and shirt. Ralph sat at the end of the table and gave his wife a smile before talking to the three children. Margret listened as he questioned the children about school, homework, and grades. Not often he got home this early and everyone was enjoying the conversation. He started in on the youngest. "Now, Janet, tell me how your classes are going and where you rank."

Janet was fourteen and no longer a child, although her father still thought of her as a baby. Janet looked at her father, a six-foot-tall, sturdily built man, with large rough hands from the work he did, and a stern face which smiled most of the time. He talked rough and tough and growled a lot but it was all for show, he had never slapped or even yelled at any member of the family. His brown eyes were staring at her. Janet smiled. "My classes are going very well and I rank number four out of thirty-one students in my class."

Ralph glared at her. "Number four. Why isn't my daughter ranked number one?"

Janet laughed, "Because there are three students who are smarter than me."

Ralph's fork of food stopped halfway up to his mouth. "Smarter than you? I don't believe what you say. Are you sure it isn't because they work harder than you?"

Janet shrugged. "Could be, Father, but you know I work hard at my homework."

"Yes, you do and I'm proud of you, keep up the good effort and maybe you will move up to number three." Ralph turned his attention to Anne, the oldest daughter, and the same routine started on her and then Ralph Jr., the brother who was a senior in high school this year. It wasn't often this happened at dinner because Dad rarely made it home until later. As often happened, while Mother was serving dessert, Dad repeated a lecture they had heard many times. "Never did get to finish school myself. My parents had six children and me being the oldest, I needed to go to work. After a while, your mother showed up. I tell you, kids, I tried hard to avoid her but she just hung around until I decided to marry her and have her do the cooking just to make my life easier. We struggled for a few years but look at us now. We got this nice house and a few bucks in the bank and I have a good job that I like. Young Casper Blakerly is a good boss except for one thing, he never knows what time of day it is. He has a bad habit of working well into the evenings and often I get stuck helping him do whatever he has on his mind. Would rather be home with your mother but he pays me well and to tell you the truth I like him. Now, you children keep going to school and your mom and I hope you will all go on to university to further your education."

The bowling went well; Margret enjoyed the evening and so did Ralph. Several times his mind wandered away, thinking about the new project he had been given.

* * *

Two years after purchasing the half-section from Old Joe, the neighbor who owned the section of land separating Blakerly land from Old Joe's land drove into the yard offering to sell and the deal was closed quickly, bringing Casper's land holdings up to ten quarters of mostly grain land. The following winter, another neighbor approached Casper about selling his three quarters. In a few days, Casper had grown to thirteen quarters and on the weekends; he spent a great deal of time working out plans for the farm. He had a herd of mixed breeds that came from the land purchases and decided a change was needed. He and the two hired men discussed the situation and Casper told them he wanted to start a herd of purebred Black Angus cattle.

After a careful search, they found a herd of fifty-three cows and two bulls for which they negotiated a good purchase price. All had registered purebred papers.

The farm was running two large combines, two four wheel drive tractors, and a complete line of equipment to get the crops grown and harvested.

* * *

Casper left the plant at eight and stopped to eat a hamburger on the way home to the farm. It had been his farm for six years, ever since his father had suddenly died from a heart attack. He lived in the house alone and had a hired man who lived two miles down the road to do the farming with the help of two other employees. Casper helped with the work from time to time. He pulled up at the rural mailbox and picked up the mail. It was mostly flyers which he left lying on the truck seat. Driving into the shop, he parked, dropped the flyers into the garbage, and walked to the house. He was feeling tired after a long day and decided to shower before going to sleep. Coming out of the upstairs bathroom, he was rubbing his body dry with a bath towel and stood looking at the bed. His bed and he had slept in it for almost all his thirty-two years. He dropped the towel on a chair and crawled in where he laid on his left side as he did every night; a few minutes later he was sound asleep.

* * *

Working the two hours and sometimes longer, before eight a.m. brought the staff in, was the best part of the day. His mind was fresh from a sound sleep and an early breakfast and he loved to work on his projects and ideas in the silence. This morning, he had cooked bacon and eggs along with whole wheat toast and strong black coffee. A big breakfast was a tradition on the farm which he had learned to like when he was just a little tyke growing up and he continued doing the same. A large hot breakfast was the best way to start a new day. On sheets of paper, he had sketches of various pieces for the log splitter. In some cases several versions of the same part. Just after eight a.m. his secretary, and general take-care-of person, walked into his office with an arm full of reports, mail, etc. "Good morning, Casper, how are you today?"

Casper's head came up and he looked around. "Oh, good morning, Mrs. Sparks, what did you say?"

She laughed. "Just asked how you are today." Casper smiled. "Last week's report from the accounting department showing all the checks written are in this pile. Now, don't you forget to look over the checks issued? It is your money that is being spent so you must make sure all of them are correct."

Casper stood up and stretched, putting his arms up and reaching as high as he could. "Right you are, Mrs. Sparks. I have laid my pencil down and will follow your orders right now."

"The dean of the Mechanical Engineering School called yesterday to remind you of your visit to the school next Thursday." She handed him a sheet of paper. "The schedule is set out for you in the morning and in the afternoon; you have invited all the grad class to take a bus to the plant for a tour."

Casper's eyes grew large. "My goodness, is it that time of the year already?"

"It is the end of March, Casper, the semester will end very soon. You make sure your clothes are ready." She laughed, "Have you given thought to what you will tell the senior students?"

"I wrote down a few ideas some time back. Will have to find them and see if what I was thinking still makes sense." Casper walked to the desk and sat down. "Now, Mrs. Sparks, give me the check list first and lay out the other papers in the order you believe they should be dealt with." Casper picked up a red ink pen and started on the list and Mrs. Sparks smiled. She knew he would go through the total report before doing anything else and any checks he didn't understand would be circled in red and a note written in the margin. She laid out the papers in the order she had already figured out and walked back to her office.

Casper diligently worked his way through the reports and letters before sitting back in his chair. He remembered the meeting Mrs. Sparks had mentioned and opened a desk drawer where he found his notes. As he read them, he smiled. *'Good ideas; must expand the notes as a reminder to myself'*. He was writing on a pad of lined paper when Sparks came back in and took away the last of the papers. When he was concentrating, he never noticed her comings and goings unless she broke the silence, which she never did unless it was important or urgent.

Mrs. Sparks watched Casper, through her office window, as he walked to the stairwell wearing a safety vest, hardhat, and steel-toed boots. No doubt going down to see his employees during the lunch break and discuss his ideas with whomever. After visiting with the groups of people eating lunch, he left when the bell ending the break sounded and walked to the marketing department. He hadn't been in there for a few days and wanted to get an update, especially about the new catalogue they were preparing. He had told them it was time to move up a notch and make the catalogue more appealing. Most often, it provided the first contact between Davenport Machinery Inc. and the public, particularly the customers who were purchasing the products being manufactured in the plant.

The marketing people had shoved together several tables and had preliminary drafts of each page laid out in order. The front cover had a good picture of a large fencepost pounder and was the only page that would be printed in color. The picture showed the name Davenport which was a decal along the front frame and a larger one on the side of the fence post storage bin. They looked good and he liked the colors, red decals on yellow machines. They discussed every page and made numerous changes. At three p.m., they were finished, and he didn't go back to his office.

He was studious and shut out everything when he was focused on a project and often people thought he had a very poor memory.

It wasn't true, he had a great memory, even though he occasionally put things aside and had to be reminded. Mrs. Sparks was very efficient at reminding him and keeping him on schedule. Casper threw his hat and safety jacket into the pickup and drove away from the plant. At the house, he gathered his sport jacket, pants, and a bundle of shirts and drove to the dry cleaners where they told him everything would be ready on Monday.

Back at the farm, he entered the workshop and walked over to where Ralph was busy building the I-Bar frame along which the splitting wedge would move as the hydraulic cylinder pushed it. Ralph looked at Casper and commented, "Looked for that portable scale you had around here and couldn't find it, you know where it is?"

Casper sat silently for a moment, stood up, and walked across the shop and pulled out a tool drawer and moved a few items around. His hand came up holding the scale. He came back and held it out, "This scale the one you were looking for?"

Ralph nodded. "Been worrying about how strong this base needs to be. Won't matter all that much if you are splitting a large chunk of Oak in the vertical position but what if someone throws a large chunk on the splitter when it is horizontal. Need to know what kind of weights we could be dealing with. Don't want the splitter to bend or break. Another thing, if the cylinder is pushing at twenty tons, it might also be apt to bend or break the splitter. This base has to carry the load, especially in the horizontal position."

"Good thinking, Ralph. You bring that metal tape and let's weight up some oak." Casper went to the wall and took down a ten-foot tie-down strap and they walked outside. The first chunk they found was thirty inches long and twenty-six inches in diameter. They wrestled the chunk to the ground and onto the strap. A bit of jiggling around and they were ready to weight and suddenly both thought, *'We can't lift this chunk of wood.'* They looked at each other and laughed. "One of the farm tractors has a front-end loader on it. It'll take a few minutes to fetch it over here, be back as soon as I can."

Ralph was sorting through the woodpile when the sound of a tractor engine came to his ears. He had found a forty-inch long piece of oak. He climbed down as the tractor came into view. They rigged it all up and Casper raised the front-end loader until the chunk of oak was off the ground. With the engine turned off, he came to look at the scale. Ralph read out the weight, "This chunk weighs 326 pounds."

"Seems like a lot of weight for one single chunk of wood." Casper paced around and finally said, "Ralph, it looks to me like we need to build heavier. The bottom piece the ram will run along needs to be strong and inflexible. We would be smart to use a box beam. Give me that pad of paper you brought with you." Casper drew the end of a box beam. It wasn't square; the upright sides were longer than the top and bottom. He drew in a half-inch plate on the top. "If we weld a plate on top of the beam, the ram can have overhangs that run under this plate to keep the ram on course and not allow a chunk of wood to drive it sideways or cause it to twist. I will draw up a spec for this piece tonight and have it for you in the morning." Casper looked around. "First thing is to put this tractor away. Be back in a few minutes."

Ralph watched the tractor drive away before he gathered up the tools and walked into the shop. He put everything away and went back to his work spot. "You might as well go home now, Ralph, and in the morning, we can have another look at what we are do-ing."

"Okay, Casper, see you in the morning." Ralph put his tools away and walked to his truck. Casper sat and looked at the piec-es laying on the floor and thought about the project. Finally, he turned out the lights and went to the wood-frame house where he had grown up. The wall clock in the kitchen told him it was ten minutes before seven. Casper wasn't musical but he liked to listen to music so he turned on the FM radio and adjusted the volume so it would be audible in the kitchen. He hadn't stopped to eat lunch, so he sliced some potatoes into a frying pan and added a slice of ham steak. While they were cooking, he shredded some lettuce into a bowl and added a few walnuts and raisins before a sprinkle of canola oil. When he sat down to eat, he did the cutting and chewing while his mind was thinking about the wood splitter.

There was a stack of farm and industrial magazines on the side of the kitchen table and Casper decided to thumb through a few of them to see what was going on; he might get a good idea. He sorted through the pages while the music filled the empty space around him; once in a while, they played a bouncy song that caught his ears and he listened more carefully. Leaning back in his chair, he looked around the large kitchen and felt lonely. His mind drifted back down the years. He had been a smart student and made good marks, but he had never been athletic and being naturally shy he hadn't fit in very well with the other students. He was good at the math and science courses with his marks always at the top of the class but, somehow, he was different than the other students. Suddenly, it hit him. He was an oddball. He had always been an oddball. He was still an oddball. He didn't know why but he never fit in well with other people. He liked people and always talked to them but he had no close friends. He had always been different, never hanging around after school or going to parties. All the years he was growing up, he had gone to school, returned to the farm where he helped his dad with the work, and spent his spare time in the farm shop building anything his mind came up with. He thumped his chair down onto four legs and slapped the table, muttering out loud, "I am an oddball who doesn't fit in, my successful business makes me happy, now I understand the long hours I work, I am lonely. Have been lonely for many years and working and sleeping is all I do."

Casper stood up and washed the dishes and put everything away before he went to bed and was soon sound asleep. He had analyzed himself and his mind was working on the problem. At two a.m., he was awake in bed his mind trying to figure out a solution. At thirty-two years old, he was still the same oddball he had always been. He didn't like to think of himself as an oddball but how in hell could he change his ways after so long? During the days, he couldn't be happier. It was only the slack times when he recognized he was different. It was five-thirty a.m. when his eyes opened and he hopped out of bed, ready to attack another day.

* * *

For the next five days, Casper spent the mornings working at the plant and the afternoons back in the farm shop working along-side Ralph on the wood splitter. At the plant, everyone wondered and speculated on what the two men were up to and no one thought to mention a wood splitter. Most of the opinions were far out. By Wednesday afternoon, Casper and Ralph had the main part of the splitter built and rigged up to plug into a tractor for test purposes.

Tomorrow was Thursday and Casper would be tied up with the university and the mechanical engineering students and their professors. Casper reminded Ralph he would be away. "Ralph to run tests on this splitter, it will have to be mounted on a strong framework. Tomorrow, why don't you weld together a test support so we can mount the cylinder and try it out?"

Ralph's head came up as he looked at Casper who smiled. "Tomorrow, I will be entertaining a group of student engineers so you will be on your own. See you on Friday." As he walked from the shop to the house his mind reverted to the thought that he was an oddball. This had happened to him several times over the last few days.

Chapter 5

Casper Edward Blakerly drove onto the campus at St. Ambrose University at nine a.m. on Thursday morning and parked the Ford half-ton. His dark brown hair was freshly trimmed and he was wearing a sports coat and gray pants with a bright red necktie hanging over his shirt. He didn't don dress shoes very often and they were shinning black from a new polishing. His sense of smell wasn't the greatest and he was unaware he had applied a somewhat larger than normal amount of aftershave lotion. He was over six feet tall and thin, from not always eating every meal, and struck a rather handsome figure. He wasn't movie-star handsome; after all, he had been raised on a farm and had the rugged good looks farmers developed due to being out of doors in all kinds of weather. Hazel eyes set in a well-tanned face and flashing white teeth when he smiled gave everyone the impression he was a hardworking man doing an important job for his employer. The clothes he wore were nice and appropriate but certainly not expensive. Only a handful of people knew he owned a successful company that was growing and building a reputation for supplying well-constructed and dependable equipment that the company guaranteed and looked after. He worked hard and put in long days because he enjoyed everything he was doing and had a head full of projects to tackle in the months and years ahead. Probably the only thing he would complain about, if it occurred to him, was the dark of night and the need for sleep to maintain vitality and good health which interfered with work. Certainly, Blakerly never did anything to give people the impression that he was important, inventive, and had a steadily growing wealth because many of his employees dressed and looked superior to him. In fact, to do such a thing never occurred to him.

Blakerly walked into the engineering building and immediately saw Dean Everly of Mechanical Engineering talking to two students in the hallway. He stepped to one side and waited. When the dean turned and spotted Blakerly, he excused himself and hurried over. "Casper, it is so good to see you again. Thanks for coming today, the graduating students are looking forward to meeting you." They shook hands. "Please come with me, I am sure the students are milling around in the auditorium waiting for you to arrive."

The two men walked in and the dean closed the door. The chatter and noise immediately started to quiet down. Most of the students were seated and the remainder hurried to find seats for themselves. Casper looked around and the first thing that registered on him was seeing three female students. It came as a surprise. When he had attended classes here, the students were all men. He smiled, *'The times are a changing.'* Thirteen years now since he graduated. The seats for the students sloped downward to where he was standing, and behind him was a low stage with blackboards, and controls for projectors and other equipment mounted on a lectern. Two armchairs were on the stage for use of the dean and himself. Dean Everly touched his arm and pointed at the steps. Casper walked onto the stage and the dean followed him up the steps. The dean turned and looked at the students. "Graduating class, it is my great pleasure to introduce to you Mr. Casper Edward Blakerly." Everyone clapped and two male students whistled.

When it was quiet again, the dean continued. "Casper is a graduate of this faculty and this is the fifth year he has agreed to come here to tell you what he thinks. By the looks of this crowd, I judge that all thirty-seven graduates this year are in attendance as are several of our professors. I plan to take a couple of minutes to introduce our guest, so you have some knowledge of who he is. Thirteen years ago, he graduated as a mechanical engineer, having obtained a master's degree and PHD with honors from this school. He is employed by the firm of Davenport Machinery Inc. which designs and builds a variety of equipment, which are reported to be among the most reliable machines on the market. I have attended his four previous talks and each time gone away with new knowledge of the real world. A real eye-opener for a professor who is penned up in this academic environment. In just a few days, all of you will graduate and receive a diploma to hang on your office wall. You have all been good, conscientious students, as was Casper, except he arrived at this university with a rather annoying habit of questioning everything. This peculiar trait of his led to many long discussions to resolve his inquisitive mind. Please don't misinterpret what I am trying to say. This unusual trait of his came from living on a farm where he spent all his free time in the workshop building all the things that came to his mind. As a result, he learned the hard way how to shape, weld, and fit together the pieces of his latest gadget or machine resulting in a head full of practical experience learned the hard way, getting cuts, welder burns, and even dropping tools on his feet. We, his professors, were faced with a first-year student with his practical experience combined with a scientific brain, which led to four years of excitement in this faculty. He graduated before his twentieth birthday and I still remember telling him and his parents that I wasn't sure whether we had taught him, or he had taught his professors. Students, I now give you Casper Blakerly, listen carefully and ask him questions, you will be surprised. Casper, the floor is yours."

Casper walked the few steps to the dais, took the microphone in his hand and kept walking. On the right side, he stopped. "Thank you, Doctor Everly. We have been good friends for many years now but, students, you shouldn't believe everything the doctor tells you. We did have many hours of great discussion, always after classes were over for the day. Doctor Everly would be late getting home for dinner and his wife often threatened me until she issued instructions to bring me home to eat with them. An engineer must always look deeply to figure out what the problem is and how to fix it and, in my case, you would find that the discussions were all about me receiving free food from the good doctor." Casper turned and walked to the left side and waited for the applause to quiet down. "Good for you, engineers, you figured out what the message was. Always remember it and you will be better engineers because often the thing causing a problem is hidden and many times a sharp mind can figure out what it is and arrive at a solution."

A hand went up in the crowd of students. "Yes, Mr. Engineer, do you have a question?"

"Yes, sir. Doctor Everly mentioned that you grew up working in the farm shop. Please tell us what you were doing."

"First, you called me sir. My name is Casper and that's the name you should use. I am a mechanical engineer like all of you. Maybe I have a couple of years on you but if you call me sir, I will start to feel old. Please treat me like I am a member of your class, happy to be completing my education, and excited about the graduation. I will not reply to anyone who doesn't call me Casper." He smiled widely and walked to the center of the stage. "You want to know what I did in the farm shop. Of course, I started by helping my dad. Running for the tools he wanted and fetching bolts or whatever and when he went to do something else, I would pick up wrenches and try to do what he had been at. You know when you are young, actions like tightening a bolt is not easy. I was too small, but a few years cured that. My dad always pointed out the easiest way to do a job. Tightening a bolt is about leverage and as I struggled one day he handed me a short length of pipe which was like magic. With the extra leverage, the bolt tightened easier. It was the first real lesson I remember, and the knowledge led to many other solutions. On my own, I got started looking after my wagon which of course needed to have the wheels oiled and greased. Out behind the shop, I found an old bicycle and dragged it in. When my dad came in from the field, I had parts lying all over the floor.

He drove me to town, where we bought two new balloon tires and tubes and he left me to figure out the rest. When it was all together again, I found I couldn't ride it. My legs were too short to reach the pedals. It was that damn crossbar. After lighting the cutting torch, I cut the bar off. When I was trying to ride the bike, my mother came and held it up while I figured out how to pedal. I rode that bike out to the hayfield to show my dad. I learned, had fun, and suffered from cuts and bruises, and fingers hit by hammers." Casper kept talking as he walked back to the left side. "First useful machine I can remember making was an electric welder." He laughed. "Still have that old welder, although there are larger and nicer looking ones in the shop now. It was my introduction to doing research. I had to dig through the library in town, study dealer literature, and everything else available and in a few months, I had cobbled together an electric welder. It was small but I was able to use it for several years. I did all sorts of things like that and then when I was fifteen, I watched my dad pounding in fence posts with a hand maul. The first really useful machine I built was a fence post driver for my dad. He hooked it to his tractor and went to work. I watched my dad driving posts and saw several ways to make a better driver, so I went back to the shop and started on a better machine. Nearby neighbors watched my dad pounding posts and I managed to sell two of the better drivers before winter arrived. Davenport Machinery has been building fencepost drivers ever since."

Stopping for a drink of water, Casper saw three hands go up. He pointed to the student on the left. "Do you have a question?"

The student stood up. "Yes, Casper, I do. Can you tell us what you do at Davenport Machinery, how many hours you normally work, etc.?"

Casper laughed. "How many hours do I work? Never really gave any thought to my hours before. Usually start at six in the morning…" The questions kept coming and Casper handled them until Doctor Everly came and touched his arm while whispering, "Lunch will be served at noon and it is eleven-thirty now. Maybe we should wrap this up and load the students into the bus."

Casper stared at the dean for a minute before laughing. He turned back to the students. "Dean Everly just told me we have run out of time. Thank you for all the questions and I hope you enjoyed the morning. There should be a tour bus outside and if you follow Dean Everly on-board, there will be lunch waiting at the plant for all of you, even your professors who have been here today. After you have eaten lunch, I was planning on touring you around the plant so you can observe the machines being built."

Casper turned off the mike and put it back in the holder. Dean Everly had already gone so he followed the students out to the bus which was rated at forty-two passengers. The last two students in the lineup were females. As the line of students moved aboard, the driver stood by the door counting. When the ladies got there, he stopped them. "By my count, the bus should be full now. Please stay here while I check." He climbed the steps and watched as the passengers found seats. There were no empty ones left. The driver came down the steps and said, "The bus is full, there is no room for you three students."

The girls looked around for the third student and giggled, realizing Casper had been mistaken for a student. Casper smiled and nodded. "I can take two ladies with me in my truck." He asked the driver. "Do you know where you are going?" The diver nodded. "Okay, we will see you at the plant. Come with me, ladies." Casper walked beside them to his truck and unlocked the door for them. It was a bit crowded, but no one complained. With the truck running, he turned on the air conditioning. Casper smiled. "The bus will go on the highway, so we will take a shortcut and be there waiting for them when they arrive." He drove off the campus and took a side road as he asked, "What did you ladies think of the morning?"

The student by the door answered. "I found it very interesting. You have had an active life and seem to be full of enthusiasm. Oh, by the way, Casper, my name is Jessica and this girl in the middle is Hellene."

"Pleased to meet both of you; Jessica and Hellene are nice names. I have been coming back to the campus for five years now and always enjoy the event. If you have any suggestions, I'd be pleased to listen."

Hellene asked, "How many children do you have, Casper?"

"Children? To be honest with you there are none. Have never had time to look at the girls, although saw a few along the way who were right pretty. Where are you from, Hellene?"

"Right here, I grew up a couple of miles from the campus and always figured on attending. Jessica is from out in the country."

Jessica jumped into the conversation. "I grew up helping my brother and parents run the family dairy farm. Enjoyed working with the cows and the calves they dropped each year but I always figured on being an engineer. My father grumbled about me wasting my time going to school but when the time came, he provided the funds I needed, which was mighty good of him. Now I'm coming out of engineering school debt-free."

"You are a lucky girl, Jessica. Coming out of university debt-free is a blessing because going to work carrying debt is a heavy burden. So, now you are going to find a job and get on with the rest of your life?"

"Well, not exactly Casper. I am hoping to obtain a summer job because I have enrolled at the university to take the one-year Master of Business Accounting degree starting in September."

"Smart move. Having an MBA along with your Mechanical Engineering Degree will broaden your perspective considerably." Casper came to a stop at a red light and turned on his left turn signal. All was quiet in the truck. He made the turn and commented, "Two miles along this road will bring us to the plant which is located along the railroad right-of-way. Much of our shipping is by truck but it is sometimes cheaper to ship in steel and other supplies by rail car and often we ship equipment orders out on the railroad, especially when they are going overseas."

Hellene asked in surprise, "Davenport ships machines built here in the plant to other countries?"

"Sure do and have been for several years now. The company hasn't put much effort into the export business because it takes most of our capacity to supply the American market. The company is now getting close to expanding the facilities and after they are up and operating, we will begin signing up dealerships to represent our products in other countries. The building up ahead on the right is Davenport Machinery Inc." Casper raised a hand to the security people and parked the Ford F150 near the main entrance and turned off the ignition. "The bus should be here any minute now. Do you ladies want to come inside with me to check on lunch?"

Hellene grinned. "Sounds good to me and hopefully it will be a little cooler in there." Casper held the door open and they walked in. The reception area was full of tables and chairs and Mrs. Sparks was directing traffic as the food caterer's staff rushed around dressing the tables with glasses, plates, and cutlery.

Casper commented, "You ladies find a table and sit down while I check on things." They watched Casper stop to talk to the lady directing the caterers before he went on through the door and disappeared. The two students walked to a table away from the windows and sat down. There were glasses of ice water and beside each plate a card with the menu printed on it. Under drinks there was water, coffee, and soft drinks, two choices for food: Mexican Tortillas or Roast Beef, and for dessert ice cream with chocolate sauce. The girls giggled together. They had been living together and cooking their own food which often wasn't very good because as students, money was always in short supply. This would be one of their better meals in some time. The sound of the bus arriving distracted their conversation and they watched as the door opened and Dean Everly was the first to step down. Casper hurried out to direct the students into the reception area. When everyone was seated, Casper announced, "There are menu cards on your tables. Choose what you want to eat and the caterer will be coming around to take your order. Enjoy your lunch."

The tables were each set for six people and catering staff came to write down the orders. Very quickly, they were coming back with plates of food. Casper was sitting with the Dean and Mrs. Sparks and three men who were going to conduct tours. The professors were scattered around at various tables. The noise level went down as the students began to eat and several asked for a second helping. The ice cream was cold and the chocolate sauce hot and very enjoyable. In three-quarters of an hour, the lunch was over. Casper stood up. "These three gentlemen are managers at Davenport and will be leading groups of you on the tours. If I recall correctly, there are forty-four of you so each group will have eleven plus the guide. I plan to come along last with my group." The guides walked over to the door and their students followed. Casper came to the table where Hellene and Jessica were sitting and handed a business card to Jessica. "Earlier, you said you were looking for a summer job. If you wish, please write a letter to Mrs. Sparks applying and enclose a resume, marks, etc. and she will arrange an interview for you."

Jessica was totally surprised. Casper hadn't displayed any re-action when she'd told him her plans. She stared at him from wide, moist eyes and finally found her tongue. "Oh, thank you, Casper, this is such a surprise. I will write a letter in the next few days. Thank you for being so thoughtful." Her hand took the card and shoved it down into a deep pocket in her blue jeans.

Casper smiled. "You are welcome, Jessica, and I hope everything works well for you." He looked around. "Why don't you six tour with me and we will see if there are a few others to go with us?" When they came outside, Mrs. Sparks was holding four students who she told to join Casper on the tour. She was handing out hardhats for the safety of the students. Casper looked around and the other tours were heading to the plant so he suggested, "It will be crowded in the plant so this would be a good time for us to start at the demonstration area where you will see our machines in operation. Just follow me." He walked around the far end of the plant where a circle of machines and company employees made a semicircle on the open land beyond the building. The students stopped to gaze in awe at the machines which started with the smallest and gradually became the largest at the far end. On display nearest to the group were electric welders with a table of welding helmets nearby. Casper walked up and told the men, "These are mechanical engineering students from the university. Please go ahead with your presentation." He stepped aside and watched as one of his employees prepared to explain the features of the two sizes of welders. Smiling at the students, the man told them, "Before any of you ask, welders are the only product Davenport sells which are painted black, everything else is painted yellow."

A student asked, "So why does Davenport use yellow?"

"The yellow color goes back to before I was an employee. Rumor has it that Casper mandated yellow because it is highly visible and is expected to reduce the number of accidents on construction sites."

The students laughed and one asked, "Is that true, Casper?"

Casper smiled. "Could be but around this place you have to be careful in believing rumors."

"Thank you for the help, Casper. Actually, black colored welders are a long time convention in the welding business and it is never wise to go against industry standards. These machines are very sturdy and reliable and are built to work all day long. Both machines are 3500 watts and work up to 190 amps maximum. The main difference between them is in the controls. The one nearest to me is meant for very heavy work and can be adjusted to fit a wide variety of welding. It also has a larger fuel tank and can run at full load for eight hours. The other machine at full load is good for three hours. Both produce an excellent weld and which one you need depends on the work you will use it for. There are metal pockets on the sides of the machines to carry welding rods, hammers, files, and even welder mitts." On a metal worktable was a pile of scrap steel, actually trim from the construction in the plant that would be going to recycling. "Before I start this welder, all of you must put on a helmet to protect your eyes while I run a weld." When everyone was ready, he started the engine and the machine came to life. It ran surprisingly quietly. He laid two pieces of steel side by side and explained the dangers before creating sparks and a bright light caused by running a short weld. When he finished, he asked if any student wanted to try welding. Two boys did and had used welders before. "Thank you for visiting our plant today. Please put your helmets back on the table before you move to the next display."

Next were acetylene welders. Actually, wheeled carts to carry acetylene and oxygen tanks, hang up hoses, and storage for rods and tools. Again, the carts were painted black. One thing everyone noticed was every machine carried a bright red Davenport label on its side. After the welders, there was a line of electric generators at 5,000 watts, 10,000 watts, and 15,000 watts all painted yellow with red Davenport labels. The man in charge explained, "The small generator is suitable for providing power to a small home, for example, the 10,000-watt machine can handle the average-sized farm, and the largest model has many applications where more power is needed—large barns full of turkeys, running pumps during floods, and industrial sites to power large tools and such. Let me start one for you so you will notice how quiet they run." He started the 10,000-watt generator and let it run for a few minutes. "People who live out in the country away from cities often have power outages and, for example, if they raise turkeys they can't be without power for more than a short time or they risk losing all the live turkeys. Many businesses have those kinds of risks and the solution is to have your own generator to take over until the power comes on again and sometimes it may be a day or two, especially during the winter months."

Next in the line were wagons, metal wagons shaped for different tasks. The first one was for general hauling such as sand, gravel, or wood planks, furniture or whatever task you had. It was wide and had metal sides two feet high and hydraulics to tilt the box back for emptying. There were two long narrow wagons set up for spreading manure on fields, one had a ground drive and the second a hydraulic drive to turn the beater fins at the back and a driven floor that moved the load back to the fins. They could be pulled by a truck or, in the case of hydraulics, by a tractor. The company man explained, "These wagons are just to show you what Davenport makes. These come in a variety of shapes and sizes to suit our customers' needs. On occasion, we have trouble figuring out what the customer is going to use his request for but that doesn't really matter, we try to give our customers what they need."

At the tree branch shredder, the man on duty smiled. "This machine you are looking at is the first size we are building. In the coming months, there will be several sizes added to the line. The company has designs for machines that will eat larger branches and logs up to six inches in diameter and other sizes will be added as time goes by."

Last in the circle were fencepost pounders. The largest was set up to allow the students to inspect the laser guidance system which could lay out a very straight line of posts. One of the students asked, "Who would need a post pounder as large as this one and with a laser on it?"

The company man laughed. "You would be surprised. Some large ranches and farms run miles of fences and they want to get it done quickly. Construction companies working on long-distance projects such as parks, game reserves, etc. have similar needs. The military owns many miles of fences and they have bought several of these machines. If you happen to be a smaller sized farm or whatever, we have smaller models which cost less and ease the workload of driving hundreds of posts. After you look at this system, go by the others. The one hooked to a farm tractor is going to pound a post for you to watch." The students listened as he explained that the laser put out a very narrow beam of light that spread several feet in a vertical direction. The post pounder followed the beam and kept the posts in a straight line. The vertical spread was to compensate for the natural ups and downs of the ground as the pounder moved ahead. When the talk was over, they all gathered to watch a post pounded into the ground. First, the operator explained the process before he started the tractor and came back to the controls. He pulled a fence post out of the bin and set it up in the pounder where two spring-loaded bars kept it upright. He stepped away and operated the hydraulic handle. The heavy weight went up and came down on the top of the post three times and it was in the ground. The operator went and turned the tractor off, came back and asked, "Anyone think they can pull the post out?"

Standing nearby, Hellene stepped forward and grabbed the post. She couldn't even wiggle it. She looked at the operator and laughed. "The post is solidly in the ground."

"You are right, Miss, and I am sure you noticed how little time it took to put the post in place. In one day, a man can pound a large number of posts."

Casper asked, "Do any of you have questions?" There was silence so he suggested, "In that case, we will go and tour the inside of the plant, should be room for us now." Casper led the way along the other side of the plant which brought them to a building projecting out to the north very near the railway. Before the students entered, he advised them, "This is where the plant receives its shipments of steel and other supplies whether they come by rail or highway truck. It may be noisy in there depending on what the men are doing. Be on the outlook for forklifts moving materials around." When they got inside, it was fairly noisy but soon quieted down as the men became aware of the students. Several sizes of undercarriages were stacked along one wall, piles of wheels and tires, plates of half-inch steel, square steel tubing, boxes of bolts of several sizes, and round steel bars waiting to be machined. Those were the items they saw while standing inside the door. As their eyes adjusted from being outside, they saw steel shelves loaded with boxes, gasoline and diesel-fueled engines, fuel tanks, hydraulic cylinders and fittings, coils of hydraulic rubber tubing, and many things that could only be identified by reading the lettering on the crates and boxes. The foreman of the warehouse walked over. "Anything I can show the students, Casper, or tell them?"

"Don't think so, Wilber. I wanted them to see the raw materials and items coming in and how we store them. We will go on to the plant." Wilber nodded and walked away. Casper told them, "Follow me." They walked along the rows of steel shelves and went through a wide opening where the steel doors were rolled back. "The administration, accounting, personnel, etc. are on two stories at the front of the building where you ate your lunch. Wasn't planning on boring you with looking at paper, that's what you have been doing for four years. If you look along the plant from here, you can see that both walls are lined with lathes, machining tools, breaks for bending steel, cutting and electric welding steel and assembling smaller parts of the machines. Down the middle is where Davenport builds the larger machines. Partway toward the far end of the plant, the painting parlors are located. Every machine receives a layer of undercoating, and then two coats of the best machine paint we can purchase. Let's start our tour off to our right, where the smaller items such as welders are being built."

Everyone followed Casper to where men were busy building electric welders. The foreman stood up and smiled. "Hi, Casper. After everyone went by, we wondered what happened to you, now here you are with your group for the tour. Do you want me to tell them what the men are doing?" Casper nodded. "Follow me, students, and I will show you." He walked them over to a stack of welding frames. "These are frames for the various sizes of welders we sell and to be downright truthful with you they are the only part of the welders Davenport actually builds. We weld the frames together, paint them, and put company decals on. All the parts are purchased from manufacturers and shipped in here mostly by highway trucks. These men are busy building welders into the frames to fulfill orders that have been received. If you break into groups of two, each group can gather around separate welders and ask any questions." The foreman watched the students for a moment before walking over to stand beside Casper.

When the students were ready, Casper led them down one side of the plant which had machine assembly along the middle and on each wall were lathes, milling machines, acetylene torches cutting parts out of sheets of thick steel, and in the center welders joining the parts to build a machine. The students were amazed at the high level of activity and kept going back and forth between the wall machines and the centerline of assembly, trying to watch everything. As they drew near the painting line, Casper suggested they follow him and led them through the closed doors into the spotlessly clean room. The manager of painting was waiting for them and started explaining immediately. "First thing we do with a new piece coming through is wash and steam it to be rid of all dust, bits of rust, etc. and then dry it with hot air. You can see this part of a fencepost pounder being washed. Now come ahead and see other parts being dried." The students watched the hot air carry away all signs of moisture. "Before painting, we dip all parts in this next tank to undercoat them for protection from rust and to provide a better base for the paint to adhere to. After the dipping, the part is hung to dry overnight. Through this next door, you will find parts already hung to dry. Come in and have a look around." The tour group crowded in and watched as the parts moved along an overhead conveyor chain which ran back and forth as it progressed across the ceiling. The room felt hot as it was kept at eighty degrees to speed the drying process. The manager continued his description. "All these parts you see hanging here will be painted tomorrow. Now, I ask that each of you don a paint mask to protect your lungs from fumes." Beside the exit door was a box of masks and each student picked one up as they passed. When the students were all masked, they were facing three painting booths where painters were spraying the parts as they came along. The manager again explained, "The parts you see being painted were cleaned yesterday. Now, they are getting the first coat of paint and will spend five hours going through a booth where the temperature is kept at one hundred degrees and then a second coat of paint will be applied and the parts will spend the night under the infra-red heat lamps being dried. Let's walk ahead and you can see for yourselves." Looking through windows, the students could see parts under the glare of heat lamps, all painted yellow. Next, they saw parts receiving a second coat of yellow paint. The manager was standing beside the exit door. "On the other side of this wall, you will see the parts being used to build Davenport machines to supply the market. Thank you for coming today and I wish all of you successful careers." Everyone clapped in thanks.

In the assembling area, men were busy building fencepost pounders, wagons of various sizes, and log shredders and all the parts were yellow. Each work crew seemed to be made up of two men aligning parts, installing bearings, and tightening bolts to hold the pieces together. Casper turned the students loose. "You wander around and look at whatever interests you and remember to ask questions of the men." Casper remained near the wall of the painting section and watched. The students had spread out all over the area in front of him and seemed to be very interested in what was going on. He glanced at his watch and was surprised to see it was a quarter to four. When he looked up, Ralph Shaw was walking toward him. Casper raised one hand and smiled. "How are things going today, Ralph?"

"Got our model wood splitter mounted on a sturdy rack for testing, all we need is a tractor for power. We could test it in the morning if you want."

"Sounds good to me Ralph How about eight?"

"Eight is a good time. I rustled up a few different sizes of logs just to see how the splitter will handle them. Some of the logs are cut on a bias and some have branch stubs so I figured it would be a good idea. If there are any problems, we can work out a way to handle them."

Casper saw the dean coming over and told Ralph, "See you at the farm at eight." Ralph hurried to get out of the way.

Dean Everly smiled at Casper and said, "Another good tour, Casper. The students were impressed as were the professors. If you don't mind, it would be a good idea to invite the professors to come on the tour every year."

"If they want to come, it will be fine with Davenport, make sure you don't let me forget about it."

Dean Everly nodded. "Will tell my secretary to make a note in the file. The other tour groups were in line to get on the bus when I came looking for you. Okay with you if I round up the students?"

Casper nodded. Everly walked out into the middle and shouted, "Bus time!" Paused for a moment and called again, "Bus time! All aboard or you will be walking home tonight." It didn't take long until all the students were gathered around him. "Back at the reception area, Mrs. Sparks has Davenport hats for each of you to take home so get your hat and climb onto the bus." Everly walked beside Casper to the front of the building. Mrs. Sparks was standing at the door to the bus with a cardboard box at her feet. As each student went by, she handed out a hat then walked over to where Jessica and Hellene were standing beside Casper and gave each girl a hat.

Hellene held her hat up and looked it over. Shaped like a baseball hat it was yellow with a red Davenport logo across the front. "Thank you for the hat ma'am." She stuck out her hand and shook with Sparks, Jessica did the same.

Sparks smiled and told Casper, "See you tomorrow, Casper."

"It has been a busy day, Mrs. Sparks. I am going to drive these two ladies home and go home myself." Casper walked the girls to his truck and drove away. Hellene directed him to the apartment block where they lived; they thanked him for the talk and the tour, before walking up the sidewalk to the outside door. Casper drove away, happy to be going home.

Chapter 6

Ralph turned off the county road into the farmyard and imme-diately saw Casper had a tractor parked alongside the test splitter and the engine was idling. He parked a safe distance away, donned his hardhat, picked up his gloves, and walked over to Casper who was leaning against the workshop wall. "Good morning, Casper. What do you think of the splitter so far?"

Casper laughed. "For a test rig, it seems to be good. Splitting a few logs will help us find out. Run the cylinder out its full length so we can check the clearance to the bottom plate." Ralph walked over to the splitter, took hold of the hydraulic lever, and slowly pushed on it. The splitter head started moving as both men watched it closely. When it was all the way out, the head was touching the plate. "Damn head is touching. We'll have to rework the spacing. Expect the head should stop one or two inches short of the plate."

"It will take a mite of time for me to make the change." Ralph scratched his head. "Most likely, we should have the bottom plate easy to set at several distances, at least for this testing." Casper walked into the shop and came back with a pad of paper and wrote down changes to the bottom plate. "I'm going to run the splitter head in and out a few times just as a check." Ralph retracted the head and extended it a second time. Casper was down on one knee watching as the head came near the plate.

"The head is going to hit the plate." Casper stood up and studied the head for a minute. "To split larger logs, we will have to have a four-way head to split the log into four sections. You best build a four-way head and I suspect it will be longer than this head. We will need the four-way head to decide on the spacing for the bottom plate. The other thing that strikes me is if we make the bottom plate removable, we will be able to take it off to change heads easier and not have to have slide bolts on the head." Casper wrote down the idea before saying, "Let's put a smaller log on the machine and see how it splits."

Ralph found a log and laid it on the test machine. When he operated the hydraulics, the head came along and split the log in half. A half-log fell to the ground on each side. Casper laughed, "We need to have a retainer tray curled up on each side to keep the pieces from falling off. And another thing, the hydraulic cylinder is going to need a higher speed when it comes out and switch to a slower speed after it hits the log. We will have to rig up a dual-speed control." Again, Casper stopped to write on his notepad. "Let's do another smaller log."

Ralph picked up a small log and placed it on the splitter. He looked at Casper who nodded and pushed on the operating handle to activate the hydraulic fluid. Once again, the test machine split the log into two halves. "Let me help you put the large log on and you operate the test machine while I watch what's going on with the parts." They started with a twelve-inch diameter log cut two feet long and carefully located the log squarely in the middle of the plunger path. Ralph kept the head moving slowly. It went through the log and split it in half. Ralph picked up one half and laid it flat side down on the test machine. Everything worked well.

Casper suggested, "Let's look for a larger log maybe two feet in diameter and try it." They found one that was close to two feet in diameter and lugged it to the splitter. When it was mounted, it made the eight-inch high splitter head look very small. "This isn't going to work, Ralph; hell this log is three times higher than the splitter head. You make a two-foot-high head and figure out how we can adjust the mounting on the cylinder. The way it is now, it would be pushing the log up in the air."

"It will take a day or two to make all these changes."

Casper was busy writing the latest problems identified to be changed on the list and answered without lifting his head. "That will be fine, Ralph. When you have everything ready, let me know. It's been a day and a half since I worked at the plant, so it is time for me to show up or Mrs. Sparks will come looking for me." Both men laughed, Ralph went to work unloading the splitter. Casper turned the tractor ignition off before climbing into his half-ton and driving out of the farmyard.

*   *   *

Casper drove into his favorite restaurant and ordered a cheeseburger and a mug of root beer. While he waited, he laughed at himself. He drank coffee at breakfast and the rest of the day had water, but he did like root beer. Root beer had a good taste but wasn't acidic or strong. He liked its smooth feeling. He found a window seat and thought about the wood splitter while he munched on the cheeseburger. As usual, Ralph had done a good job of rigging up the test model, but there were things they needed to modify, same as it had been on the other machines. Wouldn't take long to work out the wrinkles and get down to drawing plans for a machine Davenport could manufacture. When this machine was nailed down, it would be easier to scale it up to a larger sized machine. All the things he and Ralph were learning now could be applied to the second project. Casper drained the last of the root beer and took his tray to the disposal. Past time to drive down the road to the office and most likely there would be a pile of paper.

Mrs. Sparks saw him step off the elevator which he didn't ride on very often, normally preferring to walk the stairs. She followed him into his office. Casper sat down at the scratched-up old oak desk he had found somewhere and looked at her. "How are you, Mrs. Sparks?"

"Doing just fine Casper, did you enjoy the talk and the plant tour?" Casper smiled at her and nodded. "Dean Everly phoned this morning to thank you once again and had nothing but praise for the layout of the plant and the quality of the machines Davenport builds."

"Very kind of the Dean. Did you chat with him a little?"

"Certainly did, Casper." She smiled and her head canted to one side as she looked at him. He noticed a hint of a smile on her face and wondered. "Also had a phone call from a young lady named Jessica Hornsbee asking for a name she should send an employment application and resume to at Davenport."

"Hornsbee, she didn't tell me her last name. She told me she was looking for summer employment to earn money to stay at the university for another year so I suggested she might try applying to Davenport. What did you tell her?"

"I started to give her the name of the manager in human resources and then remembered you had spent yesterday afternoon with her following you around. So, I told her to send the resume to me and guess what? Miss Hornsbee already had one of my business cards which she said you gave her." She watched Casper trying to keep a smile off his face and not quite accomplishing it. "I hope I didn't do anything wrong? If you want, I can phone her back and give her the manager's name."

Casper shook his head no. "What you did is fine."

"Thank you, Casper. Now, I must get out of here so you can clean up this pile of paper."

When he was focused, Casper worked diligently, and he did all afternoon to clean up the paper and have them ready for Mrs. Sparks in the morning. Actually, the next day was Saturday and the plant would be closed. Casper shook his head and wondered how the days went by so fast. He felt like he had just started the week, maybe two days ago, and now it was over. The night guards were on duty and Casper stopped to talk to two of the men he met on his way to the truck. They were accustomed to him coming in early and staying well into the evening.

* * *

Saturday morning, Casper put a hoe, rake, shovel, and clippers in the back of the truck and drove to the cemetery where he parked alongside the family graves. Three generations of Blakerly's were buried in a row and there was unused space for several more. He worked two hours giving the graves a spring spruce up. He had noticed the headstones on the graves of his great grandparents were leaning slightly. Casper went over and knelt to have a look at them and the caretaker for the cemetery stopped his ride-on mower and walked over. Casper looked up at him and commented, "Can you get someone to straighten these two headstones and fix them in place?"

"Certainly Mr. Blakerly, I will phone one of our contractors first thing on Monday. Depending on how busy they are, it should be remedied within two weeks."

Casper stood and looked at all the headstones and once again marveled that his grandfather was named Casper also. He had only seen pictures of his grandparents. His parents had been married for several years by the time Casper was born and by that time his grandparents had passed away. He only knew them from looking at pictures and listening to stories told by his parents and one thing he was sure of. His parents had been excellent and, in that regard, he had been better off than most other children. He shrugged his shoulders and bent to pick up the tools which went into the truck box. As he drove away, he wondered why he had lost his parents so soon.

* * *

Monday morning, Casper stayed home and spent time with Ralph discussing the changes to the log splitter before he went to the plant. When he walked into his office, there was a preliminary copy of the new catalogue lying on his desk. He sat down and stared at the front cover printed in color and after a while decided it was a huge improvement from the previous black and white ones. He thumbed through the catalogue, reading every word and looking at the pictures of the company's products. Suddenly, he realized the new larger 3500-watt welder and the extra-large fencepost pounder were not included. The first ones had just been built and somehow had slipped through the cracks. Most likely, the catalogue had been roughed out before the new machines were built. He grabbed the catalogue and hurried to the elevator, wanting to be in the marketing department instantly. Casper walked at a fast pace right to the manager's office and found him talking on the phone. Sitting in a visitor's chair, he had time to cool down and calm himself, not paying any attention to what the conversation was about. Tom Greig hung up the phone and spoke, "Hi, Casper, how are you today?"

Casper held up the catalogue and said, "Been reading this draft of the catalogue and noticed the two newest additions to the company line are not in it."

Greig's face turned pink with embarrassment. "I don't know how that could happen. Thank God you noticed! Do you want to come with me to have a look at the new machines?"

Casper grinned. "Sure, let's do that and decide what we want for pictures." Together, they walked out into the plant and stopped first where the welders were built. The new welder was sitting there, the black paint shinning in the work lights. On each side, a red Davenport label was clearly visible.

Greig looked at the manager and asked, "We need to add your

new machine to the next edition of the company catalogue. Do you have a list of its size and features?"

The manager smiled and picked up the top copy from a stack of operating papers and handed it to Greig. "One of these will be put on each machine as they are built. This one produces up to 7,000 watts and 50 continuous amps output." Greig looked up. "This is a big machine compared to the existing ones we build. I'll send one of my people out here to talk to you and put together a good description of the welder's capability and what kind of work it will be used for. We will need to put together a situation to take pictures with a welder shown working. Thank you for your help. Our new catalogue is almost ready to go to the printers, so we will have to move quickly on this."

The manager added, "It has a large fuel tank that will keep it running for ten hours at full load and about eighteen hours under normal type usage. This would be a good day to take pictures outdoors. We will put together a realistic setup to impress possible buyers."

"Thank you." Greig turned and commented to Casper, "I need to run back and put one of my people on this. Do you mind waiting for a minute?" Casper nodded and Greig hurried away. When Greig returned, the two men walked past the end of the assembly area and through the open doors. The new post pounder was being tested and they watched for a few minutes. Ralph Shaw walked over to stand beside Casper. "You did a good job of designing this baby, she is working very well, and now we have the laser guidance set up perfectly. The only thing we are lacking is a job to pound a few thousand posts."

Casper laughed, which pleased Ralph. "We need to take pictures of it pounding posts and lay out a description of its work capabilities. The men will have to clean it up for the pictures so it looks brand new. The laser guidance is the single most important part, so we will need to play that feature up in the catalogue, and describe the number of posts it can pound in an hour. Can you work with Greig in putting the data together?"

"No problem, Casper, we will get right on it. You want to be here when the pictures are taken?"

"Good idea, Ralph. I will be in my office shuffling paper around." Casper walked away and Ralph began giving instructions to his crew.

* * *

Mrs. Sparks walked into his office and stood in front of Casper's desk. When he looked up, she told him, "Received this letter from Jessica Hornsbee which you should look at."

Casper leaned back in his chair. "What do you think of her qualifications and will she make a useful summer helper?"

Sparks was surprised. She had expected him to take the letter and read it. Her mind was spinning at a hundred miles per hour thinking, *'I don't know anything about hiring mechanical engineers.'* She glanced at Casper and he was watching her. *'Oh, dear me, now I am in a jackpot for sure.'* Sparks opened the letter and hurriedly found the grades. She stiffened her spine and cleared her throat. "It says here that Hornsbee has achieved a 3.81 grade point average across all the courses she has taken, which seems to me to be rather good since 4.0 is the very best any student could achieve. Also she and another female student are renting an apartment which presumably she can continue to live in over the summer. There is no mention of transportation so that is a potential problem. If she does not have a car, some means of getting to work will have to be found. The lady grew up on a dairy farm and helped on the farm for many years, which tells me she knows how to work."

Casper didn't move, he just asked, "Would you hire her for the summer?"

Sparks was again surprised. "From the little I talked to her, she impressed me as being intelligent, her grades are very acceptable, and yes I would offer her a job."

"Have you given thought to what level of compensation, insurance, etc. you would offer her?"

"No sir."

"May I suggest you phone the university and ask them what starting salaries new grads are receiving and possibly compare with the salaries we are paying to people who work for us by the month?"

"Yes, sir, I will do that immediately. Thank you for your help." Sparks turned and left his office and Casper smiled to himself. *'Very interesting, now we will see what she comes up with.'*

* * *

Two days later, Mrs. Sparks returned to discuss with Casper the starting salaries of new grads. She sat across the desk from Casper and this time she had a file folder which she opened and laid on the desk. "Sir, I went to the university specifically to ask for the starting salaries for new mechanical engineering grads and it turns out that their data ranges. They explained to me that not all grads are equal, especially in the marks they have achieved, and at the same time not all industries are operating at the same level of profits. I brought the data back to the office and spent several hours sorting through it. I have concluded that the range that would apply this year is $1245.00 to $1873.00. Since Miss Hornsbee had grades in the upper range for engineers, I would suggest Davenport should be prepared to pay her in the range of $1600.00 per month." She looked up at Casper.

Casper's mind was busy analyzing the data. When he had graduated fourteen years earlier, his class was starting at around $800 per month. Things had changed dramatically in a short number of years. Well, it certainly was a good time to sell machinery which fit in with what he was hearing. "Mrs. Sparks, you should call Miss Hornsbee and have her come in for an interview with you. See if you can find out how much her rent is and whether she owns a car. Also ask her what level of salary she is expecting. Talk to human resources and find out what insurance plans she will be eligible for. The other thing is we will have to find office space where she can do her work."

"Do you want to talk to her when she comes in?"

"Only if you run into something you need help with. Find an office for her to use and she will need a desk, chair, computer, drafting table, and tools. Oh, and ask her when she will be available to start working. Another item is steel-toed boots. Presumably, she won't have them and so Davenport will have to stand the cost of boots. We can't have her going around the plant unless she conforms to the safety rules. There may be other things to be concerned about so you should talk to some of our people for any suggestions they may make. Remember, Mrs. Sparks, this graduate engineer is looking for a summer job to earn money for her next term so be fair on the salary."

Sparks walked out of the office enthralled with the new task, although several times Casper had scared the wits out of her. The first thing she would do was set up an interview, look for an office and furnishings, and then she would talk to a few of the people for ideas.

* * *

Marketing phoned to inform Casper the photographer was coming at ten a.m. to start taking pictures of the new machines. The welder/generator was easy. They were planning to picture the machine being used as a generator sitting outside supplying power to an employee posing as a construction carpenter working on the new addition being built south of the plant. They had a table saw set up as background to the welder/generator which was facing the midday sun. Casper walked around watching but didn't make any comments.

Pictures of the post pounder were going to be shot out on the farm. Everyone packed up and drove to the farm and Casper followed in his half-ton. The catalogue wanted pictures to show the huge size and features of the machine and also pictures to display the laser guidance system. The men had pounded in a long line of posts for a new fence in an arrow straight row to demonstrate the guidance system. Now, the cameraman wanted the camera up in the air to shoot a photo looking down at an angle on the operator pounding a post and showing the long line of posts going off in the distance. The camera had to be mounted in a rock-steady place with no movement or vibration and putting it up in the air was not easy. Casper told one of the farmhands to bring a combine to mount the camera on. In a few minutes, the combine came from the yard and pulled up where the cameraman was standing. He lugged the heavy camera up the steps to the cab door and had a look. It took several minutes of moving the combine to find what the cameraman thought was an ideal location. The combine's engine was turned off and everyone walked clear, leaving the cameraman to shoot pictures. The employee posing as the operator of the machine, Ralph Shaw, was wearing coveralls, gloves, a hardhat, and sound mufflers over his ears. The post was one pound into the ground and the heavy weight was down on top of the post. Ralph had his right hand on the controls and his left out pointing at the post. Picture after picture was taken through a telephoto lens.

When the photographer was satisfied everything was moved out of the way and he began taking pictures of the machine from every angle and many from low down. He explained to the market department group that pictures taken from the lower angle should make the machine look even larger than it was.

* * *

Casper got into the passenger side of the farm foreman's pickup for a trip out to the grain fields to check the ground for seeding. The winter snows had stayed longer than usual this year so it was a tougher decision to make. Was the ground warm enough, dry enough, and was it now time to start? Today was a week behind the seeding start of last year. The air drill had been checked over and adjusted and was ready, all it needed was to be filled with seed and fertilizer. As the pickup drove along, Casper was considering. He owned ten quarters and last year had added five quarters of rental land to farm for two neighbors, giving them a total acreage to manage of 2400 acres of which 1695 acres needed seeding, 220 acres grew hay, 440 acres were pasture, and the remaining 45 acres were treed and provided some additional pasturage for the cattle. His herd of cattle had become all Black Angus and the 440 acres provided plenty of grazing, but the herd was growing and there would be a demand for additional grasslands in the coming years. The truck came to a stop and while the foreman put the soil thermometer in the ground, Casper took the spade and walked around checking for soil moisture. The foreman wrote in his notebook before looking up at Casper. "Soil temperature here is fifty-eight degrees, which is good enough for seeding."

"The ground here seems to be a bit on the moist side right now. Probably a day or two will take care of it; been nice so far today." The foreman wrote down Casper's comments.

"Casper, let's go and check the other two large fields and see what we find." When they were back at the home farm, they looked at the remarks and decided tomorrow seeding would start on the 660 acres of rental grain land; it was the warmest and the

94

driest soil on the farm. As Casper walked away to the house, he heard the foreman tell one of the men, "Please phone the fertilizer dealer and ask them to fill the B-Train with the farm's custom mix of fertilizer. While you are doing that, we will fill the tandem truck with seed."

Chapter 7

Jessica Hornsbee began working at Davenport Machinery Inc. on April 20th and spent the morning talking to Mrs. Sparks and the Employee Resource people. She filled out all the forms, was issued company coveralls, a hardhat, and a lady from Employee Resources drove her to an industrial supply store to purchase a pair of steel-toed boots. The safety supervisor briefed her on the work rules and all the safety practices. Mrs. Sparks led her to the office set aside for her to use and Jessica found a company ball cap sitting on her desk. Midafternoon had arrived and Mrs. Sparks took her to meet the three company managers, then the accounting department and employee resources.

Next morning, Jessica arrived for work at seven-thirty and found the doors unlocked. She walked up the stairs to the second floor and went into her office. She had only been there a few minutes when Tom Greig, the marketing manager, arrived and introduced himself. They chatted for a few minutes and he described for her the marketing plans for Davenport. He handed her a final draft of the company's new catalogue and asked her to read it through and advise him of any changes she would suggest.

Finally, she was alone in her office and looked around in amazement. Everything in the office seemed to be new or hardly used. The walls were bare which wasn't all that pleasant. She opened her briefcase, took out the lunch she had packed, and opened a desk drawer to store it. She put her Texas Instrument calculator on the desktop, put her case of drafting instruments in a drawer along with the plastic triangles, and stored the briefcase under the desk. She leaned back, the draft catalogue in her hand, and after a moment put the catalogue back on the desk. She dearly wanted to visit the production lines to watch the men work, talk to them, and, if there was going to be a demonstration of equipment, to be there to see the performance. With her hardhat firmly planted on her head, she picked up the leather work gloves and walked to the elevator. Mrs. Sparks saw Jessica going and smiled to herself. *'Going to get acquainted with the plant.'*

The men saw her coming wearing blue jeans, a red plaid shirt with long sleeves, a hardhat, and sure enough hard-toed boots. She was heading down the line to where the bigger machines were built and everyone watched her, trying not to draw attention to the fact they weren't paying attention to what they were working on. When she got past the painting section to where the post pounders were built, she walked up to a three-man group, one of whom was pointing at a machine while he talked. She stuck out her hand and announced, "Hi fellas, my name is Jessica Hornsbee and I have been hired for the summer months. Will you explain to me what you are doing?"

For a moment, all three men were silent before one man spoke. "Hi Jessica, I'm Gregory, the foreman on the fencepost pounder part of Davenport's operation. We are building the third of our new large fencepost pounders and think we have come up with a way to do part of it easier." Soon, Jessica was standing in the middle of the half-built machine listening to the verbal argument.

Finally, she suggested to the foreman, "Gregory, why don't you guys build this machine the new way and the next machine the old proven way and afterwards we could compare the results?"

"Good suggestion, Jessica. Alright, guys, we are going to do this machine the way Wilbur suggested."

Jessica got out of the way and sat down on a machine part, took out a notepad and after glancing at her watch wrote down the time. She watched all the moves the men were making and noted how smooth they were. She concluded that all three had been working in the plant for several years. The actual part of the machine that did the pounding arrived slung under a forklift and slid easily into place, bolts were stuck into holes, and the locking nuts tightened. The hinges were tested to find if they allowed the proper movement and everyone stepped back. Jessica noted the time and wrote it on her notepad. When her head came up, she told Gregory, "I kept notes on what you did, when you get to this stage on the next machine alert me so I can be here to do the same. Then, we can compare the notes and talk about the operation. You fellas have a good day. I am going to go out to the yard." They watched her walk away before going back to work.

Ralph Shaw and two men were testing some changes made on the first large fencepost pounder and he saw her coming. It took a moment for his memory to sort out who it was. Ralph took a few steps away from the machine and met her. "Hello, Jessica, I am Ralph Shaw, we met the other day when you were touring the plant with the other students. So you are going to be working with us for the summer?"

"Yes, I am, Ralph, started yesterday morning. What are you doing to this machine?"

Ralph laughed. "We made a few changes in the machine and have been trying them out to see if everything works better. Davenport wants its machines to be the best available on the market, at least for the sizes we build, so everyone is trained to suggest improvements when they have an idea. Davenport has a fund to pay bonuses to employees who make a significant improvement to any part of the company's operation. Come and have a look at what we are trying." At the machine, Jessica found herself lying on the ground beside Ralph as he showed her how they had changed the ground plate on the bottom of the fencepost pounder. Ralph ran his hands over the plate and explained it was now larger for improvement in softer ground and curved to add more square inches.

Above the plate, they had put in long triangle-shaped reinforcement pieces to keep the ground plate from bending. He explained, "Under normal weather conditions, the ground plate really isn't needed but when the ground is very dry, rough, rocky, or has tree roots, we need to be more aggressive. Also, if the fence line is going across a slope and one side of the machine is lower than the other, the ground plate will hold the machine in place so the fence posts go into the ground in an upright position, in line with the other posts."

"How did your tests turn out?"

"Everything worked fine here in the yard, which pleased us. Now we will have to take the machine out and try it in rougher terrain to be sure."

"When are you going to do that?"

"I was figuring on pulling the machine out into the countryside tomorrow morning and doing some more testing."

Jessica grinned at him. "Will you take me along so I can see how the tests go?"

"Don't see why not. Do you have a pair of company coveralls?"

"There are coveralls in my office, and I'll wear them for the trip." She glanced at her watch. "Thanks, Ralph, now I had better get back to my office and do the proofreading they gave me to do."

When Mrs. Sparks left at closing time, she saw Jessica sitting at her desk writing in the catalogue with a red ink pen. She thought, *'Jessica is going to cause some talking in the marketing department when they get her comments.*

'

* * *

Crop seeding was within two days of being completed. Casper

had spent considerable time helping out on the farm, even driving the tractor pulling the air seeder for a few hours but this was a job for the hired men. He only stayed on the tractor long enough to get the feel again and see how everything was running before he climbed down the steps of the tractor and turned it over to one of the men. Often, he had loaded seed grain in the tandem-wheeled grain truck and driven it out to where the air seeder was working. He also checked on the cattle herd and the new calves so the men didn't need to worry about them. Several times, he had gone at noon and picked up cheeseburgers and cokes for the men to give them a change of diet. Now, he was thinking about the office. The damn paper would be piling up and hopefully someone had been told to process it. Casper grimaced as he thought. "Should have gone to the office to arrange everything but damn, being out here during spring seeding is like having a holiday, and I have never gone anywhere on a holiday." He considered phoning Mrs. Sparks for a moment before shrugging. "She will have taken care of moving the paper or finding someone to do it. Most likely Ralph has told her where I am."

The air seeder arrived to be refilled and Casper backed up the tandem grain truck to the loading auger. He climbed the ladder and stood on top of the air tank while one of the men regulated the grain shoot on the truck. When the grain tank was full, Casper drove away in the tandem going to the yard to load more seed. He pulled under the auger and rolled the tarp over until the grain box was fully open before starting the gas engine and getting the auger moving. They were seeding wheat now and he watched the golden seeds falling into the truck box. He looked across the farmyard and saw Ralph's truck coming with a large fencepost pounder hitched behind it. He wondered, *'Ralph must be coming to do more tests on the machine?'* Casper turned off the engine to stop the auger and walked out to talk to Ralph. He wanted to know what was happening.

Ralph climbed out of the truck and smiled at Casper. "How are you this morning, boss?"

"What are you doing gallivanting around the countryside pulling my…" He stopped talking as he saw a lady coming around the front of the pickup. Suddenly, he recognized her and smiled. "Well, I'll be darned, it is Miss Jessica." He stuck out his hand to shake with her. "You sure do look good all dressed up in those work clothes."

"Thank you, Casper. Ralph invited me to come with him to witness some tests he is going to do and told me I had to be properly dressed."

"Good for him." Casper pointed at his feet and laughed. "Have my steel-toed boots on just like you have." Casper turned toward Ralph and asked, "What are you testing?"

"We built a different ground pad for the bottom of the pounding part of the machine to steady it on side slopes. Everything worked fine in the yard yesterday so now I want to do some pounding on the side of a hill. Come and have a look." They walked back to the fencepost pounder and got down on the ground to have a look. Jessica got down there with the men. Ralph explained the reasoning behind the new ground pad.

When they were back on their feet, Casper made a suggestion. "Not everyone will need a pad like that, so it can be offered as an extra which the owner can order if he needs it. You get on with your testing, I have to put on a load of wheat seed and get it back to the field before the air seeder comes up empty." They watched Casper walk back to the bin and start the auger engine. He tightened the drive belts and wheat started flowing out of the auger end. As they drove away, Casper was climbing the grain box ladder to check on the load. The tandem could legally haul six hundred bushels. He moved the truck forward twice and watched it fill up before shutting down the operation. He rolled the tarp over to cover the truck box which would keep the grain clean and protect it in case it rained. The tandem had a high horsepower engine and an automatic transmission for easy driving. Casper put the truck in gear and drove out to the county road with his load. Tomorrow night would see the end of seeding or be very close. He smiled as he watched the fields going by, *'One more day I'll give to the farm before going back to the plant.'*

* * *

Mrs. Sparks arrived for work at 7:45 and took the elevator up to the second floor. As she stepped off the elevator, she looked and saw Casper's head down over his desk, going through a pile of paper. She turned her head and Jessica was at her desk. She shook her head in amazement, *'People who grow up out in the rural areas all seem to be early risers.'* She walked to her desk to begin the day, telling herself she had better clean out Casper's out basket before he overfilled it.

When she walked into his office, Casper raised his head. "Good morning, Mrs. Sparks. How are you today?"

"Very well, thank you." She picked up the pile of paper in his out basket and turned to leave.

"Mrs. Sparks, please see if you can locate Ralph Shaw. I want to meet with him and Jessica Hornsbee." She nodded and hurried back to her desk to deposit her armload of paper.

In Jessica's office, she smiled and sat down in one of the chairs before asking, "Are you going to be here in your office for the next hour or so?" Jessica nodded and put down the machine operating manual she had been reading. "Good, Casper wants to meet with you and Ralph so as soon as I can locate him, we will set up the meeting."

"Do you know what Casper wants to talk about?"

"He didn't say but don't be worried. He will have some project he wants to tell you both about. As soon as I find Ralph, I will be back to see you." Mrs. Sparks walked away and Jessica watcher her go to her desk and dial the phone. Actually, she phoned three different numbers before she found Ralph and talked to him. Mrs. Sparks went into Casper's office and told him Ralph would arrive in half an hour, then she went and told Jessica the meeting would be at nine a.m. in Casper's office. Jessica was on her computer running a drafting program which she had started to operate on her machine. When Ralph came off the elevator she picked up a pad of notepaper and a pen and followed him to Casper's office.

Casper's first words were, "Jessica, how are you finding Davenport as a place to work?"

"The people are nice and easy to talk to. So far, I have been getting familiar with the plant and how the company operates. Likely it will be a busy place to work for the summer."

"Very astute Jessica, most of Davenport's employees are relatively young with children in school so the company has been shutting down for two weeks in July and everyone goes on holidays. The company is growing but still, there are not enough employees to keep everything running over holidays. The system may change in the coming years. We put it to a vote on when to take holidays and only specified it had to be in July or August. The employees voted for the second half of July. Employee relations told me some of the longest-serving employees will soon be eligible for three weeks' holidays." Casper laughed, "I told them to look into it and come back to me with recommendations. What I wanted to talk to you about, Jessica, is do you know how to operate a computer-driven drafting program?"

"We were using those programs in university and I enjoyed working on them."

"Great. Up to now, I have been doing the drafting of parts

plans for the machines. Would you be willing to work with Ralph and produce blueprints for the new log splitter and large fencepost pounder?"

"Sure would. Are these parts plans for the workers on the production line to use for building machine parts?"

"Exactly, because we want every line of machines we make to be the same which makes repairs or changes much easier to accomplish. Along with the drafting, you will need to specify the grade of steel to be used, milling measurements for good fit and long life, do stress analysis, and make sure each part will be able to handle the loads without failing. Finally, each part must be stamped with the machine name, size, and part number."

Jessica thought about the request for a minute and looked over at Ralph. "Which machine do you think we should start on?"

"The log splitter, it will be the easiest to do and we need to get started building them for the coming winter. Shouldn't take us long and then we can go after the fencepost pounder."

She looked across the desk at Casper. "Does that make sense to you?" Casper nodded. Jessica stood up and then stopped. "Anything else you need to tell us?"

"No, Jessica. You two get to work and keep me informed." He sat there and watched them disappear into Jessica's office. He smiled, satisfied with the meeting, and looking forward to finding out how good the plans would be.

In Jessica's office, they were busy writing out the steps to follow to get sketches of the wood splitter parts prepared so the drafting could begin. "Ralph, will we need to take the machine apart to get exact measurements on each part?"

"Most of the machine can stay together. There may be a couple of places where we will need to pull something off. The splitter is very simple. When we move on to a post pounder, there will be more need to take things apart."

"Does Davenport have photos of the machines?"

Ralph thought for a minute. "There are pictures of the post pounder but not the log splitter. I will stop in marketing and ask for copies of the pictures and request they shoot photos of the log splitter for us. Would eight by ten size photos be okay?"

"Those sizes will be good. What does Davenport have for accurate tools so we get the measurements of each part correct, especially the spacing between swivel points and the size on shafts and bearings which must fit properly to prevent premature wear?"

"The machinists have measuring tools. They may not want us to use them and if that is the case, they can send a man to do the measuring for us."

"Where can I get copies of a couple of the parts plans for the existing machines?"

"Come with me to the marketing department and they can get the part books for you." Ralph stood just as the phone rang. He stood there as Jessica reached for the phone.

"Hello, this is Jessica." She listened for a minute. "Very good, I will be there in half an hour. Thanks for phoning."

She put her hardhat on as they left chatting away about the task they had been given. In marketing, Ralph introduced Jessica and she explained her request and was assured books on two machines would be put on her desk. Jessica left and Ralph talked to Tom Greig about the photos.

Jessica arrived at the construction site for the post pounder and greeted the three men. This time, they had a chair for her. "How thoughtful." She smiled and opened her notebook before stating, "Please tell me when you are going to start."

Gregory smiled and told her, "We are going to work right

now."

Jessica noted the time and watched the three men walk over to the far wall where they lifted the pounder onto a wheeled dolly and secured it in place. Pushing the dolly across the cement floor seemed easy enough but it did take time. When they arrived, Gregory fitted the end of a chain lift to the top of the pounder and Wilber picked up the electric operating control. He pushed a button to lift the pounder above the dolly which was pulled out of the way. Two men swung the pounder into place and Wilber jockeyed it up and down until a mounting bolt was pushed into place and a locking nut partially tightened. One man pushed the bottom of the pounder back and forth until a second mounting bolt was put in place, then the two bolts were tightened. The men stepped back and looked at Jessica, who was writing the time down. She finished writing her notations on the operation before looking at them. "Do you gentlemen want to give me your opinion of which method is the best one to use before I go over my notes with you?" Loud laughing sounded behind her and she turned to look. A line of men was standing there watching. She shrugged her shoulders and turned back. The three men had their heads together and were discussing an answer.

"We agree; Wilber's suggestion is the best way to go on the construction."

"Why?"

Gregory looked uncomfortable. "It is just that we all have the same feeling. We think it was faster and also that it is safer doing it that way."

"You are correct. Unfortunately, feelings are not justified under safe working rules. There must be a study done, which we have just finished, and in this case, the data I wrote down agrees with your feelings. Come over here where we can talk without the noise from the peanut gallery behind me interrupting." The three men

106

came and listened to Jessica reading her notes. "I will type up a safety study report describing the two procedures we tried and setting out our decision. There will be a copy for each of you. If I may be so bold, I wish to state that in my mind you three men are to be congratulated."

Replying in unison the three men thanked her for working with them. Jessica stood up and shook hands with them before she walked back to her office, using the stairs for the first time.

She pulled out the safety manual and looked up one of the staff reports before she began typing on her computer. Following the format in the manual, she quickly produced a safety report with the recommendation and went on to congratulate the three men by name for being alert and safety conscious and added a suggestion that they be considered for an annual safety award. When it was finished and printed, she delivered the report to Mrs. Sparks.

Ralph came off the elevator with a bundle of photos and met her at the door of her office. "Here are pictures of the fencepost pounder and they promised to take photos of the wood splitter this afternoon." After looking through the pictures, Jessica commented, "These will be a huge help when we start on the pounder, I'll just store the photos on a shelf for now." Back on her computer, she asked, "Please give me Davenport's official name for the wood splitter and can you describe to me the company's system of assigning serial numbers, model numbers, and all the other picky little things?"

The afternoon flew by and at three-thirty when the phone rang looking for Ralph; it was a surprise to both. Ralph hung up the phone and told her, "They are ready to take pictures and want me there to advise them. See you in the morning. Jessica smiled and nodded before turning back to her computer. She brought up the drafting program that Casper had said he used and opened it. First thing she did was set up a master page with Davenport Machinery

Inc. and its mailing address and phone number in the top left-hand corner. At the top, in the middle, she typed in the name and number of the log splitter then ran a line around the page only breaking for the company name and the machine name. The two names were set to print in red and the line in black. She stored the page so it could be called up at any time. While talking with Ralph, she had decided to start with the bed of the splitter along which the hydraulic ram would push the splitting head. First, she drew a picture of the bed looking down from above. It was very easy, just the heavy bed top with the end of the box support jutting out at the left end. Next, she drew a view of the bed looking in from the right side and below a view from the left side. The right end of the bed would be securely fastened to the frame just below the hydraulic cylinder and they would move together from the horizontal position to the vertical position. She would need to take a look at the machine to get this connection sorted out. On the left end, she drew in profiles of how the end would look from a position outside the splitting end. With a machine that large, there might be several different sizes of bases and splitting ends for the hydraulic cylinder to push. They would have to devise a mounting system for the bases using a heavy steel shaft with a locking pin through one end so the bases could be changed easily. Her mind wandered around the options. It was not a small machine so it was not intended to split small-diameter logs, although sure as hell someone would do that. The main problem was to design it to handle the splitter base and head for larger diameter wood logs, say up to two feet. She mused for a moment and decided it would most likely be provided with an eighteen-inch head. If the buyer wanted, he could purchase a small or a larger head, but the machine must be able to handle the larger size without breaking. On a pad of paper she sketched outlines of heads and bases and added her first thoughts on how the quick-change mountings would be done, obviously with single pins for ease of changing. She heard a noise and her head jerked up to look around.

Casper was standing just inside her office and had startled her.

Casper grinned at her. "Miss Jessica, do you realize it is seven-thirty?"

"Oh, it can't be." She looked at her watch and the surprise was stunning. "My, I didn't know time was going by so quickly. Thank you for informing me."

"It is not a bad habit to be interested in what you are doing. I am often here until nine o'clock or so. Could I interest you in a hamburger and coke for dinner tonight?"

Being asked out by the owner came as a shock to Jessica but she quickly decided it wasn't a date, just dinner to compensate for working late. She smiled. "A hamburger sounds good. Just give me a minute to store my work away and we can go." Together they walked to the elevator which took them to the main floor. When the elevator doors opened, a security guard was waiting.

Casper spoke to him. "How are you tonight, Tony? May I introduce Miss Jessica Hornsbee?" Jessica stuck out her hand and shook with him. Casper continued, "It seems that Jessica suffers from the same malady I have—she works late and is so interested she misses the time going by. See you tomorrow, Tony." They walked away and Tony made sure the door was locked behind them.

Chapter 8

Jessica drove her car along the street, following Casper's Ford F150 which appeared to be several years old, probably at least five years, she thought. The pickup turned off the street and parked in a two-stall open place in the parking lot. Jessica pulled in along-side the pickup and walked to the door which Casper was holding open. She followed Casper to his favorite spot which featured a wide-spreading view through the windows. As soon as they were sitting, a waitress arrived with two glasses of ice water and menus. She smiled broadly at Casper and told him, "Good to see you, Casper. Have you been working late again?"

Casper laughed. "Meet Jessica, a mechanical engineer at Davenport who has the same bad habit as me. We both lost track of the time, now we need to eat."

"Good to meet you, Jessica. You take a look at the menu and I'll be right back."

Jessica had changed into her Adidas which allowed much more freedom for her feet than the steel-toed boots. She tentatively wiggled her toes as her eyes scanned the menu. She made her selection, closed the menu and immediately the waitress came across the room. "What will you have, Jessica?"

"The shrimp salad with Italian dressing. Does it come with a piece of toast?"

"You can get cheese or garlic on a soft bun."

"Bring me the cheese toast please and I will just drink the ice water, thank you."

"Casper?"

"My usual cheeseburger well done, a glass of root beer, and bring us a plate of onion rings and maybe Jessica will help me eat them." As the waitress was writing, Casper asked, "How is Ma doing?"

"She got home from the hospital yesterday and will most likely be here tomorrow for at least part of the day." Casper nodded and smiled.

The waitress walked away with the food order and Casper told Jessica, "Ma is the owner of this restaurant and her doctor put her in the hospital for a kidney stone operation. She's a tough old girl and I expect she will be back behind the counter sooner than she should be. I have been coming here to eat ever since my mother passed away and have gotten to know her and the staff. Tell me how you are making out with the log splitter."

Jessica grinned at him. "We are making good progress, the files are set up on the computer, Ralph was looking after the picture taking today, and I started drafting some of the parts, working from memory. When we have the pictures, it will improve the speed of drawing and getting the measurements and tolerances correct. Out in the plant, I can't find anyone to explain to me why the thickness and size of the parts are sized as they are. This afternoon, I developed a feeling that there has been no stress analysis or load testing done to make sure the parts won't fail while working." She watched Casper and his face didn't show any sign that he knew something she didn't.

"The best thing for you to do is make the calculations and document them for people to look at in the future, especially if problems are reported by the users. When you are working the numbers, please remember that Davenport doesn't want failures so make sure the parts are specified to be two or three times as strong as the numbers indicate is necessary. People have a habit of using the machines to do things they are not intended for, and can overload or shock load some part, causing it to fail. For sure we don't want a worker being killed or seriously injured by one of the machines we build." The waitress arrived with their meals. Casper smiled at her. "Thanks for the good service, Florence."

"You are welcome, Casper. Do you want mustard or hot sauce?" They both said no and Florence walked back to the counter.

The conversation mostly died while they were eating. Casper ate an onion ring and pushed the plate closer to Jessica who helped herself. Casper had never adapted to slow eating and finished his cheeseburger when Jessica was only halfway through the salad. He leaned back in his chair and pulled a small notebook out of a pocket and wrote a message of some kind in it. Still holding the notebook in his left hand, his right reached out and picked up an onion ring which he started eating. When the last of the ring went into his mouth, he picked up the pencil and wrote more. Jessica wondered what idea he had come up with. Or was it a solution to some problem he was worrying about? When she pushed the salad bowl away, Florence arrived immediately and asked, "Either of you want dessert?"

Casper glanced at Jessica who shook her head no. "Nothing for us Florence, please bring the bill."

Five minutes later, Florence was back and handed Casper the bill. He already had a twenty in his hand and gave it to her. "You keep the change, Florence. Thanks for the great service and say hello to Ma for me. You tell her to take it easy until her body is over the operation."

"I will tell Ma what you said Casper and thanks for the change."

Casper held the door for Jessica and walked with her to the vehicles. "See you tomorrow, Jessica."

"Sure thing, Casper, and thanks for dinner." He waved one hand and opened the truck door. He backed out, and drove off down the street before Jessica had her car engine started.

*   *   *

Lockley Simpson was sitting in his half-ton in the farmyard when Casper arrived home. It had been a while since the two men had gotten together and a feeling of happiness surged through Casper. Both men exited their trucks and shook hands. "I haven't laid an eye on you for several months, Lockley; real good to see you. Do you want to come in and have a coffee?"

Lockley laughed. "Stopped by twice this spring to see how you were doing. For a farmer, you sure don't spend much time on the farm. When I got home, I told my wife you must have changed into a city boy. Late in the day for me to be drinking coffee, so I'll pass on that."

"How's your family coming along?"

"All four of us are healthy and both of our children are in school now, riding the bus every morning. My wife has planted a garden large enough to feed three families. I told her we would have to lug all those potatoes and vegetables into the cold room this fall and next spring lug them back out and throw them away. She told me it would be healthier for me than driving into town and going to a gym and I wouldn't have to pay."

Casper laughed. "Shannon is a fine lady and you are lucky she agreed to marry you and now she has given you two children. Hell, you are probably the most spoiled husband in the county."

Lockley leaned on the front fender of his truck and fell quiet for a minute or so. "Cass, I came over to ask for a little help. Haven't finished my seeding and the darn drill broke down. Was wondering if you might have time to come over and finish the

113

seeding for me."

"No problem, be proud to give my best friend a helping hand. What do you have left to seed?"

"Was seeding corn when the drill broke down so there are probably about forty acres left to be done? Also need to seed fifty acres of green feed for the cattle to eat next winter."

"Do you have everything you need to finish, like seed and fertilizer?"

"Everything is in storage on the farm."

"Okay, Lockley, follow me into the house so I can phone Fred Aitchison, my farm foreman." Together, they walked into the house and Casper dialed the phone and listened to it ring. When he heard a hello he said, "Fred, this is Casper. My good friend Lockley Simpson is here and he needs a little help to finish his seeding. Any reason we can't run the equipment over to his farm in the morning?"

"We can do that, what does he want seeded?"

"He estimates forty acres of corn and about fifty acres of green feed for his cattle. I'll see you in the morning and come along to help out. Good night." Casper turned to Lockley and commented, "There, everything is arranged. It will take a few minutes to get the equipment hooked up but we should be there before nine in the morning."

At seven a.m., Casper was backing a tandem grain truck out of the large machine shed. The fuel gauge was at the full mark so he let it run for a few minutes while he checked the grain box and found it swept out. All the tires seemed to be properly inflated when he hit them with a hammer. He opened the driver's door and stood on the step to turn the engine off and looked over his shoulder at the sound of a truck and watched Fred drive into the yard.

Five minutes before eight a.m., Casper led the way in his Ford

F150 with two tractors coming along behind him, one pulling a corn planter and the second a grain air seeder. Fred followed the seeding equipment, driving the tandem grain truck. It would be just over two miles to the Simpson farmstead. Lockley was out in the farmyard when they arrived and they gathered to discuss the seeding. Lockley, Fred, and one hired hand would tackle the corn planting, while Casper helped the hand who would seed the green feed for the cattle.

Lockley had his truck grain box full of corn seed and told them another truck with a tank of liquid fertilizer was in the field. Fred asked, "How many pounds of corn seed per acre do you want going into the ground and how deep?" Lockley handed him a sheet of paper with the numbers written on it. Fred read the numbers and handed the paper to the tractor driver. "Lead us out to the field so we can set the seeding rates, fill the machine, and get ready."

Fred rode in the grain truck cab with Lockley to lead the way to the field with the tractor following and Casper and his hired hand bringing up the rear. The field was half a mile long and six hundred and sixty feet wide with a good tight barbed wire fence on all four sides. It wouldn't take long to seed the corn. All four men helped to fill the planters which were mounted on thirty-inch spacing over a span of twenty-five feet, a total of eleven planters. Fred checked to make sure the seeding rate on each planter was set at twenty-six pounds per acre. The liquid fertilizer was set for Lockley's expectation of one hundred bushels of corn yield per acre. Just after nine a.m., the corn planter started down the field seeding corn. The men watched for a few minutes before going back to the yard to load the air drill with seed oats.

By coincidence, the fifty acres to be seeded to green feed matched the capacity of the grain tank on the air seeder so it was filled with oat seed. The air drill had two fertilizer tanks and the small one was left empty while the larger tank was filled with a fertilizer blend of nitrogen and phosphate to provide a good start to the oats. Actually, it was a blend that would have worked well on the corn also except the other planter was set up for liquid fertilizer. It took twenty minutes to fill the air drill with seed and fertilizer and Casper and Lockley drove out to the field behind the tractor and air drill and watched him start down the field, throwing up a dust cloud from the actions of the ground openers. Both side windows on the truck were open to allow the morning breeze to keep the truck cab cooled off. After watching the action for a few minutes, Lockley asked, "How wide is the air drill?"

"The drill is forty-five feet wide and seeds just over two and a half acres on each half-mile pass down a field. The farm bought it four years ago and now the men are starting to ask about trading for a wider machine because we have more acres of land to seed. They are right about how good it would be to have a wider air drill but if we trade drills we also have to trade for a larger four-wheel-drive tractor and that amounts to a fairly large amount of money. There's another solution which I haven't suggested to them, we could run the air drill two 12-hour shifts each day and double our capacity."

Lockley laughed, enjoying the remarks. "You have always had a different way of thinking about problems."

"Farming is a business and the first requirement of a business is to make a profit or it won't be around for long. Living on a farm is a great way to live, but you also must apply yourself so the farm can keep up with changing times. Farming is much different today from what it was when our fathers started and thirty years from now it will be much different than it is today. Always figured a man has to keep changing, adapting, and growing to keep up with what is developing around him."

"Expect you are right, Casper. The wife and I have talked about it and decided to make sure our two children go to school, hopefully right through university, so they will have the opportunity to make choices. When they do choose, we hope it will be the right way for each of them to go."

"Very wise Lockley. Never know, they may opt to come back to the farm. Still, it might be nice to have a high-powered doctor or lawyer to watch over."

Lockley pointed at the air drill. "He has turned and is coming back south. Let's walk over and have a look at how the seeds are being placed in the ground." The two men got out of the truck and took a screwdriver with them. When the drill arrived they were standing on the first set of seed rows. The tractor turned and went back past them, leaving a third set of seed rows. Down on their knees, they gently removed the topsoil and sure enough, down about two inches they found an oat seed and nearby a sprinkling of fertilizer. The soil was moist but not wet. Lockley commented, "This should be enough water to help the seeds germinate and hopefully we will get a shower of rain in the next week or two."

"Early to be seeding green feed Lockley. Hell, you will be baling this crop when your neighbors are looking to see if their seeds are going to grow. You got a cool, shady place where you can store the bales?"

"My dad's hay shed is on the north side of a double row of elm trees so they will be away from the sun and in the shadow of the trees. We have been using it to store green feed for many years now." The two men who had been old buddies, going back to when they started grade one, drove the pickup back to the field entrance, turned the engine off and got out, put the tailgate down and sat on it to watch the seeding operation. It wasn't often anymore that they found time to sit and talk. "How many cows do you have in your herd now?"

"We have two hundred and twelve Black Angus cows although fifty-two of them are last year's heifers coming up on their first breeding season. Of course, there are the one hundred and fifty-four calves the cows dropped this spring. There hasn't been time to sort them out and brand so far but we will get to it in a few days. There should be close to seventy-odd new heifers. More than likely the farm foreman, old Fred, knows the count, except I haven't gotten around to asking him yet."

Lockley laughed and slapped Casper on the shoulder. "Some farmer you turned out to be. You don't even know the numbers yet."

"Got real good men working for me and I try to stay out of the way and let them do their work without interference. Doesn't mean I don't know what is happening but there is no hurry for me. When they put in their reports, I will know as much as they do." They watched the air seeder as it came toward them and Lockley started to relate what his two children, Quinton and Isabella, were doing and how they were fairing in school. From the sound of his voice, Casper understood that Lockley was proud of them and he listened to the story being told. After a while, he commented, "Sounds to me like you are lucky to have two children doing so well."

"Credit for their good performance in school belongs to their mother. She keeps a close eye on the results the children bring home and never misses a school event. Shannon knows all the teachers and which ones are the most interested in passing on their knowledge so she tries to steer the children into those teachers' classes. Quinton hasn't shown any interest in athletics but his younger sister is now a member of the school tennis club and is learning to play the game. If nothing else, it is very good exercise for her." Casper listened to what was being said but his mind kept wandering to other things he needed to think about. Finally, the seeding of green feed was finished and the two men helped the hired man clean out the tanks on the air seeder and put it into transport for the trip home. After the air drill left, they drove out to check on the corn planter. As they arrived at the field, the planter came to a halt and was ready to be cleaned out. When the corn planter started out of the farmyard to go home, Casper walked to his Ford half-ton to follow along behind.

Lockley came running to stop the truck. "You figure out how much I owe you for doing the seeding for me."

Casper smiled. "Well, when you get a bill from me, make sure you pay it on time." He laughed quietly as the truck rolled toward the county road. He had no intention of charging his long-time friend for helping him out when he was having equipment problems. What good were friends if not to help when there were problems? By the time they had everything put into storage, it was mid-afternoon and Casper decided to stay home. He had enjoyed the day, out in the fresh air and talking to his old friend.

* * *

Casper was happy when he walked into his office at six-thirty in the morning and found his in basket empty. Good, now he wouldn't have to spend several hours wading through a pile of invoices and requests. Yesterday, while spending time with Lockley, he had been thinking about the new product catalogue and wondering why it wasn't available. Now, he would go and ask. The catalogue was a key part of the plan to boost their sales, which was a priority. Casper hung up his jacket and donned his hardhat before he headed to the stairwell.

Tom Greig, market manager for Davenport, saw Casper coming. He had a stack of new catalogues on his desk and was reading one. "Good morning, Tom. Came to ask you about the new product catalogue…" His eyes took in the pile. "Well, I'll be damned. Here I am worrying about getting a copy and you have them right here."

"They arrived late yesterday and I was just looking through this one for presentation and mistakes. Sorry we were so slow getting it printed. The new lady you hired, Miss Jessica, held us up for a few days."

"Why did she do that, Tom?"

"It wasn't a problem, Casper. You told me to have her look it over and offer suggestions to make it better. Well, she came up with so many it took time to make the changes." Tom held up a copy machine printout with red ink marks on every page. "I have been going through checking the printed version with her editing suggestions. So far, every change she suggested has been made and I must confess the final printed version is much better than it would have been."

"Show me."

Tom took a printed version from the top of the pile of catalogues and handed it across the desk, then he leaned forward and placed the red ink version in front of Casper. "Look at the magazine's front covers and see the improvement her suggestions made. Next, go through the first two or three pages and do the same." Tom sat back and watched as Casper studied the cover before he opened the catalogue. It took several minutes before Casper's head came up.

"The improvements are amazing. Look at the cover; it is something we can all be very proud of. The inside pages are the same. Now I wish we had spent the money to print the pages in color. My gut feeling is this catalogue is going to boost the sales of our equipment. You better start keeping track of the orders and sales of machines so we can compare the catalogue's effect on our shipments." Casper took off his hardhat and leaned back. His hand came up to ruffle his hair. "Tom, how do you suppose Jessica learned about laying out the artwork and wording in a magazine? Hell, she graduated as a mechanical engineer the same as me and there were no courses in stuff like this."

"Can't answer that question, boss I plain don't know. One thing is for sure, we have been lucky to have her on hand, helping to put the finishing touches on this catalogue. Our first attempt at producing a catalogue and none of us had much in the way of knowledge or experience."

A huge smile lit up Casper's face. "You aren't finished checking for mistakes but please let me have two copies. I plan to march right into Jessica's office and tell her what a great job she did." Tom picked two copies off the pile and handed them to his boss. Casper set the hardhat on his head, tucked the two catalogues under his arm, and stood up. "See you later, Tom." He walked away and disappeared into the stairwell.

Jessica was working busily on her computer, doing design work and did not hear Casper as he walked in and settled himself in a chair. It was the chair squeaking as its springs adjusted to compensate for the additional weight that caused her head to turn. "Oh, Casper, how long have you been there?"

Casper grinned. "Seems like most of the morning, Jessica."

"No, you haven't. Ralph was here just a few minutes ago." She swung her desk chair around so she was facing him. "Is there something I can do for you?"

"Take a look at this." Casper held out a copy of the new catalogue.

Jessica leaned forward and took the catalogue before leaning back to gaze at the front cover. It had 'Davenport Machinery Inc.' in large block letters across the top. At the bottom were the words, 'Product Catalogue Number Six' and in smaller print down below were the words, 'Issued June 1991.' Filling the page between the two headings was a color picture of a large fence post pounder. A man wearing a baseball-shaped hardhat and coveralls was operating the machine. It was painted yellow with white wheels to carry the two air-inflated tires. On the side of the hydraulic cylinder in large print was the word Davenport. The Honda engine was painted red. The operator had his hand on the operating lever and a line of perfectly straight fence post stretched away in the distance. Jessica laughed. She knew the post pounder was not running in order to get very clear photos which would not be possible with moving parts creating dust and noise. A pile of fence posts filled the lowest part of the picture. Jessica's eye switched to look at Casper. "This catalogue has a good looking cover. Bright colors, the details are clearly visible, and the operator is wearing the proper clothing."

Casper snorted. "He better be since Davenport has a strong belief in safe working conditions. What the buyers do is their business but our company recommends a safe working environment. Don't want anyone going to the hospital with a serious injury. Down in the marketing department, Tom Greig tells me they owe a lot to you for your concerns and recommended changes. Want to add my thanks."

"I didn't do much, just read through the draft copy and made a few suggestions."

"Hell, yes, and you did it in red ink. Tom had your corrected copy on his desk and the changes were more than just a few. You tell your story however you want but remember I said thanks."

Chapter 9

Tom Greig kept his people busy for two weeks shipping out catalogues to the company's dealers. Eleven dealers were the largest sellers of Davenport equipment and each was sent one hundred copies to give away. The smaller dealers received fewer copies but in every case, the cover letter gave instructions for ordering more copies whenever needed. During the third week, Greig phoned the sales managers at each of the eleven large dealers and talked to them about the catalogue. He kept notes of their comments. Five of the managers asked when someone from Davenport would be stopping by to talk to them. Greig discussed the request with Casper and they decided that they would make a tour, especially to the west coast where three of the large dealers were located, one each in Seattle, Portland, and Sacramento. On the way home, they would stop and talk to the dealer in Denver.

Sunday morning, the two men drove to Des Moines to catch a flight to Seattle. Casper was riding in Tom's car which was only one year old and he looked at the controls without saying a word and settled down enjoying the drive. Tom wasn't speeding and was courteous to other drivers in the traffic. This was early June and the public schools were still operating so those families wouldn't be out on holidays cluttering up the hotels. Tom's secretary had made room reservations in a hotel at the Seattle Airport for both men for Sunday night. Tom talked to the Seattle dealer and made arrangements for them to go to the dealership first thing on Monday morning. At eleven a.m., Tom had the car parked at the Des Moines Airport and they checked in with the airline. They had two and a half hours before departure so went into a restaurant to eat where Tom put away a good-sized steak while Casper ordered a shrimp rice stir-fry. Tom was in charge of this trip so Casper told him to pay the bills.

The plane to Seattle was a direct United Airlines flight which was scheduled to arrive at five p.m. The plane was ten minutes late when the wheels touched down on the runway. After deplaning, it took thirty minutes to wait to receive their luggage, which was only one suitcase each and they were standing at the hotel registration desk a six o'clock. With his room key in his hand, Casper asked, "What time do you want to meet for breakfast in the morning?"

"Meet you at six-thirty at the dining room. Will take most of an hour to drive to the dealership and I told them we would be there by eight-thirty."

"Okay, Tom, see you in the morning." Casper walked away with his suitcase and a thick briefcase. Casper didn't know what Tom had planned for the evening and he didn't want to know. From the rumors he had overheard around the plant, Tom was likely to be going to a party or meeting some lady. Casper was only concerned with results and so far Tom had done a very acceptable job. Casper owned the company but had no intention of trying to run his employee's private lives. Most likely, they did all sorts of things he wouldn't approve of but as long as he didn't know about those activities he was only concerned with results. If something along those lines came to his attention, in all likelihoods he would fire the person involved.

At eight-thirty a.m., the rented half-ton was parked in a visitors slot alongside the dealer's building. Casper was wearing a sports coat over an open-necked shirt, his dress shoes brightly polished. He held the door open to allow Tom to enter with his briefcase. A man Casper estimated to be as tall as six foot six inches was waiting for them. It was several minutes before Casper noted the man had only half his left arm. The man's face was rugged, deeply tanned, he spoke in a solid deep voice, and his hair was turning white. Tom introduced him. "Good morning, Ernest, great to be seeing you again. May I introduce Casper Blakerly?"

Ernest smiled and stuck out a long arm to shake. "Very pleased to make your acquaintance, Casper, welcome to our dealership." The two men shook hands and Casper knew he would like this man who was most likely all business. Ernest asked, "Would you fellas be interested in seeing the pieces of your equipment we have on hand right now?"

Tom jumped right back into the conversation. "Seeing the equipment would be an excellent place to start, Ernest." They followed along behind Ernest as he walked across the showroom to the far side. There on the floor were two sizes of Davenport welders, all three sizes of engine powered generators, an all metal wagon set up for manure spreading, one of the first in the Davenport line of tree branch shredders, and a stack of yellow painted metal toolboxes with Davenport decals. On the far side were two sizes of Davenport fencepost pounders. Every machine had a copy of its operating manual wired on and a small table against the wall had a stack of the new product catalogues. Ernest picked up one and waved it in the air. "Inside this catalogue, I see Davenport is developing larger fencepost pounders and log splitters. When will they be available for shipping to dealers?"

"The new machines are being tested right now. Probably around the end of August there should be log splitters coming off the assembly line and ready for shipping. The men testing the splitters tell me they have made all the changes they wanted to increase the size and strength of the machine." Casper smiled and waved an arm at the pounders. "The two new, much larger fencepost pounders are taking a little longer to test out. We don't want to sell a machine to a customer and find out there is a weakness. We have two machines being tested right now and there should be new machines available in the fall. The company is being extra careful because we anticipate they will be used on long fences, often crossing hilly and rough terrain. Requests for these pounders have started coming in from the military, large ranches, and government parks but there are many contractors, mining companies, etc. that we fully expect to become customers. If any of your customers show interest, it would be a good idea to get in contact with Tom and let him know."

"Thank you, Casper. We have a lot of large operations scattered around and it will be a surprise to me if they show no interest." Ernest walked to a window and pointed out into the yard. "We have a number of trade-ins out there in the yard. Are you interested in having a look at them?"

"I want to, but don't want to waste your time. Do you have someone who can walk me around while you and Tom go over the records and talk about the coming months?"

"Good idea, Casper. Tom, you go into my office over there." He pointed at the office. "I'll get one of our people to take Casper out to look at the trade-ins." Ernest walked Tom to the office door before hurrying off to find someone to act as a guide.

The guide was about the same age as Casper and his name was Maurice Bingman. Together, the two men walked out into the yard and Maurice led the way. He explained, "We have customers who work their machines hard and want to trade them in on a regular basis. One fella told me by trading they save downtime and it saves money because in the backcountry and mountains, repairs are often costly." Maurice watched as Casper started going over the machines, looking at every detail. He wasn't missing dents or scratches anywhere and finding details that Maurice didn't know existed. He was surprised when Casper took a small 35mm reflex camera from his pocket and became busy taking close up pictures of details and writing notes in a small pocket-sized notebook. One of the used fencepost pounders was all twisted from an accident when the truck hauling it had gone off a road and rolled. Casper was noting all the damage and looking carefully at how each part was bent. His collection of pictures and notes grew noticeably and when they were finished, it had taken almost two hours. Casper went over a well-used metal wagon that had been traded in, again taking pictures and making notes. Maurice didn't ask why the careful inspections were going on but he finally surmised the information being gathered would result in changes to future machines.

Casper finally asked, "I don't see any old welders."

"To be honest with you, we have never had a welder traded in. We have sold a large number of Davenport welders over the years and continue to do so but they just go out there and disappear. We sell a lot of welding rods and a few times an owner has come in wanting a new set of cables. Of course, we also supply tanks of oxygen and acetylene for the gas welders."

Casper wrote another note in his little book. "Have any of your customers complained or suggested changes to the machines?"

"No one has ever suggested any such things to me, although a few times someone comments on how much they like the machine they bought. Tell you what. I will talk to the other employees and if there are any comments they can recall, I will send them to you."

"Thank you, Maurice. Davenport wants to build the best, most reliable machines on the market, and we are always looking for ways to improve so anything you can tell us will be a big help. Your company has a well-organized place to do business, well cared for buildings, the yard is neat, and machinery is parked in an orderly manner."

"Thank you, Casper. We sell a lot of large equipment to the logging companies, miners, etc. and doing their repair work keeps a staff of mechanics busy. We also have attracted a growing number of individuals who buy equipment for their own use on their yards and acreages. Is there anything else you would like to look at?"

"Don't think so, Maurice, thank you for taking the time to show me your trade-ins."

"It was my pleasure. You are the first one of our suppliers that has ever spent so much time looking over the trade-ins. It suggests to me why everyone seems to be happy with your machines." Together, they walked back to the display building where Tom and Ernest were waiting.

Casper looked at his watch. It was eleven-thirty so he asked, "Do you gentlemen have time to go for lunch with us?"

Ernest laughed. "Thank you for inviting us but we can't do it today. The owner has set up a noon hour meeting for all of us so we will have to say no. Next time you come, we will try to keep our noon hour open to eat with you." After shaking hands, Tom and Casper walked away to their rental pickup. Ernest and Maurice watched them drive away before Ernest asked, "What in the world were you two doing out there for over two hours?"

Maurice laughed. "Casper was going over our trade-ins with a fine-tooth comb. He took pictures of any damage he found and wrote pages of notes in a little book. I finally figured out he was looking for ways to improve the construction of their machines. He even asked if any customers had complained about the machines."

Ernest stared at Maurice for a minute. "Davenport builds real good machines. No one has ever complained to me and maybe the reason is that Davenport is doing a fine job of construction and it sounds like they are still looking for ways to make their products better."

* * *

The Davenport boys ate lunch and drove back to the hotel,

paid their bills, and, after collecting their luggage, walked to the airport terminal where they checked in for the flight to Portland. They spent Tuesday in Portland, Wednesday in Sacramento, and Thursday in Denver. Friday morning, they caught a morning flight back to Des Moines. Just after the lunch hour, Tom drove them into the yard at the Davenport plant. It had been a successful trip and the dealers had been happy to have them drop-in, there had been effective discussions, orders for more equipment which Tom had written up, and Casper had a notebook and camera full of things he wanted to discuss with his staff.

Casper took his suitcase to the Ford F150 before he hurried to his office with a bulging briefcase. He was pleased to see his desktop clear of paper and the in basket empty. He unloaded the briefcase, making piles regarding several different items. He was putting the briefcase under his desk when Mrs. Sparks walked in. "How did you find your equipment dealers, Casper?"

"Very well thank you, Mrs. Sparks. We had good meetings with all of them and Tom brought home orders for more of our equipment. How did everything go while I was away?"

"Quite well after the first day when I was fighting with your three managers and telling them they were responsible for processing all the invoices and paper coming to your attention. Tuesday morning, I marched into their offices and laid a pile of paper on each desk with word that I would be back in two hours to pick up the processed items."

Casper stared at her for a moment. "Did they do a good job of sorting through the paper?"

"Yes, they did, although they may all three be in here to register complaints about how I treated them."

Casper was quiet for a few minutes and Mrs. Sparks stood watching him. Finally, he shook his head. "It seems to me we are in need of a change in policy around here. Since you have a process working, from now on you pick out the items you specifically believe must come to me and divide the remainder between the three managers."

Sparks smiled. "Excellent plan, Casper, except for one thing. It seems to me you must establish a dollar amount each manager can approve and anything above that amount must also receive your signature."

Casper laughed. "You have been thinking about this issue, haven't you?"

"Yes, I have, mainly because it seems to me there are more valuable things which should receive your time and attention. For example, the development of new lines of machinery, the expansion of the company in terms of hiring people and providing ample space for everyone to do a great job, and of course your talent for designing and properly building machines to do a first-class job for our customers."

Casper was amazed and stared at her for a moment. "Thank you, Mrs. Sparks. Now, please ask Jessica to come to my office." When Jessica walked in, Casper picked up a pile of paper sitting on his desk and walked to the drafting table. "While I was traveling, I used my spare time to go over these drawings of yours, Jessica. To give you fair warning, I used a red ink pen to put in my suggestions. Hopefully, you will realize I can be quick to pick up on someone else's ideas. You, of course, deserve credit."

Jessica nodded and looked down at the first drawing. Her finger followed the red lines as she read the remarks and when she looked up she smiled. "Very good suggestions Casper, may I expect the ones on the other pages are just as remarkable?"

"Certainly, but you must understand, I don't want you accepting something just because I suggest it. If you don't agree, make sure you tell me why and we will argue about what is best. On our trip, I took pictures of damage on traded-in machines and wrote notes. Monday afternoon, I would like to get together with you, Ralph, and Ned Ambrose the Manufacturing Manager to decide if there are changes warranted in machines we build in the future. You take this pile of drawings with you and look them over."

Jessica walked away with her pile of paper and Casper sat down at his desk and picked up the phone. He was lucky this time and Ralph answered. "Ralph, this is Casper calling. Do you have time to come to my office and talk about the testing on the new machines?" Casper listened to the answer and hung up. They met for two hours and went over the testing. The firewood splitter was ready and Casper asked when the drawings would be available for the manufacturing people to use in starting to build sales models. Ralph estimated by next Wednesday the line drawings would be finished and building could start. There were still nitty little problems with the two large fencepost pounders and Ralph figured it would take another two weeks to work the problems out. Casper didn't like that and said so but finally backed down and accepted what Ralph was saying. He was in a hurry but quality was more important and he told Ralph he agreed.

* * *

In the Ford F150, Casper drove the nine blocks to the camera and photo shop. He walked in with his camera and set it on the counter. The store owner hurried over and smiled at Casper. "What can I do for you today, Casper?"

Casper pushed the camera toward him. "There are twenty-three photos on the disc inside the camera. I need an 8 x 10-inch color print of each picture with a number on the front starting at one. Need to have the prints on Monday morning for a meeting." The owner was filling in an order form. "Mrs. Sparks will come to pick up the prints. Please put a new disc in the camera for me." Casper was out of the store in less than ten minutes and drove to his favorite restaurant.

When he walked in, he looked and sure enough Ma was sitting at the cash register. He headed straight for her. "Hi, Ma, very good to have you back here. How are you feeling?"

"Doc tells me I am fit as a fiddle." Ma smiled at him. "Course, I never told him I still feel a little on the weak side but getting stronger every day. Are you here to eat?"

"Ma, you tell Florence to bring me a cheeseburger and a root beer."

"Coming right up, Casper. You go over there to your favorite table and your food will arrive in a few minutes." Casper walked to his table from where he had a good view. Florence followed him and put a glass of water on the table.

Casper's mind was full of plans for the future and the few minutes went by in a flash. Florence startled him when she brought his food. His head came up. "Ma is looking pretty good, Florence, a mite pale around the gills, but for sure her head is working fine."

"You are right, Casper. We've been keeping a close watch on her and insisting she go home when she starts looking tired. She growls about us giving her orders but has always left when we told her."

"Ma isn't a teenager anymore and probably won't admit that. Sounds good to me to know you folks are looking after her." Florence left and Casper got started on the cheeseburger.

He waved to Ma as he left the restaurant and drove back to the farm. He hadn't talked to Fred since the previous Saturday and wanted to catch up on what was happening. When the pickup drove into the yard, he stopped beside the three men who were preparing to go home. Casper rolled down his window and leaned on the door. "How are you fellas doing?"

Fred Atchison walked over and leaned on the truck and his two men stood nearby. "We were just fixing to go home, worked these two lazy no-goods hard all week branding the new calves and figured they need to catch up on their rest."

Casper laughed. "Good to hear. Now, you guys go on home." The two men walked to their trucks and drove away. Fred fished in his shirt pocket and pulled out a folded sheet of paper which he handed through the window. Casper glanced at the paper and saw calf numbers so he set it down on the truck seat. "You go on home, Fred. Your wife will be surprised to see you this early in the day."

Fred smiled and tipped his hat with one hand as he walked away. Casper watched him go before driving the pickup into the garage. He turned off the engine and picked up the paper Fred had given him. In total, they had branded 154 calves and according to Fred's count there were 81 heifers and 73 bulls now turned into steers. It was good news. Over the past few years, there always seemed to be fewer heifers, now they had a year when heifers exceeded half the total number. Casper banged one hand on the steering wheel and smiled as he added the numbers. *'By damn, we now have 293 cows on the place. Fred and I better start thinking about more grazing land before those cows eat us out of grass?"*

*   *   *

Casper had a head full of ideas from things he had seen and heard about on the visit to the western dealers. He had heard complaints about tree branch shredders that weren't built sturdy enough to stand up to more than regular homeowner use. Saturday morning, he was in the office at the plant working at his drafting table. From the answers he received to his questions, he was focused on two sizes of tree branch shredders. The smallest model would take branches up to ten inches in diameter, while the larger shredder would handle branches up to fifteen inches in diameter. He visualized both machines being towed behind a tractor providing seventy-five horses of power to the smallest and one hundred and fifty horses of power to the biggest one. The first models would be for tractor towing and powering. In the future, wheel-mounted models powered by diesel engines would be added.

These would be big machines and produce great piles of wood-chips so he wanted to enable the machine to blow the chips into a wagon or truck box. He drew a view of the machine from above showing it with a wagon parked alongside. After studying it for a few moments, he noticed that the feed hopper would be very close to the wagon. He didn't like the arrangement and reworked the drawing with the feed hopper set off at a thirty-degree angle. After studying the picture, he thought it would work. The tree branch would be approaching the chipper rotor at an angle that would expose a larger area to be chipped. After thinking about the idea, he decided the rotor would need a larger number of chopper blades to enable it to eat the branch at a good rate. The workmen feeding branches in would not be caught in a small workspace. Good for working and much safer if anything went wrong.

He started sketching out the main parts for the smallest machine in what he considered to be a practical manner. For the rotor, which was the heart of the machine, he debated with himself for a few minutes and finally settled on thirty inches in diameter with a large solid weight to provide rotational momentum and decrease the chances of stalling. The rotor would have heavy heat-treated steel blades mounted on it which could be reversed to present a new cutting face. On the forward rotation, the blades would be locked in place to provide maximum impact when hitting a tree branch. At that point, he stopped drawing and sat back to think. Looked to him most likely the system would work well, provided the branches were kept moving forward. His first thought was that a man tending the machine would have to push on the branches and then a second thought hit him. It would be hard work and the man would tire out. After a few minutes, he decided there would have to be a spiked roller to keep the tree branch moving ahead. At the rotor level, the width wouldn't be very wide. On a ten-inch model, a width of two feet seemed logical to him. The spiked roller to move the branches should be mounted about six inches in front of the rotor. Casper drew a sketch and then realized one roller by itself wouldn't work. There had to be two rollers to put the proper pressure on the branches. He changed the sketch to show the bottom roller mounted in one position and the top roller capable of moving up and down from five to twelve inches, dampened by springs which would always keep a downward pressure on the top roller to stay in contact with the branch as it went past.

Casper turned his attention to the rotor, which would be thirty inches in diameter. It needed to be heavy. To start, he assumed the rotor would be one inch thick. He grabbed a calculator and ran the numbers to calculate the cubic inches of volume. The calculator came up with 706.86 cubic inches. Tool steel weighed 0.2833 pounds per cubic inch and multiplying the two resulted in a weight of 200.46 pounds for the rotor. Casper leaned back in his chair and considered. Two hundred pounds sounded like it would be enough to provide momentum to the rotor. At a one inch thickness, would the rotor warp over time? This concerned him. After a few minutes of thinking, he decided the back of the rotor would need bracing by long steel ribs running out from a central hub and the hub would provide a way of mounting the rotor onto its driveshaft. What size of driveshaft would be needed? All the shredding would take place on one side, which might be enough to throw the rotor out of balance. Cutting the branch at thirty degrees would result in an oval-shaped shredding face. Another calculation was required. Casper used the calculator to run the numbers on an oval-shaped face, coming up with a vertical radius of five inches and a horizontal radius of six point six inches. He ran out the area formula for an oval and read out the number of one hundred and three square inches. To shred at thirty degrees, the shredding blades would have to be more than thirteen inches in length. Laying out a large white sheet of drafting paper, he used a drafting divider to draw a ten-inch diameter circle, left a space for a side profile and drew another ten-inch circle. With a T-Square and clear plastic triangles, he started drawing in a shredder blade, then added another at one hundred and twenty degrees across the circle and a third at two hundred and forty degrees. This drawing represented the front cutting side of the rotor. The second circle represented the back of the rotor and since he was considering a two-inch diameter shaft to turn the rotor, he drew in a scaled-down two-inch circle to represent the inside of the slide on the rotor hub. On the same spacing as the blades, he drew in support ribs to keep the blades from wavering as they came around and hit the tree branch each time. He left where the hub would be blank until he had a chance to talk to the purchasing people on Monday and got their recommendation on what hub to use. He wrote another note to himself in his notebook. Next, he considered mounting bearings and decided a roller bearing to support the rotor would be better than a ball bearing. He wrote another note to ask about the available sizes of roller bearings since he couldn't find them in his supply of catalogues.

Looking back through his sketches and drawings, he thought he had enough to start building a test model. Casper wrote a note to Ralph to leave on his desk for Monday morning saying to come to meet with him. He turned his mind to considering the drive system. It would provide power to turn the rotor and drive a fan to blow the wood-chips out the top of the machine, and there should be a clutch the men could use to stop the machine if anything went wrong. The clutch should also be adjustable to automatically stop the rotor if it began to slow down from being jammed. Casper started sketching a drive system. A knock on his office door brought his head up and he turned to see who it was.

Jessica was standing inside the door smiling at him. Casper was surprised. "My goodness, Jessica, what are you doing here on a Saturday?"

"Been here for three hours and decided I was hungry; thought possibly you could be talked into taking me out for dinner."

"We will do that…" Casper stopped talking as he looked at his wristwatch. He stammered, "My goodness, where in the world did the day go? It is already four-thirty."

Jessica laughed. "You have been working all day and your stomach never told you to stop and eat lunch?"

"If my stomach was talking to me, I didn't hear it. Where do you want to have dinner?"

"Do you eat Mexican food?" Casper nodded. "Good, there is a restaurant a few blocks from here that looks well cared for and I have been meaning to eat there. What about that?"

Casper stood up and stretched. "Let's go now. If you will drive, I will be happy to ride in your car." He turned off his office lights and together they walked to the elevator. A security guard was tipped back in his chair where he could see everything from the entrance doors to the elevator and the stairwell. Tony stood up when the elevator lights blinked. Casper followed Jessica out of the elevator and smiled at the guard. "How are you doing, Tony?"

"Just fine, Mr. Blakerly. It has been a very quiet day around here."

"Have you met Jessica?"

"Oh yes, Mr. Blakerly, she is noted for coming in early and staying late. How are you today, Jessica?"

"I am very good, Tony. See you on Monday." Tony stood there and watched them leave. He noted they left in Jessica's car, which meant Casper would be back, at least to pick up his truck. Tony took the elevator to the second floor and checked all the offices and found the power was turned off. He walked the stairs back to the ground level. Another hour and his replacement would be there to relieve him.

Chapter 10

Jessica drove into the parking lot and stopped her car near the front door of the restaurant. She looked up at the words in large letters above the doors. Las Mexico Food, which she read out loud for Casper's benefit. "Never have I been here before, Casper, but it has always looked inviting."

"If this restaurant looks inviting to you and the food is half as good as Las Mexico looks, everything will be fine." They exited the car and Casper held the restaurant door open for her to enter first. She told herself it was nice to be spoiled a bit like Casper always did. A slim Mexican lady approached and Casper told her they wanted a table for two. She picked up two menus and led them to a stone-topped table in a corner with windows on two sides. There were a few people sitting at tables, probably because it was a little early to be eating dinner, unless you had missed lunch as Casper had. When they were seated, the hostess laid a menu in front of each and came back a minute later with two glasses of ice water.

"Would you care to order a drink?"

Casper looked at Jessica and she noticed a twinkle in his eyes as he looked at her. "How would you like to drink a margarita while you eat your food?"

"That would be very nice, Casper, as long as we both have one."

"You heard what she said, Miss. Please bring the margaritas when the food is ready. Give us a few minutes to look at the menus and choose what to order." They opened the menus and started looking at what was listed. After a few minutes, Casper leaned forward and whispered, "I have no idea what to order, do you have something to suggest?"

Jessica looked at him. "I have eaten Mexican food a few times but really don't know very much about it except that I like the tastes. My usual order is enchiladas with refried beans, rice, and hot sauce."

"Sounds good to me, please order the same for both of us." Casper smiled and closed his menu. Jessica continued to look at the different food items for a minute, before closing her menu. Almost immediately, the waitress was back with her order form.

Jessica told the waitress, "We both wish to order your enchiladas with refried beans, rice, and hot sauce." The waitress wrote the order down and told them it would be a few minutes. Jessica asked how the trip to the west coast had been. Casper started telling her how he had spent two hours looking at the scratches, dents, and wear and tear he had seen on traded-in Davenport machines. He was leaning forward, gesturing with his hands when the food arrived. Casper stopped talking mid-sentence and sat back from the table. Jessica was thrilled she had asked and wanted to hear the rest of the story after they were eating. Right after the food was on the table, the margaritas were set in front of them. Casper picked up his glass and took a sip. He got a mouth full of salt off the rim and a rather acidic taste of the liquor which he had very little experience with. He watched Jessica cut the end from an enchilada, put a few refried beans on it, and a bit of sauce. She chewed on it and swallowed before sipping the margarita. He followed suit and found he liked the taste. He tried the rice and found it very good with a touch of refried beans.

Until now, Casper had always sounded very serious when he talked around the plant but he was quite humorous as he related the story of the west coast trip. Jessica enjoyed hearing the details between bites of Mexican food. She had never been to the west coast, the result of coming from a family that ran a dairy and had to milk cows twice a day. You couldn't tell the cows to turn off the production of milk for a week while you took a trip. Her mother's parents lived across the river in Indiana and she had gone there several times when her mother went to visit. Other than that, she had not traveled out of Iowa in her twenty-one years. Hearing that all four dealers were anxious to obtain the new fencepost pounders and the log splitter she was drawing production plans for caused her to feel elated. The plans for the splitter were done and being copied now. She probably needed another month to finish the fencepost pounders production drawings. Ralph Shaw would be happy on Monday when he learned the drawings for the pounder were ready. It would get him off her back for a few days at least. She smiled and ate another bite of enchilada.

Eating their dinner took more than usual time as they carried on a detailed discussion. When Casper told her what he was working on, her ears really perked up. She would love to be involved in designing the large tree branch shredder but she was already busy drawing the fencepost pounders. The operating manuals for the new machines were being written in the marketing department. Casper sketched on a paper napkin as he explained how he wanted the feed-in chute to be adjustable to provide more working space for the men while blowing the wooden shreds into a wagon or truck. He regaled her with his story of figuring the angles and how much work it would be for the machine. He had liked forty-five degrees and settled on thirty degrees as the best compromise.

The waitress came and refilled their water glasses. The conversation stopped and both looked at their watches. "It is almost seven-thirty and Saturday night is when I do my laundry. This week, I'll have to do the laundry on Sunday morning."

"It is my fault entirely for talking and telling you so much, please forgive me."

141

"Nothing to forgive, I enjoyed hearing about the trip to the west coast and all the things you saw and heard and the new machine you are designing sounds really interesting. Now, it is time for me to go home." Casper paid the bill and they walked out to the car. They were both home by eight.

* * *

Casper put the F150 away for the night and walked over to the corral to lean on the rails. An Angus cow and her twin calves were still being held there. He turned on the tap and filled the water tank to the top before he pitched one forkful of fresh hay over the fence. He watched them walk over to the tank and stick their noses into the water. The twin calves were only four weeks old, had been small, and were just starting to grow. His eyes switched to the sky and noted it would be dark in a few minutes. One of the calves came over to the corral fence and sniffed at Casper's pant leg. He reached down and scratched one of the ears. The calf shook her head and partially withdrew. After a moment, she stuck her head forward again. Casper scratched the other ear. The little heifer was friendly. He talked to them for a minute before walking away to the house.

As he approached the door, he could see a sheet of white paper hanging on the inside of the screen door. He recovered it and went inside. With the lights on, he read the note. The writing was scrolled in pencil.

'Cass: You haven't sent me a bill for the seeding. Lockley'

Casper laughed and walked to the phone where he dialed the number for Lockley. It rang twice before Shannon answered. "Hello, Shannon, it is Casper calling."

"Hi, Casper, do you want to talk to Lockley?"

"Not at all, rather talk to you any day. You tell that no good husband of yours he doesn't owe me anything. He was broke down and we have been friends for most of thirty years. Anytime a friend needs help, I am happy to be able to assist."

"Casper, that is so nice of you. I will tell him."

"Thank you, Shannon, goodbye." Casper hung up the phone, dropped the note in the waste paper basket, and went into the living room where he had a book he was reading. It had been over a week since he had last picked up the book.

Sunday morning, Casper stayed in bed for most of an hour after he woke up. He was feeling weary and decided he would take the day off and laze around. After showering and dressing, he mixed batter and ate pancakes and sausages for breakfast. He drove the pickup out to the pasture to have a look at the cattle herd and didn't find anything amiss. He parked and watched the animals moving around as they grazed; all the little calves were following their mothers and prancing around. It was relaxing to sit quietly and watch. When he went back to the farmstead, he noticed the grass had grown long so he got out the mower and rode it around the yard. He was cutting the grass at three inches and leaving swaths of cut grass behind the mower. It would need cutting again in a few days.

In the afternoon, he lay down on the chesterfield and closed his eyes. When he awoke, it was surprising to find he had slept for over two hours. Looking in the refrigerator, he decided it was time to go shopping. From De Wit, he drove home with a load of food and refilled the fridge, throwing out all the older items. Now he would start the week with a supply of fresh food and vegetables. He wandered out to look around the yard and finally found himself standing at the corral. The water tank was full and fresh hay lay on the ground, so Fred had been there to look after and check on the cattle. Leaning on the rails, his mind wandered and finally he acknowledged he was lonely. It was Jessica. He liked her and enjoyed the time they spent together. She was a very nice girl and a hard worker and he… hell; he didn't have a clue on how to date a woman. He had never had a girlfriend, well not one to date; he had gone to school with girls and was always nice to them but had never gone out with one. Now he was thirty-two, had a fast-growing business, and there was money in the bank. He kicked the corral railing and wondered. Did he dare to walk right up to her and ask her to go out to a movie or maybe dinner? What if she said no? The little heifer calve stuck her head threw the rails. He sank on one knee and scratched her ear. Out loud, he muttered to the calf, "Why don't you tell me how to go about dating a girl?" The calf shook her head and walked away. Casper laughed. "Just what I am afraid Jessica will do."

Walking back to the house, he considered. Jessica has been working for Davenport for just over two months now and it's not like we are strangers. *'We have gone out to eat three times now. This last time she came and invited me. Now damn, if she can do the inviting why can't I?'* He figured he could but deep down he knew he would have to think about it for a while.

* * *

Casper sat at his drafting table, hard at work on the shredder design when Mrs. Sparks arrived in the office. She sat at her desk sorting papers until the phone rang. When she walked into Casper's office, his head came up, she told him there were pictures ready and she was going to drive to the camera shop to pick them up. Casper jumped off his seat as he told her, "Mrs. Sparks, please wait a minute." He hurried to his desk and found the note he had written to Ralph. "Please give this to Ralph and tell him to come to a meeting in my office at two." She walked away and he returned to the drafting table where he worked until Jessica arrived for the meeting.

A minute behind her came Ned Ambrose and Ralph Shaw. Casper was using a knife to open the envelope of pictures. "Thank you for coming. As you know, I was out on the west coast last week visiting four of our largest equipment dealers. I spent a lot of time looking at the machines which had been traded in and took a few pictures. I wanted you to see the pictures and hear my comments. It may be possible to find a few ways to improve our designs. Let's sit down over at the table." They walked over to the table and when they had all selected chairs, Casper started laying out the photos one at a time, explaining what it was, and read the corresponding note he had written. It took them two hours to go through all the pictures and discuss them. By that time, Ned had made several notes on a pad of lined paper. He told Casper he would return in a few days to tell him what changes could be made. Casper replied, telling him he should talk to Jessica, who would be in charge of redrawing the construction specs from which every part was made. Jessica noticed Casper was throwing out little jokes or antidotes which were unusual in Davenport's business meetings. When the meeting was finished, Casper asked Ralph to stay for a minute.

At the drafting table, Casper pulled out his sketches for the tree branch shredder and explained to Ralph his idea to have an inlet hopper that could be moved sideways up to thirty degrees. Ralph asked, "Why do you want to be able to move the hopper?"

"This is going to be a large machine and I visualize it blowing the wood shreds into a wagon or truck box. My reason for being able to move the hopper is to make larger and safer workspace for the operator."

Ralph grinned. "Now I understand and it is a great idea. Will the hopper be able to move to both sides?"

Casper scratched his head. "Good idea, Ralph, I hadn't thought about that. You are a smart old devil despite what your wife has to say."

"Whatever she says is probably right; we've been married a long time and she is the one who runs the family."

"You're a good sport, Ralph. What I am trying to get sketched here is the main working parts of the machine around the rotor. When I get the sketches done, you come back and talk to me about it before we start building a test model."

"Sure thing, Casper. You phone when everything is ready?" Ralph walked out of the office headed for the elevator and Casper sat down at his drafting table again. He didn't realize that most of the company's employees would be leaving in just a few minutes. A security guard coming around at eight p.m. found him working and asked if everything was okay.

Casper sat back in his long-legged chair and looked at his watch. "My goodness, it is eight o'clock already. Time for me to shut down and go home, give me a minute and I'll ride down the elevator with you." Casper went to his desk and got his briefcase which he stuffed with some of the papers, just in case he had trouble going to sleep. He and the security guard went down in the elevator and Casper said good night to him before going out the door to his truck. For dinner, he made a piece of toast and put slices of onion and cheese on it and sat at the table eating and drinking root beer.

Wednesday afternoon, Ned Ambrose put a few of his line people to work making the parts for the first log splitter. They all had very precise construction drawings, a noticeable change, which drew comments from several of the machinists. In the title block on each drawing was a note which read, designed by Jessica Hornsbee.

Ralph was meeting with Casper and they were going over the

pencil drawings he had made for the shredder to get rid of large tree branches. Casper wasn't going to give up his originals. Mrs. Sparks had run the drawings through the copier and Ralph would take the copies away with him. "Talk to Ned and ask him to have his people make these parts for us. The rotor will be critical and tell him we are open to any changes he feels will make it work better or decrease the chances of the rotor warping. While they are manufacturing these, see if you can weld up a test rack so we can see how the rotor works. I am going down to purchasing to talk to them about shredder blades, roller bearings, and a hub for the rotor."

"Okay, Casper, I am on my way to talk to Ned. See you later." Ralph walked over to the elevator and disappeared.

Casper's visits to the purchasing people were infrequent but always entertaining and most of the time they had been able to step up to solve his problems, whatever they were. They watched as he came through the door with a handful of papers. Mike Osborn, who managed the purchasing department, came out of his office to greet Casper. "Good afternoon, Casper, you haven't been here to visit with us for a long time."

"Sorry about that, Mike. The last few months have been extra busy. Made a week-long trip to see our dealers on the west coast and it was very worthwhile. They all said their customers like our products." Casper looked around at all the people working on their computers in the large common room which housed them, mainly so they could throw questions and answers at each other without leaving their desks. It could be scary to walk in there and be faced with all these hard-nosed buyers who searched for and purchased the materials Davenport needed to build its equipment. He smiled at them. "How are all of you doing today?"

He was answered by a chorus of voices and laughs. One of the senior buyers called out, "Where have you been hiding, Casper?

We had about decided you had gone into retirement."

"Now, Bernie, you know I will still be here when you are retired and forgotten." They all laughed. "Truth is I am working on a new machine our dealers want us to build and have come here to get some help and advice. Can we use that table over there, Mike?"

"Sure thing, give me a minute to remove those three-ring binders." Casper followed Mike to the table and as space became available he started laying out his sketches. "First thing, Mike, this is my drawing of the main rotor which will shred the tree branches. It will be rotating at around seven hundred and fifty revolutions per minute and when the blades hit the branch, it will tend to set up vibrations. Ned is starting to put together the rotor but what I am looking for is a large sturdy hub that will keep the rotor steady and transmit the power from the PTO easily. Came to ask what our chances are of finding such a hub on the market."

Mike scanned the drawing and lifted his head. "Bernie, please come over here and look at this drawing."

Together, they discussed the rotor and Bernie asked, "Casper, how heavy will the rotor be?"

"The disc itself will weigh two hundred pounds. When Ned gets the other parts made the total it will probably weigh at least two hundred and thirty pounds. We have designed it to slide fit on a two-and-a-half-inch driveshaft."

"Let me show you something, Casper. These support arms going on the back side of the rotor are shown as being welded to the central hub. It seems to me rather than buying someone's standard hub, we should have our machinists turn a hub on their machines and make it with straight walls the arms can butt up against for welding."

Casper grinned. He shuffled through his sketches and pulled out one of them. "This is the first drawing I did and it is the way you are saying, Bernie. Afterwards, I started thinking maybe a heavy cast iron hub would be better. I'll talk to Ned about doing it this way. Thanks for looking at this with us, might still be a good idea to check on what hubs are available." Casper picked up the drawing and laid out another. "Mike, we need to buy a few of these shredder blades each thirteen inches long. When we start building the machines, we can make them but for this test model we might as well buy them on the market."

Mike commented, "Sounds right, how many go on the rotor each time?"

"Three blades go on the rotor each time, so buy a dozen to start with. If we find three isn't enough on the test machine, we may add more blades. Now, Mike, please get someone to check on sturdy roller bearings to go on the shaft right beside the rotor hub. We want endurance and support to keep the shaft steady. The other end of the shaft will run in a standard heavy-duty ball bearing. Thank you, fellas, now I am going to talk to Ned." Casper picked up his drawings and waved to everyone as he left.

He spent an hour talking to Ned before they had gone over everything and Ned said they would move ahead and see how the results came out. Casper went back to his office.

June thirtieth was approaching fast and that was the date of Davenport Machinery Inc.'s year-end. The next month would be busy putting together the year-end financials, inventory records and then preparing tax forms. Casper dialed the phone for Ronald Smith, CA, Davenport Company's chief financial officer. "Hi, Ron, it is Casper calling."

"Good to hear from you, Casper, we have a year-end coming up very soon. We should sit down and run through the information we have and look for any items that may present a problem."

"When will you be ready to do that, Ron?"

"This is Thursday, how about next Monday morning?"

"Sounds good to me, Ron. I will come to your office Monday morning. Goodbye." Casper wrote the meeting in his day timer before going back to the drafting table to continue drawing sketches for other parts of the tree branch shredder.

Friday morning, Casper asked Mrs. Sparks to come and talk to him. He started out asking how her family was doing and listened to her reply. When she finished, he wanted to know how the children were doing at school. Mrs. Sparks looked carefully at Casper as she answered and then asked him, "Is there something bothering you, Casper?"

Casper's usually ruddy face turned redder. He squirmed in his desk chair. "Well, yes, there is. You see, Mrs. Sparks, I have never had a date with a lady, never gone out with a lady, and don't know anything about how to go about asking a lady if she would like to go out."

Mrs. Sparks' smiled. "Can I take from your comments that you have met a lady you like?"

"Yes, Mrs. Sparks, you are right. She is the first lady that has ever attracted my attention. By that, I mean have me take notice of her, but I have never mentioned this fact to her. What if I talked to her and she said to go away? I would feel terrible."

"Now, Casper, you are a grown man and as such you have to learn to take chances. Just think of all the things you have done over the years, building this company and making all these different machines. You have had things go astray on you many times." Suddenly, Mrs. Sparks' intuition kicked in and she thought she might know the lady. She stifled a smile and asked, "Would this lady be anyone I might know?"

Casper's faced turned red again and he hesitated before screwing up his courage. He leaned forward with his arms on the desk.

"To be honest with you, the fact is you do know her. It is Miss Jessica, the mechanical engineer we hired for the summer."

Sparks' face broke out in a wide smile. "How wonderful, Casper! She is a very nice lady and I am so pleased you like her." Casper suddenly relaxed and slumped back in his high-backed desk chair now that the embarrassment and tension had eased. "So, Casper, what do you have in mind, to take her to a movie or out for dinner or some stage show taking place in Davenport?"

"Yes, any of those things or all of them, but I must tell you, I don't know what she is interested in, what she likes to do, or where she likes to go. How do I ask her out on a date if I don't have tickets to something or know what she would like to do?"

"This is Friday morning and you should go to her office right now and ask her to go out to eat dinner with you Saturday evening. If she says yes, ask her if there is a particular restaurant she would like to go to. If she agrees to go with you, tell me and I will phone for a dinner reservation for you. Now, while the two of you are eating dinner, tell her you would like to see her again and ask her if there is a show or movie that particularly interests her."

"You said to go and ask her right now. What if she says no? It will ruin my weekend. What will I do after that?"

"Casper, you are a grown man and a very successful one. If she tells you no, ask her why, maybe she has another appointment she can't break away from. You can always ask her out for another date. Hell, maybe she will tell you she is already married and has four children."

Casper broke out laughing. "She is not married and certainly there are no children. You are making fun of me."

"You are correct, Casper. This is something you want to do and you are making it seem like the end of the world. Go now and talk to her and I will sit right here waiting to find out how you make out." Casper squirmed around in his seat and twice started to speak but no words came out. "Casper Blakerly, you are a grown man, not a small wee pasture vole who is afraid of everything. When you tell me to do something, you do not give me days to think about it, you expect me to act right away. Now you have a wee task to do and you are frightened. Get up on your feet and go ask her for a date."

Casper stood up and raised his arms in a useless gesture. She watched him walk across the office and turn down the hallway. She smiled, he wasn't moving at his normal no fooling around pace. She kept her eyes on the window and waited.

Casper stood in the doorway and finally rapped on the door. Jessica was head down over her computer and she looked around. Her face split in a wide smile. "Hi, Casper, how are you today?"

Casper swallowed and answered, "It has been a busy day, Jessica." He sat down in one of her office chairs and looked around. Jessica waited, wondering what was going on. Finally, Casper built up his courage and started. "Miss Jessica, I want to ask you something." She sat upright in her desk chair and looked at him. He did seem to be tensed up about something. I hope I didn't make a mistake on one of the drawings? What could it have been? She was getting worried. "Miss Jessica, in all my life I have never been on a date with a girl. I came here to ask if you would be so kind as to accept my invitation to go out for dinner tomorrow evening."

Jessica sighed in relief and then her face broke out in an ear to ear smile. "It is very kind of you to ask me out for dinner. I will be pleased to have dinner with you."

Casper's relief at her reply was evident as he relaxed. "Thank you, Jessica; do you have a restaurant you want to visit for dinner?"

"No, I do not, Casper; anywhere you want to go will be fine with me. Will you pick me up at my apartment?"

"Oh yes, Jessica. Mrs. Sparks may know of a good place for us to go, I will ask her to phone for a reservation." He stood up. "Thank you for saying yes." Casper hurried away and Jessica watched him go. She was so happy she almost cried out in joy but managed to control herself. Several times she had wished he would ask her out and had almost given up, now it had happened.

Casper went back to his office, walking with a swinging stride. Mrs. Sparks knew the answer before he told her. "Mrs. Sparks, do you have a recommendation of a high-end place for dinner?"

"What time do you want your reservation for, Casper?"

Casper rubbed the top of his head. "Would you approve of seven p.m., Mrs. Sparks?"

"An ideal time, Casper, let me make your reservation and I will write out the details for you."

Casper paced around his office, finding he was too excited to go back to the drafting table. Mrs. Sparks came with a note all typed out for him. He walked back to Jessica's office and told her where they would be going for dinner and he would pick her up at six-fifteen. Back in his office, Casper finally put on his hardhat and walked to the elevator. Mrs. Sparks and Jessica both watched him go. He walked along the assembly line, stopping here and there to greet workers, say a few words, and sometimes ask questions. Every one of the workers noticed Casper was in a great mood. It was very near closing time for the plant when he walked into the financial department and asked Ronald Smith's secretary if there were any reports regarding the year-end he could read over the weekend.

"Yes, certainly, Mr. Blakerly, we have just been gathering several reports together and I was to take them to your office in a few minutes. Would you mind sitting down for a moment while I check?" Casper sat in one of the visitor chairs and waited. A few minutes later, he was handed a six-inch thick stack of reports and thanked her. Casper didn't feel like going back to his office so he took the reports and walked to his truck. He stopped at the barber and had his hair trimmed. On the way home, he wasn't thinking about driving, his mind was on Saturday evening.

Chapter 11

Two days before, he had made a beef and bean soup with jalapenos for heightened flavor and he planned to have it again for his Friday night dinner. First, he put the coffeepot on a cook stove burner to boil before a bowl of bean soup went into the microwave to heat up. He found himself humming some long-forgotten tune and reprimanded himself for acting like a teenager. Casper smiled and spoke out only for his own ears to hear. *'Nothing wrong with that, you may be thirty-two years old, but tonight you are feeling like a teenager, and even better prepared to go on your first date with a real live lady.'* The coffeepot was steaming so he walked over and pulled it off the heat. Next, he removed the soup from the microwave and set it on the table. From the cupboard, he brought a coffee cup, a saucer, and a soup spoon. He filled his coffee cup and sat down thinking, *'Tonight, soup and coffee and tomorrow night a fancy dinner with a beautiful woman.'* Out loud he shouted, "Damn, Casper you are a lucky old farmer."

Halfway through the soup, he told himself to smarten up, stop thinking of Jessica; you have a pile of proposed year-end financials to study. Get serious. He finished his dinner and washed the dishes, wiped off the tabletop, and looked around to be sure everything was in proper order. With a determined step, he took the year-end papers and walked to his home office. It was six-thirty when he sat down and started on the papers, using a red pen to write notes and questions in the margins. As was normal for him when he got started working on a project, his mind became completely focused. It was nine-twenty when he put down the pen and stood up to stretch. When he saw what the time was, he walked away from the work.

Casper locked the house door, brushed his teeth, and was pulling on his pajamas when he remembered he had forgotten to pick up the mail. First thing in the morning, he would recover it, there might be something important that needed attention.

Saturday morning, he spent two hours sitting in his pickup watching the cattle. Nothing seemed to be out of place. He drove over to the hayfields and checked to see whether the hay was ready for cutting. He stood up from doing a hand test on a broom handle thick roll of hay and it wasn't quite ready. Walking toward his pickup, he saw Fred's truck coming along the trail on the side of the field. At the pickup, he leaned on a fender and waited. Fred pulled up alongside Casper and rolled his window down. "Is the hay ready?"

"Almost ready, probably another two or three days will do it."

"About what I figured, will keep an eye on the fields and as soon as it is dry enough, we will start cutting and baling."

"How are the grain crops coming along? I haven't been out to look at the soybeans for some time now; are they doing okay?"

"Everything has been sprayed and there doesn't seem to be much in the way of weeds. The corn could use a good rain to keep it coming on normally. The soy is doing fine although a little rain would be good. It should be ready for combining by the end of July or early August. Hay wants things dry and grain wants water, hell of a dilemma for a farmer to face up to."

"Always been that way, Fred. One way or another, we always seem to get the work done. My dad never showed much in the way of worry over rain but my mother was always checking and talking about the wind, how dry the fields were, and how were we going to get all the work done."

"A fine woman your mother was, hell of a shock when she had that accident. Your pa was never himself afterwards."

Casper shrugged, he didn't like being reminded although

enough years had gone by so he no longer got emotional when someone brought it up and usually an old neighbor was the culprit.

"Did you have a look at the cattle herd?" Casper nodded. "Fine looking cattle we have there. Black Angus produce a fine brand of beef with good marbling and superior muscling. We haven't sold any young cows for several years but the yearling steers do alright. Tough specs to stay qualified as being Black Angus but so far we have stayed within the limits."

Casper smiled. "My dad said about the same as you but back in those early years we only had a small herd. Which reminds me, Fred at the rate the herd is growing are we going to need more pastureland. You better have a look around and see if there is anything to buy or rent."

"Will do, Casper, I'll talk to some of the neighbors around us and spread the word. Could be we will have to split the herd, depending on what acreage we can get our hands on."

"Real good, Fred, do the best you can. Time for me to go back to the office to read a pile of year-end financials the accountants laid on me." Casper lifted one hand to say goodbye, climbed into his truck and drove away. He worked diligently reading the financials until one o'clock before stopping for a small lunch. He was saving stomach space for dinner. He finished reading the papers just before four-thirty.

He could feel himself getting excited and hurried to shower and bring out the suit he was going to wear. With a brush, he spruced up the dark blue suit and went to the basement to shine his dress shoes. They didn't really need shinning but he had always been careful about his shoes. At five-thirty, he was ready and felt it was too early to start driving. He checked and his wallet was in a suit coat pocket and his hand went into the pants pocket and came out with a folded-over pack of money. Quickly thumbing through the bills, he found it added up to just over six hundred dollars, far more than enough for their dinner. The Ford F150 fired up at a quarter to six and Casper headed off down the highway to Davenport staying below the speed limit. He arrived five minutes early and parked at the curb. He had never been to the apartment but Jessica told him it was on the second floor with door number 208. He heard the door-bell ring and stepped back one step before the door opened and Jessica stood there smiling at him. Casper smiled back and asked, "Are you ready to go out for dinner?"

Jessica grinned. "Most certainly. To be truthful, I have been ready for an hour and started worrying that you might not get here on time. Now you have arrived and I am mighty pleased to see you." She stepped through the door and turned the knob to make sure it was locked. She put her arm through his and together they walked down the hall to the stairwell. Casper opened the pickup door for her and closed it after she was seated. The pickup was running when she asked, "Did you work in the office today?"

"Not today. I drove out to check on the cattle and talked about haying and the grain harvest with Fred. Everything is looking right on schedule so likely the haying will start this coming week. That was the fun stuff after which I spent the day reading draft reports for the year-end financials. For the next few weeks, the year-end reports will eat up a goodly portion of my time."

"The plant will be shut down the last two weeks of July for holidays."

Casper smiled and looked at her. "Yes, it will but the June thir-tieth year-end still has to be finalized and the budget for the next year nailed down. A lot of work and time is required."

"You don't go on holiday?"

"Never have and in any case, July wouldn't work for me. Where would I go all by myself? I would be so lonesome on holidays I might go out of my mind. Also, there is the farm with haying and harvesting to get done. It is a very exciting time with everything that will be happening. Holidays for me have to be in the winter when no one notices Casper is not around."

"Makes sense. My father runs a dairy farm and he has never been on a holiday more than a few hours long. The only time I have ever been out of the state was when I went with my mother to visit her parents over in Indiana."

"Are your grandparents still living in Indiana?"

"Well, they are still there but we buried them several years ago. My uncle is on the farm now." During their talk, Casper had turned onto Utica Ridge Road and was driving along. Jessica wondered where they were going. Finally, Casper turned off the road into Biaggi's Italian Restaurant and pulled into a vacant parking spot. "I hope you like Italian food."

"Oh yes, Casper, Italian food is very tasty." Casper walked around the truck and opened the door for her. After he locked the truck, they walked to the large front doors and he opened one for her. After only a moment standing there, a waiter approached, "How are you this evening?"

"Very good, thank you, we have a reservation under the name Blakerly."

"Ah yes, Mr. Blakerly, please follow me." He led them to a corner table with walls on two sides. He pulled out a chair for Jessica and helped her to sit. Casper was moving the chair on the other wall for his seat. They would be sitting around the table corner from each other with walls behind them and a good view out across the dining room which appeared to be about half full. The waiter arrived with two glasses of ice water and positioned them on the table. "Would you care to order a drink or possibly wine to go with dinner?"

Casper looked at Jessica. "Do you care to eat seafood tonight?" She nodded and Casper told the waiter, "Bring us a bottle of good white wine which you would recommend." The waiter nodded and hurried away.

Jessica asked, "Are you familiar with the restaurant's menu?"

"When Mrs. Sparks made our reservation, she insisted Biaggi's send out a menu to her immediately. I got to look at it yesterday and chose what I thought would be good, although I must admit to not having eaten the food before. Are you enough of a risk-taker for both of us to order the same items?"

Her tingly little laugh thrilled him. "Of course, although I cannot guarantee I will like everything."

"If there is an item we don't like, we will pretend to eat it, must put on a good face to impress the staff." The waiter arrived with a wine bottle and held it out to Casper who read the label. "Please pour us a taster." After a dollop was in the bottom of a wine glass, he handed it to Casper who held it up and looked at the color, swished it around in the glass and held it up to his nose. He sniffed the aroma and commented, "Smells very aromatic. Here, Jessica, smell the aroma and tell me what you think." Jessica sniffed the wine and agreed. "Good, now for a taste." Casper took a sip and sloshed it around in his mouth for a moment before swallowing. He smiled, "An excellent choice, waiter, please pour for my guest." When both wine glasses were half full, the wine bottle went into an ice bucket to keep it cool. Like magic, the waiter produced two menus and laid them on the table. Casper nodded and commented, "Please give us a few minutes." After the waiter left, he leaned toward Jessica with a soft laugh. "Did I do everything correctly?"

"Oh yes, Casper, you were very impressive."

"Thank you, Jessica, this is the first time for me and I hope not to do anything stupid. If you don't agree with something, please kick me under the table. You know I feel like a green stage actor but to be truthful it is fun and I am enjoying myself." Casper picked up a menu and opened it. "Let me show you what I was planning to order and if there is anything you do not want we can change the item. To start with, the minestrone soup, followed by a salmon salad. The main course will be Sea Scallops. I'm not much on eating dessert so we can decide on that after dinner. What do you think?"

"I think you have done an amazing job of selecting menu items, please go ahead and order for both of us."

Casper picked up his wine glass and took a sip. After a minute, he commented, "Have never been much on liquor, but you know, this wine tastes very nice. It is smooth and no trace of acid. I do believe it is okay for dinner."

Jessica set her glass down and agreed. "The wine tastes fine to me but I must be honest with you. Only rarely have I tasted wine and most of it was probably cheap. In my judgment, this wine is of much better quality. We should remember the name of the wine for another occasion."

Her remarks pleased Casper and he struggled not to show his elation. If he heard right and interpreted right, she was saying they should go out for dinner again. He was sipping the wine when the waiter arrived and asked, "Are you ready to order, sir?"

"Yes, we are. We will both start with the Tuscan minestrone soup. The second course will be seared salmon salad and our main course will be the sea scallops." The waiter was writing in his order book. When he finished, Casper asked, "Please bring me a Biaggi business card with your name written on the back."

The waiter walked away, smiling to himself. *'I wonder who these people are. The lady who phoned to make the reservation was very insistent. He must be an important person and, who knows, he may become a regular customer. Certainly, they are well dressed and seem very presentable.'* As head waiter, he had some influence and hurried in to discuss the food order with the chef. He explained the situation and asked for a special effort to make sure the food was excellent. While he waited for the soup, he went to the reception counter and picked up a business card and wrote his name on it. When he arrived with the soup, he noted that Mr. Blakerly's wine glass was almost empty. As usual, he served the lady first and then Blakerly. After they started eating, he picked up the wine bottle and refilled the glasses. He had sensed early on they liked their privacy. From a distance, he watched them eat and talk and it was an intense conversation which made him wonder. He waited until the lady finished her soup and sat back in her chair. Blakerly said something and she laughed. After a moment, he went and picked up her plate with the empty soup bowl and asked, "Was the taste of the soup agreeable to you, madam?"

"Very good indeed and please give my compliments to the chef."

"Thank you for your kind remarks, madam." He picked up the second soup bowl on its serving plate and walked away. Five minutes later, he came back with the seared salmon salads and placed them on the table before holding up the long wooden pepper grinder. "Would either of you care for fresh ground pepper?"

Casper looked at Jessica. "No, thank you we will keep the flavor as it is." Neither of them had touched their wine glasses so he left them alone. It took longer than usual for them to clean up the salads. Once again, he wondered what they were talking about. It had to be more than just polite conversation.

He was picking up their salad plates when he heard the lady speak. "Casper, there is Professor Sprague, his wife, and two friends. He is looking at you. It would be advisable to wave to him."

Casper looked across the room and smiled. His hand went up and waved. Immediately, Professor Sprague started to walk to their table. Casper stood up and held out his hand to shake. "Nice to see you, Christian, and how is your lovely wife doing?" Casper stepped past the dean and hugged Christian's wife. "Did you have a pleasant dinner?"

"A lovely dinner and we were surprised to see you eating here. Do you come here often?"

"Not really but the food is excellent. Is this one of your favorite places to go in Davenport?"

"Oh yes, as often as my husband will agree to take me out. As you know, these old university professors are rather a boring lot. This time, my brother came to visit so he had to perk up his eating habits."

"Don't listen to her, Casper. I could take her out every evening and she would still complain. Tell me how is Jessica working out at your plant?"

"Very well, sir, she wears her coveralls, steel-toed boots and hardhat and gets right into things climbing inside, over, and under the machines we build. I do believe she will make a good mechanical engineer."

Sprague laughed and looked at Jessica. "It's great to hear Casper say you are doing good work for the company. We best be on our way, don't want to hold up your dinner. Nice seeing both of you again." They walked away to the door and Casper sat down. He was only nicely settled in his chair when the waiter arrived with the sea scallops, topped up their wine glasses, and asked if either wanted freshly ground pepper which was turned down. Jessica took a part of a scallop and chewed it thoughtfully. "Very good, Casper, you have turned out to be a great connoisseur."

Casper cut into one of his scallops and ate it. "You are right, Jessica, it is very tasty." He lifted his wine glass and took another sip. "I am even starting to like wine. Did you know you are a bad influence on me?"

"We could get into a long-winded debate over who is a bad

influence on the other. This food has been great and I have enjoyed the whole evening. Wait until I have told everyone at the plant what a great connoisseur you are and what an excellent taste you have in food."

"Don't you dare, Jessica, you would be embarrassing me. Besides, no one would believe you anyway, they all consider me to be a lost farm boy."

"Mrs. Sparks doesn't, she is always telling me how smart you are, how hard you work, and points out the success you have had. Sometimes, she even brags about what you will do in the coming years."

Casper stared at her with his mouth hanging open for a moment before he recovered. "Mrs. Sparks shouldn't be talking like that; she is ignoring all the help and advice I receive from the employees and our dealers. I never knew she was such a gossip."

Jessica frowned. "She is not a gossip, she is very discrete but on some occasions she believes she must act like a mother to you, to make sure you don't forget something or go off without finishing a job. You are very lucky to have her working for you."

Casper laughed. "Right you are, Jessica, she is great, but in the future don't believe the wild tales she is telling you. These scallops are very good and the taste is out of this world. How are yours?"

"Excellent, Casper, thank you for inviting me to have dinner with you."

"There is no one I'd rather have dinner with than you. We will do this again very soon. They sat back and sipped their wine, the plates empty in front of them. The waiter cleared the table and asked about dessert. Casper looked at Jessica who shook her head no. "No dessert for us, just bring the bill when you have a moment."

When the waiter returned, he laid the dinner bill on the table and handed Casper a business card. Casper looked on the back before putting the card in his shirt pocket. "Can I pay you here at the table?"

"Certainly, Mr. Blakerly." Casper reached into a pocket and brought out a folded pack of bills. The bill was for one hundred and five dollars. He added fifteen percent, which brought it to one hundred and twenty-one dollars. He peeled off a hundred and two twenties and handed them over. "I will return with your change in a moment."

"You gave us good service this evening so keep the change, we appreciate the excellent food."

"Thank you, Mr. Blakerly, please drive carefully on the way home." Jessica held onto his arm as they made their way through the doors and into the pickup. Neither of them was drunk but they had finished a bottle of wine. Casper made sure he was below the speed limit as he drove Jessica home. When they arrived, he opened the door for her and escorted her to the front doors of the apartment building. He looked at her. "It has been a fine evening, thank you for going out to dinner with me. I will see you on Monday."

Chapter 12

Jessica unlocked the apartment door and entered. She was slightly dizzy from drinking wine and her feet felt like they were walking on air, not the hard, well-worn carpet. Now she was sure Casper liked her. She walked to the window and looked down in time to see the pickup drive away. She laughed gaily. Casper had been very nice to her although there was much she didn't know about him and still he drove around in an old farm half-ton pickup truck, or Ford F150, use whatever name you wanted for his vehicle. She was first attracted to him by his down to earth, hardworking, farmer-like attitude with no putting on of airs. The fact that he was a skilled and inventive mechanical engineer was another large attraction. She smiled again. Just imagine two engineers getting along and being together. Well, they weren't together but she could hope Casper would get around to thinking about being together with her. The coffee she had on was boiling so she went and poured herself a mug to drink. Sitting down on the sofa, she found herself feeling elated, she needed to talk to someone, and who indeed could that be other than her mother? She picked up the phone and dialed while having another sip of coffee. She waited as the phone rang, hoping she wasn't getting them out of bed.

"Hornsbee Dairy Farm, how are you?" Jessica smiled at the gruff voice.

"Hello Dad, are those cows of yours still putting out milk?"

"You're darn tooting they are; how are you doing, daughter?"

"Working long hours and learning to be a design engineer. The company has so many projects lined up ahead of me I should have a staff to help me get the work done. Ten or twelve hours a day with positive results and the best of all is my steel-toed boots never get cow manure on them."

The gruff laugher of her dad came over the line again. "Suppose you want to chat with your mother?"

"Please give her the phone, Dad, and keep on doing a good job of dairying." Her dad held out the phone and Elizabeth took it from his hand.

"Thank you, Karl. Hello Jess, why are you calling this time of the day?"

"Just wanted to talk to someone and you have always been the best. I was out on a date tonight and everything went well."

"Go on, tell me who you are dating, where you went, and what you had for dinner." She glanced at Karl and noticed he was watching and listening to her conversation.

Jessica laughed happily. "I had a date with Mr. Blakerly who came to my office on Friday and explained carefully he has no experience with women. When he asked me to go out for dinner, of course I agreed, to be honest, it is what I was hoping might happen. He came and picked me up in his truck and took me to an Italian restaurant named Biaggi and it is very exclusive. I found out his secretary made all the arrangements and she must have put pressure on the staff because we drew the head waiter. We both had the same food, minestrone soup, salmon salad, and brazed sea scallops. He even ordered a very fine bottle of white wine which we drank."

"Sounds very elegant, Jess, and the food tasted well, like it was carefully prepared?"

"Oh yes, Mother, nothing could have been better than what we had. He even suggested we should eat there again."

"Sounds very nice Jess, but to tell you the truth I am surprised to hear my daughter was drinking expensive wine."

"We were both drinking the wine, Mother, and neither of us really knew what we were doing. The wine had a smooth taste although I tried to be very careful."

"I see and am glad to hear my daughter is still able to think about what is best. What does this friend of yours look like?"

"Well, I wouldn't claim he is real good looking but to me he is handsome and sturdy. He is thin and taller than me, I estimate about two inches over six feet with broad shoulders and appears to be very strong. People around the office have told me he grew up having fights with other students because he is very intelligent and mostly was two years or so younger than his classmates. He has hazel eyes and when he becomes upset their color changes to almost dark burnt brown. He is rugged looking and well-tanned from working on the farm which gives him a ruddy complexion and shows off his white teeth. He is very inventive and industrious and when working his mind blanks out everything around him. At first, I didn't think he liked me until I discovered he is very shy around women. We get along very well now and have many work issues to discuss. A fact you may be interested in hearing is he grew up on a farm not far from Davenport and since his parents passed on, the farm is his and he runs it with the help of hired men."

"Sounds like a very industrious and likable man. Now, you remember the talks we had over the years and don't do anything foolish."

Jessica laughed. "Mother, you drilled the facts of life into me so many times I have always been afraid of men. To tell you the truth, I find Casper to be different. He is quiet, hardworking, and shy; maybe bashful would be a better description. His mind is almost always on a problem that needs solving and when he gets started working, he becomes so involved he doesn't know what else is going on around him. Last Saturday, I went into the office to finish off a drawing I was doing and he was working at his drafting table. It came to light that he had eaten breakfast at six a.m. and worked right through lunch hour. It was five-thirty when I interrupted him. I do like him, Mother, and so far he hasn't even held my hand. I do hope things might progress from there."

"Very good, you are a grown woman with a university education, just take care of yourself and make sure you always know what is going on around you. Thank you for calling, Jess, and please do it again."

"Goodbye, Mother." Jessica hung up the phone and reached for her coffee mug. It was cold so she emptied it in the sink and got a refill. Talking to her mother was always beneficial and now she felt solidly back on earth.

*　　*　　*

Casper arrived at the financial department at eight-thirty and asked the secretary where the meeting was being held. "Just down the hallway on the left." Casper walked along the hall and turned in at the meeting room. Two accountants were already seated. A rather stout looking lady told him, "The others will be arriving momentarily. Please find yourself a seat near the end of the table where Ron will want to sit."

The meeting took all morning and by noon they had identified many alterations and corrections that needed to be made. As the meeting broke up, Ron told Casper, "We will have these reports changed and have a few more pages ready so expect we will bring you a stack of paper."

"Real good, Ron. I will be waiting." Casper picked up his papers and walked through the door. He decided to stop and talk to Jessica so when he came out of the stairwell and saw Mrs. Sparks sitting in Jessica's office he was surprised. He kept going to his own office and stacked the papers on the credenza. For sure there would be a lot to read over next weekend. After sorting through the telephone messages, he decided there weren't any that required an immediate return call. Going to the drafting table, he stared down at the drawing he had been working on last Friday. He spotted where a few more details were required and sat to start working. An hour later, he had the drawing finished and sat back to consider the details. He didn't find any detail that wasn't the way he wanted. His mind started considering which part of the machine he should draw next when Mrs. Sparks walked in.

"Good morning, Casper. Did you have a good weekend?"

Casper turned to look at her and smiled. "It was a very good weekend, Mrs. Sparks, and my thanks to you for arranging the dinner Saturday night. Such a nice restaurant with an excellent staff and they serve well prepared and great tasting food."

"You are welcome, Casper, and you make me happy saying you enjoyed the dinner. I will have to ask Jessica what she thought of the food."

"Yes, please do that. I hope she was happy with the evening because I would like to ask her to have dinner with me again."

"If you wish, I can check for other high-end restaurants where you may want to go."

"An excellent idea, Mrs. Sparks, eating out in fancy restaurants is not something I have been in the habit of doing and certainly the Biaggi is one place I will return to. Of course, I must be aware that Jessica may prefer other types of food."

"I will talk to the city's tourism board and ask for a list of the top-rated places to go for a fine dinner. Sorry for interrupting your work." Sparks turned and walked back to her office, suppressing a smile as she considered what was happening between Jessica and her boss.

Casper worked through the afternoon and into the evening

drawing plans for machine parts. He wanted to get done and have a test model built. There was a very good chance that one more day would get him to that point. As he turned out the lights for the night, he thought it was strange Ralph hadn't been to his office with a progress report. He filed a mental note to see Ralph in the morning. It was eight p.m. and as often was the case, he was the last one to leave at the end of the day. He chatted with two security guards on the way to his truck before driving home.

* * *

On Thursday, Ralph had the test rig for the rotor ready to try and Casper went out to the yard to watch the action. A farm tractor was hooked up to power the rotor at 540 RPM during this test with the feed-in hopper coming in from the back. Plenty of heavy box tubing for worker safety and a piece of heavy pipeline steel piping was enclosing the rotor. The sole purpose of the rigged up machine was to try the rotor and judge its performance. It was an in-house research project and the public would never hear or see the setup. There was a pile of tree branches, some dry and others green for testing the rotor and most of them appeared to be in the five to eight-inch diameter range.

Ned Ambrose came out from the plant to stand beside Casper and watch the trial. He told Casper, "I hope the rotor the way we built it will work well. Damn thing is plenty heavy, which should be a good thing when it is chewing up a large tree branch. If it isn't, guess we will have to find ways to make it better."

Casper smiled. "This is just a test and I wouldn't be surprised if we find things that need to be changed."

Ralph started the tractor and after a moment, kicked in the power takeoff although he left the tractor engine running at low RPM. Everyone carefully inspected the turning rotor and there were no kinks to be fixed. Ralph sped up the engine to PTO and

171

they could hear the rotor turning. Still, everything seemed to be running smoothly. Ralph's helper picked out a dry three-inch diameter branch and stuck it in the rotor very carefully. The branch was going straight in and the rotor was chewing up the end of it. After a minute, Ralph shut down the tractor and everyone went to look at the rotor. Other than a pile of shredded wood, everything seemed to be fine. Ralph cleaned all the wood-chips off the rotor to make room for another test run. They chewed about two feet off a six-inch diameter branch and were satisfied. After cleanup, Ralph told his helper to select an eight or nine-inch diameter branch. The test started out fine but as the helper pushed harder, the rotor slowed down. As soon as he eased up, the rotor returned to full speed. The trial was repeated several times and was always the same. When everything was shut down and quiet was reestablished, they inspected the rotor. Casper and Ralph found nothing to complain about with the rotor and decided it needed a higher rotational speed.

"Ralph, let's try a test with around a thousand revolutions per minute. The other thing we should test is having five shredder blades instead of three. Could be with more blades the slower rotation speed will work well."

"Okay, boss. First, I will go to the plant and talk to Ned about making another rotor. I will have to drive to a farm equipment dealer and buy a thousand RPM speed PTO connecter to fit this tractor. Will let you know when we are ready to run another test." Ralph took the keys out of the tractor cab and hurried into the plant. Casper watched him go before turning his eyes to the test rack and thinking about other options—if there were any? He wondered to himself if they were being too conservative, maybe the rotor should be turning at a higher speed, maybe something like two thousand RPM.

* * *

Casper finished drawing the plans for the parts of the ten-inch branch shredder and gave them to Ralph. He heaved a sigh of relief, happy to have finished that project. He needed to spend more of his time on the year-end. Well, first they had another test to run on the rotor for the shredder and he donned his hardhat and with his leather gloves in his hand started for the elevator. The doors opened and Jessica stepped out. He received a happy smile from her and suggested, "We are going to run another test on the tree branch shredder. Why don't you come along with me and watch the test?"

"Great idea, Casper. Just give me a minute to get my gear together." Together, they rode the elevator down to the ground floor and walked through the plant to the end door. They stopped several times to talk to men working on building machines and the trip took longer than expected. Outside, it was sunny and quite warm but regardless you had to wear the safety equipment and follow all the rules. Ralph was waiting for them and immediately showed Casper what had been changed. The rotor now had four blades to do the shredding and his crew had rigged up a jack-shaft for the tractor PTO to turn with a chain drive from the jack-shaft to the rotor axle. There were three different sizes of toothed sprockets to power the chain and create different turning speeds on the rotor. He explained, "These three drives are 2 to 1, 3 to 1, and 4 to 1, so we can get three different speeds, namely 1000, 1500, and 2000 RPMs on the rotor."

"Have you tried them out?"

"No, sir, I figured you should be here to make your observations. Ideally, it seems that the lowest speed which provides a good steady cut without any hint of slowing down should be the best. To tell you the truth, I don't know which speed will be the most efficient."

"Ned tells me we have a heavier than normal rotor so it may be possible for us to use a slower speed with the rotor providing good steady momentum. In any case, Ralph, let's get started and see what everyone thinks."

Ralph grinned. "As you saw, the chain drive is on the 3 to1 sprocket. Okay with you if we start there?"

Casper smiled and waved his hand in agreement. Ralph started the tractor and the tests began. Jessica was keeping notes on her observations as the test proceeded. They were using an eight-inch diameter branch and the two highest speeds did a good job. Jessica wrote that down and noted the fifteen hundred revolutions were adequate. They didn't have a ten-inch branch so couldn't do a test on the largest size. Casper looked around and asked, "Well, tell me what you think. Ralph?"

"Casper, the 1000 RPM is too slow. The other two did a good job and I think for now we should go with the 1500." Ned nodded. Casper turned his head and looked at Jessica.

She responded immediately. "I agree with Ralph, except I have a different approach. This is a big machine and a ten-inch branch will have fifty percent more material in it compared to an eight-inch. I am inclined to suggest we leave both sprockets on, well labeled, so the user of the machine can switch to the highest speed if he runs into a branch with overly strong wood and needs it."

Casper thought about what Jessica had said and finally smiled. "Are all ladies as cagey as you are, Jessica?"

"Just trying to be helpful, Casper, down the road if we find it's not necessary; the machines can be put back to one speed."

"Ralph, I agree with Jessica and we will go her way for now. The first few machines will have two speeds. When you are fin-ished here, come to my office and we will go over the other finished drawings." Ralph watched them walk away before he and his crew started cleaning up. When Ralph arrived, Casper spread out his drawings and they discussed what he was planning. Ralph left with copies of the drawings.

* * *

It was the last week of June, the kids were out of school, the weather was warm, and it was the financial year-end for Davenport Machinery Inc. In a few days, Casper would receive another set of yea-rend financial reports to review. He was sitting at his desk leaning back with a sketchpad in his hand. His mind was dreaming about another line of equipment he wanted to start. A second plant was under construction and would be ready by fall. He was thinking and sketching pictures of the line of tractors and attachments he wanted to put on the market. The market was full of small mowers and fifteen to thirty horsepower tractors of various makes, which wasn't the market he was thinking about. Davenport would focus on fifty to one hundred horsepower units with a wide variety of attachments, front-end loaders, forklifts, backhoes for trenching and a variety of digging, powering equipment such as water pumps, generators, wood splitters, chippers, small shredders, winching, pulling wagons, three-point hitches, and PTO for running garden equipment, and he was sure there would be other opportunities coming along.

A fifty-horsepower tractor would be first and he had gathered a stack of catalogues, magazines, and textbooks, all of which provided information on how the tractors were built, repaired, and on and on. What he needed first was to find a source for good reliable engines to build a tractor around, both gasoline and diesel-powered. Thinking about it for a few minutes, he decided fifty horse tractors and larger built by Davenport would be diesel fuel-powered. If there was a demand for gasoline engines, they could be added sometime in the future. Finding a suitable source of engines was a project for the purchasing department. Casper stood up and headed for the stairwell.

Mike Osborn saw Casper coming and stood up from his desk. He watched as Casper came directly to his office and plopped into a chair. "Hi, Mike, how are you doing today?"

A smile split his face as he looked back at Casper. "Life is treating me alright, Casper. You look like you have a head full of problems and are looking for help."

Casper laughed. "My dad always told me I would not be a very good poker player. He always said my face gave everything away. Anyway, there aren't many secrets around here. For a couple of years, there has been an expansion project running around in my head and now the new plant will be ready this fall so here I am to ask for help."

"We are here to help. Do you want to tell me what a bunch of old experienced buyers can do?"

Casper nodded. "I have a plan to start building tractors and need a good reliable source for fifty to one hundred horsepower diesel engines suitable for farm tractors. I figured your people were the logical ones to have out looking and getting recommendations."

"We will do our best, Casper. Do you have any specs on what you want in an engine?"

"Reliability, not loud and noisy, good starting in cold weather, which means some kind of preheating, ease of servicing, design to run at different RPMs without causing engine damage, and long-term supply. Don't want to start with a good engine and have to change five years or so down the road."

Mike was busy writing down what Casper was saying. When he finished, he looked at Casper. "Quite a list you have. When do you want the information?"

"The sooner the better; after we find an engine which will do what we want, we will have to look at them, do tests, and start on the design. With the new plant going to be ready this fall, I want to start construction as soon as possible thereafter. Of course, that does not mean the day the plant is available but a reasonable time afterward."

"Okay, I will get a couple of our people started. If I may be so bold to suggest, you might be wise to talk to Jessica Hornsbee, and ask her to check with the university to see what they may have in one of their libraries."

Casper stared at him for a moment. "A great suggestion, Mike, might I ask why you are suggesting her?"

"I have not dealt with Hornsbee but she is often in here talking to one or another of my people and they tell me she is sharp, very quick to understand, and can become angry if she is not receiving the information she is seeking."

Casper nodded thoughtfully. "Thank you, Mike. I will talk to her. Please let me know how your search is going." Casper stood up and walked out of Mike's office.

As he came out of the stairwell, he saw Jessica working on a drafting table. He walked in and spoke to her. "How is all of your work going today, Jessica?"

She looked over her shoulder and then swung around to look at him. She grumped. "Do you know how much work there is to do around here?"

Her stern manner set him back a few paces. He slid into a chair and looked back at her. "We are all working quite hard, that I know. Was there something particular that is bothering you?"

She starred at Casper for a minute and her face began to un-wind. Finally, she shrugged her shoulders, and with a sigh held up both hands. "Oh, it is nothing really; it is just that I can't get my work done with all the interruptions. Someone is always phoning with a problem or walking in that door and asking for help or wanting me to come to witness a test or approve a safety feature. All important matters but so is my project."

Jessica could see the smile hidden is Casper's eyes. "So have you figured out what to do about these interruptions?"

"No, not really."

"Let me tell you a little company secret. *'Welcome to the head office'.*" Casper grinned at her and after a moment's thought, she laughed. "What you do is take charge of your time. When someone wants you to come and look at whatever they are concerned with, give them a time when you will do it, today or tomorrow, so be it. When they find out you will not jump every time they yell, things will start to change for you."

"Thank you, Casper. I know I only have two months plus experience and have much to learn."

"How would you like to spend some time away from Davenport's offices?" Casper surprised her. "I need someone to go to the university and dig out data from their libraries."

"You always treat me so nicely, Casper. What is it you want from the libraries?"

"I will type up a description and give it to you tomorrow. Now, with the university data out of the way, may I ask if you would like to go for dinner with me on July 4th?"

"Oh yes, Casper, I would love to have dinner with you again. Surprise me with where we will be going, just come and tell me what time you will pick me up."

Casper smiled and stood up. "See you tomorrow and keep your chin up, your eyes sharp and your fists ready to put up a fight." He walked out of Jessica's office and she watched him go.

Chapter 13

Once again, Jessica demonstrated her superior mental capability as she sat in Casper's office and read over the outline he had prepared. She told him, "Most of this data, if it is in the university's libraries, should be accessible from my computer where I can print it out for you. There may be some things that will require a trip to the campus to gain access."

"Excellent, Jessica, we want to establish a listing of the best engine candidates for use in our equipment. We will have to consider where they are being built which may be a factor but for now, ignore it. Start on this as soon as you can."

Jessica left his office and a few minutes later, Mrs. Sparks entered to hand him a list of the top five fine dining locations in the city. He noted immediately that Biaggi's was rated number four. "What kinds of food do these top three serve?"

"One is a French restaurant and the other two serve the usual American food, steaks, roasts, fish, and seafood."

"May I suggest you go and talk to Jessica and see if she has a preference?"

"Of course, Casper, and what time would you like to dine?"

"Damn, Mrs. Sparks, the time never occurred to me. What would you suggest?"

"I would think around six so there will be time for other activities since this is one of the major holidays during our year."

"Sounds fine, Mrs. Sparks, but make sure you suggest it to Jessica and get her reaction." Mrs. Sparks left and Casper went back to work. He was planning for the production of the new line of tractors and what the future might hold for their sales and the accessories which might be sold along with them. Finally, his mind wandered to the new plant being built and after a minute he stood up and grabbed his hardhat. Mrs. Sparks was sitting in Jessica's office when Casper went by. He walked into the new plant and stood inside the door. In many ways, it looked like a mess due to the piles of finishing board, construction tools, boxes, and other items and he laughed. Construction of a building like this was entirely different from what Davenport did. Out in the middle of the floor was a portable skid-mounted office shack. A shack probably wasn't the right term but he didn't have any other word to describe it. Casper walked over to the shack and stopped beside one of the foremen who greeted him. "Good morning, Mr. Blakerly, welcome to our inside circus operation."

A wide smile broke out on Casper's face. The foreman had talked louder than was necessary and as he wondered, he saw another man go into the trailer. His suspicions were confirmed when the manager of construction came out of the trailer. Casper continued to look at the foreman. "Haven't been over to see how things are going for a couple of weeks so I have come to have a look around."

The foreman smiled back and commented, "As far as I can tell, the construction is on schedule although some days a man has reasons to wonder."

Morley O'Brien arrived beside the foreman. Casper put out his hand to shake with the manager. "Good to see you, Morley. I haven't been around to look at your progress for a while so here I am to have a look at where you are with the building."

"You are most welcome, Casper. Would you like a tour around?"

"Certainly, Morley. Let's go around so I can find out how construction is progressing. Sorry for not phoning ahead but to tell you the truth, the new plant popped into my mind and I decided now was the time." He looked at the huge size of the new plant from where he stood. It still amazed him; on the blueprints, it hadn't seemed to be this big. He sighed knowing full well this was reality and not theory like it had been on the plats. This building was wider, longer, and the distance up to the steel roof girders above was farther than in plant number one. He had purchased plant number one and was stuck with the way it had been built. Plant number two was all one story with no flights of stairs to climb. He was standing in the main area of construction and on other sides of the walls were offices, material storage for supplies coming in, painting facilities, and at the far end storage for finished and painted machines being readied for shipment. On the railroad side of the building were washrooms for the workers, change rooms, work areas for crews to assemble subsystems for machines, and other areas not yet designated to specific functions? This large central area where he was standing was where parts of the new machines would be built and assembled. It was a large expansion for Davenport Machinery and caused worry for Casper, although the funds to pay for it were in the bank. He was personally opposed to debt except in specific short-term cases. Only he and a few of the financial people knew funds were easily available because of this specific quirk in his nature. The two plants were inline along the railroad with a wide-open yard separating them where equipment could be tested, stored, and semis coming in to deliver or pick up items could maneuver. A new, large parking lot was being built for future employees. Casper admitted to himself that it was exciting to be building and expanding. He looked around and asked, "Where are the Davenport construction people?"

Morley dispatched one of his men to find them. "We are using this large space to store materials and tools while the crews work on completing all the side rooms along both sides. Insulation is going on first, then the sheeting crews move in to seal up the walls.

Ahead of all that, there are electricians running power, phone, and computer lines in the walls, including the undesignated color-coded lines you specified for future use."

"Very good, Morley, we tried hard to plan for the future, whatever it may be. Let us stay here until some of my people arrive. It will probably only be a few minutes." It was four hours before Casper had toured the whole building and satisfied his curiosity and he was the only one who didn't notice they went right through the noon hour. When he left, they laughed and joked about his ways before sitting down to eat their lunches. It was mid-afternoon when Casper came off the elevator and walked to his office.

He turned from hanging up his hardhat and found Mrs. Sparks standing by his desk. "Jessica thought any of the restaurants would be fine but I got the distinct impression she would prefer to try the French food."

"French food sounds excellent, Mrs. Sparks, except I have never eaten such food. How will I know what to order?"

Mrs. Sparks smiled. "I anticipated your answer and have already phoned and asked the restaurant to send us one of their menus. When they objected, I told them to put the cost of the menu on your food bill."

"You are a sly one. When we get the menu, Jessica and I should look at it together and figure out what we want. I have already surprised her once and no sense doing it again."

"There is a phone message for you from a Mr. Hiram Weinstein, who said he attended university with you and would like to drop by to talk to you."

Casper dropped into his office chair and thought. He remembered the name except who was he? After a moment, it came to him. A rather short overweight boy who made good marks. "Yes, I remember him now as I think about it. How about tomorrow morning for a meeting, did he say what he wanted to talk about?"

"No, he didn't. When I asked, he said he had always liked you and wanted to renew the old acquaintanceship."

Casper opened his day timer. "Please invite him to come in at ten a.m. and best you give him directions to find us." He wrote the appointment on the page.

"What about lunch, Casper? Do you want to take him out to eat at noon hour?"

Casper shrugged. "A very good idea, Mrs. Sparks but I would prefer to find out what he is like now. If he has turned into one of those snobbish know-it-all types, I may wish to cut our meeting short. I will decide tomorrow and let you know."

"Thank you, Casper. I will phone him back and invite him to come at ten o'clock."

He leaned back and watched her walk away. Hiram Weinstein, if he remembered right, had done quite well at university and if he recalled correctly was three or four years older than Casper so was now probably thirty-five or more. Weinstein was of Jewish descent which meant he wouldn't eat pork. *'Well, that is his right and there are probably other things I can't recall or maybe never knew. I wonder what Hiram has been doing the past dozen or so years?'* His mind wandered around and he recalled several other students from mechanical engineering he had attended classes with. It was not often his mind went back into the past because he was always so busy planning and working with his mind on the future. Mrs. Sparks interrupted his thoughts. "Mr. Weinstein said to tell you that ten a.m. will be perfect."

"Thank you, Mrs. Sparks. Please ask Jessica if she has time to come and talk to me."

A few minutes later, Jessica arrived. "Hiram Weinstein, who went to university with me, is dropping in at ten a.m. tomorrow.

Don't know what he wants but if the conversation seems useful, I may have Mrs. Sparks order cheeseburgers and root beer for lunch. Would you be available to eat lunch with us?"

"Certainly, Casper. If you order in, please ask Mrs. Sparks to advise me." Jessica walked back to her office with her mind whirling. *'Why would Casper want me to attend a meeting with a fellow student of his? There must be a reason so I will have to be alert and note anything subtle or implied in case he asks me for my impressions.'*

It was four-thirty on Casper's watch and he decided to go home to check on how the haying was coming along.

* * *

The first field was dotted with large round hay bales. To Casper's eye, it appeared to have been an above-average crop. He drove to the next field and there was the baler running along dried up and tender swaths of hay. Once again, it appeared to be an ample crop. Across the fence line, he could see a tractor and mower cutting hay. They had been lucky with the weather the last two weeks. He looked around for Fred's pickup and couldn't see it anywhere. As he drove forward to watch the mower operate, he pulled up at the wire gate in the fence and parked. Some ten minutes later, Fred drove up beside him and turned off his engine. They got out and leaned on Casper's pickup. "Looks like you are getting more bales than has been usual."

"The number of bales seems to be running around fifteen percent higher than last year and it is good hay."

"Just what I thought, if nothing changes on the number of bales and assuming we don't get a real tough winter, we should be able to feed the cattle herd through till spring."

"Expect you are right, Casper, and we are lucky once again."

Fred removed his baseball cap and wiped the sweat off his head. "A couple of weeks ago, you told me to check with the neighbors for grazing land that might be available. Had a phone call from the owner of a section of grazing land over west of here about six or seven miles right on the north side of the Wapsipinicon River. The river makes a turn to the south to go around some hilly land and this section is in that bend. I wanted to talk to you before going to look. The owner says there are some trees on the land and the river cuts through the south-east corner of the section."

Casper considered for a few minutes. *'Blakerly Farms land goes west and northwest from the home site. Probably a gap of three, maybe four miles from the farm's current land holdings. Well, that wouldn't be such a long move for the cattle.'*

"Did the owner say what he wants to do?"

"No, sir, he did not and we didn't get into a discussion of selling price or rentals. That is something you should probably be handling. I can go and look and tell you what I think of the land. If you decide you might be interested, I can go with you but I'd prefer to leave the money talks to you."

"One thing about you, Fred, is you are consistent." Casper laughed happily. "Okay, you talk to the owner and make arrangements for the two of you to tour the land and discuss water, trees, grass, and anything else you want. You will need to estimate how many head the section will support for feed."

"Will do, Casper. I will phone this gentleman tomorrow morning and see what happens."

"How many days do you need to finish up the haying?"

"If the weather holds, the field behind us will be done baling tomorrow and this one here will need another two or three days to dry up the swaths and a day and a half to be baled. If things go right, we will be done in about five days."

185

"Sounds real good, Fred. What about the soy crop?"

"I figure four to five weeks and we will be ready to combine. You want to take a drive over and see for yourself?"

"Hell of a good idea, Fred. You drive and I will be a tourist." The two men climbed into Fred's pickup and drove away. The soybeans were planted on a little higher land and they had to go in a circle to get there. Fred pulled into the first field and stopped. Casper stood out away from the truck and looked at the plants. Fred said, "If you get the light coming from the right angle, the plants are starting to ripen up. I figure three weeks or a little longer and the plants will be almost dry." They walked out and picked a few beans. They were still green, but when shelled out, some of the beans were starting to change color.

"Nice fat beans, Fred. Let's hope we can bin a good-sized crop."

"If you walk along the rows, it is darn hard to find any weeds so our spraying worked real well. What the weather does will be the most important factor from here on in. Good weather and it should be a good crop. Let's go and look at the other fields." Fred drove around from field to field looking at soybeans, corn, and wheat. They had a good, relaxing talk about crops, harvest, and next year's seeding. It was almost dark when they got back to Casper's truck and the baling and mowing was shut down for the night.

"Thanks for the ride, Fred, and the discussion. See you in a day or two." Casper waved and started his engine to drive home for a late dinner which he would have to cook for himself. At least Fred's wife would have food ready and waiting.

* * *

Casper was in before six a.m. and tore into the final drawings for the ten-inch shredder. He wanted to get it out of his way and leave Ralph to build the first test model. He glanced at the calendar and by golly, it was July third. Tomorrow was a holiday and he had a date with a fine young woman to eat French cooking. His mind wandered for a few minutes until he settled down again. He glanced at his watch and in one hour he had a meeting with Hiram. He put his head down and went back to work. When Mrs. Sparks knocked on his office door, it startled him. She smiled. "Your ten o'clock appointment is here."

"Oh yes, Hiram." Casper smiled at her. "Please bring him in."

Mrs. Sparks returned a few minutes later with a relatively slim, gray-haired man following her. Casper stuck out his hand to shake. "It is good to see you again, Hiram. Please come in and have a seat so we can talk for a few minutes."

Hiram Weinstein heard the few minutes and reminded himself to not waste time. Casper was undoubtedly busy and appeared to have a sizable operation he was responsible for. Briefly, he wondered who the owners were. "Thank you, it has been several years since I last talked to you when we were on the university campus. Do you go to the campus often?"

Casper smiled. "Not often, probably on average once or twice each year. Tell me about yourself, Hiram; what have you been working at, where you have been living, and family… I see from your finger you are married."

"Very observant, Casper. My wife and I have been married for twelve years now and we have two children, both of whom are doing well in their studies. We live in the Detroit subs and I am working for the Ford Motor Company doing research and design work. Frankly it is not a challenging task because there is a lot of repeat work, especially in the research area. Right now we are on vacation and visiting my wife's parents, who are the owners of a retail grocery store over in West Branch, about forty miles from here. If you can spare the time, I would love to visit and catch up on the years but to be honest with you I am looking for a career change that will provide more challenge."

"Very interesting Hiram but first please bring me up to date on your children and wife."

"How kind of you Casper. We are very proud of our children who are both well above average students although they are not yet in high school. Our son is ten years old and loves to play soccer which the coach tells me he is advancing rapidly in both knowledge of strategy and skill. He even hints that with determination, the boy has a reasonable chance of possibly becoming a pro player after several more years of practice. Whether he can maintain his high grade-point average in school and also advance as a soccer player is a worry to us. Our daughter is two years younger and an exceedingly good student who is on the honors list. She is now taking tennis lessons but does appear to be somewhat on the awkward side which we hope she will outgrow. You know, raising children is not the easiest task a man can have but my wife is excellent in keeping track of what they are doing and the timing of their games. My wife is somewhat on the tinny size and always seems to eat small meals but she is healthy and maybe her cooking and eating have had a good influence on me. You may not remember but I was rather chubby while at university, now I have slimmed down. My wife graduated from university with an education degree and taught for several years before our children arrived. She often dreams of returning to the classroom, since she loves children and teaching. I am fortunate to have a fine family but have reached a point where I am looking for a more challenging career with more freedom to innovate and put forth new ideas. It is very hard to find such positions in large companies and all too often, the managers up above are academic and very short-sighted. They make far too many restrictive decisions and rarely understand the expertise of the employees, plus they do not want to rock the boat, so to speak. It can be very hard to convince them to try anything that is not already in place for fear they will be caught making a mistake."

Casper held up a hand. "Thank you for telling me your family story. Now, before we go into careers there is a young mechanical engineer who I would like to ask to join us. Before I do that, do you have time to stay here over noon hour?" Hiram nodded yes. "Good and do you eat cheeseburgers?"

Hiram laughed. "Most certainly, both of my children are always insisting on having a hamburger."

"Good, give me a minute." Casper dialed his phone. "Mrs. Sparks, would you please ask Jessica to join Mr. Weinstein and me and also come in with her so you can order food for us." Casper hung up the phone and told Hiram how hardworking and effective Jessica was, although she just recently graduated from university. Both men stood up as the ladies entered the office. Casper made the introductions before telling Mrs. Sparks, "We are getting close to the noon hour and I want you to bring food for us. For me, a cheeseburger and fries along with root beer from Ma's Restaurant would be excellent." He turned his head to look at the other two. "Please tell Mrs. Sparks what each of you will have."

Jessica smiled. "I do believe I will have the same order as Casper although ketchup would be nice."

"Please, Mrs. Sparks, order for me the same as Jessica."

Casper added, "If you care to, get the same order for yourself."

"Thank you, Casper, but I have a lunch stored in my desk so I will decline." She smiled and walked out of the office.

Casper pulled another chair across the floor and positioned it for Jessica. "You sit here, Jessica. I wanted you to eat with us and listen to our conversation. Please feel free to jump in anytime you want especially if I get to talking more than I should." Everyone laughed and relaxed. "Hiram, please tell Jessica the last bit you told me about academics."

Hiram's face showed his surprise at the request and complied. Casper told Jessica, "Wanted you to hear the fact, I have worried about the over-educated under-experienced academics for years and how to keep them from slowing down our operations. Hiram and I took our mechanical engineering degrees together so now we have the problem of three mechanical engineers all cooped up in one room. Seems to me such a gathering is an ideal equation for disaster?" They all laughed and Casper could tell Hiram was relaxing. "Now, Hiram, tell us where you have been employed and what types of projects you've worked on."

"I'll send you my full resume when I get home. After graduation, I worked two years for a military supplier of small items they require in semi-trailer loads. Security door locks, seats for trucks which were much better than the ones the truck builders were using, radio communicators for interpersonal data exchanges, and on and on. From there, Case Farm Machinery hired me to help design better and more efficient tractors and make them easier to service on a less frequent basis. I worked on everything from small ride on lawn mowers up to one hundred and fifty horsepower tractors. I ended up working for Case for eleven years before moving to Ford Motor. The last two and a half years have been with Ford doing research, which to be honest is boring so I have decided to look around and see if there is anything challenging enough for me to make a move."

Casper asked, "Does Case design and build all the different sizes of engines they use?"

"Far from it, they build the larger engines for tractors, combines and other similar equipment and the bigger sizes of two-wheeled farm tractors but in most cases, those are designs that have been used for many years with some of the newly designed and required add-ons, like for example to reduce environmental damage. For all the other equipment, we purchased engines from manufactures located all over the world but the greatest number came from Japan and Korea. Their small engines are very well designed and built and they sell thousands of them each year so the price is usually attractive as well. The only real problem with this approach is that you end up with stacks of design material coming from all the manufactures. This is particularly true on the low horsepower engines where they only use a particular design for two or three years before it is replaced with a new design."

"Are all the engines Case purchases from an assortment of reliable manufactures or are there constant needs for mechanics and replacement parts to keep them running?"

Hiram smiled and looked at Jessica. "You are correct. You have to be careful to buy established engines from large steady suppliers who have been in the business for a long time. Honda for example is very dependable, as are many others, but often their prices are higher than others who know they have to undersell to get a piece of the market. It may sound complicated but actually, it only takes a short time to steer a course through all the sub-quality builders of engines."

There was a knock on the door and they all looked to see Mrs. Sparks coming in with packages. Casper cleared the table they were sitting at and they spread out the food. Casper wasn't much of a time waster. While the other two were getting organized, he was eating his cheese-burger. He finished well ahead of his two guests. Jessica felt a bit embarrassed by this and kept chatting with Hiram as they ate and both ignored Casper. While he waited, his mind was on the year-end statements and he wrote several notes to himself. When everyone was finished eating he brought his metal wastepaper bin and they cleared the table.

Casper had made up his mind while listening to Hiram. "Hiram, our company is currently building another manufacturing plant out in the yard in alignment with this building. We plan to introduce additional lines of equipment. Would you have any interest in joining Davenport Machinery Inc. as a design engineer? To be fair about it, as Jessica can testify, we have a kind of open free-flowing structure so no one is confined to any one phase. How many different types of projects have you worked on, Jessica?"

Jessica smiled. "To be honest, I have no idea how many. Each day, I receive several calls from the production people asking for help of various kinds. I find it stimulating since each one has to be approached in a particular way. I also witness test runs on new machines and help to make amendments to the design. My main task is the design of new pieces of equipment so test models can be built. When we have a machine ready to be manufactured, there are drafting people who produce the production line drawings. Also, the marketing department drafts operating manuals for each machine. This company is unique because its basic intent is to produce the most reliable machines on the market, sell them, and make a profit. Everyone is focused on that intent and there is very little red tape to slow things down."

Hiram laughed happily. "Very interesting, Casper, I am very interested in working for Davenport."

"Good. When you return home, send us an application with your resume attached and we will consider whether you will fit in around here. While you are here today, would you like to take a tour of the facilities?"

"Most certainly! I would like to see some of your new machines and watch the employees doing their jobs."

Casper looked at Jessica. "I know you are very busy but would you have time to walk Hiram around and explain what is going on?"

"No problem, Casper. I could use a change from the computer

on my desk. Come along, Hiram, and we will find a hardhat for you to wear and we will try to keep your nice clean clothes from getting dirty."

Chapter 14

Jessica stood at an apartment window and watched the farm F150 pull in to the curb and park. Casper got out wearing his suit and walked toward the front door. She hurried to a mirror and checked her hair and makeup one more time. She was wearing her second-best dress this time, just to be different. She waited impatiently for the doorbell to sound. When it did, she walked across the living room and opened the door. "Hi Casper, oh my I do like that suit of yours. It makes you look very successful."

Casper smiled. "Thank you, Jessica, and you are looking like a rich New York model who has come to Davenport to do a clothing revue." They laughed together and she stepped out into the hallway. Arm in arm, they walked to the truck. In many ways, he was a mystery to her and she wondered why he lived in an old wooden house at the farm and why he drove a five-year-old Ford F150. He didn't act and behave like a wealthy businessman and yet there didn't seem to be any shortage of money. She had concluded that Casper continued to live the way he had grown up and preferred not to display his success. She hoped her conclusion was correct; after all, she knew she wanted to marry him. She had very little experience with men, was still relatively young at twenty-one years, and Casper had not even held her hand, although they had gone out to eat together several times. All she really knew for sure was her happiest times were when they were together; agreeing or arguing over design details, testing new machine models, joking, or eating dinner. He had included her in the talks with Hiram Weinstein and she didn't understand why, still it made her happy to be asked. She was sure they would talk about what had turned into a job interview. She sighed quietly and thought Casper certainly didn't behave like she would expect from the owner and president of a company like Davenport. Although he spent many hours running the company, he always seemed happiest when he was down and dirty working on a new machine. She shook her head. Well, tonight she would begin by grabbing his hand and hanging on so tight he could never get away and by damn if he didn't kiss her soon, she would buck up her courage and kiss him.

She sat thinking how quiet the trip to the restaurant was when she realized Casper was driving into 115 E 3rd Street and parking at the Duck City Bistro. Jessica laughed and told Casper, "Mrs. Sparks told me this is one of the top-rated restaurants in Davenport and the Mississippi River is right over there only a short walk away. This Fourth of July holiday has brought a large number of people out to celebrate."

Casper came around the truck and opened the door for her. After he locked the truck, she reached down and took his hand. Her grip was firm and while it startled him at first, he found he enjoyed it. They were arriving at just after five o'clock and already people were sitting inside the windows. For whatever his reasons, Casper had asked for an earlier reservation. She thought to herself, *'Maybe he thinks there will be time to talk me into going to bed with him. Well, he is going to get a big surprise if he tries. I would like to cuddle and kiss with him, but no more until after a wedding.'*

She heard Casper say, "This is a nice area, maybe after we finish dinner, we should walk over to the river and see what is going on."

"What a great idea, Casper. After living here for four years, I have only seen the river a few times." Casper held the door for her and they entered.

"You have a reservation for Blakerly."

The hostess looked down at her table layout. "Thank you for arriving on time, Mr. Blakerly, please follow me." She led them to a table on a slightly raised deck at the side of the restaurant and a waiter followed to help seat them. They had an interesting view of the city through the windows.

The waiter brought a glass of ice water for each of them and placed menus on the table. Casper asked his dinner partner, "Would you like to have another bottle of the same white wine we enjoyed?" Jessica nodded. Casper ordered the wine and opened his menu. When the wine came, Casper went through the ritual and agreed he liked it. The waiter poured each of them a glass. They raised their glasses and took sips before smiling at each other. Jessica ordered a small Caesar salad and grilled salmon for the main course. Casper ordered lobster bisque soup and horseradish crusted salmon. While they waited, Casper asked her what she thought of Hiram Weinstein and she launched into a report on the plant tour and the interest he took in various phases of the operation. "He was very impressed by the new plant and the way it is designed to provide the best possible efficiency and speed of operation. It took us two hours to make the tour before he went to his car and left for West Branch. He told me he had the materials we asked for in his briefcase and would send them by mail immediately. In my opinion, he is very interested in obtaining a position at Davenport."

"Do you think he would be a positive and productive employee for the company?"

"Yes, I do, although in fairness it is hard to judge."

"Of course, Jessica, and if he is not a good employee I will fire him immediately." Jessica noted the hard cast of his face. "It is never easy but I've learned that when you find an employee is not correct for the job, do not waste time. The employee always knows they are not properly fitted to the job long before we recognize it. Enough of business discussions let us enjoy our dinner and time together."

"An excellent idea, Mr. Blakerly. I must say that I have enjoyed myself every time we go out to eat and I get to talk to you. When I told my parents what we ate at Biaggi's they thought we were being extravagant and my mother was shocked by the wine."

"Are your parents that restrictive?"

"Not really but they live a rather sheltered life. With the requirement to milk the cow herd twice each day, they seldom get off the farm for more than a couple of hours. They are very average citizens and very caring parents who do not have the liberty to travel." The salad and soup arrived and the conversation stopped for a few moments.

Casper looked up from his soup and asked, "Have your parents never traveled outside Iowa?"

Jessica swallowed her bite of salad. "My father has never traveled outside the state since he finished school. He even met my mother at a church party. Mom traveled regularly to Indiana to visit my grandparents but now with them gone, she has no reason to go." They finished the food and the waiter cleared the table.

"When was the last time you were back to the farm?"

"During the Easter break, we had a good visit. When you hired me for the summer, my mom was both proud and disappointed because I wouldn't be home to see them."

"In ten days, the plant will be shut down for two weeks for the annual vacation. You should drive home and visit your family." The main courses arrived and they turned to eating. Jessica's mind was busy analyzing their conversation and she saw the opportunity to play a joke on Casper. She waited patiently for the right moment.

Casper was on his second forkful of salmon when she asked, "Is the food hot and spicy with the horseradish?"

"No, not at all, it is not near as spicy as I expected. How is your salmon?"

"Very good and cooked just right so the meat is firm." They continued to eat their dinner and Jessica waited.

When they finished their dinner, the waiter took the empty plates away and Casper looked at his dinner partner and told her, "You didn't reply to my suggestion."

"I have been thinking about it and to tell you the truth, a trip home would be very enjoyable but I can't do that."

"Why can't you?" His voice became harder, the way it had a habit of being when someone was arguing with him. Jessica had been in that position several times and learned. "I told you to take some time off and go home."

"What you say, Casper is true but there are three reasons. First, there is a tremendous amount of work ahead of me which must be done because in sixty days I will be back in university. Secondly, I am working to earn money to pay for another year of classes. Thirdly, I am afraid you might decide to fire me for not working properly."

The silence lasted several moments and Casper's face hardened before he began to smile. "You are a sneaky little devil, throwing my own words back at me." Jessica's face split open with a hearty laugh and Casper joined her. The waiter wondered what they could be talking about. "To be honest with you, I would much rather have you stay right here and work with me through the holidays. Still, it has to be your decision."

"Thank you, Casper. I will be here every day until the end of August." Jessica watched his face and thought she saw what she was intending. She had launched a campaign to persuade him to want her badly and to realize it; he wouldn't want to be separated from her. He was a great leader in many ways but his shyness with women was interfering. Somehow, she needed to encourage his mind to get off machinery and think about her. She had established a deadline for the end of August to subtly convince Casper that he wanted to be married to a mechanical engineer.

The waiter came and poured the remainder of the wine into their glasses and laid a dessert menu beside each of them. Jessica opened her menu. "Casper, we have never eaten dessert but they have a chocolate dessert here we could eat together if you are willing."

Casper waved a hand at the waiter to come back and told him, "We would like one serving of this dessert with two spoons." The waiter nodded and wrote the dessert in his book. When the dessert came, it looked enormous but they tucked in and after a few spoonful's, Casper told her, "It is very good but we don't have to eat it all."

Jessica laughed and nodded. She finished her wine and told him, "As good as it is, I do believe I would be happier walking over to the Mississippi to see what is going on."

Again, Casper waved at the waiter and when he arrived told him, "We are finished; please bring me the bill." When the bill arrived, Casper looked at it and added fifteen percent and took out his folded money and laid two one-hundred-dollar bills on the table.

"I will be back with your change in a moment."

Casper smiled at him. "The dinner was very nice and we have enjoyed ourselves, please keep the change." Jessica held his arm as they walked from the restaurant and then switched to holding his hand on the way to the river. Her campaign was off to a good start.

* * *

In the July sixth mail, Mrs. Sparks noticed a brown envelope addressed to Casper. She slit the end open and walked into Casper's office. "Here is a letter from Hiram Weinstein addressed to you. I took the liberty of opening it for you."

199

Casper took the envelope and leaned back in his chair before pulling the contents out. There was a one page letter to him, a Davenport employment form filled out, and several pages outlining Weinstein's history of employment. Casper read every word and when he came to the section of working for Case, he took out a highlighter and ran a green line along the side where the words concerned designing, testing, and buying various engines, both gasoline and diesel. Hiram had much experience in various areas of endeavor but his small engine years were what Davenport was looking for. The company intended to start a line of tractors in the fifty to one-hundred horsepower range to which various attachments could be added to do a variety of operations. The project would take time, probably several years, to reach full development. Casper sat back in his chair and considered all aspects of the project once again. For two years now, he had mentally planned and thought about how to go about developing this line of equipment and since he had only marginal personal exposure to this size of engines he needed someone who could be his right hand in making the project come to life. After much contemplation, he decided Hiram Weinstein was the right person to hire. Casper hadn't known Hiram very well back in school and in fact had some trouble remembering him when he came to talk on July third. Hiram had rattled around in Casper's head ever since the meeting and now he had made a decision. Unless Hiram made some far out demands in terms of compensation, titles, or whatever, the company would hire him. As was his usual habit, he set the material aside and decided to inspect the new plant and see how the construction was progressing. That was a little trick he had to make sure every detail had been considered.

Casper put on his hardhat and carried his leather gloves as he walked to the elevator. Mrs. Sparks watched him go. A few minutes later, she decided to drop in and ask Jessica how the dinner had been. After all, two days had gone by now.

Jessica heard the footsteps coming and looked up from the design details she was preparing and watched Mrs. Sparks come through the office door. Yesterday had been a very busy day with little time to converse, except about various projects so both were happy to spend a few minutes together. Mrs. Sparks smiled and asked, "How are you today, Jessica?"

"Very good, thank you but there is so much to get done and there are times when I feel over loaded and there is only until the end of August to finish them."

"May I give you some of my motherly advice?"

"Please do."

"Casper hired you for the summer and that period ends when August is used up. On September first, you will be free to tackle your studies again. Any work you have not completed will be Davenport's responsibility, not yours. My advice to you is to do the best work you can and at the end of August move on to your studies. There is another factor which is obvious to me. Casper is brilliant, focused, and devoted to his company and most often only thinks about things in the immediate future." Mrs. Sparks laughed. "I have never figured out whether the immediate future is one day or maybe a week. You may not see it but of all the people employed by Davenport you are in a very special position. And may I add, it is doubtful Casper is aware of it either. When it finally hits him and registers in his brain that you are leaving, he will be terribly upset. The number one fact is that Casper has fallen in love with you and still doesn't recognize it."

Jessica starred at Mrs. Sparks for several minutes. Her eyes slowly became damp. She opened a desk drawer and reached for a tissue to dry her eyes. Mrs. Sparks watched her and laughed softly. "It has been obvious for several weeks and I have worried about both of you because neither of you seemed to be aware. It makes me happy to see that you are in the same dilemma. In the last several weeks, Casper has taken you out to dinner more times than I could count and what else you two have been doing only God knows. My most fervent hope is that you haven't jumped into bed with him."

Jessica was suddenly over her sadness and laughed. She held up her left hand. "Do you see a ring on my third finger? There will be no bed until after I am married. The facts are he has just started to hold my hand when we walk along the street. He hasn't even tried to kiss me and I want him to, very badly, but it never seems to come to his mind. We enjoy our dinners and our time together but you are correct, his mind is never far from his work. When he talks about the projects, his eyes become intense and he is totally focused. Little old me just disappears."

"It is the way men are, they are unpredictable, which is probably a key factor in their business success. They can focus. They have one track minds. Sometimes, I talk to my husband and he doesn't answer which used to annoy me greatly before I realized he was thinking about his work. After he returns to the real world, I tell him what I wanted to say. Now in your case, if I may be so bold, at some point Casper will wake up and when he does you will feel like you are locked in a cave with a runaway semi that has lost it steering and is swerving all over the floor throwing up dust and trying to run over you."

"Tomorrow wouldn't be too soon to suit me." Jessica smiled. "On the other hand, I have another year of university ahead of me."

"Yes, you have and you should plan to work hard and rack up good marks. Be sure you always remember to keep your back to a wall against the time Casper loses his steering and starts roaring around under full steam."

"Thank you, Mrs. Sparks, you have given me good advice and I needed it." Sparks stood up and walked away. Jessica sat there reviewing their conversation. Mrs. Sparks returned.

"I came to ask how your dinner was at the Duck City Bistro."

"We had a good dinner with fine white wine and afterwards walked over to the Mississippi and along the bank, watching the water and the people. Casper got me home just as it was turning dark."

"Happy to hear that, Jessica and may I suggest; if Casper doesn't kiss you in the next few days you must ask him to do so."

Jessica smiled at her. "Thank you, Mrs. Sparks." She went back to work with her brain divided, half on the project and half on Mrs. Sparks and Casper. Several times, she giggled softly to herself as her mind wandered back and forth on both projects. She was hard at work when near four-thirty Casper walked into her office with a brown colored envelope.

"This is an employment application from Hiram. If you can read it over this evening, we should get together in the morning and decide what to do. Got to check on the haying at the farm so am in a hurry, see you in the morning." Jessica watched him go into the elevator and the doors close. She looked at the eight and a half by eleven inch envelope and decided, *'What the hell, I might as well read it now and not have to carry it home tonight.'* She spent an hour reading the application and making notes. Everything looked good to her. She noted the highlighting Casper had put alongside the notes pertaining to engines and smiled. So, that is what he is planning for the future. Tonight, she would dig out her textbooks on engines and brush up. Maybe she could startle these two old men with her up-to-date knowledge. She laughed out loud and put away her papers for the night.

She didn't have a good night's sleep, her mind kept bringing back to her the conversation with Mrs. Sparks, then switching to her rather restricted upbringing, and the talks and warnings of her mother. In her mind, she argued both sides of the question of kissing and finally accepted that kissing couldn't do any harm as long as nothing further occurred. It wasn't something she would ever tell her mother, Elizabeth had rather restrictive beliefs. She walked into her office at six-thirty a.m. feeling rather tired and pulled out her gear to get started. With her personal Texas Instrument calculator, she went to work punching in numbers and checking what had been put on her latest drawing. Particular attention was necessary on the tolerance of fittings between two moving parts. The fittings had to be right to reduce wear and extend the life-cycle. She was making good progress and the drawing would be ready in a few minutes. Footsteps intruded into her space and she looked over her shoulder. It was Casper. She swung her stool around.

"Good morning, Jessica, why are you looking so tired this morning?"

"Didn't sleep as well as normal because these darn plans kept disturbing my mind. Do you want to talk about Hiram's application?"

"If you have the time, right now would be good for me." Jessica opened a desk drawer and pulled out the application and spread it out on the desk. For the next hour they went over the information Hiram had provided and discussed and argued over what was significant. They were left with the dilemma of what title would be best to bestow upon Hiram. Finally, Casper told her he would have Mrs. Sparks set up a file on Hiram and find out what salary range would apply. He would think about a title.

Jessica watched him walk away thinking, *'Titles aren't considered important around Davenport, in fact I don't ever remember Casper using a title, he just signs his name. For those people dealing outside the company, titles are necessary.'*

Chapter 15

Hiram Weinstein reported for his first day of work on August first and human resources occupied most of his time signing him up for various programs. At midafternoon, he was delivered to Casper's office where they looked in the door and saw Casper bent over his drafting table drawing another part for a new machine. Ron Smith, Manager of Financial, rapped on the door. Nothing happened. He looked at Hiram and smiled. "Casper, can we interrupt your work for a few minutes?"

Casper's head came up and he looked at the doorway. "Oh, hi Ron. What can I do for…Ah, Hiram, please come in both of you." Casper hopped off his stool to shake hands with his new employee. "I suppose Ron has had you wrestling with paper all day?"

"True, Casper, but now they tell me I am all signed up, covered by insurance, and need to go and buy steel-toed boots to wear around the plant."

"Yes, they have the rules to enforce." He held up one foot showing his steel-toed boot. "We are very serious about safety around here and Ron has the responsibility of enforcing the rules. Are you going to drive Hiram over to the safety company to get boots?"

Ron laughed, "I wasn't planning on doing that, Casper. Mrs. Sheldon will fill in for me and they will go as soon as you free us up."

Casper glanced at the clock over by the door. "It is getting well on in the afternoon. Ron, why don't you send Hiram to get his boots right now? Afterwards, Hiram, you go on home for the night. In the morning, come and talk to me. I must tell you I am very happy to have you join our company. You will have to get used to our somewhat informal way of working around here. We are not much on titles and formality but I must give Ron credit for trying to drag me into the corporate world. Which reminds me, Ron, when will I receive the final financial reports for the year just ended? It has been a whole month, you know." Casper winked one eye at Hiram and laughed.

Ron smiled, commenting, "We are going to give them one last review tomorrow and if we don't find mistakes to correct, they will be ready for you."

"Real good, Ron, see you fellas tomorrow." As they walked out, Hiram glanced back through an office window and Casper was already on his stool at the drafting table.

* * *

One thing Hiram had learned during his first day at work was that these people weren't eight hour-a-day workers. Beyond that, he realized there were other things he needed to discover. On this his second day, he walked off the elevator at seven-thirty and was shocked to see Jessica in her office, Mrs. Sparks working on her computer, and Casper signing checks at his desk. Obviously seven-thirty wasn't considered early around here. He walked to Mrs. Sparks' desk and asked her, "Do you have an office for me to use?"

"We certainly do, follow me down the hallway." They stopped to say good morning to Jessica before continuing along the hall. Mrs. Sparks turned into a large office. "This is where Casper said to put you, although you may not have been told your permanent office will be in the new building when it is opened."

Hiram looked around thoughtfully. "Very nice Mrs. Sparks. When do you estimate the new plant will be ready?"

She smiled at him. "No one has told me as yet but I do know

that Casper is expecting it to open in late September or October. In the meantime, you will be hanging your hat here."

After walking to the desk and laying his briefcase on the top, he pulled open a drawer before looking up. "All this furniture appears to be brand new."

"It is, Hiram, the big boss himself went down to talk to Mike Osborn, our manager of purchasing, and told him what to get for you. If there is anything not suitable to your work habits, please inform me and we will arrange changes."

"Changes will certainly not be necessary, Mrs. Sparks, this furniture is far better than anything I have ever worked with in the past."

"Thank you for the comment, Hiram, You are fortunate there was no used furniture sitting around when you were hired and besides all the management employees work long hours so Casper insists they be comfortable. For your information, Casper only likes people who work hard and don't complain and he is anti-bureaucracy. No red tape, the emphasis is on getting things done, manufacturing top of the line machines, safety, and when someone comes up with a better way to build a part, to switch over right now. You may find this place to be disturbing for a time but don't worry, once you get used to the way we do things, you will be happy. Let me know when you are settled in and I will set up your meeting with Casper." She turned and walked out of his office and Hiram stood looking around for a minute.

He sat in the desk chair and found it was comfortable, un-packed his large bulging briefcase and filled two drawers before taking his drafting and drawing tools over to the drafting table. After tipping the drafting table up at an angle which would work for him, the drafting instruments and a bundle of colored pencils went into the tray which ran all across the bottom of the table.

It took three trips to his car to carry in boxes of textbooks and place them in the large bookcase. He had made a good start. More books and files would arrive when the movers brought all the family possessions from their Detroit house which was now listed for sale. Hiram was hoping to catch one of the summertime home hunters, who wanted a house before the schools opened in the fall.

For a few minutes, he sat and looked around to make himself feel comfortable in the space. The walls were bare so one of the things to do was select pictures to brighten them up. Finally, he dialed the phone. "Mrs. Sparks, whenever Casper is ready for the meeting, please let me know."

When Hiram arrived, Casper was still signing checks. Mrs. Sparks picked up the pile of signed check and took them away as Casper told her, "I will process the rest after Hiram and I finish our meeting. Now, Hiram, tell me, where is your family?

"All three of them are at home packing up personal and private items to bring down. We have to find a school for the children and my wife is always fussy about the school's record. Our house is listed for sale and we hope it will be sold before the end of the month."

"What are you going to do about finding a home for your family here in Iowa?"

"When my wife arrives, we will start looking."

"There is a Realtor that has done many house searches for new Davenport employees. If you are interested, ask Mrs. Sparks to phone him. Where you live is your business but let me remind you that the further you live from the plant, the less time you will spend with your family. From out west at West Branch, you would be driving a couple of hours each day, a lot of wasted time."

"Good point, Casper, thank you."

"Your wife will need help in looking at houses so feel free to take off time to help her. Also, do the same when your belongings are brought in by the moving company. If you need help, just ask and we will do the best we can. Now let's talk about what you will be working on here at Davenport. For several months, on and off, I have sketched out ideas for a line of tractors and attachments that we want to add to our equipment list. Right now we plan to start with a fifty horsepower tractor, front-end loader, forklift, backhoe bucket, etc. Let's go over to my drafting table and look at my sketches. As we go along, we intend to add larger higher horsepower machines up to one hundred horsepower and probably larger." The two men walked over to the drafting table and Casper began passing out the sketches and they discussed each one as they slowly went through them. It was several hours before Hiram walked back to his office carrying an armload of papers. The last thing Casper suggested to him was to go down to the line where the current machines were being built and observe how and why things were being done in certain ways. Hiram got a drink of water and followed up on Casper's idea. There were many things to see, people to talk to, and work parties to be watched. He hadn't gotten to the end of the construction line before the bells sounded and the plant began to shut down for the night. He sighed and told himself, *'Tomorrow I will return and finish my trip. There is a lot to see and observe in this plant. Most amazing, almost all the people are workers and very few are supervisors. This must be one of Casper's moves to cut out red tape and protect against academically minded bureaucrats with no practical work experience.'*

Hiram worked in his office till six o'clock before starting the drive to West Branch where he was staying with his wife's parents. He was thinking about what Casper had said about wasting time, and for sure he would soon become tired of the hour long drive.

* * *

When Casper had arrived home the evening before, the farm

crew was out in the first field combining soybeans. The first field was ready. He had finished his breakfast and cleaned up the kitchen and now was out in the yard waiting for Fred Aitchison to show up. Harvesting was the most exciting time of the year on the farm— it was long, hard, dusty work, and some years full of problems. Casper always felt like a teenager when the combines came out of storage and dearly wanted to drive for a couple of hours to get his feel for riding the combine again. When Fred arrived, he grinned at Casper. "I told the boys yesterday you would be showing up today. All of us got into an argument about whether you are qualified to drive one of these big machines."

Casper laughed happily and replied, "Every year when the combine's startup it makes me feel like I am sixteen all over again. Think you can let me drive for a couple of hours?"

Fred laughed. "You know you can drive all day if you want. Just remember there is one of our hired hands not getting to do his job while you are out there hogging his machine."

"A couple of hours are all I ask for. Maybe other times during harvest you will let me go at it again. Like say lunchtime." Casper got a grease gun from the service truck and greased the combine while Fred followed him around and checked belts and chain drives. Engine oil and antifreeze were fine. Casper drove the combine over to the fuel pump and filled the combine with diesel while Fred washed the windows. The inside of the cab was clean. By the time Casper was ready to start combining, the two hired men were getting the other combine ready for the day. Fred followed Casper into the cab and rode beside him as they drove to the soybean field to start straight cutting for the day. Casper waited for Fred to correct him or suggest an adjustment but for two hours they just talked and not once did Fred interfere. Casper wondered to himself if it was because he was doing a first-class job of combining or because he owned the farm. Fred claimed to be in the cab in case something went astray and needed to be adjusted, which he would do and keep Casper clean.

Casper pulled up to the B-Train and dumped his last load before climbing down the ladder from the cab and telling the hired man to take over. His dump had filled the trailer and he sat in the cab as the combine moved away and rode to the yard with Fred driving. The B-Train pulled up to the unloading auger and the two men loaded the soybeans into a large steel storage bin. Before walking away, Casper told Fred, "See you this evening."

Driving the combine was exciting and he was pleased with the yield of the soy crop as he drove the F-150 to the office. He came off the elevator with a happy, bouncy step and stopped in Jessica's office. When she looked up at him, he smiled and told her about his morning. Listening to him talk about the combining, Jessica realized how much he loved his farm and there she sat missing her parents' farm. She listened until he finished telling his story and told him, "I would love to get back on a combine again but the dairy farm is too far away."

Casper plopped into one of her office chairs and looked at her for a moment. "Tomorrow is Saturday, why don't you drive out to the farm and ride a combine for a while, haul soy with the semi, and see what our farm is all about? Only bad thing you will face is eating my cooking."

Jessica looked at him for a moment. "I will. What time do you want me to be there?"

"The men will get going about eight-thirty or so. You come by then or any time after and I will find a spot for you."

Sitting back in her chair, she laughed out loud at him. "While I am out combining and trucking you will be in the house peeling spuds and fixing a big dinner to keep my strength up."

"Now, I didn't promise anything like that, maybe we will go

out for a hamburger." Casper stood up and added, "Glad you are coming and make sure I take you around to see the farm, grain, and cattle."

Jessica watched him walk away and told herself, *'A lucky break for me, now he has asked me out to the farm so whether he knows it or not, it is him who is being aggressive.'*

Walking into his office, he spotted a pile of reports on his desk and hurried to see what they were. He sighed, now he had the year-end reports and could sit down this weekend and read through them and find out what position Davenport was in. There would be taxes to pay and the cost of the new plant and retooling it. Well, he looked forward to finding out where the company and he stood, which would make it easier to plan ahead. He already had a fair indication from editing and helping to reword parts of the reports but still, it was always wise to see the final numbers. He packed the reports in a large leather briefcase and set it by his office door, ready for the trip home.

With his mind on the year-end, he decided to visit the new building and see how it was progressing. Dropping the steel safety helmet on his head, he decided to ask Hiram if he wanted to go along. Together, the two men walked through Plant No. 1 and across the open yard to Plant No. 2. Morley O'Brien was parking an electric run-about after having made a trip to purchasing. Casper asked Hiram, "Have you met Morley, the manager of construction on Plant No. 2?"

"No, I haven't. Is that him getting out of the electric cart?" Casper nodded.

As they got nearer, Casper waved at the manager and called, "Morley, come and say hello to Hiram Weinstein. Hiram is a well experienced mechanical engineer we have hired to work on developing a new line of products." Morley arrived with his hand outstretched and shook with Hiram. Casper continued, "I want to get up to date on the progress of construction and when you believe this plant will be completed."

"Let's go to my office and I will tell you and estimate the end of construction the best I can." The three men gathered around Morley's paper-laden desk and began. They spent two hours mostly listening except for Casper questioning some of the projections. Morley ended by saying that he expected construction to be over right around the end of September.

Casper asked about the timing on the office spaces along the side of the building. Morley pointed at the outside walls and commented, "We started insulation at this end so the spaces for offices are now ready. I hadn't planned to start putting up walls until August fifteen but if you are in a rush, I can reshuffle and start sooner."

"You stick to your plans, Morley. August fifteenth will be fine. Thank you for the update and you can expect me and/or Hiram to start showing up more often from now on. We will get out of your hair for now. Thanks." The two men left and walked back to their offices. It was after four so Casper decided he wasn't going to start on any project, he was going back to the farm to watch the harvest.

* * *

Jessica drove into the farmyard just before nine a.m. and found Casper helping to unload a highway semi-truck and trailer filled with soybeans. She parked near the farm workshop, put on her hardhat, and walked over to watch the men. A smiling Casper came to greet her. "I thought it would be wiser to take you out to look around the farm, check the crops, see the land, and inspect the cattle. This afternoon will be warmer and a good time for you to ride a combine."

She smiled back at him. "Sounds like a good plan, Casper."

"Okay, jump in my truck." Sitting in the truck, Casper told her, "The house was built by my grandfather and is where I grew up and live now." Jessica looked where he pointed and saw a nice old two-story house well painted and with vines growing along the open-air porch. Partially visible on the porch was a chain-suspended swinging two-seater probably made of wood. They drove around the yard looking at the workshop, a two-vehicle garage, a long line of large steel grain bins, a large barn with a corral, and huge hay storage shed now full of round bales. Around another corner were machine storage buildings, the doors on the combine building standing open. The truck left the farmyard and went along a farm-owned lane with pastures on the left lower land with a herd of Black Angus cattle grazing, on the right of the lane was a hayfield. A mile out, they turned north and came on wheat and corn fields not yet ready for harvesting. Next, Casper pulled up at the gate where the combines were straight cutting soybeans. After watching for a few minutes, he continued to drive west past more of the farm's crops. Several sets of buildings went past the windows and Casper explained they were part of the farm and were rented out. He turned south and drove downslope toward a river which he explained was named the Wapsipinicon and flowed into the Mississippi River. A mile up the road, he stopped to open a gate and drove through before closing it. "This section of grazing land, we started renting last spring. It has water from the river, and two small ponds, and is all in grass. Presently, there are three hundred cows and calves grazing here. We are considering putting in hay storage to provide winter feed although there may be a water problem in the real cold months." He laughed. "Cows can't drink frozen water."

Stopping on a rise, he turned off the truck and they had a far-ranging view with the river going past on the other side of the south fence. Casper explained, "With these four quarters of rental land added, we have nineteen quarters of land, ten of which we own, gives us a total of fifty-five acres over three thousand. These six hundred and fifty-five acres of grass bring our grazing to a total of one thousand and ninety-five acres of pasture so we have enough for several years with the cattle."

"There is a beautiful view of the countryside from up here."

"Yes, there is but this land is somewhat remote and doesn't have the greatest access roads. I sat up here last spring and thought this was a far-seeing spot to build a home. The trouble is it is not located on a good all-weather road. In any case, it is a good place for me to come and think and from here you can see most of the cattle." He handed her a pair of binoculars and Jessica was surprised by the strength of the lenses. She slowly scanned around the grasslands and there were places where clumps of aspen trees blocked the view but she watched a large number of cows with little calves following them. She smirked, the calves weren't so small; four or five months had put a lot of growth on them. She looked out across the river and then up at the sky and clouds. Jessica spotted an airliner and followed its flight until it started descending into the Davenport airport.

She handed the binoculars back to Casper. "It is a beautiful view and looking over all the countryside gave me a feeling of being a spy." They both laughed.

The truck clock showed it was almost one o'clock so Casper asked, "What do you say to me taking you to our little town where we buy supplies and having something to eat?"

"A very good idea, Casper, let's go." Casper got them back out on the road and drove north for three miles and turned right to get to DeWitt. Just a little town on Highway Thirty with people and vehicles moving around all busy about whatever was important to them. He parked the truck with the nose pointing at a rather small building with a sign reading 'Big Joe's Deli.'

Jessica wasn't sure she was impressed but didn't say anything as they got out of the truck. Casper held Jessica's door open for her and she noticed he didn't bother to lock his truck. She smiled inwardly, noticing that in small-town America people trusted each other. A man not much over five feet tall raised a hand and called out, "How are you, Casper? Haven't seen you in town for several weeks."

"Now, Big Joe, if you lazy town people would work decent hours, you would see us come in for supplies and food. Joe, I want to introduce you to Jessica Hornsbee and she says she is hungry enough to eat a dried-up old boot."

Joe laughed. "Pleased to make your acquaintance, Jessica, but I must warn you we are fresh out of old boots."

"Disappointing news, Joe, but I am sure there are other things on your menu which will be just fine." She followed Casper to a corner table from where they could see the parked truck and traffic going past on the highway. Joe followed, carrying menus and two glasses of ice water.

"How are your wife and kids getting along, Joe?"

"Real good Casper, the three kids are all in school now, or will be come September first, and my Phillis is back in the kitchen handling the cooking. Our special today is fried potato strips mixed with beans, roasted ham bits, peas and mixed in with a dash of hot Chile and you get a slice of cheese toast to go with it."

Casper smiled. "You put me down for your special and bring me a root beer."

Jessica smiled up at him. "I will have the special also but tell your wife to make it a small order, I don't eat the way Casper does and the order is dependent on you leaving this menu here for me to look over."

Joe smiled and wrote her order down, picked up Casper's menu, and walked to the kitchen. They could hear him calling out the food order to his Phillis. Jessica started studying the menu items. A few minutes later, Phillis arrived at their table. She was no taller than Joe and slim as a toothpick and good looking, except for a red face from the heat of the kitchen. "Now, who is this lady who wants a small order of my fine cooking?"

Jessica stuck out her hand and they shook. "My name is Jessica from a dairy farm over west of here and to tell you the truth I have never been a big eater."

"You don't need to tell me, Jessica, just looking at you, it is plain to see. Now, you tell me what the heck are you doing with this no good Blakerly fella who my husband and I attended school with. For your information, he was always causing problems."

"Doesn't surprise me, Phillis, everyone around warns me to watch him real close."

"Good for you, my girl. Now, Casper, how are you keeping and what are you doing with yourself?"

"I am ailing something terrible, Phillis. Got bad knees and a sore back and can't stop working to support myself. Why, if I had a working wife like you, I could sit on the porch swing and rest up."

Phillis frowned. "Now, don't you be trying to feed me any of your no-good bull? Big Joe tells me everyone says you are rolling in money and won't spend a cent of it. Hell, how are we working people going to make a living with guys like you not spending?"

Big Joe arrived with their food and frowned. "Now, Jessica, don't you be paying any attention to my Phillis, she can talk all day and not say a darn thing worth hearing. Do you want more hot sauce, shredded cheese, or anything else? Do you want something to drink?"

"No, thank you, Joe, I will drink the ice water. Thank you for cooking up this food while I was talking to your wife."

Joe and Phillis walked away and they dug into their food

and found it delicious. It looked very plain but the mixture had a yummy taste and the way Casper was eating, his plate would end up clean. Finally, Jessica stopped eating for a moment and asked quietly, "You went to school with those two?"

Casper smiled. "Sure did, all through public school, we all rode the school bus together and these two took a liking for each other real early. They've been married for must be twelve or fifteen years now. They got married and moved into DeWitt and now they have their own business. From what I hear, they are doing just fine."

On the way back to the farm, Jessica found herself feeling stuffed. She had eaten more than usual and enjoyed every bite. Casper pulled into the soy field and stopped beside the B-Train, which Fred was driving. "Fred, Jessica here grew up on a dairy farm and she would like to drive one of your combines."

Fred couldn't keep a look of doubt off his face for a moment before he smiled. "Sure thing Casper, as soon as one of the combines comes to unload, we will get her on it. You going to need some help, Jessica?"

"Oh yes, Fred, I have driven combines for many hours but I am sure these machines have gadgets my dad has never purchased. Send your man along with me to prevent any troubles."

Fred began to relax. When the combine came alongside, he took Jessica up the steps to the cab and told the driver what the arrangement was. When they drove away, Jessica was in the driver's seat. Fred and Casper watched for a while and soon Jessica was up to the proper speed and doing fine. When the second combine came in to dump, the semi was full so Casper rode with Fred to the yard to unload. It was a close thing. They barely got back and parked when Jessica pulled alongside and dumped. She waved happily at Casper and went back to combining. Casper helped with the trucking and the hands on his wrist watch were reading six o'clock when Jessica came down the combine steps and walked to the truck. She was happy and her wide smile gave the secret away. "What a glorious afternoon, Casper! The sun shining and me in the driver's seat of a combine. You have a wonderful machine there with all its computers and gadgets which your hired man spent the time teaching me how to set and read." They got into the truck and Casper started the trip to the buildings. Jessica was sitting sideways with her blue jean-clad left knee up on the seat so she was looking right at him. In a serious-sounding voice, she told Casper, "For the right amount of money, I could drive a combine for you all summer."

Casper glanced at her and started laughing. "We can arrange things that way, provided you agree to work the rest of the year at the plant for the same wages."

Jessica frowned at him, "To get high-class help like me to work on your farm, you will have to pay a much higher wage than those poor boys are getting."

"Sorry, girl, the farm can't afford people like you who make staggering high salaries." Jessica laughed along with him and turned toward the front of the truck. At the farm, he sent her to the bathroom to wash up while he started cooking dinner.

Chapter 16

Hiram had spent the last three weeks drawing up plans for a fifty horse-power tractor in between house hunting and moving his family to Davenport, Iowa. Mrs. Sparks had helped by lining up the Realtor for him who had shown him and his wife several houses, but so far nothing that appealed to them. One big worry off his shoulders was the sale of their previous home and now the money was in the bank. His wife had found a school that she considered to be up to her standards and the two children were now registered for when classes started. Today, he was moving. His new office in Plant No. 2 was ready and staff from the purchasing department were packing his things and hauling them to the new office where he was busy unpacking and putting various items where he wanted them. Just past four p.m., he heard Jessica's voice and turned around. There she was standing in the door of his office. "Hi, Hiram, I have come to say goodbye to you."

"Goodbye to me? I don't understand, where are you going?"

Jessica laughed. "I have been working on a summer contract; this is my last day of employment. I am now going back to university to start work on my Masters of Business Administration degree." She held out her hand.

Hiram shook hand and held on, "I didn't know you weren't here full time, I will miss you and being able to discuss programs together."

"Yes, I will miss those things also, but education is important and so I must move on. Have you talked to Casper today?"

"No, I haven't. Goodbye, Jessica, and all the best in your studies."

Jessica hurried away. Hiram had been her last stop and now she would load her car. In her office, she sat at the desk and wrote a note to Casper, sealed it in an envelope, and dropped it on his desk. She had two briefcases and three boxes to pack into her car, which only took a few minutes. She went back and hugged Mrs. Sparks and said goodbye once again. As she walked to the elevator, she stopped and looked through the window of Casper's office for a moment, bringing back many good memories. It was sad missing Casper on her last day and she would try to stay in contact with him, maybe things would work out in the long run. Her eyes became wet and she wiped them with a tissue as the elevator doors closed behind her.

It was two days later before Casper left the grain harvest and showed up at his desk. When Mrs. Sparks arrived for work, he was sitting there holding the note Jessica had written to him and he looked terrible. She went to talk to him and saw he had been crying. Never before had she seen him with wet eyes. "What is wrong, Casper?"

He didn't answer, just held out the note to her. She sat down in a chair and read the words. Casper finally spoke. "What am I going to do without Jessica here to work with me? She is such a good engineer and planner and I totally forgot she was only hired for the summer, and I liked her company."

Mrs. Sparks sat up, straightened her back, and very pointedly asked, "Those are kind words, but tell me, honestly, what are your feelings about Jessica?"

Casper started twice before he found the words he wanted. "I like her very much, thought we would be together forever, and now she is gone."

"Casper, very bluntly, do you love her, do you want her to be your wife?"

"Yes, that is what I want, except I never could figure out how to tell her. I have no experience with women and what would I do if she told me no?"

Mrs. Sparks pointed a finger at him. "Casper, you are the smartest, kindest, most hard-working man I have ever known. You want Jessica to marry you so get out of that chair and go find her. When you do talk to her, tell her how you feel, and by damn you ask her to marry you."

Casper stared at her for a minute. "Yes, yes, you are right. I will leave right now and drive to her apartment and tell her." He jumped out of his chair and ran out of the office to the stairwell.

Mrs. Sparks watched him go and wondered, *'Talking to women is the only weakness I have ever seen in him and now he is off on a personal mission. He does talk to women like me for example but the ones he likes clam him up.'*

* * *

Casper never broke the speed limit but he was doing it now as the truck raced down the streets. He parked in front of the apartment building and hurried through the door and up to the second floor. He rang the doorbell and waited. He rang it again, still no answer. He paced around on the hall rug and tried to think but his mind was blank, nothing came to him. He rang the doorbell again, still no answer. He leaned his head against the door and tried to think. He was interrupted by a rather firm voice, "Is there anything I can help you with, sir?"

Casper found himself looking at an older man, probably Fred's age or more. "Please can you tell me where Jessica is?"

The old man smiled, so this was the fella she told him about. "Two days ago, I helped her unload her car and carry all her belongings into this apartment but she didn't say anything about going away so presumably, she is now out shopping for groceries or maybe other things she wants."

"Not much of an answer, at least not what I wanted." Casper thought, well the answer did cheer him up somewhat. "No sense in me wandering around town looking for her; I will sit in my truck and watch for her coming home. Thank you for your kind words and for helping Jessica in unloading her car." He shook the old man's hand and walked away. When he came out of the building, the first thing he saw was a city policeman sitting on the hood of his truck. His mind whirled, trying to think what he had done.

The policeman watched him come along the sidewalk and asked, "Is this your truck, mister?"

"Yes, it is, Officer. Is there something wrong?"

The officer's gruff voice answered, "That depends on how you see things. You left the driver's door open and the keys in the ignition, not a wise thing to do." The officer held out a key ring and dropped in into Casper's hand. "You should be more careful in the future."

"Thank you, Officer." Casper leaned on the fender beside where the officer was sitting. "You see, I am trying to find my girlfriend to ask her to marry me and she is nowhere around, at least right now."

"This is a very serious problem for a young man to have. Been married almost twenty years myself and usually, I have found that waiting is the best solution to many a problem. Of course, if your problem is very serious I could ask Police Headquarters to put out an APB describing her and asking for help in locating her."

Casper stared at him, wondering what an APB was. The police officer smiled. "The initials stand for All Points Bulletin."

A loud laugh came from Casper as he stepped back. "My goodness no, if Jessica found out we had done that, she would beat both of us to a pulp."

"Can't have such a travesty happening, now can we? Good luck." The officer walked away along the sidewalk and Casper watched him go. A minute later, he shook his head, wondering what he should do now. Glancing at his watch, he found it was five minutes after ten a.m. *'If I sit here all day and she doesn't come back till evening, I will be a nervous wreck.'* He paced around for a few minutes before getting into the truck and driving back to the plant.

Mrs. Sparks saw him coming. "No sign of her at the apartment. Had a nice chat with the janitor and a city policeman, but didn't find Jessica."

"I have phoned the apartment twice this morning and got no answer. Have you considered that Jessica may have driven home to the dairy farm to visit her family?"

Casper's face lit up. "I didn't think about that!" He paced around for a minute. "I don't know where the farm is and Jessica never gave me a phone number." Mrs. Sparks held out a sheet of paper with the information written on it in bold black ink. As he read the notes, his face lit up. "By damn, I will phone there right now." He rushed into his office, grabbed the phone, and was dialing as he sat down in his chair.

A female voice answered. "Hornsbee Dairy Farm, how are you today?"

"Hello, ma'am, my name is Casper Blakerly and I am trying to find Jessica Hornsbee. Do you know where I might reach her?"

There was silence for a moment as Jessica's mom turned to look at her daughter and silently mouthed, *'CASPER.'* Jessica's face lit up with an ear to ear smile as she rushed to the phone. "Hello, Casper."

"Jessica! Oh, Jessica, I have been looking everywhere for you!

Will you marry me?"

She tried to answer and nothing came out. She forced herself to take a deep breath and let the air out first. "Yes, Mr. Blakerly, I would be pleased to do that."

The loud voice almost broke her eardrum and she moved the phone away a short distance. "YIPPIE, MRS. SPARKS, JESSICA SAID YES!" Jessica tried the phone a bit closer to her ear; the voice was still loud but more comfortable. "Mrs. Sparks, I am going to have a wife! Jessica said she will marry me."

"That is very nice, Casper, and I am so pleased. Is Jessica still on the phone?"

There was silence for a moment before a soft voice asked, "Are you still there, Jessica?'

"Yes, I am, Casper, and very pleased to be talking to you. Thank you for asking me."

"Jessica you must hurry home so we can get married tomorrow."

Jessica laughed. "It would be very nice to do that, Casper, but you have forgotten I have a family and they will want to be at the wedding."

"Oh, yes, yes. We must plan, Jessica; you should come home today so we can be together. Let's have the wedding soon, very soon."

"I hear you, Casper, but I must talk to my mother. I will phone you after a while when we have considered the best things to do."

"I will stay here in my office all afternoon, waiting for your phone call."

"You do that, Casper, and thank you for phoning and asking me to marry you."

"I should have asked you weeks ago but I was afraid you might laugh and say no. Now it is done and all we need is the wedding."

"True, Casper, but there are many things to plan; the wedding, a reception, dinner, how we dress, flowers and many others. Now you sit back and relax and I will phone you this afternoon." Jessica hung up and her mother came to hug her.

"Jess, I am so happy for you. Your Casper must be some kind of character but I know you have loved him for some time now."

"He is a bit of a character, Mother, but it is because he is a very intelligent man and was an honor student all through his schooling. His mind is always working on business and designing equipment and running his company and the little things in life just go past him without being noticed. You will be impressed when you meet him."

"I am sure you are correct, dear, now we better walk out and tell your father." It was a bit of a cool day so they put on jackets and walked across the yard. Her mother called, "Karl, where are you?"

"In the shop, Elizabeth, come in and see me." Karl had a wheel off a cultivator and was replacing the bearings. His hands were all dirt and grease. He watched them come and wiped his hands on a rag which left them still dirty. The rag went back into a rear pocket in his coveralls. He smiled at the ladies.

"Dad, my good friend Casper has asked me to marry him and I agreed. We just came to tell you the news."

"Congratulations! Your mother told me you had found the man you wanted but it sure seemed to take a long time."

"Yes, I suppose that is so, but you must understand, Casper is a brilliant man and the common, ordinary things in life just slide past him. It often seems his mind can't get down to the level of us ordinary people. We need to talk because Casper is not used to de-lays, in fact he told me to drive home today so we could be married tomorrow."

"Nonsense, what did your mother say?"

"Not a single word simply because we want to talk to you first. If you two agree, I would prefer a small wedding with just the family; you must remember that Casper's family are all in the cemetery and he is alone in the world. Besides, while he is friendly and nice to everyone, he considers large gatherings a waste of time."

Karl wiped his hands again. "I see, well it might be best if we all go to the house and sit down to talk about what to do about this wedding. Your brother will be coming in with a load of hay bales before noon and we should include him and his wife in the discussions." Karl peeled off his coveralls and led the way to the house.

By the time they got to the house, Jessica had her mind made up. It would be a small wedding with just her immediate family and Casper. In her mind, she compromised and decided her grandmother would have to be invited also. Her mom and dad would argue in favor of inviting their brothers, sisters, uncles and aunts but if they were invited it would no longer be a small wedding. Jessica started gathering her arguments to support a small wedding, knowing full well that in the end, she would be standing alone, unless of course Casper were here to support her. Suddenly, she realized this matter had not been discussed with Casper. Which side would he come down on? Why did her life always have to be so complicated?

Jessica and her mom started making sandwiches while Karl phoned Teresa, his daughter-in-law, and asked her to bring her husband to have lunch with them. When the five people were all seated at the kitchen table, Jessica looked around at her mom and dad and her brother Trace and wife Teresa. Everyone was looking at her. This unusual event had obviously alerted all of them to something different and they were waiting on her. She cleared her throat and started. "Casper has asked me to marry him and I have agreed. There are questions about what kind of wedding we should have and this little gathering is to discuss the alternatives."

Trace leaped out of his chair yelling, "Congratulations, sis! We have been waiting for your wedding for weeks." Trace came and hugged her while Teresa stood in line to get her turn. "Why isn't your Casper here to celebrate with us?"

Jessica felt happy with her family's reaction but now the matter of the wedding had to be discussed. She watched Trace pacing around the table obviously happy. "We have a list of all the relatives at our house so the invitations will be easy to do. Oh, what is the date for the wedding? We will have to reserve the church and the hall and you women will have to go shopping for a dress. What about at Thanksgiving for the wedding?"

Karl held up his hand. "Might be a good idea for you to sit down son, your sandwich will be getting cold. You have supported your mother and my feelings about the wedding; except your sister has expressed a different approach."

Trace looked puzzled. As he sat down, he asked, "What different approach is there?"

"Trace, I am marrying a man who has no family except for a row of graves in the cemetery, three generations. What you are proposing is we fill the church with our relatives and Casper will be sitting all by himself. I have suggested a small wedding with just our immediate family in attendance."

Elizabeth spoke up, "Son, there is much we do not understand about Casper, not one of us has even met him. Jessica has told all of us that he is highly intelligent, probably a genius, and often does not understand the routine things which we consider normal. Why, this morning he phoned and asked Jessica to marry him and when she accepted, he wanted her to drive to Davenport today so they could be married tomorrow."

There was shocked silence for a moment until Trace laughed. "Why the hurry, sis, are you pregnant?"

Jessica smiled, this question she could handle. "No, Trace, I am not." She held up her left hand. "There are no wedding rings on this hand and until there are, there will be no bedding. You all must understand that Casper is a creator, a doer, and never wants to wait. In his mind, we agreed to become married and his approach is to do it now. Which reminds me, I am arguing for a small wedding and I have not discussed the wedding with Casper. I assumed he would support me. I shall call right now and get his advice." She walked to the phone and dialed Casper's number. Mrs. Sparks answered. "Mrs. Sparks, it is Jessica calling."

"I am so happy you phoned. First, may I offer my congratulations on your engagement? How lovely!"

"Thank you, Mrs. Sparks, I am very happy that Casper finally screwed up his courage and stopped just looking at me. Is he available?"

"Just hang on for a moment, he has been flustered all day, so don't be too hard on him." The phone buzzed and immediately Casper answered.

"Jessica, where are you?"

"I am having lunch with my parents and my brother and his wife. We have been discussing the wedding and I find myself a one-person army fighting with the family. I am arguing for a small wedding with just my immediate family while they want all the extended family to be invited. Can you imagine a church with seventy or eighty of my relatives carrying on while all you and I want is to become married?"

Her statement had suddenly focused Casper on the problem which was what he spent his days doing. "So, when would this Jessica Hornsbee family hold the wedding?"

"We haven't discussed a date, but my brother did suggest Thanksgiving."

"Thanksgiving is too far away, Jessica. May I suggest that you go along with what the family wants and invite all your relatives but get a closer date, say the middle of October? Would that be satisfactory, make your family happy, and get me a wife?"

"I do believe your suggestion will work and may I tell you, Mr. Blakerly, you are the most underhanded man I have ever known."

"Thank you, Jessica, and may I ask when you will be coming home?"

"Probably the day after tomorrow, then I have to start attending classes."

"Please come to see me when you get here."

"You can count on that, Mr. Blakerly. I will phone you this evening at the farm. Goodbye."

Jessica came back to the table, sat down, and bit into her sandwich. As she chewed, her mind was reviewing the conversation with Casper. All her family had heard her talking but hadn't any idea what Casper had told her. Finally, Karl asked, "What did your future husband have to say about the wedding?"

Her head came up and she smiled around the bite of sandwich she was chewing. She swallowed and answered, "He will be a wonderful husband who believes his future wife is brilliant and he is very supportive of my ideas."

"Please explain."

"Certainly, Father, Casper wants the wedding to be in mid-October. No argument, he was adamant. Beyond that, he asked me to turn the Hornsbee's loose with the freedom to invite all their relatives to the wedding to eat, drink, and be merry and he will pay for the reception."

"Wonderful, Jess. Your man must be every bit as smart as you claim. You and I will go to talk to the minister this afternoon and get the date nailed down. Teresa, please locate the mailing list of guests from your wedding. Oh my, we will need invitations printed, a wedding dress, and a caterer for the reception. All of us must get into gear if we are going to have a wedding in five or six weeks and it seems to me sending out the invitations must have a high priority so our relatives have time to make arrangements."

When they sat down for dinner in the evening, the wedding was the main subject of discussion. The wedding would be on Saturday, October fourteenth and Jessica had called Casper and got approval for that day. Teresa arrived with the list of invitees from her wedding and the ladies went through it and put a red checkmark on each name which should be sent an invitation. Jessica would add any names Casper would like included. Based on Teresa's invitation, they prepared a copy for the printer which they would take tomorrow. Also tomorrow, Jessica and her mom would look at and purchase a dress. Karl had phoned the church ladies, who agreed to cater the reception and they were working on a menu for Karl to approve. Trace had the responsibility of purchasing wine and liquor. Each time another task came to their attention, it was assigned to one of them to run with.

Before going to bed, Jessica phoned Casper and read the wedding invitation to him and got approval and explained all the tasks being done to prepare for the wedding. Casper's only comment was that they had to buy rings.

* * *

Hornsbee Dairy Farm was located two miles north of Newton, Iowa. There were fifteen miles into Des Moines and about one hundred and fifty miles to Davenport. It would take her two and a half hours to drive to Davenport and she wanted to get there early in the day, so Jessica left after a hurried breakfast. She was gone along the road when Karl was still eating his bowl of porridge and at nine-thirty pulled to a stop at the security gate for Davenport Machinery Inc. She turned off the engine and opened her door. Three security people came in a hurry and smiled at her. The senior man commented, "Good morning, Miss Hornsbee, there is no need for you to stop at the gate. Your usual parking place is waiting for you. May I be the first to offer the congratulations of the Safety Group on your oncoming marriage?"

Jessica was astonished and it showed. "Thank you and all the people in the Safety Group for your gracious greeting." She closed the car door and the guards waved her to the usual parking space. She retrieved her briefcase from the backseat and walked to the plant door. It opened and a security guard was grinning at her as he waved her in. She waved at a group of workmen as she crossed to the elevator. When the elevator doors opened, there stood Mrs. Sparks smiling broadly. "Please follow me, Madam, and I will take you to the supreme leader."

When they reached the door to Casper's office, Mrs. Sparks knocked and announced. "Miss Jessica Marie Hornsbee is here to meet with Mr. Casper Edward Blakerly."

Jessica was laughing gaily as Casper stood up and hurried toward her. He grabbed her in a bear hug and held her tight, whispering, "It has been a week since I last saw you." When he loosened his grip, he asked, "Can I have permission to kiss you?" Jessica didn't hesitate; she grabbed his head between two hands and kissed him.

Mrs. Sparks laughed and clapped her hands as they both turned to look at her. "Well done, very well done."

Chapter 17

The days flew past, especially for Jessica, as time raced to the wedding day. Casper helped where he could, still planning a wedding was a specialty of ladies, so most days he worked on the farm or the business of Davenport Machinery. Jessica was going to classes four days each week and reading, writing, and studying her course materials. Casper offered her the chance to come and live at the farm but she refused, holding up her left hand with only one ring on the third finger. He knew she was sending a message. One thing that changed was the kissing and often they sat together all entwined in arms and legs and smooched and no one's hands strayed.

Thursday, Jessica drove to Newton and now on Friday morning, Casper was packing his car to make the trip. He had reserved the best hotel suite in Newton and they planned to stay there until Sunday or even Monday. He had given Jessica the names of Lockley Simpson, his wife Shannon, and two children Quinton and Isabella, and Mr. and Mrs. Sparks to be sent invitations. He had asked Lockley to stand up with him as best man and after Jessica was wearing her engagement ring, they went to the Simpson farm for dinner. The ladies got along great and Casper spent time teasing the children. Now, he had prepared and was ready to go and climbed into the pickup. The truck stayed under the speed limit and Casper figured he would arrive in Newton before noon.

He lugged his suitcases into the lobby and registered. The suite was already paid for until noon on Monday. After unpacking and hanging up his clothes, he phoned the farm. He smiled when Jessica answered and told him how to drive to the Hornsbee Dairy Farm. He had neatly dressed in casual clothes and checked his appearance before starting the drive, which only took a few minutes. The Hornsbee's were in the yard waiting with Jessica out in front. She hurried to the truck and kissed him while all the Hornsbee's lined up behind her to greet Caspar. Jessica handled the introductions which took considerable time. "Casper, this is my mother, Elizabeth." They shook hands and Casper hugged her. She told him, "It is so nice to finally meet you; welcome to our farm."

Next in line came Karl. "This man is my father, Karl Hornsbee." The men shook hands and Karl noticed Casper's grip was firm.

"This beautiful woman is my grandmother…" and so it went until the last Hornsbee had been greeted.

Elizabeth Hornsbee called out, "Lunch is ready, everyone. Come to the kitchen and fill a plate. We don't have enough chairs so leave them for the ladies; you men are on your own."

Casper sat with Karl, Trace, and two uncles to eat and found the wooden benches to be comfortable. Karl suggested, "After we finish eating, would you like to take a tour around the farm Casper?"

"Yes, I would, thank you." The men chatted and joked while they ate and finally Jessica came with mugs and Elizabeth poured coffee. Casper enjoyed the farm tour. The milking parlor was clean, well lit, and had the latest equipment to speed the milking of two hundred and eighty cows. The barns and hay storage had been recently remodeled. The steel grain storage had been on the farm for several years and was well looked after. They sat in the workshop and talked farming until Trace announced, "Time to milk, Dad. The hired men will be getting everything ready." The two men left and the others walked back to the house. Casper ended up talking to a group of ladies and he only remembered two of the names. They teased him and told Jessica she would have a tough job making Casper into a good husband.

There were holiday trailers parked in small spaces all around the farmyard and when Casper commented, one lady laughed and said, "Wait until you see what arrives during this evening and Saturday morning."

During the drive to the wedding rehearsal, he asked Jessica about the answer and she smiled. "The Hornsbee's who are here, life nearby. Tonight and tomorrow, the rest of the Hornsbee's will show up."

The rehearsal went well and afterward everyone gathered at the farm to eat, drink, exchange family news, and look over Casper. He left at eleven to go to the hotel after Jessica followed him to his truck and kissed him goodnight.

Jessica's mother had warned Casper to stay away from the farm until the wedding was over so the next morning, Casper sat in the hotel lobby reading a book and waiting for the Simpsons and Sparks to arrive. They were all early risers and by nine-thirty, everyone was there. Casper explained, "The wedding is at two o'clock so I have a reservation in the dining room for all of us at eleven-thirty, then there will be time to get dressed. I was told to be in the church by one-forty-five."

When Casper walked into the church with his group, the place was swarming with Hornsbee family members. Karl stepped into the aisle and greeted Casper and his guests before asking, "Where are the rest of your family?"

Casper smiled. "We are all here and we will all sit in the front pew."

Karl was surprised and it showed. "You sure no one else is coming?"

"If they are, they don't have an invitation. I did notice there are Hornsbee family members all over the church. If you don't have sufficient seating, please send some of them over to the Blakerly side of the aisle."

"Thank you, Casper, you beat me to the matter and my family will be very happy. If you will excuse me, I shall spread the word." Casper and his group watched as Karl made the announcement in a loud voice. The only change he made was to suggest they leave one empty pew behind Casper. One of Jessica's uncles was the first to bring his family and sit in the third pew. When they were seated, he came and shook Casper's hand and thanked him. Casper whispered in the uncle's ear, 'bring all the Hornsbee's you wish.' The uncle did even better; he walked to the back of the church and told the ushers that all the empty pews were available.

At two p.m., the organist began playing, the door opened, and Elizabeth Hornsbee walked down the aisle, left a space for Karl and sat down. To match Casper, there was only one bridesmaid and it was Jessica's sister, Elizabeth, named after her mother.

When Jessica came through the door on her father's arm, there were gasps of pleasure at the sight of the pure white dress. Someone clapped and quickly the whole church erupted. Jessica was totally 'unphased' by the clapping and lifted her hand in greetings. She was a tall girl, only two inches shorter than Casper, and walked to the front of the church and stood proudly beside him. The minister heard her whisper to Casper, "Did I ever tell you I love you?" The minister cleared his throat, stopping Casper from replying. There were two photographers taking pictures and they were both members of the congregation.

When the service ended, the minister stepped forward and announced, "I have been instructed by the new Mrs. Blakerly to tell you the reception and dinner will begin at four p.m. in the church hall. Just take the steps down from the front lobby. Also, the photographers are reminded they have one hour to take pictures and then the new couple will walk away from them. Now, folks, and as far as I can tell you are all Hornsbee's, please stand and greet

Casper and Jessica Blakerly."

There were only six people in the wedding party and they were all well-mannered and congenial so picture taking went quickly. They arrived in the church hall at three-forty with the photographers following along. The hall was full of Hornsbee's and Jessica worked a path through them with Casper following. Promptly at four p.m., the food started arriving and the happy chatter and laughing gradually died away. Many of the guests had long drives ahead of them and Jessica wanted them to be on their way early. The ones from nearby would stay around till Sunday or even Monday. Not unusually, the church ladies served a roast beef dinner. Dessert was apple pie with ice cream and when everyone had their dessert in front of them, Karl stood up.

At the mike, he told the crowd that he was acting as emcee for the program which he promised would be short. "First, I wish to congratulate my daughter and her new husband." The crowd reacted with cheers. "I must admit that for several months I had deep doubts about this Casper fella. Our daughter was very open about her love for him but he wasn't responding to her and we never got to meet him until yesterday morning. Now, I am here to tell you he is a fine fella and the only thing that would make him better is if his last name was Hornsbee." The room echoed with the cheers and laughter. "Our main speaker today will be my new son-in-law, Casper Edward Blakerly."

Casper kissed his wife's cheek before standing and looking around. "Do you Hornsbee's have any idea how scary all of you are?" There was a roar of laughter that Casper joined. "Please believe I am the only Blakerly alive. I came to Newton to marry Jessica with no warning of how many Hornsbee's there are. All she mentioned was her parents and occasionally talked of growing up on a dairy farm. Let me start by thanking Elizabeth and Karl for letting me marry their daughter, to thank Elizabeth and all who helped her put on this wedding, and my new sister, Elizabeth Hornsbee. Sitting here beside me is Lockley Simpson, who was my best man today and has been my friend since we met on the school bus to grade one. At the table is his wife Shannon, son Quinton, and daughter Isabella. Also at the table are Mickle Sparks and his wife Susann. Mrs. Sparks has worked with me for it must be eleven years now and she keeps me on track and completes everything I request of her. I do tend to get deeply involved in projects I am working on and Mrs. Sparks sees to my schedule, papers to be signed, and generally growls at me when it is necessary. I owe you my thanks Mrs. Sparks for being so diligent."

"Now, what do I say about my wife? Do you Hornsbee's know that she graduated last spring from Ambrose University with a mechanical engineering degree and is a good one? Now, she is back at the university working toward her MBA. When she started working at Davenport Machinery, I soon discovered she was not only a good worker, but she also knew what she was doing, and when I disagreed with her, she fought back. We had a few great arguments, her eyes would glare at me, and never once did she back off on her conclusions. Sometimes, I did it just to see how she would react." Jessica led the laughing.

"Gradually, it dawned on me that I more than liked her but to be honest, I had no idea how to proceed. She scared me. I wanted to marry her but was afraid to ask her, what if she said no? Since arriving in Newton, I have decided she is a typical Hornsbee, smart, hardworking, has the determination of a Missouri mule, and likes to laugh. Mrs. Sparks tried in her subtle way to guide me and slowly my courage grew. But, at the end of August, I was away from the office for two days and forgot Jessica was going back to university. She left without saying goodbye and it was devastating. Mrs. Sparks and I finally tracked her down here visiting her parents and I phoned and asked her to marry me." Casper laughed and held up his arms. "She said yes." The hall erupted in laughter. Casper sat down and Jessica leaned over and congratulated him.

Karl took the microphone and announced, "Our final speaker is Jessica or I should say the new Mrs. Blakerly."

She stood up and smiled at the room. "Thank you for being here today, Hornsbee's. There can't be another family in Iowa as large as ours is. My new husband is also a mechanical engineer from Ambrose and the first time I met him was when he came to the university to speak to the graduating engineers last winter. When I told him I was looking for a summer job, he didn't react at all but later in the day, he handed me a business card for Mrs. Sparks and told me if I wanted a summer job to contact her. I got the job. Casper is not a normal individual. At first, I thought he was kooky but Mrs. Sparks straightened me out. He is highly intelligent and was an honor student all through school before graduating as an engineer when he was nineteen. He has an uncanny ability to focus. To wipe out and forget everything except what he is working on and Mrs. Sparks has developed her ways of interrupting him when she needs him to sign checks, or meet a visitor, etc."

"Besides running a large machinery manufacturing business, Casper also owns the farm his parents raised him on. In August, he agreed to let me drive a combine and stood around all afternoon while I raced up and down the field straight cutting soybeans. I may have neglected to tell him I have many times driven combine for my dad. Casper and I will be living in the house his grandfather built while I finish my MBA and then we will tackle the world as a team of mechanical engineers. You will have noticed that we kept the wedding small and simple because I surely didn't want to over-load him with more than all the Hornsbee's. It seemed to me that I was gaining the upper hand by trusting all my relatives to talk to him about a multitude of endeavors and so far he has been able to keep his sanity. Once again, our thanks to all of you for coming and making this day one to remember."

Chapter 18

Lockley agreed to drive Casper's truck back to the farm and left with his family late in the afternoon. Mickle and Susann Sparks stayed over till Sunday before driving back to Davenport. The last thing she asked Casper was, "When can I expect to see you at the office?"

"Mrs. Sparks, I will be there on Tuesday morning." She smiled and rolled up her car window.

Early in the evening, the Blakerly's disappeared and no one saw them till Sunday afternoon. Hornsbee's were packing up and leaving and they walked around talking to any who had the time and waving at the vehicles driving away. After a couple of hours, Jessica went and packed her belongings, leaving her wedding gown hanging in the closet of her well-used bedroom. She smiled wryly, thinking about moving into her new home. Casper carried her luggage to the car and filled the trunk, well almost, he reminded himself, there were their items at the hotel. Mother Hornsbee watched the preparations with wet eyes. Finally, she asked, "When will you be coming to see us?"

"I have a busy schedule at the university but we will be back, maybe at Thanksgiving. I will phone you regularly." They hugged each other. "You tell Dad goodbye for me."

"Yes, honey, I will." She watched the car drive out of the yard and turn south before going into the house.

They parked the car and hurried to the elevator. Casper locked the door behind them and clothes started dropping along the floor on the way to the bedroom. Casper put a nipple in his mouth and his hands started exploring. Jessica took it as long as she could before scrambling on top of him while thinking, *'If this is what married life is like, we will never get any work done. Hell, who cares, this is glorious.'*

At ten-thirty on Monday, they checked out and drove the car to the Blakerly farm. Casper lugged all the suitcases into the house, locked the door, and pulled her into the nearest bedroom.

*   *   *

Mrs. Sparks was waiting. "Good morning, Mr. Blakerly, it is very nice to see you back in the office. There are checks to be signed sitting on your desk. Ralph was here earlier wanting to talk to you. You will find a list of other people who have called."

Casper smiled at her and walked past into his office. First, he would sign the checks. Next, he would go and find out what Ralph needed. He was almost to the bottom of the stack of checks when Ralph arrived. "Just give me a minute to finish up these checks."

"Boss, we have the wood splitter and both the new sizes of post pounders on the production line and it will take a while to fill all the orders that have come in. You know that Davenport catalogue you sent out is having a big effect on our business. Now Hiram is nagging me to start building test parts for the tractor he has designed. What I am here for is to find out what you want me to work on first."

"It will take me an hour or two to catch up on the projects. What have you been working on the last couple of weeks?"

"We have just finished testing a few little modifications to the manure wagons which will greatly improve their performance. Sure wish that darn Jessica had stayed with us. She was very good at making production drawings. Guess I will have to get the supply department to do drawings for us." Casper smiled at Ralph's lack of knowledge.

241

"You do that, Ralph, and as soon as I clear up some of these things piled on my desk I will come around to see the changes you have made." Ralph walked away and Casper smiled to himself. His marriage to Jessica hadn't been publicized because he didn't want the employees feeling obliged in any way. Now, it would get out simply because her company files would have to be updated. She had agreed to him putting her on temporary leave at half salary. "Mrs. Sparks, can you come here for a moment?" She came with her notebook and sat across the desk from him. "Mrs. Sparks, I have told Jessica that I was going to put her on temporary leave at half salary until next spring. Please talk to personnel and have them update their files as of September first. Doing this is going to cause all the employees to learn about our marriage. I do hope they will just accept it and not make a big fuss."

Mrs. Sparks smiled. "You should wish anything you want, Casper, but on this you may well be wrong. It wouldn't surprise me, if we ran an employee poll, to find Jessica is more popular than you are."

Casper leaned back. "I have never tried to be popular, and it would please me if they like her much more than me. I have finished signing all the checks for you."

"Thank you, Casper." She stood up and gathered the stack of checks into her arms. "If I were you, I would sit very loosely in that chair to avoid any sudden surprises." Casper watched her walk away, wondering.

He fidgeted around for a few minutes before picking up his hardhat, planting it firmly on his head, and walking to the stairs. He needed to get out in the plant, talk to the production people, watch them work, and get back into the swing of things. He spent an hour watching the three new machines being built and decided they would be very useful to the people who needed them. He didn't manage to locate Ralph so he went to Plant No. II. Hiram was at his desk so Casper stepped in and said hello. Hiram grinned, "Good to see you, Casper. When you have a few minutes, we want to show you the plan we have roughed out for the fifty-horse tractor."

"Would eight tomorrow morning be a suitable time for all of you?"

"Very good, Casper, there are a couple of people who will come with me."

"Would it be easier if I came here?"

"Thank you, Casper, doing that would make the whole operation easier. Everything we need is right here and easy to get at. See you in the morning."

Casper wandered down the center of the plant where machine tools were being installed and came back through the north attachment where storage, parts, raw materials, and offices were located. He made a mental note to check with personnel on how recruitment was going. Also, he had to sit down with Ned Ambrose and work out how the two plants would be operated and who might be ready to be production manager. At the very least, they needed a manager for Plant No. II. He decided to go and talk to Ned first.

Ned seemed to be tied to his office most of the time doing paperwork. That is where Casper found him. "Well, Ned, it seems your paper piles are as large as mine."

"You are correct, Casper, and mine are growing since the new machines have begun construction. Don't want to hold you up but have you given any thought as to how we are going to run two plants? Have been thinking about it. Plant No. II has to have many of the services we have here to keep ahead on raw materials, parts, storage, etc. Then, there is what you mentioned. We have to be able to coordinate production, acquiring parts, etc. For example, bolts are used all the time so there should be one buyer who purchases all the bolts and other things so we have control of supplies."

"Should we have purchasing put people out in each plant?"

"Might be the best way and I have been intending to go and talk with Mike Osborn but haven't found the time yet."

"Be okay with you if I go by and talk to him?"

"Great idea, Casper. Could be he will want to handle the planning on this and if he does it would suit me to a tee." Casper grinned, held up a hand and walked away. He headed straight to the purchasing department and walked into Mike Osborn's office.

"Hi, Mike, I am here to talk to you about how we are going to control the purchasing in the two plants. Have you given any thought to it yet?"

"We have been working on it for several weeks. There are basically two kinds of supplies. First, there are the common items which both plants will need such as paint, bolts, nuts, washers, welding rods, gloves, helmets, hydraulic fluid, and on and on. The second section is specialized items. For instance, Plant No. II is going to be building tractors and I understand the first one will be fifty horses. Well, when we receive engines they need to go the Plant No. II. The engines can be stored and be where they are needed along the production line. This company has always kept paper records and it is now apparent we must go to a computer system which everyone can look at. I hired a computer system consultant to work with my people to rough out a plan of what we need to keep track of supplies, where each item is stored, and to alert us to place orders for replacements. Another week or so and the rough plan should be ready for us to review."

"Well done, Mike. Keep the pressure on so we can get a good operating system up and running as soon as possible." Casper walked away and Mike watched him go, smiling at how down to earth and practical his boss was.

Casper came out of purchasing and Mrs. Sparks was walking toward him. "Casper, I have been looking for you. Please come with me to talk to Shelbie about what you are doing with Jessica." Casper shrugged and walked beside her. When they entered the personnel department, he smiled as he read the sign on the manager's office window which read, 'Mrs. Shelbie Cox, Manager of Personnel.' As they entered, Mrs. Sparks greeted the manager. "Good morning, Shelbie. Casper agreed to come with me to inform you of an employee's change of records."

"Thank you for coming, which employee is your concern with?"

"Jessica Hornsbee, who chose to leave Davenport at the end of August to return to university." Mrs. Sparks smiled as she watched for the answer.

"Ah yes, Jessica, we have just finished closing down the file on her. What is it you wish to talk about?"

"Casper asked me to have you put her on temporary leave and reduce her salary by fifty percent beginning September first."

Mrs. Cox's eyes grew large and she looked back and forth between them. "Most unusual, I must say. Jessica Hornsbee was a temporary hire for the summer and left as scheduled. What possible reason can there be to continue paying her? If my memory is correct, she was going back to university to further her education."

"That's true, Shelbie, but last Saturday, Jessica was married. In fact, she married Mr. Blakerly and is now living at his farm from where she is driving to university. They discuss Davenport projects every day and Jessica will continue to use her office whenever her time permits."

Cox's eyes flared again and the silence went on for a minute. "Jessica married Mr. Blakerly? Are you talking about our Casper?"

"Yes, I am, Shelbie." Casper held up his left hand and the gold ring was shining brightly. Shelbie stared.

"Oh my, most unusual! Yes, the file, please excuse me for a moment." She stood and walked out the door and they could hear her talking. "Mrs. Young, please fetch me the personnel file for Jessica Hornsbee. Jessica and our Casper have gotten married."

Mrs. Young replied, "Our Casper is married? When was the wedding, why didn't we get an invitation? Oh, Shelbie where did they get married? Ladies, did you hear? Shelbie says our Casper is married now."

"Mrs. Young, I need the file, please produce it for me and then you can celebrate with the other employees."

"I am sorry, Mrs. Cox, just give me a moment." A moment was all it took and Mrs. Cox came back to her office.

She sat at her desk and opened the file which she scanned. She picked up a pen and asked, "Now, Mrs. Sparks, this file must be changed to a temporary leave of absence beginning on September first and the salary will be reduced by fifty percent. Is that correct and do you know the date Mrs. Blakerly will return full time?"

"I don't know the date she will return, it will be sometime next spring. I suggest you put a note in the file and leave it open for now."

"We will do as you say, Mrs. Sparks. We will prepare the notes to the file and bring them to you for signing." Her eyes switched to look at Casper. "May I be so bold as to congratulate you Casper and wish you many happy years together?"

Casper smiled and spoke for the first time. "Thank you, Shelbie, we are very much in love and I will tell Jessica what you have said."

Casper stood up to leave with Mrs. Sparks' right behind him. When he opened the office door, the reception area was full of people. Almost all were ladies from young high school grads to older women. Casper could see they were happy, excited, and maybe a little scared of what the big boss would do. "My goodness, ladies, have all of you completed your duties for the day?"

There were laughs and titters and Casper grinned. Almost in a practiced chorus way, he heard voices yelling congratulations in various forms. "Now, ladies, there are too many of you for me to kiss all of you and besides doing that might make my Jessica jealous. Thank you for the best wishes. I have been a bit slow in finding a wife but when I began to understand Jessica, I knew she was the lady for me. I didn't really understand until she left to go back to university and suddenly my life was in turmoil. Mrs. Sparks is to blame, she talked and pushed me until I dialed her number and proposed over the phone. I give you permission to hold Mrs. Sparks at fault." The ladies got a good laugh.

They made it back to their offices, both knowing that within minutes all the employees would hear the news. Casper sat at his desk and realized he wasn't going to get much work done that day. After a few minutes, he packed his briefcase, told Mrs. Sparks he was going to a meeting and left for the farm. At least on the farm, there wouldn't be constant interruptions and it would be peaceful. Fred was in the yard when he arrived.

"What are you working on today, Fred?"

"I was figuring on going out to check on the cows and calves. Want to come with me?"

"Hang on while I change clothes, be right back." Fred was driving a one-year-old F150 and it was nice to ride in. Casper climbed in and suggested, "Let's go over west on the river and look around." Fred drove along the road at the usual slow pace most farmers used as they scanned the countryside and commented on what they saw. Casper opened the gate so Fred could drive through the fence, closed the gate, and they walked over to the north bank of the Wapsipinicon River. Standing in the shade of a large aspen tree, the slight breeze felt cool as they studied the area. The water level in the river was at its low stage and the exposed mud was full of cattle tracks. "Sure would be good for the farm if we got an inch or two."

"Guess so, Casper, if it doesn't rain soon, we will be getting snow. Rather get rain."

There were a few head of cattle within eyesight. "How many animals are in this field?"

"We took the bulls home a couple of weeks ago so now there are two hundred and twelve cows and eighty-one heifer critters in here. In total, two hundred and ninety-three animals are left here to graze. The breeding bulls are back in the pasture and the seventy-three steers are out in the small pasture." Fred removed his cap and rubbed the top of his head.

Casper laughed at him. "Hair is getting a bit thin up there on top."

"Expect you are right, Casper, the years pile up on a man." He put the cap back on. "We got to decide on these cows. We can leave them here for the winter and haul hay bales to them. Or else, we can take them home where we put up bales to feed them."

"Which way are you leaning, Fred?"

"It will be more work but I am inclined to leave them here. Could be a shortage of water before spring but unlikely the river will freeze over. Seems to me it would be a good thing to leave the home pastures this winter with no cows cropping the grass. Give the plants a chance to grow stronger for the future. Figured if we get a real tough winter this time, we can always move the cattle home when the time comes."

Casper leaned against an aspen tree and considered. Fred was a canny old man who had spent his life with cattle and he was doing a good job of running the farm. In fact, thinking about it, he rarely had to make a decision and usually, it was because the amount of money was large. By nature, Fred wasn't a spender. Casper's usual participation came on the decisions to trade machinery. He smiled quietly. Now with a wife who came from a farm, there would probably be many discussions about what to do between the two of them. "Fred, I like your idea of leaving the cows here for the winter."

"Figure it will most likely result in better pastures. Any chance we might be able to buy this section? I figure if we owned it, we could drill a couple of water wells to ease the shortage. If we were to put up hay storage, then the winters would be easy. If you take a look, there is a power line along the north side of this section."

The silence lasted for some time as both men considered. Finally, Casper asked, "You heard anything?"

"Couple of weeks back, the Misses and I ran into the owner's wife up at DeWitt while buying groceries. In the conversation, she mentioned that her husband wasn't feeling so well anymore and might just sell his land. Might be there is more land than this section."

"Fred, why don't you drop in to see how the owner is getting along and have a chat about farming? Which reminds me, on November first, the land rental is due. When we get back, I will write a check and you can take it to him. If he is reasonable in setting his prices, we may be able to put together a deal with him."

They drove over to the small bull pasture and parked along the fence. The bulls had water and grass and were well fed. Fred commented that two bulls were getting old and should be replaced in a year or two.

Next stop was outside the steer pasture. "There are sixty-nine yearling steers out there that are ready for market whenever you say."

"Have you talked to any of the buyers?"

"Two buyers have phoned. One advised me we should hold off a while. The selling price has been edging up this past week but seems to me if we are hit by a big snowstorm it will push prices down."

"You are right; if it snows many of our neighbors will put their steers on the market and weaken prices. Let's gamble a little and wait another week. You keep a check on the prices." Fred nodded.

After another few minutes sitting there, Fred suggested, "Reckon I will drop you off in the yard and head on home. You never know, maybe the old girl will feed me."

* * *

Casper walked into Hiram's office at eight o'clock. Hiram gathered up his gear and files and they walked to a large table set up in an entrance area. There were three employees waiting for them. Hiram picked up a drawing and held it out. "We have to build and test the system first but this is a sketch I made of what it could look like when we finally build a complete tractor. I borrowed these three men from Ned for a few day and they have been drawing and making suggestions. In fact, many of their suggestions are downright amazing and if we use them, our tractors will be market leaders."

"I know these three well. They have been working for Davenport a long time." Casper smiled at the men, "How is Hiram for a boss?"

The comedian of the group spoke up, "He is pretty good although he may have spent too many years sitting in a fancy office somewhere." Everyone laughed and Casper noticed Hiram laughed as loud as any of the men. *'A very good sign, Hiram can take a joke, the men will like him and he will fit in'.*

Noon hour was fast approaching when they finished looking at the sketches. Everyone took part and seven changes were suggested, two from Casper and five from the crew. "Hiram, we need production drawings with dimensions so the men can start building parts for testing."

"I have started on drawings but to speed up the process, two more people would sure be a help."

"Let me ask around. Ralph Shaw might be available. He has worked with me several times to make the early drawings on projects. Jessica isn't with us anymore; guess I will go to the purchasing department and ask if they have anyone they can loan us." He looked around and everyone was smiling. "What the hell are all of you guys laughing about?"

The comedian answered, "There is a rumor going around the plant that some down and out no good farmer ran off with Jessica and married her. You know anything about that?"

Casper smiled. "Sounds like something she would do. Okay, it is true; Jessica and I were married on Saturday at her family farm. I came from a family where I was the only kid and she married me without disclosing the Hornsbee's are existing in the hundreds."

Hiram stuck out his hand and they shook before Casper shook with each of the men. "Thank you, fellas."

* * *

Casper went to his office and dug into the piles of paper. It was six o'clock when he had cleared his desk and moved the piles onto Mrs. Sparks' desk. It was six-fifteen when he climbed into his truck to drive home. He didn't want to be late, hell they had only been married for four days.

He pulled in to the garage and parked beside Jessica's car. When he walked into the house, there she was pounding away on her laptop, working on a paper for university. He watched her for a minute before she looked up. "Hi, honey, how has your day been?"

Her face broke into a shining smile. "Glad you are home, what do you want for dinner?"

Casper grinned. "You are working on your homework so I will cook." He came and kissed her before going to the bathroom and washing his hands. She focused on her report and could hear her husband humming as he worked at the counter. By the time he was moving to the cook stove, she had blanked him out. First, he fried sliced potatoes, then strips of bacon, and finally scrambled eggs. While the bread was being toasted, he brought plates and silverware to the table. Next, he came with the butter dish and a bowl of salsa and told her to put the computer aside. "Bring your plate over to the stove and help yourself." She did and as usual, didn't take her full share. Casper filled his plate and sat across the table from Jessica. He handed her a slice of toast before buttering his own. They talked and ate at the same time. Jessica had to admit the food was good. Typical farm fare as per her husband, who it turned out was a fair to middling cook. Well, he had been living alone for several years and hadn't starved to death and he was no fool so had learned. *'Four days we have been married and he didn't throw me on the floor to make love. Guess the marriage is getting old and has cooled off.'*

She grinned and thought, *'Just wait until the eating is over and the kitchen cleaned up, his hands will be searching and patting and probing and he will have me screaming with delight. It is amazing what he has learned since our first time on Saturday evening when neither of us knew what to do and we fumbled around. It is amazing what we both have learned.'*

Chapter 19

First thing in the morning Casper went to talk with Ned. "Ned, when I walked through the plant yesterday I noticed it is very crowded down at the end where the large machines are being built. Why can't we move the construction of the two large new fencepost pounders over to the Plant No II?"

Ned frowned and rubbed his chin as he thought. "Don't see any reason why we shouldn't and for sure it will open up space in this plant. Let's walk down there and look around, maybe talk to the men and get their input." It had been a long time since the men had seen Ned and Casper walking around in the plant and it alerted them that something new was in the air. When they arrived at the construction area, Ned walked around looking at the activity. Finally, he called the men working on building the two large sizes of pounders to talk. "Casper and I are concerned about how crowded your working area is since these large pounders have started being built. To solve the problem, we are considering moving your operation over to Plant No. II. Do you fellas see any reason why that won't work?"

The foreman spoke right up. "Hell no, a few days back we talked about moving and figured it was a good idea. When do you want us to move?"

Ned smiled. "Thank you for agreeing. You have two machines on the go here so finish them. In the meantime, I will have the crews over at Plant No. II clear out a space for you and arrange for the parts to be shipped over there. How much time do I have?"

The foreman glanced at the state the two machines were in. "Two more days and these machines will be done. We will need to move our tools and other gear over which will mess up a day. I figure you have three days."

"Okay, Hank. I will get on it right away. Thanks, fellas, for your help." Ned and Casper decided to go to Plant No. II and make the arrangements for the construction space. Two hours later, Ned was in full swing and Casper excused himself, happy with the progress being made.

Next, Casper went looking for Ralph and found him sitting at his table. Ralph saw him coming and stood up. "Good morning, Ralph, need your help with the tractor project. Hiram is busy drafting production drawings for a fifty-horse tractor and says he needs two people to speed it along."

"Thanks for telling me, Casper. I will head over there in a few minutes. If you are looking for another man to help out, go to purchasing and ask to borrow a fella by the name of Brian McCullum. He has worked with me several times before and is good."

"Thanks, Ralph, and ask Hiram if he has a drafting table for you to use. I expect McCullum can do his work in purchasing where his gear is located. Talk to you later, Ralph." Casper walked away in the direction of the purchasing department.

Casper stopped in the doorway of Mike Osborn's office and said hello. Mike's head came up and he smiled. Casper asked, "You have a fella named Brain McCullum whom I need to borrow."

"Come in, sit down, and tell me why."

Sitting in a visitor's chair, Casper related the project to Mike. "Very well, Boss, there is just one problem right now. Two days ago, Brain was coughing and sneezing so I sent him home rather than have the whole staff get sick. In my opinion, Brian had caught up with the flu bug. If you will wait, I can phone his house and ask when he will be back at work."

Casper nodded and Mike dialed the phone. It rang four times before there was an answer. "Hi, Brian, it is Mike calling from the plant. How are you feeling?" Mike listened carefully and finally smiled. "Real good, Brian, see you on Monday. Goodbye."

"You want me to send Brian over to talk to Hiram on Monday morning?"

"Good idea and I will explain to Hiram. You have yourself a good weekend."

Mike held up one hand. "There is a rumor around the plant that Casper went and got himself married, is that true?"

"Yes, it is, Mike, finally managed to talk Jessica Hornsbee into marrying me."

"Great news, Casper. Congratulations!" Mike hopped to his feet and stuck out his hand. They shook and Mike slapped Casper on the back. "Please tell Jessica how happy I am for her."

"Will do, Mike, and thanks." Casper walked out the door and headed for Hiram's office where he reviewed the arrangements he had made. It was into the afternoon by the time Casper arrived back at his office. Mrs. Sparks frowned as he walked past her.

She followed him into his office holding the form Mrs. Shelbie Cox had sent her. Casper read the note and handed it back. "You can sign this, Mrs. Sparks."

"Yes, I knew I could but wanted you to read what had been written and thought you might want to sign it."

Casper smiled at her. "This lady is just another employee and does not deserve special treatment."

Mrs. Sparks laughed loudly before replying, "I dare you to go home and tell Jessica she is just another Davenport employee and there is nothing special about her."

Casper joined the laughter. "A private joke between us, Mrs.

Sparks. To me, she is the most special woman in the world and she knows." Mrs. Sparks walked away still laughing to herself as she returned to her desk.

At the desk, she picked up a black ink pen, signed the form, turned, and walked away to the personnel department.

* * *

At mid-morning on Saturday, Fred drove into the yard and parked near the house. When he rang the doorbell, Jessica came to answer. Fred hurriedly doffed his cap. "Good morning, ma'am. Does that husband of yours happen to be around?"

"He certainly is, Fred. Please come in, you will find him in his office."

"Thank you, ma'am, I will just wander down the hall and say hello."

Casper looked up from the papers he was reading and smiled. "Good morning, Fred, come in and have a seat." They chatted about the need for rain, how the prices for steers were doing in the local markets, and then they started wondering once again about selling the steers. "Seems to me steer prices can't go much higher than they are now."

Fred nodded. "I expect you are right, yesterday the prices hit the high they set a month ago, and it is time to sell. You want me to phone a couple of buyers or take them to an auction market?"

"Try the buyers, Fred, and if they make an offer close to yesterday, take it. If they try playing games with us, get trucks and take them to the market."

Fred grinned. "I will try to sweet-talk the buyers a little, maybe one of them will have a weak moment. Went and had a visit with Ted about the section of grassland. He said to thank you for sending the rent check. Fact is, he is thin and looking rundown, won't surprise me if before long we will be saying goodbye. As I recall, he is about ten years older than me. We old farmers have a good life but over time the hard work takes a toll on us and looks to me like Ted is near the end. When I raised the question of his selling the section of grass, he thought about it for a few minutes and sort of nodded. He told me, Might be a good idea, Fred. My kids have all moved away and don't have any interest in the farm. They get hold of the land, they will just sell. That section of grassland isn't flat, kind of rough with all the high ground, but it does have water down there on the south end. Ma and I have two quarters here where we have lived the last fifty-five years and it is fairly good grain land. Do you think Casper would be interested to buying our six quarters?"

Fred smiled at Casper. "Told him I didn't know, you just asked me to deliver the rental check, but I could carry the message. Well, we talked about the land for a while before I asked, Ted, do you have a price range you can give me and maybe what your grain crops have been yielding?"

"Just as I figured, old Ted had been thinking and was ready, he opened a drawer and took out a sheet of paper with everything written down and told me to bring the paper to you." Fred reached into his jacket pocket and took out the folded sheet and handed it across the desk.

Casper unfolder the paper and started reading and right at the top the writing said, *six quarters of land for sale as a package.'* Listed first was the grassland at six hundred and thirty-eight acres with a description and a price that seemed a bit on the low side to Casper. He went on to read about the grain land which had three hundred and fifteen acres plus the farmyard and his eyes wavered a bit on the price listed. Now he understood the low price on the grass, it was a loss leader to get what Ted wanted on the grain land.

Casper took a calculator from the desk and started punching numbers. When he looked up, he told Fred, "It says here that his corn yielded a hundred and seventy bushels per acre and the soybeans thirty-seven per acre. What were our yields this year?"

Fred thought for a minute. "Our soy came it around forty-five bushels per acre and the corn about a hundred and ninety per acre."

"How do you compare his soil to ours?"

"Looking at it from the truck, I figure the land is about the same. He is up more on the flats so his black soil could be a bit deeper. This is only a visual from the road. Ted's grain land is just south of Highway 30, straight west of DeWitt."

"What kind of buildings come with the land?"

"Ted has a large two-story house like so many farmers built, much the same as yours, seemed to be well cared for and painted. Don't know if it is insulated or not. There is a barn all painted red with attached corrals. It was most likely built for the horse days but now is used for cattle. No grain storage unless there are some out in the fields. No up-to-date run of machinery sitting around so I guess he is getting the land custom farmed."

Casper rattled his pencil on the desk before asking, "Anything else you got to add?"

"No, sir, you got the whole story. If you aren't busy this afternoon, might be a good idea for us to drive up there and take the roads around his land. Never know what we will see."

"Great idea, Fred. How would it be if Jessica and I drive over to your place and pick you up after we eat our lunch?"

"I will be waiting, Casper, you come when you are ready." Fred left and Casper could hear him talking to Jessica on his way through the kitchen.

While eating lunch, Casper told Jessica about the possible land deal. As he expected, she was immediately interested and wanted to help him evaluate the land. He told her Fred's suggestion and she laughed. "I do believe Fred is a great guy." Together, they cleaned up the kitchen before backing the car out of the garage. Casper drove and when they arrived, Fred was sitting on the porch waiting. Jessica moved to the backseat so the two men could converse easily, but she was listening. Ted's two quarters of land were the east half of a section so there were roads on three sides. The entrance to the farm building site was from the south so they drove along that road first. Jessica had her 35mm camera and she shot pictures of whatever seemed interesting. The buildings were just north off the road and plainly visible now the trees were losing their leaves. There were a few older buildings, one had been a chicken coop and a second probably housed hogs at one time. The only buildings of interest were the house and the barn. It was black soil and as Fred had opined it appeared much like Casper's own land. There was no road on the west side so Casper turned the car around and drove back to the southeast corner and turned north. Now there was a full mile of Ted's land ahead. The north quarter was the better of the two with no buildings and only a few trees. It would be good to farm. Casper stopped the car and he and Fred crossed the ditch, climbed through the fence, and walked out into the field to check on the soil. When the men were back in the car, Casper looked at Jessica and told her, "Real good soil, Jess, hard to tell any difference from our own but as Fred says, it may be somewhat deeper up here."

To check the distances, Casper drove one mile north to Highway 30 and turned east. It was six more miles into DeWitt. Fred commented, "Good roads coming this way."

From DeWitt, Casper drove back to where Fred was living and let him off. "See you on Monday, Fred." Fred nodded and Jessica moved to the front seat. The big question facing them now was determining a fair price to pay for the land and could they afford it?

Using the kitchen table for a desk, Casper and Jessica worked through the numbers. From a file he opened, Casper told her, "Back in the early eighties, good land was selling around two thousand an acre but for several years now the price has been between one thousand and twelve hundred dollars per acre."

"This seller has three hundred and fifteen acres of grain land and dividing that into his asking price it comes out to twelve hundred and forty dollars per acre, which is high. Casper, what value do we put on the buildings?"

Casper tapped the table with his pencil, "Don't really know but we could probably get two hundred a month in rent. We could subdivide it out an acreage and sell it but then down the road, we would probably have a junk pile of old cars and whatnot causing an eyesore."

"You could put a hired man living there as long as he agreed to mow the grass, paint, and generally look after the place."

"Good suggestion, Jess. I like that better than selling it. We would still be in control. At twelve hundred and ten dollars an acre, what would the grain land come to?"

Jessica worked on the calculator and stated, "At your price per acre, the grain land would cost three hundred and eighty one thousand, one hundred and fifty dollars. The grassland at five hundred and twenty dollars per acre would come to three hundred and eighty thousand, eight hundred dollars. Added together it is a total of six hundred and sixty-one thousand, nine hundred and fifty dollars. Adds up to a big pile of money, Casper."

Casper leaned back and considered. "The grain land on a per-acre basis is the most valuable. If we made an offer at twelve hundred and ten dollars per acre, we would be right on last year's land sales. What did that come to?"

Jessica did the calculation. "In round numbers, three hundred and eighty-one thousand dollars which would be a saving of just over eleven thousand dollars."

"There are a lot of grain land evaluations circulating and an offer at that price would be right on the dot. I like the philosophy of that price. Makes arguing for a higher price hard to justify. Now, on the other hand, the grassland is a lot harder to put a value on. Run out what six hundred and thirty-eight acres comes to at five hundred and twenty per acre."

Jessica punched in the numbers. "In round numbers, three hundred and eighty-one thousand, a saving of just over thirty-eight thousand dollars."

Casper had written numbers down and added them up. "Jess, it feels about right to me. In total, we would be paying seven hundred and thirteen thousand, four hundred and ten dollars for all the land. Ted would receive full value for his grain land and hopefully, we would get a deal on the grasslands. Next spring, the grain land can be seeded while on the grass we need to drill two water wells and put in storage for hay bales. Maybe even plant a few trees. We can use those things to justify our bidding price."

Casper threw his pencil on the table. "Let's leave the numbers for a few hours, there might be something else we will come up with that needs to be considered." The silence extended for several minutes and Jessica knew it was because Casper's brain was still on the land deal. Jessica went around the table and sat on her husband's knee and murmured, "We have been married for a week now and this is the first day my husband hasn't carried me off to the nearest bed. Could it be I am losing my charms and his interest is waning?" Casper laughed with her and pulled her in close for a kiss. His hands slid down and pulled her blouse out of the jeans she was wearing and crept up to undo the bra clasp. When they came back to the front and started playing with her nipples, she squirmed and ran her tongue into his mouth. It might have been as long as two minutes but no one was keeping track when Jessica jumped up, grabbed his hand, and pulled him toward the staircase leading to the second floor.

* * *

Sunday morning arrived and most of it passed by and the Blakerly's didn't notice. They were resting up, snuggled together, letting their bodies enjoy the rest. Waking up, squirming around a little to change positions, and dozing off again. It was nearly noon when Casper arose and walked to the bathroom where he turned on the shower. Jessica donned a housecoat and stripped the bed, took the sheets and pillowcases downstairs, and filled the washing machine. She turned it on, threw in soap, and went back upstairs. In the bathroom, she dropped the housecoat on a chair and opened the shower door. Casper was surprised but also welcoming. He soaped her body all over and began to rinse her off. She became vaguely interested but noticed an important part of her husband was hanging loose. She smiled and turned the water off and Casper followed her through the door. With fresh clean towels, they dried each other before looking for clean clothes to wear.

Casper asked, "You want to drive to DeWitt and have lunch?"

"Sounds like a splendid idea to me." He backed the F150 out of the garage and drove to the porch to pick her up. The truck didn't speed and it was only a short distance until it was parked just to the right of the entrance door to Big Joe's Deli. Jessica walked in and Joe looked at her, wondering where he had seen her before and then Casper came in.

"Holly Jumping Jehoshaphat, I will be danged if it isn't old Casper himself and he still has that good looking girl with him. Now, let me see, was your name Jessie?"

Jessica laughed. "Close, Joe, my name is Jessica and since you

262

last saw us, we have gotten married."

Joe stared for a moment. "You up and married this old hound dog? I don't believe it. Hey Phillis, come out here and see the catch Casper made!" Phillis arrived at the counter and Joe told her, "Can you believe it? Old Casper talked this good looking lady into marrying him."

Phillis laughed, enjoying the joke. "Now, Jessica how did he talk you into getting married? Did he force you to drink a bunch of liquor and get you so drunk you lost all your judgment?"

"Something along those lines, Phillis. He said he wouldn't give me a raise in salary unless I married him. Being a poor girl, what else could I do?"

"You could run, girl; be the smartest thing a girl can do for herself."

"Darn, I never thought of running. Just goes to show you, we young girls have a lot to learn."

"Young you may be, dearie, but you sure got good looks. Old Casper probably fell in love with you before he even heard your name." Phillis and Jessica both laughed and looked at Casper to see him frowning.

"Joe, you send your wife back to the kitchen. Next thing I know, she will have talked my wife into looking for a divorce lawyer. We drove all the way here to eat, not listen to Phillis run off at the mouth."

Together, the Blakerly's walked to the table they had sat at last time. Joe came with glasses of water and menus. "You want coffee along with your food?"

"Sounds good to me, Joe. Why don't you bring the coffee while we read the menu?" Jessica grinned at him.

"Sure thing, Jessica, be right back." Joe hurried behind the

263

counter and poured two mugs of coffee. Brought them to the table and came back with cream and sugar.

"Joe, the last time I was here, you had a dish with potatoes, beans, and ham. It was really good and I would like to order it again, if you have it on your menu."

Joe smiled. "It is not on the menu but Phillis can stir it up for you. How about you, Casper, what would you like?"

"The same order as Jessica for me, Joe." Casper looked up. "Do you and Phillis have your children all in school now?"

"Sure do and Phillis found a neighbor lady who keeps a watch on them when they get home from school. In fact, they are coming here to eat their lunch, should be arriving anytime now." Joe walked away.

While they waited, Jessica asked Casper if he had come up with anything new on the price for the land they were looking at. He laughed at her and said he hadn't had time to think about the land because he had a wife who kept him sidetracked. They were smiling at each other and sipping coffee when Joe came with their lunches. A minute later, he came with a bowl of hot sauce for them. Jessica found the food even better than the first time and was digging in. Casper was also busy eating. They hadn't had a meal since late Saturday afternoon and both were hungry. The door opened and the sound of little voices caused them to look up. Three children aged six to probably twelve had arrived. They seated themselves on counter stools at the far end of the cafe. They were neatly dressed and Jessica surmised they had just come from attending Sunday school. Joe went along the counter and stopped in front of them. They talked and Joe wrote their food orders down and left. The youngest was a girl and she was sitting in the middle. She was telling the older two a story of some kind and her tiny arms were waving as she explained. The talk was loud enough for the Blakerly's to hear but not loud enough for them to make out the words.

Jessica looked over at Casper and asked him, "Aren't those kids adorable? The way they are dressed seems to me to indicate they have been at church."

"Probably right, Jess. Their mom is always neat, clean, and well dressed. I imagine she hasn't changed much over the years and is passing it along to the kids."

More people were arriving and filling the cafe and Joe was busy taking food orders. When the Blakerly's were almost finished eating, Joe arrived and refilled the coffee mugs. Jessica had her fork lying across her half-finished plate and was sipping coffee while watching Casper eating the last of his food. Joe asked if they wanted dessert and both declined. Jessica told him, "Excellent food, Joe, you thank Phillis for us."

Casper commented, "Good looking kids you have, Joe."

"Thank you both. We are proud of our children and Phillis is doing a great job of raising them."

After finishing the coffee and paying the bill, they walked out to the F150 and drove away. Casper headed west and Jessica wondered until he turned south and drove to the north quarter of land. They stopped on the road and looked out across the quarter. "Darn good looking chunk of land, Jess. See if my binoculars are in the glove compartment." Jessica pulled them out and Casper scanned the land before handing her the glasses. Jessica spent several minutes carefully looking at the quarter.

She commented, "Don't see anything to be concerned about. The land is almost tabletop flat and no sign of grain storage." Casper drove down to the northeast corner of the southern quarter and stopped. Jessica was busy with the binoculars. "There appears to be two metal grain bins west of the barn, mostly hidden by windbreak trees. Here have a look."

Casper scanned and agreed with her. "Figured there had to be some, he was raising cattle and needed to feed them. Buildings look to be well cared for." The truck drove south and kept going until suddenly they were at the northeast corner of the section of grassland. They didn't enter, Casper wanted to leave the cattle alone after having been in there yesterday. "Fred and I figured to drill two water wells up here on the north side of the section. There is a power line right above us or we could buy a couple of wind-mills to pump water. Will need hay storage alongside one of the wells."

After a while sitting there looking around, they drove south to the river and turned for home. Jessica felt happy, her husband had turned out well, she loved the farm, although she hadn't yet seen everything. She didn't like living in a city and now that was over. She hadn't asked about bank accounts, how much money her hus-band had, wills, or insurance, figuring he would be looking after such things and would sit her down and communicate when he was ready. She was in no hurry and if he didn't tell her soon, she would ask. After all, she was a full-time student at the university and wouldn't have the time to be a full participant in the farm and Davenport until after graduation.

Chapter 20

Mrs. Sparks phoned Wilford Black's number and arranged a meeting for Casper. She walked back to his office and told him, "Mr. Black will be here for your meeting at ten-thirty." She watched Casper write the appointment in his daybook before she left. Casper sat still for a moment. Wilford was the son of Reginald Black, who had been his father's lawyer and now their firm represented Casper personally, Blakerly Farms, and Davenport Machinery Inc. Wilford was much closer to Casper in age. Combined, his companies were the largest client the firm of Black and Black had. As Casper's companies grew, so did the law firm. He needed to tell Wilford of his marriage, discuss the corporate documents, and have any needed changes made. He also needed to discuss the land purchase with the lawyer and there may well be other things involving Davenport that Wilford would bring up.

Getting ready for the meeting, he made four piles—one for Davenport, one for Mid-West Holdings, one for Blakerly Farms, and finally a pile for his marriage. He moved the piles, putting two on one end and two at the other end, leaving room for Wilford and himself to sit across from each other. He glanced at his watch and was surprised to see it was two minutes to ten. While waiting, Casper doodled on a pad of paper, considering the land purchase. He was surprised when Mrs. Sparks walked in and told him, "Wilford Black is on the way up, should I bring him in?"

Casper watched the elevator doors open Wilford came out carrying a large briefcase and he stood up. Wilford came through the door and grabbed the extended hand. "Thanks for coming over to meet with me, Wilford, please be seated." Wilford sat down and glanced at the four piles of documents, thinking there was more to the meeting than just buying land. He waited until they got glasses of water and Mrs. Sparks went out and closed the door.

"Wilford, there are several items we need to deal with and of course you may have others. First, let me inform you I got married a week ago last Saturday. I married a wonderful girl and we need to rearrange any documents requiring such."

Wilford was startled and finally said, "You didn't tell me you were getting married."

"No, I didn't; firstly because it took me weeks to get up the courage to ask her. Secondly: because as you know, I live a quiet life with only a few friends and a great many acquaintances. Also, my wife is now at university studying for her MBA which leaves little spare time. As you know, Davenport is owned one hundred percent by Mid-West Holding Company so now we have to figure out how to arrange for Jessica to become an owner. Of course: I will depend on your advice when you are ready." Casper sat back and smiled.

"I will need to go through all the documents and build a good plan, Casper. Let's just talk about the corporate structure. Davenport is a private company owned one hundred percent by Mid-West. You are the only share-owner in Mid-West, which has one hundred thousand shares approved, of which you own fifty-one percent. As I recall we did it to allow you room for other family members or you could sell shares to outsiders. On the face of it, your wife could receive forty-nine percent of the shares. A complicating factor is since you are now married, there may well be children in the future. To avoid a serious tax problem, we must proceed carefully. After reviewing all the documents, tax decisions made in Washington, etc., I will draft a rough proposal and go over it with my father. When we have what we consider to be a good plan, I will come back to meet with you again. Have there been any changes made at Davenport?"

"You must check that also. Davenport's business is growing rapidly. We are just finishing constructing a large new plant, to be known as Plant No. II, which when in full operation, will more than double our production of machines. It will most likely lead to an increase in international business. Also, you should be aware that my wife is a mechanical engineering graduate and by next spring will have her MBA. I intend to appoint her as Vice President of Corporate Planning to guide Davenport's growth and expanding business."

"When Mrs. Sparks phoned, she said you wanted to meet to discuss the purchase of additional land and you blindsided me. Is there actually a land purchase in the works?"

Casper laughed. "Yes, there is, Wilford. We are looking at six quarters of land and have been figuring out a reasonable bid." He handed a sheet of paper across the table. "Here is a handwritten brief on the deal which Jessica, my wife, wrote out for you. We thought it would be a good idea to have you check the land titles, mortgages, loans, or any form of encumbrances. It is a deal we would like to make, provided it is clean and nothing is hidden away to come back and haunt us."

Wilford read the handwritten notes. "All right, Casper, we will get copies of the titles, etc. and let you know what the situation is in a few days."

"Very good, Wilford thanks for coming over to see me this morning. If there is any other information you need, call whoever you believe will have it. I should remind you that buying land is the most urgent item to deal with before someone else comes along and buys it. When your studies are complete, call us to set up another meeting. We dealt with Davenport and Mid-West and that leaves Blakerly Farms Inc., in which my wife will be involved."

"Of course, Casper. I will get back to you as quickly as I can." They stood up and Casper walked him to the elevator.

It was noon hour and Casper wanted a cheeseburger. He drove to Ma's Restaurant and put in his usual order before sitting back to relax in his window seat. It made him happy to see Ma looking well and healthy. Florence seemed to be her usual bubbly self. He hadn't been there for a couple of months and immediately felt relaxed. While he waited, he reviewed the meeting with Wilford Black. When Florence arrived with the burger, she asked, "How are you, Casper? You haven't come to see us for a long time."

"We have had a busy summer, Florence. Real good to learn Ma is feeling better now. I have been coming in here to eat for more than ten years and Ma had been operating her business for a long time before then." Florence nodded and went to pick up an order for another customer. Casper's mind immediately went back to the meeting he was sorting out in his mind. On his way out, he stopped to chat with Ma for a minute and felt refreshed when he got back to the truck.

Casper drove directly to Plant No. II and went in to see how the transfer of the large post pounders was going. He watched the crew begin to assemble one of the largest fencepost pounders now on the market. Soon, he sat down in a chair to continue observing. A few minutes later, Ned Ambrose arrived and pulled up another chair to sit beside Casper. "One thing we accomplished with the move is these guys sure can't complain about being crowded."

Ned looked around the large plant. "You are right, Casper. Looks to me like this operation isn't using even five percent of the plant's space."

When Casper was satisfied with watching the assembly of the pounder, he walked to the truck and drove to the farm. The most urgent thing to get done now was the land deal before some other farmer showed up with an offer. Fred was in the farm office waiting to weight a load of soybeans. Not only was this the farm foreman's office but also the truck weight scale was alongside, with the controls inside a large window. "Howdy, Boss, come in and sit, got to wait for the boys to finish putting a load on the B-Train."

"Fred, I got to thinking we best go and drive around on Ted's land to make sure we have seen everything. You want to phone him and ask for permission?"

Fred dialed the phone from memory. "Hi, Ted, this is Fred calling. Had a chat with Casper about your land and he is wondering if we could drive over there and have a look around." He listened carefully before replying, "Thank you, Ted. Casper and I will be there within an hour to pick you up. Will be good having you along." When the B-Train pulled onto the scale, Fred went and worked the computer and filled out the shipping ticket. Standard soybeans weighed sixty pounds per bushel so he divided the grain weight on the truck by sixty and came up with sixteen hundred and ninety bushels. The truck driver took a copy of the weight ticket to give to the buyer and Fred filed the other two copies. "Shannon Hogs phoned and wanted a load to keep their feed supplies up so now it is on the way."

They drove Fred's F150 to Ted Arson's farm to pick him up. Casper got out of the truck to shake hands. "Good to see you again, Ted."

Driving slowly around the farmyard, they looked at all the buildings before Ted directed them west into a pasture and sure enough, there were four steel grain bins, mostly hidden by surrounding aspens. The pasture was small and the grass tall. Ted explained, "Haven't used this pasture since you rented the grassland, now the pasture grass is growing tall. There is a gate up ahead which will allow us to climb up to the flat land." Casper hopped out and opened the gate and closed it after the truck went by. The truck climbed a gentle slope and came out on a stubble field. "This land had corn on it this year and on average produced about a hundred and seventy bushels to the acre. Looks likely we will receive around three dollars per bushel."

Fred drove east and turned south past the farmyard, went across the south side and north up the east side. They toured the north quarter and ended up in the middle of the field. Fred stopped the truck and he and Casper got out and walked around. Several times, they got down on their knees and dug into the soil with Fred's small shovel. They didn't go down far but the black soil was more than a foot deep. Both men took a handful of soil and examined it. Ted watched them carefully as they discussed the soil and he wondered what they were saying to each other. One thing for sure, Casper hadn't changed, he was still careful. He might make a mistake on the land price but it would be a small mistake, of this Ted felt sure.

The men came back to the truck and Fred dug a clean rag out of the carryall that spanned the box back of the cab. After wiping their hands clean as best they could, the men got into the cab. Fred asked, "Looks like we have seen everything, unless you have something else to show us."

Ted grinned. "You men have seen everything there is to see." Casper remembered he and Jessica had valued three hundred an fifteen acres so they had been generous because close to fourteen acres was in pasture. Looking over the stubble, one thing he for sure liked was no sign of weeds so the crop spraying had worked. Ted told them, "Had soy in here this year and we combined around thirty-seven bushels to the acre. Price of soy has followed corn down and probably we will get around eight to eight-fifty per bushel. What you think about buying the land, Casper?"

"First thing, Ted, I apologize for not having an offer form filled out. We are interested in making a deal with you but keep in mind my lawyer told me it is only a deal if he is satisfied on all the facts. We came today after I remembered we hadn't had a look at all the land and I sure wanted to do that. Thank you for taking the time to show us around. It is good grain land. My wife and I sat and talked about an offer using three hundred and fifteen acres, which I now know was high, and when we finished, we gave the grain land a value of three hundred and eighty-one thousand dollars."

"You are a good man, Casper, and I understand nothing is for sure until the lawyer says everything is okay." Ted grinned. "You know you are looking mighty spry for an old married man."

Casper grinned. "We have only been married for ten days."

"Before you can turn around, it will be twenty years, isn't that right, Fred?" Fred smiled and nodded before Ted asked, "What are your thoughts on the section of grassland?"

"We didn't know but assumed six hundred and thirty-eight acres. Old Fred here has become a problem. If we buy it, he says we have to drill two water wells and put up a hay storage building, so there is going to be capital costs along with the purchase price. We argued about the section for a while and finally decided we could afford to pay two hundred and eighty-one thousand for it."

Ted starred out the windshield for a few minutes as he thought about the offer. "Tell you what, Casper; it seems to me you are a touch low on the grassland and maybe a touch high on the grain land. In total, at six hundred and sixty-two thousand, I can sell it to you, subject to your lawyer coming up with a clean sheet."

"Thank you, Ted. I can shake your hand on that." The two men shook and then Ted turned and shook hands with Fred. "It will be a few days before the lawyer finishes his checks and when he does, I will phone you and pass on his comments."

"You are a gentleman, Casper. If the deal is approved and you give your lawyer the check, bring your wife to the farm so we can meet her. Hell, bring old Fred along also."

Fred dropped off Ted at the house and drove back to the farm.

Casper put his truck away for the night. It was six o'clock when he got to the house and Jessica was busy in the kitchen cooking dinner. Casper watched her from the doorway thinking, *'Marriage sure has changed my work habits, haven't stayed late at the office since the wedding.'* He closed the door and Jessica turned to look. Her dazzling smile pleased him. "There's that husband of mine. How are you, Casper?"

"Fair to middling, girl, fair to middling. Spent most of the day with a lawyer and when they get through digging out everything, you know your head is ringing like an empty bell tower. A few minutes with you and I'll have my perspective back. How was the schooling today?"

"It turned out to be a great day. The professor this morning made me stand up and read a paper I wrote before our wedding and then defend what I said against the class. Almost everyone in the class graduated from university years ago and the way most of them see things, I am not sure they were even in university. After it was over, the prof congratulated me, telling the class it was one of the best papers he had ever received and they lost every argument they made against my conclusions. Hard for a girl like me to remember she is normal when all she receives is praise."

Casper came and kissed her and whispered, "You have other talents I could tell your class about."

"Don't you dare, Casper Blakerly or I will stand up and tell everyone you are a liar and live in a fantasy world." She got kissed again and patted on her butt.

While they ate dinner, Casper told her about his meeting with Ted Arson, touring the land, and discussing their offer to purchase the land. When he told her Ted had verbally accepted, she laughed happily and clapped her hands. "Wonderful! Now tell me how you are going to pay for it."

He laughed happily and started talking but what she was hearing wasn't an answer to what she asked. "Honey, with this deal added in, we now own twenty-one quarters of land and have five more on rental. In total, it comes to 4216 acres. The other way of looking at it is we have 2796 acres of grain, 1155 acres of pasture, 220 acres of hay, and 45 acres of wasteland. Also, our cattle herd is up to 293 cows and heifers and this year's 76 spring steers."

* * *

Casper started the day cleaning up paperwork, signing checks for large amounts, and answering a few phone messages. When his desk was clear, he went to Plant No. II. He started by checking on the construction of the fencepost pounder and then went to Hiram's office. Ralph and Brian McCullum were busy at drafting tables and Casper talked a few minutes with each of them before walking into Hiram's office. "How are things going, Hiram?"

As was usual, Hiram smiled. "We are making good progress now and starting to turn out construction drawings. All of which is good, except now I need people to start building and testing the things we design."

Casper wasn't surprised, he had been thinking about this. "Have you talked to Ned Ambrose?" Hiram shook his head no. "Well, go and talk to him today. He goes through this on every new machine we design and will fix you up. What about an engine for the test tractor?"

"Purchasing has the descriptions of three engines I recommended and are in the process of contacting the companies. One is American made and the other two engines are from Japan. I told them to make sure the companies knew we were going to start building and selling tractors and want their best engine for the job, also a good price. They are smart and will know that if we like their engine, it will mean sales of a lot of engines in the future. Purchasing is going to ask for the latest test data on their engine so we can do an evaluation. This is an exciting project, Casper, and something I have been wondering about is the wheel sizes. All tractors on the market have small front wheels but when you consider the attachments we are planning, there are as many on the front as there will be on the rear. It seems to me we should be looking at making this fifty-horse machine along the lines of the four-wheel drive farm tractors. It will give the tractor more weight and strength to support whatever attachment is put on it." Casper was now sitting up straight and very interested. "Such a design may not look as pretty but be much more practical."

Hiram noticed Casper was staring at the wall deep in thought and waited. Casper's mind was whirling. He hadn't thought of the four-wheel design and it seemed to make sense. The steering would be simpler, the front-end would be stronger, and it might have a lower cost to build. Finally, he asked, "Are the engines you are looking at suitable for such an arrangement?"

"I don't see why they wouldn't work for both types of tractors. When we get the data, we may find one is more suitable than the others. Both front and rear will need hydraulics, power takeoffs, and three-point hitches along with towing bars. These are tractors that will not be running around putting on miles but working on a project using PTOs and Hydraulics to do the work. It seems to me to be very important to provide a stable, strong work platform."

Casper exclaimed, "I like your ideas, Hiram! Carry on and keep me informed. In fact, you will have trouble keeping me away from this project. It is very interesting." Casper stood up and walked away without saying goodbye.

As he left Plant Number II, Casper was thinking about a conversation he'd had with Wilford Black yesterday regarding international trade, manufacturing, and markets and now it all came back to him. His mind must have been working on the problems they discussed because now he knew. Davenport had to expand outside the USA; the big dilemma was where to locate? Canada they were already supplying. Mexico appeared to be attractive with lower labor costs and lower taxes so it would have to be studied along with other countries further south. Europe was a market they were shipping some machines to already and he had never been there, so his pool of knowledge was small. Seemed likely they were heavily unionized, taxed, and would have intense human resource costs. He didn't know so again it would have to be studied. Asia was a definite possibility but it was far from the markets Davenport served. All this was exciting but he didn't have the knowledge so a consultant company had to be found. The answer was simple. He would go and talk to Wilford and ask him to find a consultant and to keep the project quiet so the current employees didn't become worried about their jobs. He was standing still in the yard, his attention all focused on what he was thinking about. Employees were passing by him, going about their work and wondering what the big boss was doing. Casper didn't notice. Now, he was thinking about the financial strength of Davenport. Yes, the money was important and so he would go to financial and talk to Ron Smith and get the latest numbers which they received late every afternoon from the bank. Yes, that was what he would do, these were major decisions and it was exciting. It was past time for him to be making a move. Was it because he had married Jessica? Could be, she had a way of making suggestions, asking questions, and wanting to know. He smiled and smacked his fisted right hand into the palm of his left and that brought him back to the present.

Casper looked around. Yes, employees were going about their work but he could see they were wondering about him. He laughed, feeling a great sense of accomplishment in having finally thought about this issue and formulated a rough approach to it. Now, he would start. At a brisk walk, he pointed himself at the office complex located at the front end of Plant No. I.

Ron Smith saw Casper coming and wondered. The boss sure

seemed to be full of energy. He waited. Casper marched into the office and smiled at Ron. "Please give me a copy of yesterday's financial numbers from the bank." Ron opened a desk drawer and pulled out a three-ring binder which he opened, removed the top page, and walked to a copy machine. He came back and handed Casper the copy. Ron watched as Casper's eyes went over the numbers. To his surprise, Casper turned and walked away. What in the devil was Casper up to? We send a copy of the report to Mrs. Sparks every day so obviously Casper had forgotten the fact or his mind was so far away he didn't think about it.

Casper stomped up the stairs and into his office. Sitting at the desk, he went over the numbers again. Millions of dollars where being cared for by the bank with the money in a variety of accounts, term deposits, and short-term high-return funds. He dialed the phone and asked to speak to Wilford. When the voice came on the line, Casper started, "Wilford, yesterday we talked about international business for a few minutes. My mind has been wrestling with thoughts ever since and now I need to meet with you to lay out an initial plan to investigate the idea. What time would suit you for me to come to your office?"

Wilford was taken back by this approach. Never before had Casper come to their offices. His mind raced as he looked in his daybook. "Would one o'clock be suitable for you, Casper?"

"Very good, Wilford, see you at one, goodbye." Wilford hung up the phone and sat at his desk thinking. Finally, he pushed the button on the intercom and told his secretary to cancel all meetings between one and three p.m. This was unusual because it was Casper Blakerly; it had happened with other clients for a variety of reasons over the years. After considering for several minutes, he got up and walked to his father's office, he just happened to have no client in at the moment. "Dad, I just had a call from Casper Blakerly. He is coming over at one p.m. to discuss taking Davenport to other countries to do business. I am sorry to say I do not have much in the way of international experience."

Reginald Black smiled. "Neither do I. First thing I will do is have my secretary check the resumes of all our lawyers in case one of them has had exposure. Now tell me what this is all about."

"Casper got married two weeks ago and we met to discuss what corporate documents would need to be amended. In the course of our meeting, the subject of going international came up but only for a few minutes. We have noted over the years that Casper has a way of pursuing a wide range of ideas with no forewarning. I guess that since yesterday, his mind has been thinking about going international and now wants to draft a proposal of everything that will need to be done.

"Well, son, you may soon have international business law to add to your resume."

"International business law would be fine but right now I am more concerned about what we should do to get the damn project launched without me showing my ignorance."

"Have Casper tell you what he is considering and get any facts you can, such as when he wants to accomplish this. First thing is to discuss which country he has in mind. There will have to be a team set up to visit the country and engage a local legal firm and investigate the local business laws, etc. Davenport will have to set up a company, write corporate documents, obtain a banker and set up accounts, office space, and on and on. That will keep us busy for several weeks so don't worry about today. If during the meeting, you wish to call me and ask me to come and sit in the meeting, please do so. I suggest you go back to your office and make a list of all these things. While you do that, I will see if any of our lawyers have worked overseas."

Five minutes before one o'clock, Casper was standing at the reception desk asking for Wilford. She had been warned about this client coming to the office and watched him intensely. "Please have a seat, Mr. Blakerly, while I call and tell Mr. Black you have arrived." She punched the button for Black's office and his secretary answered. "Please tell Mr. Black that Casper Blakerly is here for a meeting with him." The receptionist pretended to go back to work but she was watching; word that he would be here had gone through all the secretaries in a matter of minutes. With a sigh, she noticed his left hand wore a wedding ring.

Wilford came through the entrance wearing a suit jacket which caused her eyebrows to rise. "Ah, Casper, good to see you, please come with me." They shook hands and walked away silently. Wilford got him seated at his office table and his secretary came in with two glasses of ice water. As she left, she closed the office door. "You are full of surprises, Casper, so please tell me what it is you have on your mind." While he talked, he had placed a fourteen-inch long legal notepad on the table and taken out a pen.

"We are nearly finished building a second plant and since yesterday my mind has been churning with expanding our business to more international locations. As you know, we have many times shipped machines to other countries, particularly in Europe, but now it is time we build a plant overseas."

"In which country are you planning to build, Casper?"

Casper smiled. "Don't have the faintest idea yet. A country that speaks English would be easiest but not necessary. There are so many things that need to be considered, it is staggering. What I would like today is for us to outline as many of the considerations as we can think of and map out a strategy to get started, including what type of consultants we will need."

"Well said, Casper. Just give me a minute to write down your brief description at the top of this page and we will…"

Three hours later, they sat back in the chairs and looked at each other. Wilford told him, "We have made a major beginning. My secretary will type my notes up and send you a copy with the envelope noted as 'for Casper Blakerly only to see.' The most important item for us to get done is selecting a country where you will be comfortable going into business and we will find out who is available to help us. Also, I will have people assigned to start producing draft documents for a new corporation which will be finalized once we have a target country. If you don't mind, you might give some thought to whether the new company should be owned by Davenport Machinery Inc. or Mid-West Holding. There are probably good reasons for both but if you have any thoughts, pass them on to me for consideration. Oh, before I forget, we should have your 'Offer to Purchase' ready tomorrow."

Together, they walked to the reception area and said goodbye.

Chapter 21

Casper spent the morning processing paper and touring the plants to keep up on the status of machinery construction and projects. Just before noon, Wilford arrived with the Offer Sheet which Casper signed and wrote out a check to Black & Black. They told him the finalized offer could be given to Ted Arson in the morning. Wilford handed Casper a large envelope which contained the minutes from the previous day's meeting. As soon as Wilford departed, Casper phoned Ted. "Hello, Ted Arson here."

"Hi Ted, this is Casper calling. The lawyer just informed me the deal is closed and you will get a copy of the offer sheet and a check tomorrow. I told him to send them to me and I would deliver them to you. What time would be best for you, Ted?"

"Not planning on going anywhere tomorrow so come when it suits you."

"Real good, Ted, see you tomorrow." Casper hung up the phone.

Noon hour had been over for some time and since he wasn't feeling hungry, he decided to wait for dinner. Sitting down at the desk, he started reading the remarks from yesterday's meeting. Partway down the front page, he grabbed a red pen and started making changes. Some were spelling mistakes, other places had material missing so he kept marking the sheets, thinking how lucky he was to have gotten a good education and how little you could trust people to do things right. In his mind, it was obvious that Wilford had not proofread the material. In the morning, he would drive over with this mess to leave at Black & Black and while there pick up Ted's money. He looked at his watch and was surprised to see it was six-thirty. He packed his briefcase and hurried to the F150 for the drive home.

Jessica was waiting for him with a pizza she had bought on the way home. She fired up the stove and popped the pizza in. While they waited, Casper told her he was going to deliver the purchase check to Ted Arson tomorrow and asked if it would be okay with her if he invited them to go to Big Joe's Deli for dinner tomorrow night.

As was her way, she smiled at him and said six-thirty would be a good time to meet the Arsons in DeWitt and she would be home and ready to go before six. The buzzer on the stove sounded and Jessica pulled the pizza out and set it aside to cool down before slicing. From the fridge, she got a large bottle of root beer to put on the table. Casper watched her working and muttered to himself, *'Damn woman seems to be good at everything. I was very fortunate she said yes when I asked her to marry me.'*

They ate pizza, drank root beer, and talked. Together, they cleaned up the kitchen so it was shining. Jessica set up her laptop on the kitchen table and worked on another course paper she was writing. Casper went to his office and updated the farm accounts, which reminded him once again it was time to hire an accountant. The farm had become too big an operation for him to continue to carry the load which he had done since a few months before his father had died.

* * *

Casper went to marketing and walked into Greig's office. "Morning, Tom, how are things going around here?"

Tom Greig looked up. "Busy, Casper, damn busy. We are shipping the most equipment in our history. For one thing, it will take several months to supply the requests for the new large fencepost pounders. Don't know how the Parks Department heard about them but they have many miles of fences all over the country and those fences are a constant problem. Got to keep the elk, bears, and now buffalo inside where they can't take advantage of the public."

"Davenport is the company that can help them out. How many pounders do they want?"

"We have an order for ten now and I suspect they will want more than that. I meant to have someone find out how many parks there are in the country and forgot to do it."

"It would be interesting to know the count, Tom, so get the number but we also have to realize the pounders can be easily moved around, even between various states. They can fence in the northern states in the summer and the warmer ones in the winter. Lots of variables come into play. Plant Number II is starting up and the production of machines will increase in the months ahead. Can you take a look at how many machines we have sold overseas and where at? As our production speeds up, selling overseas will become much more important to the company."

"I will get back to you in a couple of days, Casper."

"Thanks, Tom, and maybe you should talk to Ned about speeding up the pounders."

Casper arrived back in his office to find a messenger from Black & Black waiting for him. He took the young man into his office and opened the envelope. There was a copy of the 'Offer to Buy' agreement signed by everyone and a check in the right amount. Casper put them in his briefcase and handed the messenger an envelope with Wilford Black written boldly on the front. "Thank you for bringing this material to me and please give this envelope to Wilford."

"Yes, sir. Have a good day, sir." Casper watched as the messenger got into the elevator on his way out.

The office clock was reading ten a.m. so Casper picked up his briefcase and went to the truck. At the farm, he picked up Fred and together they drove north to see Ted Arson. When they arrived, Ted stood in the doorway and waved for them to come in. "Come in, boys, and sit down, the wife has coffee on and you may as well join me." He called out in a loud voice, "Clemi, come and meet the boys."

Clemi was a white-haired, stout, older lady and Ted explained, "My wife's name is Clementine but I shortened it to Clemi many years ago. This here is Fred Aitchison from Blakerly Farms."

Clemi stuck out her hand to shake. "I met you several years ago, Fred. How are you?"

"Mighty well, Clemi, although must admit to having put on a lot of years."

"This here is Casper Blakerly who you have heard me talk about." Clemi shook Casper's hand and smiled at him.

"Casper pleased to meet you. Knew your mom and dad away back, and now Ted is telling me you went and got yourself married."

"That is true, Clemi, and she wanted to come with me but couldn't. She is back at the university working toward another degree. Jessica told me to ask you and Ted to join us for dinner tonight in DeWitt at six-thirty."

Clemi looked at Ted who nodded yes. "Be pleased to join you tonight. Six-thirty you say and where are we going to eat?"

"Long-time friends of mine own Big Joe's Deli and my wife loves to eat there. The food is very good and Joe and Phillis like to tease me, which they have been doing since we were schoolkids."

"Will be nice to see you tonight and meet your new wife. Now you men sit down and I will fetch the coffee." As they were settling in around the table, Clemi arrived with a dinner plate full of fresh-made donuts along with cream and sugar. She came back with coffee mugs and the big coffeepot and poured.

Ted told the two men, "Clemi and me attended the wedding when Joe and Phillis were married, must have been some fifteen years ago. We stop in at the deli once in a while to eat. They tell me they have three little ones now."

Casper smiled. "Their youngest just started grade one last September."

Ted pushed the donuts toward Casper. "Help yourself, boys." After they each got one, he helped himself and they munched and sipped coffee for a few minutes.

Casper brought an envelope from one pocket and laid it on the table. "Your check is inside, Ted." Ted nodded, pulled it over, and left it beside his coffee mug.

Ted walked to the kitchen and came back to refill the coffee mugs before asking, "Blakerly got all the harvesting completed?"

"Sure did, Ted, everything went in the bins dry and we have been shipping a few loads, mostly to local hog and turkey operations we usually supply." Fred smiled. "On the commercial side, we usually wait until after all the farms that sell right from the combines have slowed down and grain prices regain what they lost."

"Good management, Fred, most years I did the same. Remember one year it wanted to rain and shower all the time and we had tough grain. Had to sell to get loads out of every bin but the moisture was the driver, not management."

The men finished their second donuts and Fred pushed his chair back. "Casper, I reckon you should get me back to the farm; our semi will be coming in for another load anytime now."

Casper shook hands with Ted. "Thanks for making this deal with me, Ted, and tell Clemi we will see her tonight. Good coffee and donuts your wife makes." Ted stood in the doorway and watched them drive away.

* * *

The days were a blur and weeks went by. Jessica phoned her mom and said they couldn't make it for Thanksgiving. Now, Christmas was only a few days away and Jessica wanted to go home for the celebration. She drove to the plant and parked. It took her a while to get past all the people who wanted to say hello. Finally, she stepped off the elevator and grinned at Mrs. Sparks. They met partway and hugged before chatting for a few minutes. Jessica walked to Casper's office and stood in the doorway as her hand knocked loudly on the open door. Casper's head came up and he looked at her before he began smiling. "Come in, Jess, come in." He stood up and hugged her tightly.

"Sit down here at the table. Oh, it is so good to have you in the office. Is there something you need?"

"Yes, there is, Casper. Christmas is only a few days away and I am here to tell you we are going to drive up to Newton and have a happy yuletide with my folks." She smiled as Casper started to talk and held up her hand, palm toward him. "Now, honey, please don't starts giving me reasons not to go. You have been working far too hard and seven days a week. You never gave me an explanation and I haven't asked. The simple fact is you need a rest and so do I." She stood up and told him, "Now I have delivered my message and I shall leave, see you when you get home." She held her head high and walked to the elevator, afraid he would ask her to come back. He didn't and she rode the elevator down to the ground floor and walked to her car.

She was surprised when he arrived home at five-thirty. It was agreed they would drive to Newton on December twenty-third and return on the twenty-sixth. During the drive and while walking together around the farm, he told her what he was doing. The excitement in his voice made her happy and now she understood why he was so busy. On the drive back to Davenport, she confided in him her news that she was two weeks pregnant. He became so excited he almost put the F150 in the ditch. At her graduation in April with an MBA, the gown she was given to wear hid her waistline which was expanding.

While legal and financial committees researched and worked on documents for a new European company, the committee to look for a suitable location had narrowed it down to three cities—Lisbon, Portugal; Budapest, Hungary; and Milan, Italy. Lisbon was their number one choice so it was time for decisions. Casper arranged a trip to Lisbon to have a departure date two days after Jessica's graduation so she could accompany him. Ron Smith and Mike Osborn were leaving two days ahead of them and would meet them at Humberto airport when they arrived. They had located two industrial sites they believed were suitable and now Casper would have a look at them and the city. Not a new city, it had a history that went back centuries before Rome came into existence. Lisbon enjoyed a Mediterranean climate, averaging year-round temperatures between the mid-fifties and high seventies. More important to the committee, Lisbon was located on the Atlantic Ocean and the Tagus River with excellent railroads to the rest of Europe. It was not a large city, having a population within its borders of around half a million people.

The plan was to fly on United Airlines leaving from Chicago. Casper dialed the phone and talked to Wilford about the trip and being prepared to carry out any legal negotiations required, particularly if they had a site Davenport liked. Wilford informed Casper that Black & Black had talked to three legal firms in Lisbon, had found the one they believed was most capable, and the fact that Portugal did contracts with companies from outside Portugal in the English language would make it much easier for an American company. This arrangement seemed unusual but was common practice in Europe.

Casper sat proudly watching his wife as she waited to receive her MBA Degree. When her turn came, she walked to the university president and received the certificate. He held on to her hand and had a brief conversation with her, which caused many people to wonder. Casper had a reservation at Biaggi's for dinner and drove her there as a surprise. Once again, they ate sea scallops and he was amused she wouldn't have anything else, just watched him eat minestrone and a salmon salad. She was being careful and protecting their baby, which was due in five months. When the eating was finished, Casper brought out a gold case and handed it to his wife. She opened it and removed a business card which said, 'J. Blakerly, ME MBA, Vice President of Corporate Planning' with of course the company name, address, and phone numbers. She smiled and asked, "Does this mean I have to report to the office?"

Casper smiled. "Of course and work long hours, and I might mention your new office has been prepared for you."

"New office? I don't understand, there is nothing wrong with my old office."

Casper frowned. "If you had told me before, it would have saved Davenport considerably money. But, alas, your old office has disappeared; now you have a new one and you will be the only Davenport executive with a private bathroom."

Jessica stared at him, bewildered. "Are you playing another of your jokes on me?"

"Not at all, Jess. And, Mrs. Sparks has requested she be allowed to act as your tour guide. Tomorrow, you can ride to work with me and get all the details yourself. You have two days to prepare yourself before we are off to Lisbon."

Jessica's face became serious. "Never have I traveled before.

How will I know what to do, how to dress, and what about conversations?"

"Neither of us has traveled, especially internationally, but we will do it together and learn. We will enjoy seeing an old, old, city that has existed for thousands of years and has more history than any other city I know of. Just be yourself and make me happy, what anyone else thinks is not important."

"Okay, Mr. Big Shot, I will relax and depend on you for guidance."

* * *

They were seated in first class, Jessica was having a nap, and Casper was reading the guidance papers the lawyers had prepared. The plane landed at Humberto Delgado Airport on time and when they came out of customs, Ron Smith and Mike Osborn were there to meet them. Jessica gave each a hug and told them, "It is so nice to see familiar faces. You know this is my first trip outside of Iowa." Everyone laughed. The men had a rental car and drove them to a hotel named Olissipo Lapa Palace located in the diplomatic quarter of the city. When they entered the hotel suite, it was impressive, with large rooms, a large open-air balcony, and plush furnishings and a quiet, polite floor steward who spoke really good English. Casper asked the men when they wanted to visit the proposed sites and they answered tomorrow. He smiled and told them to pick up himself and Jessica at eight a.m. In late afternoon, they went to the dining room and ate dinner, came back to the room and relaxed out on the balcony. During the drive to the hotel, they had seen intriguing parts of the ancient city and Jessica was excited about touring as much as they could. The Portugal steward for the second floor had obtained several brochures on the main attractions and they looked through them. As darkness descended, they watched the city lights with delight.

There were two sites for them to inspect, both located on the railroad in the Grande Lisboa Sub-region in the municipality of Oeiras along the waterfront in southwest Lisbon (the English name for Portuguese Lisboa). It was the noon hour by the time Casper had finished tramping around both sites, looking at and checking every detail. All the buildings were in good shape and needed to be cleaned out of left behind machines, boxes, and crates. Casper was impressed with the access to railcar loading both sites had. It was an important factor. In the first few months, most of the parts would come from Iowa and the machines would be assembled here and then shipped by rail to places all over Europe. How things would change in the future was debatable. Jessica went where her husband went and came away with a detailed knowledge of both sites. Casper had spent time looking at the electrical supply facilities and finally wrote out a list of questions about the services and gave it to Mike Osborn with the directive to obtain the answers from the power provider. Luckily for Osborn, the Black & Black lawyer sent over to Lisbon had arrived with a lawyer from the Lisbon law firm and they were sitting in a car parked beside Davenport's rental. He walked over, explained to them what was going on, and gave them the written list plus a request to the Davenport lawyer to go to the USA Embassy and ask for guidance in business dealings with the Portuguese government. He watched the car back out and leave.

They sat outdoors at an open-air restaurant and ate a small lunch while discussing what had been seen. Casper wanted to know the floor space of each building, the size of the land each site was sitting on, a copy of the survey plats for both, ownership documents, debt records if any, and copies of agreements with the federal government and/or the City of Lisbon.

In the afternoon, the Port Authority took them on a tour of the waterfront to look at the ship loading and unloading facilities. The tour guide explained that Lisbon had recently completed construction of the dock facility they were touring and was determined to build more facilities to become the biggest port facility available in Europe. Combined with excellent rail shipping facilities, they were expecting to be among the lowest port costs available.

Next morning, they had breakfast with Ron, Mike, and the two lawyers and reviewed the many information requests Casper had generated. The meeting adjourned just before noon and the men took off on their tasks. Casper was in one of his thinking moods and it lasted almost an hour. Jessica suggested, "There are many old historic sites in Lisbon, we could tour some of them while we wait on the men to return."

"Have you something you would like to visit?"

"I made a list from the materials the floor porter gave us. Top of the list is Lisbon's Belem Tower and the Jeronimos Monastery which are UNESCO World Heritage Sites. There are others but I believe these two are more than enough to fill the rest of the day."

"We were close to both of those sites when the Port Authority took us to look at the ship docking provisions."

"True, but now I would like to see them up close and walk inside and learn their history."

Casper didn't answer; he picked up the phone and dialed for the concierge. "We wish to rent a limo with a driver who is knowledgeable about historic sites to drive us around this afternoon." He listened for a few minutes and agreed. Looking at his wife, he declared, "Madam Blakerly, your limo will be waiting in twenty minutes." It was a rush to change into casual clothing and footwear to make the walking and climbing easier. When they walked across the hotel lobby, the doorman was waiting for them. Their driver was most likely in his fifties and very knowledgeable. He kept pointing out historic sites and notable buildings. He drove them along the northern bank of the Tagus River and parked by a small bridge which gave access to the Belem Tower. When they exited the limo and stood there for a minute looking at the building which had been built in the early 1500s, the driver told them he would be there waiting for their return.

"Oh, Casper, look at the massive size of the tower! It must be a hundred feet high and looks like a solid block of limestone and I think there are four different floors. What magnificent architecture."

"It was built almost five hundred years ago to house canons to fight against ships trying to enter the harbor. You are looking at the decorations."

"Mr. Blakerly, it was built in four years starting in 1516." Jessica was staring at him with a hand on each hip. "If you would be so kind as to set your engineering diploma aside for a few minutes, we will have a much-improved tour."

"You win, Jess. I will try to behave myself for the rest of the day."

"Thank you, Mr. Blakerly. Now, when we cross this bridge, you can pay for two passes for us." He did and they got tickets and a touring manual.

They were entering on the northeastern corner of the lower bastion, where, along the riverside, there were openings in the limestone wall for seventeen canons with heavy stone arches isolating each window. Casper looked out and commented, "There is a great view of the entrance to the river and no place for a ship to hide, those gunners must have had a field day shooting at ships."

The oval-shaped ceiling was supported by half circle stone arches that were massive and decorated with carvings. In the center, the ceiling appeared to be twenty feet or more above the floor. Probably to provide ventilation when the canons were firing and creating clouds of partially burnt gun powder. The stone floor was large rectangles of stone that were clean and relatively smooth although in places the edges left little ledges to trip up a walker. Jessica looked at everything and often ran her hands over the stone surfaces, commenting to her husband about the work that had gone into shaping and setting each piece in place. When they walked out on the second floor of the bastion, it was open-air with a marvelous view over a low wall. There were a few chairs and the Blakerly's sat down and enjoyed the scenery. To the south, there was a river and ocean with ships passing by in both directions from the port facilities. In the other directions, was the city of Lisbon which combined new and old buildings everywhere within their sight? There was a magnificent view of the Jeronimos Monastery a short distance away which was also on their list to visit. They sat there for the best part of an hour, talking, looking, and Jessica taking pictures. The intricately carved stonework was amazing in its detail and must have taken days to carve. Casper found he was relaxing after seeing so much ancient history and workmanship which was new and unknown to him.

In the tower, the first floor was occupied by a vaulted cistern which warned visitors that the tower was mainly a daily living space. On the second floor, they found a sort of porch along the south side covered by laced and intricately carved stonework with a roof that slanted toward the river creating a very nice space to walk along or sit and look out. The stonework again intrigued Jessica for its beauty and the amazing talent needed to create it. The northeastern corner had a statue of Saint Vincent of Saragossa and in the northwest corner Archangel Michael, both set in niches. Jessica looked carefully at both statues and read what was written about them in the manual she had received. On the third floor, there were twin windows on the three walls away from the river. The fourth floor was encircled by a terrace enclosed by a low wall with pyramidal merlons which to Casper looked like small towers with steeply sloped stone roofs. This had obviously been a watch and lookout with views in all directions. Surprisingly, the roof of the fourth floor was a terrace. Casper could imagine army guards being stationed in these places to watch for an enemy trying to invade Lisbon.

They took the spiral staircase back to the ground floor. Casper checked the time and it was late afternoon, time to go to the hotel. He followed Jessica around as she looked again at the stonework. When she was satisfied, he took her arm and walked her to the rental limousine. On the car ride home, the driver asked if they had enjoyed their visit. Jessica answered, "It was a great tour, so much history and the workmanship is awe-inspiring. I must return there again sometime in the future."

When the car pulled up to the Olissipo Lopa Palace, Casper told the driver, "Thank you for a good tour, there are other places we want to go to so in a day or two we will request the car again." He held out a twenty USA dollar bill to the driver. When they entered the hotel, they stopped to talk to the concierge. Davenport's lawyer was at their side in a few moments to inform them they had met with the Commercial Attaché and were scheduled to meet again at nine a.m. in the morning. They were welcome to attend if they wanted to. Also, the American Ambassador had invited the five Americans for lunch in the embassy at one p.m. Casper thought about the invitation for a moment before telling the lawyer they would meet him at the embassy at nine.

Jessica and Casper ate dinner in their palace suite and were in bed at nine p.m.

Mike parked the rental car at the USA Embassy at 1600-081 Lisboa five minutes before nine a.m. and they walked to the modern-looking embassy building first occupied in 1983 and registered. Jessica took the seat across the table from the Commercial Attaché with two men on each side of her. Casper left a seat between them and where he chose to sit and prepared to listen. He could tell the Commercial Attaché was wondering why the president of Davenport was not heading the meeting for the company. Casper kept his face bland and smiled inside. The embassy staff started the meeting by describing how the Portuguese government liked to do business deals with companies from other countries. They reviewed the regulations and laws that were prevalent and reminded the Davenport people of several loopholes they should look for and not accept even though they would be presented seeming innocently. They were warned that if they had any doubt about a contract, to write to the US Attorney General and Davenport would receive an answer within thirty days. The embassy staff also talked about banking and mentioned the Export Import Bank of the United States. Casper listened and wrote down a list of items and contract pitfalls to avoid. He was not interfering but also was learning many new things.

At eleven fifty the meeting shut down and the attaché suggested they visit the washrooms before he took them to the dining room. Casper washed up and waited in the hallway for his wife. When the attaché showed them into the dining room, it was immediately apparent that Jessica was the only female in attendance and secondly that everyone, including the ambassador, was drinking wine. A waiter came with a tray of wine glasses and of course, offered first to Mrs. Blakerly who declined as did her husband. Ambassador Briggs arrived and started a conversation with Jessica and Casper. As usual, Casper was observing and the embassy had everything well organized. There were name cards at the settings and Jessica found herself sitting on the ambassador's right while Casper was at the other end of the table with the commercial attaché on his right. It was all carefully crafted to give Davenport information but also to gather details of the company and their intentions. Ambassador Everett Briggs had been appointed on April 1st, 1990 by President George Herbert Walker Bush and seemed quite competent to Casper. When the dinner ended, Davenport's lawyer had several items he wished to discuss with the embassy legal staff and he was left to attend his meeting. It was midafternoon, so Casper invited Ron and Mike to come to their hotel suite to discuss the meeting and schedule for the next day.

Jessica and Casper invited the two men to join them in the hotel dining room for dinner. The Portuguese were known to be great fishermen and the menu was loaded with choices in seafood. The men shared a bottle of great white wine and ate well. Jessica drank water and ate a large shrimp salad. They talked and laughed until near nine p.m. before the men departed and the Blakerly's retired to their suite. Before going to bed, Casper suggested, "Hopefully we will spend the morning going over the conditions and I will be able to break away for the afternoon to take my wife to tour the Jeronimos Monastery." Jessica kissed her husband and nodded happily.

The morning meeting moved along rather quickly. The lawyer had copies of the survey plates and notes from the power supplier explaining the details they were concerned with. Casper deliberately kept the meeting moving ahead. "We have the surveys and all the other data on the two locations. We need to decide which site will best suit our needs. Please, each of you, tell me your choice. Jessica, what is your opinion?" He listened carefully to all that was said and it came down to three choosing the smaller building and only Mike Osborn arguing for the largest. Casper sat with his fingers steepled as he considered and the other four watched him. In his mind, he ran over everything one last time. He looked up at them and smiled. "You are all good people and employees but ever since starting this company, I have carried the burden of always having the final say. Often, it is not easy. I have just reviewed all the data and discussions and in my mind, called a share-owners vote, and that dumb single share-owner said he had two reasons for telling me to buy the largest building. The reasons are: this is our entrance into Europe and hopefully the business will grow and surpass the capabilities of the largest building. Secondly, I believe the much larger area of unused land will be important to store machines awaiting shipment, supplies of steel, and parts coming in from Iowa."

There was silence for several minutes and Casper waited. Jessica broke the tension by laughing. "Husband, I have known for some time that you have vastly more knowledge and experience than I. You are a brave man to oppose your wife and these fine gentlemen." She clapped her hands and the men joined her. Casper smiled at her.

After the decision, the meeting moved along at a fast pace. The men all had assignments to work on and as they left, Casper picked up the phone and dialed the concierge number.

Chapter 22

The limo driver dropped them off on the far side of a huge garden where they stood quietly looking across at the immensity of the monastery. Jessica's eyes finally looked down to study the garden. "Oh, Casper, look at the size of the building, looking at it makes me feel so small and insignificant and we are far away from it. This huge garden is beautiful and being carefully trimmed and look at the size of the perfectly round fountain! It must be glorious to see at night with the lights on."

Her husband took her hand and led her across the street into the garden where they spent an hour looking at the fountain with all the carvings of various municipal coats of arms from around Portugal. The trees and hedges were kept well-trimmed. Finally, they walked out the other side of the garden and entered the monastery via the main entrance. Casper stopped her when the interior of the church became visible. Both their heads swiveled to allow their eyes to see everything, but there was so much to look at. Finally, Jessica's head tipped back and she stared at the ceiling. She gasped, "Casper, the high arched ceiling sitting on the octagonal pillars is beautiful, it is breathtaking! And, the only light available is coming through the stained glass windows. It makes me feel small like tiny bird droppings on the floor."

Casper felt the same. "Would you like to sit down in a pew while you study the interior?" She nodded and they moved to a pew. Jessica sat trying to absorb everything—an impossible task, she decided—and took out her little camera and snapped pictures. Everywhere she looked, she saw details she had missed before. In her mind, she thought about the construction beginning in January of 1501 and continuing until 1601 and of course there were many changes and additions over the years. She gasped, thinking this place is almost 500 years old. Where could they have found all the greatly talented workers needed to build this beautiful church? Every time her head turned, she spotted a detail she had missed before. It was over an hour before she suggested in an awed voice, "Let's walk forward and see more of this church."

Every stone column was carved with figures and many other items and the view kept changing as they moved forward. It was a slow trip simply because there was so much to look at and discuss. Finally, they came to the entrance to the cloister and Casper paid the entry fee so they could see the inner sanctuary, which they were told was considered to be the most beautiful in the world. The golden limestone walls seemed to glow in the light pouring through the stained glass windows. It seemed to Casper that every surface was ornately decorated with carvings of planets, animals, and religious themes. From the cloister, they entered the refectory where the monks who once lived, had gathered here to eat dinner and hear readings from the Bible. They walked up the steps to the choir balcony from which there was a fabulous view of the upper church. The balcony had large rose-colored windows and a statue of Christ along with polished wooden seats for the singers to occupy. They sat themselves down to better absorb the atmosphere and look at everything. Their thoughts were interrupted by a priest informing them it was five p.m. and the doors would be locked at five-thirty. By the time they made their way back, the front doors were locked and a priest smilingly let them out.

They hurried back across the large garden and found their car. The chauffeur smiled and welcomed them. On the short drive to the hotel, Jessica filled his ears with descriptions of what she had seen. Casper paid him for the car rental and added a large tip. He knew his wife would want to return to the monastery to see more.

Dinner was ordered from room service and Casper was prepared. He knew Jessica would be talking about all she had seen and speculating on many other items. He was amazed by her enthusiasm, awe, and wonder at what she had observed and learned during the afternoon. Also, she had a handful of documents and pictures, giving descriptions of many more famous carvings and paintings than they had seen.

*   *   *

Casper started the morning meeting by asking the Black & Black lawyer if all papers, titles, etc. had been checked on the property they were proposing to purchase. "Yes, sir, we have gone over all the papers, titles, and opinions of the seller and everything is in order."

"Fine, have you gentlemen discussed the asking price with our Realtor?"

"Yes, we have, Mr. Blakerly and yesterday afternoon we told him the asking price was too high. We gave him a list of the things we felt were wrong, such as the building not cleaned out of machines, crates, and junk. The yard is equally junky, the inside of the building needs to be painted, and we found the office space to be inadequate. The Realtor said he would talk to the owner's representative and inform him the asking price would have to be reduced substantially or his client would purchase a different property."

"Good and when do you expect to hear back from him?"

"We told him he had till noon today to come back and discuss the deal. As soon as we have discussed the deal with him, we will inform you."

"Thank you, now what about the government queries we wanted answers to?"

"We haven't heard back as yet. When this meeting is over, I

will phone my contact and inquire."

"Very good and are you satisfied with the answers received from the power company, hydro, telephones, port landings, and the permits to bring in supplies from the USA and to ship out of Portugal the products Davenport plans to produce? What about safety regulations, government-employed or hired inspectors, and taxes?"

"Mr. Blakerly, to all the first items you mentioned, we have written replies which seem satisfactory plus the safety regulations. On the question of inspectors and taxes, we are waiting on replies, although the government representative did say the government was pleased to have an American company wanting to start manufacturing in Portugal since they have very little in the way of companies doing such things."

Casper laughed and replied, "Let us hope their pleasure is sufficient to ease our way to a conclusion. When do you think you will have the paperwork all pulled together? I have been away from Iowa for over a week now and it is time to fly home."

"We will try very hard to have everything by this evening or in the morning. Would you be willing to sign the property purchase agreement on the condition the Davenport check cannot be deposited until we have everything that is still missing?"

Casper rubbed his jaw as he thought about it. He looked at Jessica and after a moment, she nodded. "Yes, I would be willing to do so under the provision the agreement and the Davenport check is left with our Portuguese legal firm with the understanding they cannot do anything with it unless they obtain a written approval signed by both me and J. Blakerly." Casper looked at his watch. "Time is approaching the noon hour. Ron, please accompany our lawyer this afternoon. Mike, I would like you to go with Jessica and myself to look over the property and outline what we will need to do with it."

* * *

With the limo parked across the driveway, the three of them walked to the gate and looked at the building. Casper asked, "Jess, do you have a pad of paper to write on?" She pulled a pad out of her briefcase and held up a pen. "Mike, when we close the purchase deal, the first thing to do is close this gate and put a big padlock on it and contract security people to guard the place. Fencing has to be inspected and any breaks or cut wire replaced so it is personnel tight. There is nothing in this yard worth keeping, so get it taken away. Now, let's go and look at the insides and see…"

Time was closing in on six p.m. when they finally decided there was nothing else to consider. Jessica said she would type up the notes and make copies for everyone and Casper said he was going to call United and reserve two seats to fly to Chicago on Friday. During the drive to the hotel, Casper invited Mike to join them for dinner.

It was a happy time because they all believed the purchase deal would go ahead. Mike ordered a steak, Casper told the waiter he wanted lobster, and Jessica asked for a shrimp salad. Mike got red wine and Casper white, while Jessica stuck to her water. While eating, they discussed the deal and no one suggested any changes or additional items. Jessica looked at her cellphone and checked messages while the two men ordered ice cream and refills on the wine. It was after nine when Mike said good night and the Blakerly's retired to their room. Casper called United as he had stated while Jessica typed her notes into her laptop. The two of them crawled into bed, snuggled up to each other, and fell asleep.

* * *

Casper was pleased to find that all the paperwork was in place with the exception of a letter from the minister in charge of commerce which was promised to be delivered by noon. All that was left to be discussed was the purchase price to buy the property. The lawyer phoned the Realtor and asked him to join them where they were meeting in the Portuguese law firm's offices. He also asked their Portuguese lawyer to sit in. It took the meeting over an hour to talk and consider what the Realtor was telling them before Casper asked him to leave the room. "Well, folks, what do you think?" He turned and looked at the local lawyer. "Do you like the price they are asking on the property?"

In his accented English, he replied, "Mr. Blakerly the owner agreed to reduce the asking price by thirty-five percent, which is a large drop. It is probably happening since the property has been listed for sale for almost two years. It is my opinion, you have negotiated a very reasonable price and Davenport should find it working well in their planning."

Casper nodded and looked around. "Anyone else have an opinion they wish to offer?" No one spoke up. "Well, I take your silence to mean you all agree." They smiled back at him. "Okay, call the Realtor back in and we will fix up the purchase offer so he can go and get the seller to sign it." The lawyers checked the offer agreement over and while Jessica and Casper signed it, Ralph Smith wrote out a check which he and Casper signed. The local lawyer held the check while the Realtor went to present the purchase offer to his client, promising to be back within an hour. When the door opened and the Realtor entered, Casper looked at the clock. It had taken sixty-five minutes. The legal firm got the check and the original of the offer, Casper got a copy to take to Iowa, and Mike Osborn received a copy to use in taking over the property.

When the Realtor and the local lawyer left the room, Casper invited everyone to come to the hotel and join him for dinner.

Next day, the Blakerly's packed their suitcases and took the limousine to the airport. The plane departed on time and they settled down to wait on arrival in Chicago.

*   *   *

Casper used the weekend to catch up on farm activities. The cows had finished dropping new calves and Casper wandered around with Fred looking at the newcomers while Bess, the farm's brown and white Collie, wandered around looking at cows. Out of two hundred and ninety three cows, there were only five that hadn't dropped a calf. "Fred, how many head of cattle do we have on the farm?"

Fred pulled his notebook out of a pocket and found the page he wanted. "Right now, we have two hundred and ninety-three cows, two hundred and eighty-eight new calves, and seventy-three steers to market in the fall which comes to six hundred and fifty-four animals in total. Along with those steers, there are five cows that didn't drop calves; they might as well go to market."

Casper laughed. "Selling seventy-eight animals will put us under six hundred to graze. Hell, Fred, I always figured we were farming and here you have turned this place into a cattle ranch."

"Guess you can think of it that way. Me, I always viewed them as two separate operations; a large grain farm operation and a fair-sized cattle operation. Something we need to think about is grazing; right now, we got a little over two acres of grass for each animal. Another year of growth like just happened and we will have a crick in our backs."

As he paced around thinking, Casper kept an eye on the cows. Some of them could get downright mean if you got too close to their calves, but usually Bess provided the defense needed. Finally, he walked back. "Fred, we better drill those two water wells we wanted here on this river section and put up a metal covered hay storage building for winter feeding. Could be we can even irrigate some of the land with well water. Have you heard of anyone who has grassland for sale?"

"Haven't heard of any for sale, maybe I should take a drive up along the river for a few miles and talk to the landowners."

"Do that, Fred, and if you scare up anything, we will take a look at a deal. If you don't find anything, we best call that Realtor we used a couple of times and ask him to look around." Casper rubbed his chin. "You know, I have always thought about getting land close to us. Maybe we should give a little thought to land a few miles away and move the cattle back and forth with a trucker."

Fred smiled. "We could buy a cattle liner to pull behind our semi."

"Hell of a good idea, Fred. You know there is a big world out there, even when you get beyond Clinton County. You got time to drive past some of the grain land and have a look at it?" The two men stopped several times to walk on the land and feel the soil for temperature. When they arrived back in the farmyard, the air drill was hooked up to the tractor. "When we going to start seeding?"

"We are ready, just waiting for the soil to become a mite warmer and we will start planting soybeans. This farm is going to be a busy place in the next few weeks." Casper thanked him for the tour and walked to the house, he had reports and recommendations to study on the Portugal deal and the planning for the next few months.

Jessica was vacuuming the rugs when Casper arrived. She turned off the machine. "Casper, we need to go shopping for groceries, will you take me?"

"Certainly, honey. I will go and get the F150 out of the garage and pick you up." Jessica looked at herself in a mirror and patted her hair. Her waistline was starting to protrude but was still not greatly apparent. She reflected for a moment and decided to wear a lightweight jacket. Casper drove to DeWitt and parked in front of the food store. He pushed the cart as they patrolled the aisles and Jessica took items off the shelves. There were a few other farmers in the store with their wives and Casper talked to each of them, mostly about seeding crops. They were almost finished when a farmer Jessica had never seen before stopped his cart beside Casper. "Mr. Anderson, how good to see you. It has been a year or two since I last ran into you." Casper noticed he had lost weight and didn't seem all that steady on his feet.

"Good to see you also, Casper. Is this your new wife?"

Casper grinned. "It sure is, Mr. Anderson. Say hello to Jessica." Jessica shook hands with Anderson.

"Now, Mrs. Blakerly, your husband has always called me Mr., but such is not necessary, my name is Harold and I would appreciate you using that name."

"Certainly, Harold, it is very nice to meet you; are you a farmer in the area?"

"Yes, I am, Jessica. My farm is several miles east of where you live. I first got to know your husband many years ago when he sold me a fencepost pounder and started calling me Mr. Anderson at that time. If my memory serves me correctly, your husband had just started university. I apologize for interrupting your shopping and must confess to doing it because I wish to talk to Casper."

Jessica smiled. "May I suggest you two men go and sit in the chairs at the front entrance to talk while I finish my shopping?" She watched the two men walk away before she continued down the aisle. When she got into line for the checkout, Jessica glanced at the men and they had their heads down in a serious discussion. Jessica wondered what they could be talking about as she started unloading her cart. She chatted with the clerk while the items were scanned and put into Jessica's cloth shopping bags. Unexpectedly, Casper showed up at her side, pulled out a wad of folded money and proceeded to pay the bill. Jessica glanced around and Mr. Anderson was gone. Casper pushed the cart out to the truck and loaded the groceries into the truck box, pushed the cart to the storage, and came back to open the door for her.

Inside the truck, he told her, "I invited Harold to eat dinner with us at the deli." He grinned at her. "He has asked me if we would be interested in purchasing his farm." Jessica's mouth fell open, shocked. Her mind kicked into gear as she stared through the windshield. Always so much going on around her husband and she had no doubt he would look at the Anderson farm but, my goodness, the farm was not small now. She wondered how large the Anderson farm would turn out to be. She didn't say a word on the short drive to the deli.

It was a bit on the early side for dinner so when they entered the deli, they were the only customers. Both Joe and Phillis came to greet them. Casper asked, "We need a table for three, Harold Anderson is coming to join us."

In their seats, Phillis asked, "How you doing with that baby you told me about?"

"Very well thank you, Phillis, my waist is starting to bulge a little but otherwise I feel fine. By any chance, are you making your special dish of meat and vegetables?"

Phillis laughed. "It is not on the menu right now but if that is what you want, I will be happy to make it for you."

Casper suggested, "Here comes Harold so we best wait to order." Phillis hurried away as Harold walked slowly to the table. Casper pulled out a chair for him and got him settled. Joe came with menus and glasses of ice water.

Joe grinned at Casper. "You can order anything on the menu and my chef told me she is also prepared to make her special meat and vegetable dinner if you want it." Joe turned away.

"Harold, you order whatever you would like. My wife and I will order the chef's special which we like."

Their guest smiled at them. "Are you having the special, Jessica?" She nodded. "Fine if you are having the special, so will I." Casper looked at Joe and held up three fingers. Joe smiled broadly and went into the kitchen. Harold continued, "Jessica I have told Casper I am planning to sell my farm and asked him if he would be interested in discussing a deal."

Jessica's eyes switched to look at Casper but her face didn't change. "So, that is what you two men were talking about. Do tell me, Harold, where is your farm located relative to ours?"

Harold smiled. "I live about ten miles east of you near a small town named McCausland. You live north of the river and I live south of it. The roads between us are very good. Will you be coming with your husband to look at my farm?"

Jessica laughed gaily. "If he doesn't invite me to come with him, I will give him a terrible beating with my broom."

Harold smiled. "You are a wife just like mine was until I lost her three years ago. When you come to visit with me, I will give you a paper that lists our lands, buildings, machinery, etc. and I apologize for not having a copy of the list along with me."

"No need for you to apologize, Harold. My husband will no doubt want to drive to your farm tomorrow, which will be soon enough." Joe came with three plates of the chef's special and went away to get hot sauce for them. They began to eat dinner and Jessica asked, "Please tell me about McCausland."

Harold nodded. "A small town with around three hundred people living there, some of whom work in Davenport, and I have heard the others have a variety of jobs around the area. Mostly friendly people occupy the town and they seem to like living out in the country rather than the busy city. Occasionally, some of them come out to my farm to go fishing in the summer and hunt for elk and other meat providers in the fall. Was a time when I knew most of them but as I grow older, it seems the people I knew have either died or moved away. Not a place for you to go shopping for groceries."

Quiet descended as they focused on eating until Harold added, "This here DeWitt is a good place. My wife and I came here for years to do her shopping. Can't say we ever discovered Big Joe's Deli, my wife would have liked coming here. Good food."

* * *

During the drive home, Casper and Jessica discussed what Harold told them. From home, Casper dialed Fred's phone and told him they were going to look at Harold's farm at noon the next day and he was welcome to come along. Casper retired to his office and worked on the documents while Jessica finished her vacuuming and cleaning.

It was one-thirty when they drove into Harold's yard and it was a nice yard although a bit rundown. In the house, Harold had the land surveys, title deeds, and assorted papers listing machinery, cattle, buildings, and other items laid out on the kitchen table. As Casper expected, everything was paid for. Harold gave a verbal rundown of the farm. "These buildings are sitting on a half section of good grain land on which we have been growing corn and soybeans for several years. There are two quarters of hay land, some of which we have put into grain now and again. When you go north from this house, you are getting near the river. Most of the hay land could be farmed but the land has rolls so I have usually grown hay. Besides these four quarters, there are three others of pasture along the river. Altogether there are seven quarters, except an odd place where the river cuts off a few acres. My cattle herd is down to one hundred and twenty head of mixed breeds. All the land is tight fenced," his face broke into a smile, "thanks to a post-pound-er Casper sold me some fifteen years ago. Any questions?"

Casper replied, "Thanks, Harold. We will have questions to ask you later on. Can we go for a drive and have a look around?"

Harold stood up. "Doubt all four of us can be comfortable in a pickup, Casper. Why don't you drive my truck and Jessica and Fred can follow us around?" The two trucks toured the black soil grain land which would need seeding very soon and then the hay land. As he had told them, the hay land was more rolling but looked like it was producing good hay crops. The three quarters of pasture were lower in elevation down toward the Wapsipini-con River and there were patches of trees which would be good shelter for cattle. As Harold had said, the fences were tight and kept cleared of bushes and trees. Harold asked, "You interested in buying the cattle herd?"

"My cattle are all registered Black Angus, wouldn't be wise for me to mix them together."

"Figured that, Casper. If you buy the place, the cattle can go to an auction market to sell. You ready to go back to the farm site?" Casper nodded and turned toward the buildings. "Got some darn good buildings and steel granaries you should have a look at." Casper was busy thinking and Harold kept quiet on the trip back. Harold went into the house while the three visitors toured around the yard. He watched through a window and smiled to himself. He hadn't told Casper of the talk he'd had with his old friend Ted Arson and how he had heard nothing but positive comments on how Casper had treated him. Ted said Casper did his own evalua-tion of what value the land had to his operation and made his offer to purchase based on that. Land prices hadn't moved much in two years, so Harold had figured out what the offer to him was likely to be. He would wait and see. He had a large brown envelope filled with copies of all the paperwork which Casper could take away and work with.

It was late afternoon when they came to the house. "Harold thanks for the tour and your description of everything. Alright if we come back? There will be things we will want to look at."

"No problem, Casper. You come whenever it suits you and go ahead whether I am around or not." He picked up the large envelope and handed it to Casper. "There is a copy of everything lying out on the table inside this envelope. If you need more information, please contact me."

Casper held out his hand and they shook. "Thanks for coming over to talk to me yesterday and we will be back." Harold shook hands with Jessica and Fred. He sat in the kitchen and looked out a window to watch them drive out of the yard.

* * *

The F150 was well under the speed limit as Casper drove home talking about the deal. "The cultivated land looked very good to me, not really any different than the half we bought from Ted Arson. What did you think, Fred?"

"I agree, it is good grain land, maybe a little lower than Ted's and being so near the river it may get more rain. Much of the hay land has a good roll in it so haying will be a little tougher and there could be problems with the cut hay drying out even. The good side is buying the hay land would more than double our hay acreage and solve one of our looming problems."

Casper laughed. "Right you are, Fred. Jess, do you agree with what Fred said?"

"Mostly. I like the grain land and believe it would be a good asset for the farm. The hay land is less attractive. If we buy it, Fred can do the haying, I'd probably get dizzy going up and down those rolls."

They all laughed. "We haven't talked about the grassland and the buildings. Seems to me we should go back tomorrow afternoon and take a closer look at their value. Jess and I will list the acreage the surveys show for each quarter and especially on the grasslands we will have to decide if the numbers are correct. Beyond that, we will have to decide what our offer to purchase should have for numbers."

Monday morning, Mrs. Sparks was waiting for them. She was happy to have Casper back but she hugged Jessica. "How are you feeling?"

Jessica giggled. "Very well, thank you, but I am about to bust out of my regular clothes. My husband keeps me so busy with Davenport's affairs there has been no time to enter a store."

"You must file a complaint with human resources, and they will straighten Casper out." She put a frown on her face and looked at Casper. "You are not being a good husband." Casper smiled, nodded, and walked into his office where he found Mrs. Sparks had his work all lined up for him. He unpacked his briefcase and sat down. When he looked out, he could see Jessica and Mrs. Sparks in her office and it seemed obvious Jessica was telling her about Portugal. He settled down to sign checks.

Harold Anderson watched Casper's half-ton drive through the farmyard and enter the nearest hayfield. He smiled to himself, it made him happy that Casper was doing his usual thorough checking and also was a strong indicator that an offer would be coming. It was nearing four o'clock when the truck parked in the yard and they entered the barn, checked the machine storage buildings, and went to the steel grain storage. Harold settled back in his favorite rocking chair and opened his book again. From his vantage point in the kitchen, he could look out over his farmyard. His stomach was

313

telling him the time to eat had arrived when they drove away.

The phone rang at noon on Tuesday and it was Casper asking to come to the farm and discuss the Offer to Purchase he had put together. At two p.m., Casper, Jessica, and a lawyer who said his name was Wilford Black arrived. Harold poured coffee for them and they sat in the kitchen. Harold settled into his rocking chair. He glanced at the offer price and knew they had a deal. He settled down and read every word. All the quarters of land were listed with acreage and use description and also included were all the buildings, fences, water wells, and fuel storage. A special paragraph excluded the herd of cattle, farm machinery, and personal items. He was aware they were watching him as he read. He leaned back and looked out the window for a long minute before his head turned and he looked at the lawyer. "Mr. Black, in this document I see Casper has done his usual careful job of listing what makes up this farm. He has long been known for the way he does things. Did he tell you I made my first deal with him when he was just starting university?"

Wilford frowned, Jessica and Casper, laughed. "No, he did not tell me."

Harold laughed. "He was just a kid, although I must admit a very intelligent one, and was starting to build fencepost pounders. I purchased the very first one he sold and now he sells them by the hundreds all over the world. It disappoints me that he does not want the pounder back now."

Wilford frowned again. "Are you suggesting the pounder be included in the list of items being sold in this document?" Harold nodded. "As you wish, Mr. Anderson, are there any other points you wish to discuss?"

"Just one, Mr. Black, I do not like the price of $903,600 dollars."

Wilford's face twitched. "May I ask what price you have in

mind?"

"Certainly, you can, Mr. Black. I was born in this house and have lived here all my life. The time has come for me to sell the farm. Casper came along asking if he could look the place over which he did very thoroughly. In fact, I haven't talked to my lawyer nor have I hired a Realtor. Casper saved me several thousand dollars. I want the price changed to a nice even $900,000." He smiled, "Always did like round numbers."

Wilford had prepared himself for a hefty increase. "Mr. Anderson, may I confirm that you are asking us to reduce the offering price?"

"Yes, I am, Mr. Black and if he wishes, Casper can tow the fencepost pounder home today, which will save one change for you."

Wilford shook his head in wonder and took out a black ink pen to make a change in the offer number. Harold signed as did Casper and Jessica. Casper wrote out a check for the offer price, they signed, and Wilford put it away in his briefcase. "It will take my firm a couple of days to do all the paperwork before the check will be delivered to you."

"Thank you, Mr. Black, just give the check to Casper and he will bring it to me."

Chapter 23

When they arrived home, Jessica made tea and they sat together in Casper's office to discuss the land purchase. Jessica fought to contain herself but didn't succeed. "Casper, do you realize you didn't say a word during the negotiation? Your old friend Harold was having fun playing with Wilford and kept it up as long as he could."

"Yes, he did, Jess and I knew early in the conversation he was going to go for the deal. Poor Wilford hasn't spent much time out in the real world and can't read between the words. So, I sat back and let Harold have his fun."

Jessica broke out laughing again. "All the time we sat there, I felt like laughing and that would have spoiled Harold's joke, wouldn't it?" Together, they laughed and Casper put his arm around her and squeezed. After they calmed and returned to normal, Jessica proposed, "Let's sit here and make a list of all the land of Blakerly farms." Casper opened a desk drawer and brought out a Scott County map which started on the south side of the Wapsipinicon River and the Anderson Farm was in. He had marked their existing lands using three different colors. He quickly colored in the new purchase and spread out the map. Jessica picked up a pencil and a fourteen-inch pad of paper and Casper called out the name of the former owner and the acres. She was making three columns, owned, rented, and total. They slowly worked their way through all the grain, hay, and pasture lands with Casper ticking off each quarter with a pencil as he went over the map.

When Jessica added up the numbers, it was staggering. She had 3156 acres of grain land, 580 acres of hay land, and 1635 acres of pasture land, and there were 49 acres of wasteland that was not farmable. The total came to 5420 acres. "How many head of stock do we have?"

Casper smiled and told her, "There are 654 cows and calves, of which 142 will be sold in the fall. Also, there are five riding horses on the farm. If my memory serves me correctly, there is also a brown and white collie dog that is the same age as my wife."

Jessica's face lit up. "If what you say is true, I am the only pregnant six-year-old human in the country."

In the morning, Casper informed Fred the deal with Harrold Anderson had been completed. Fred thought about it for a few minutes. "We now have some 3156 acres to seed. This morning, we are starting on soy and we will seed all the acres we want around here before moving to the Anderson farm where we will plant soy and switch to corn before we come back here to continue with corn."

*   *   *

The expansion and start-up of a plant in Portugal soon forced changes in how Davenport Machinery Inc. operated at the corporate level. You couldn't just open the international plant and go home, you had to operate it, provide operating management, marketing, purchasing, and accounting. Casper faced up to the changes and backed off from his heavy day-to-day involvement in the Iowa plant while Jessica had direct responsibility for corporate affairs, and she dug in. The first large change was the promotion of Ned Ambrose to Vice President of Manufacturing with responsibility for the current and future plants. Casper watched warily as Ned and Jessica mapped out their strategy and promoted and hired the people they wanted. The changes were easy enough in Davenport but a search was necessary in Portugal to find a man with hands-on experience and who spoke Portuguese and English. It was two months before a Manager of Operations was hired and they started adding assembly line personnel. Shipments of parts from Davenport began to flow to Lisbon and that emphasized the need for marketing in Europe.

Ted Greig was promoted to Vice President of Marketing and with help from Jessica, he reorganized and expanded. It was vital to have marketing personnel in Europe and additional marketers in North America. The hard reality was they had to be dispersed and couldn't all reside in Davenport or Lisbon, the market areas were widely separated. Greig promoted one of his people to be a marketer in Davenport and began to lease space in Oregon, Maine, and Virginia. More would be added when Casper became comfortable with these first ones. An experienced marketer was hired to work out of Lisbon to get dealers and distribution organized. Ted Greig accompanied him to visit three dealers who had taken Davenport machinery in the past. One was located in England, one in Germany, and the third in Austria. Following would be all the other countries in Europe. Potentially, it was a huge market area but Casper wasn't going to incur the cost of setting up dealers everywhere so growth would be coordinated as production and sales grew.

Shelbie Cox, who headed personnel, sent one of her people to Lisbon to oversee installing their computer systems and process new people being hired, he would also temporarily oversee paychecks to the personnel for Ron Smith until financial people were put in place. He was also handling local purchasing for Mike Osborn until the need for people was obvious.

Ron Smith, VP Financial, and Mike Osborn, VP Purchasing, rotated in and out of Lisbon supervising the remodeling and equipping of the Lisbon plant for two months until Ned Ambrose found the man he needed to manage the plant. Even after the hire, they continued to watch until the new man learned Davenport's ways of doing business. The Lisbon plant had a large sign on the front of the building reading 'DAVENPORT' with smaller words in Portuguese 'Lisbon, Grande Lisboa'. The yard fence was tight, security strict, and safety rules posted before the first employee was hired. Inside the building had been cleaned of trash, painted, and assembly machines and tools put into place. The office space was reconditioned and painted and the men purchased desks, chairs, computer systems, and many other items for the workers; both workers loaned from the US or hired locally. Casper and Jessica flew in once each month to see how the process was going, approved and changed plans, and never stayed more than two days at a time.

It was a fast-moving and tiring process and as he planned another trip to Lisbon, his wife told him she wouldn't be going. He hadn't recognized their baby was due within a month. She kissed him goodbye and told him to hurry back. Her mother was going to come to stay with them and would arrive in two weeks. Jessica was in the office every day working on all the affairs of the company and overseeing the expansions and plant production. The year-end financials had been an eye-opener for her, company profits were very high and half was set aside for company use and half was paid as a dividend to Casper's holding company, Mid-West Holdings, which already had tens of millions in cash and investments. Suddenly, she realized they were rich in money and assets, even though they lived like their farm neighbors, who always treated them as belonging. Her husband had not changed one wit from when he was a kid. She sat at her desk thinking for some time before deciding she had a husband who was most unusual and also very wise. After the surprise of her discovery was over, she had no desire to spend all the money, the only thing she would like was a new house to raise her children in and, when the time came, to give them the best education they were qualified for. She smiled thinking, *'The first child is still three weeks away and here I am thinking about education twenty years from now.'*

* * *

Casper paced around the hospital waiting room while his mother-in-law, Elizabeth Hornsbee, sat watching him. She had never seen him like this, he was always so calm and quiet and now he couldn't sit still as he waited for the baby to arrive. Jessica had been in labor for over seven hours and the baby had to arrive soon. They had driven Jessica to the hospital just after three a.m. Finally, Elizabeth stood up and asked Casper if he would like a cup of coffee. "Do you want to come with me?"

"Oh, yes, I will walk with you. Do you know where to go?"

Elizabeth smiled. "We will find coffee just down the hall." They walked out and were standing at the counter waiting for their coffee when Mrs. Sparks arrived.

"Good morning, Elizabeth. How is our girl doing?"

"The nurses say everything is fine."

Mrs. Sparks held up her briefcase. "There are documents in here that Casper must sign if he will agree to sit down and take the time to look them over." Casper frowned and both women smiled at him. Once Casper got started, he was distracted from Jessica and hurried through the papers, signing each as he finished reading it.

Elizabeth whispered to Mrs. Sparks, "This is the best thing you could have done, he has something to occupy his mind and not be worrying." They smiled and continued to watch Casper.

A quiet voice behind the ladies said, "Ahem."

Their heads turned and the nurse said in a loud voice, "I am here to tell you Jessica has just delivered a fine-looking seven-pound six-ounce son for the Blakerly family." Casper's head came up and he stared at the nurse. He jumped to his feet. "A son! I have a son!" He clapped his hands and hugged each of the ladies before asking, "How is my wife, is she okay?"

"Your wife is very happy and waiting for you to come to see her." Casper took off along the hallway. The nurse smiled and told the ladies, "Please give us a few minutes and then I will take you to see the baby."

When they entered the hospital room, Casper was sitting in an armchair with a blanket-wrapped bundle in his arms. Jessica was tired but she was smiling at him. His eyes were fixed on the tiny face and he didn't seem to recognize anything else around him. They watched for a few minutes before the nurse walked over and gently told Casper, "Mr. Blakerly, it is time to give your baby to his mother." The nurse laid the baby on his mother's body and very soon she had him nursing.

Casper kissed his wife and patted her head. "Is there anything you want? Is there anything I can go and get for you?"

Jessica shook her head no. Grandma Hornsbee was aching to hold the baby and look at him as Casper paced around the room. Mrs. Sparks came and looked closely at the baby before asking, "Have you picked a name for him?"

Casper stopped pacing and looked at Jessica, his face furrowed in thought. He started to say something and she held up her hand. "We will talk about names after I have a good sleep." Casper nodded. When the baby stopped nursing and went to sleep, Jessica closed her eyes. Casper took Mrs. Hornsbee with him and they went to a florist shop and ordered flowers to be sent to the hospital room. It was now early afternoon and Casper didn't feel like going to the office. He dropped Mrs. Hornsbee off at the hospital and drove to the farm. It was early September and combining was in full swing. The men were almost finished straight cutting soybeans and Casper climbed into a combine, sat in the driver's seat, and took off up the field, combining soy. He was bursting with happiness and driving the combine cleared his mind, he suddenly found himself back to normal. He dumped into the semi twice before he climbed down and told the men he had a brand new son. They all shook his hand and congratulated him.

Fred informed Casper, "When this field is finished, we will move over to Anderson's. Looks likely we are going to get a good crop on the new land."

Casper drove to the hospital. The unnamed baby was in the nursery with Grandma keeping an eye on him, Jessica was sleeping with her room full of flowers. Casper sat in the armchair and closed his eyes. When Grandma came in, she saw everyone sleeping and went out, silently closing the door.

Two days after the birth, the doctor told Jessica she could take the baby home. Jessica smiled and told him, "We have named him Jeffery Edward Blakerly, thank you for looking after me and the baby." Casper drove Elizabeth's SUV with Jessica and Jeffery in the backseat. The rear of the vehicle was full of clothes, gifts, and Jessica's suitcase. Gramma sat in the front with Casper and when they arrived, she carried Jeffery into the house while Jessica and Casper unloaded the SUV.

In the morning, Casper went to the office without his wife and he missed her but he stuck out the day. Five days later, Jessica carried Jeffery from the SUV into Davenport's offices and stopped constantly to let people peek at him. When she and her mom stepped off the elevator, Mrs. Sparks came running to see the baby. Casper looked up at the noise and grinned as he walked out of his office to greet his son.

* * *

Davenport had installed a computer check-signing system that automatically printed Ron Smith's and Mike Osborn's signatures on the checks. Another task had been taken off Casper's shoulders. The hard reality was another layer of senior management had been established due to the necessity of having a system that could operate fast-growing production and shipping of machines, including a new line of tractors and accessories. The fifty-horse tractor was selling well and hundred-horse tractors were just starting to be produced. Marketing had hired engineers to design and draft production drawings to keep up and now they also needed Portuguese language versions as well. Already, plans were being discussed to decide where another assembly plant should be built. Casper and Jessica found themselves overlooking the larger corporation, setting policy, directing planning, keeping an eye on finances and a dozen other things as well as traveling.

Christmas was around the corner and baby Jeffery was three months old. Jessica looked around to check on the baby who was asleep with his nanny sitting in a nearby chair reading a book. She stood up and walked to Casper's office and knocked on the door as she entered. He leaned back in his high-backed chair as Jessica sat down across the desk from him. "Mr. Blakerly, our son is now three months old." Casper smiled and nodded. "Do you realize we have not taken him to meet my family and the Christmas season is nearly upon us?"

Casper laughed loudly. "So, my darling wife wants to take a Christmas holiday."

"You are correct, but even more important, I wish for you to purchase a new SUV to give me for Christmas so I can safely haul our son on trips. I will leave the selection of the vehicle to you as long as it is large, heavy, safe, and is either blue or red." Casper stared as she smiled at him, stood up and walked back to her office, and Casper's eyes watched her go.

He tapped his pen on the desk and murmured, "Damn, now why didn't I think of this? She is right, his grandfather still hasn't seen Jeffery." Casper stood up and walked to Mike Osborn's office. "Mike, do you have someone on your staff familiar with the car dealers in Davenport and their SUVs?"

"Yes, I do. Does this mean you are going to give up that worn-out half-ton you drive?"

Casper started to get angry and then saw the humor and laughed. "I had not thought of doing so. Damn, Mike, you may have a very good idea there. My wife has informed me she wants a new SUV for Christmas and it has to be large, heavy, safe, and either blue or red. I will add on my own initiative that it must be loaded with bells and whistles. To follow up on your suggestion, all our personal vehicles are Fords so talk to Ford Dealers first and it will be Blakerly Farms Inc. who is the buyer and we will want one in blue and one in red. Jessica can make her choice and I will drive the one she doesn't want." Mike watched as his boss turned and walked out of his department. He couldn't help himself, he laughed. All the years he had worked for Casper, the absentmind-edness of his boss always amazed him.

As he walked down the hall, Mike remembered the agent he wanted would be in a staff meeting. He knocked on the door and went in. There were six people in the meeting and they looked at him. "Gentlemen, I apologize for interrupting your meeting but I have two important items that must be purchased as expeditiously as possible. As you are all aware, the Blakerly's have a new baby. Casper just left my office after informing me his wife asked him to purchase a new Ford SUV which has to be large, heavy, safe, and either blue or red. He also told me the vehicle is to have all the bells and whistles. He ended by telling me to get one of each color and Jessica can choose the one she wants and he will drive the other color. Oh, by the way, the two vehicles will be purchased by Blakerly Farms Inc." Mike laughed again and the six men joined in. "We have all been working hard the last few months and I thought we could all use a good laugh. Thomas, you do the truck purchasing around here so this is your project. Remember these two people own the company. They are great people, friendly, hardworking, and have very large decisions to consider, as a consequence, many of the regular everyday things just slide right past them. We are all lucky to be working for two people who are this way. Thomas, you keep me informed of your progress, it is unlikely Casper will inquire but be damn sure Jessica will. Okay, guys, back to work." Mike closed the door behind him.

The six purchasing men sat there with smiles on their faces. The chair of the meeting laughingly said, "We just got a good laugh we all needed. We are lucky to be working for the Blakerly's. Thomas, you are excused from this meeting—go and get started on your side project."

Thomas went to his office, donned his suit coat, and drove to the Ford Dealer where they purchased and leased mostly trucks. He walked into the fleet department to the office of the man he always dealt with. The meeting was over when Thomas left after thirty-five minutes, leaving the fleet man fully informed. These vehicles were for the heads of Davenport Machinery and they were a large customer. The dealership needed to do a first-class job or the truck business might be endangered. He went to his boss and together they went to the general manager, who decided he would discuss the SUVs with the owners of the dealership.

* * *

Casper arrived back in his office and felt uneasy. After thinking about it, he got his steel-toed boots and hardhat out of storage and dressed for the plant. He needed to get back to the basics. He walked through the old plant and talked to several of the long-time employees. Next, he crossed over to the new plant and walked slowly along the assembly lines. He found it interesting but was sorry because he knew so few of the new employees. The longer time men smiled and waved to him and he stopped several times to talk. It had been months since he'd last done this and found himself enjoying getting back to the basics and having a chance to talk to people who had worked with him for years. He wasn't going to all parts of the plant and hurried through shipping, receiving, raw material storage, and came to the offices. Hiram Weinstein was meeting with several people so he waved and kept going. Suddenly, he was face to face with Ralph Shaw. Casper laughed happily as they shook hands. "Damn it is good to see you, Ralph. Where are you headed to now?"

Ralph laughed also. "It is noon so I was going to eat my lunch."

"Lunch, is it lunchtime already?" Casper looked puzzled for a moment and then said, "By damn, Ralph, where is your truck? You drive me and I will take you out to lunch so we can catch up on things." Casper directed him to Ma's Restaurant, sat at his special table, and ordered his favorite cheeseburger and root beer. Ralph ordered the same. Their conversation roamed over many things and Casper laughed several times at funny little stories. They were an hour late getting back after the plant's lunch break. Casper was back to his old self and walked with Ralph to his desk and they drew sketches of an idea Ralph had.

His old lively step had returned, his head was high, and he walked back to his office feeling light-footed. It felt like a whole new day. The hardhat and boots went into storage and Casper dug into the contracts he was checking out.

* * *

Casper and Ned Ambrose flew to Portugal and were going to take a tour with the new marketing man to the dealers who were selling Davenport's machinery across Europe. The plane left on Sunday and they expected to be back on Friday.

Monday afternoon, Mrs. Sparks walked into Jessica's office and told her, "A Thomas Westbury from purchasing phoned and wanted to meet with you. I told him to come."

"Thank you, did he say what he was coming here about?"

"No, he did not and frankly I did not ask him."

"Okay, you bring him in when he gets here." Jessica's head went back to the pile of paper on her desk. Maybe, just maybe she could clean it up today. Casper had phoned her early in the evening and he was in Lisbon and would be spending the first day at the plant meeting with the people and especially getting to know the new ones hired since his last trip. Lately, everything had been running smoothly in Lisbon since the plant had been through the routine several times. She would dearly love to go back to Lisbon for a few days of holidays to continue getting familiar... Jessica shook her head and sighed. *'Stop daydreaming and get back to work'.* She started reading a proposal from a company Davenport had never done business with in the past. On the second page, she read and reread a paragraph she couldn't understand. She ran a yellow highlighter over the words and set it aside with a note attached to have the lawyers review it. Her head came up when there was a knock on the door.

Mrs. Sparks offered, "Jessica, this is Thomas Westbury from our purchasing department."

Jessica came to her feet and walked around the desk. "Pleased to meet you, Thomas, come and sit down." She walked back to her chair and Thomas's eyes stared. *'By gosh, she is a beautiful woman, tall and slim, and very smart.'* "What did you want to talk to me about, Thomas?"

Thomas hesitated a moment while he got his head back to normal. "Casper came to purchasing a week ago and asked us to look for an SUV for you. We have looked at several and have two set aside for you to look at."

Jessica's face lit up and she sat back in her chair. "Where are they, Thomas? And when would be a good time to see them?"

"The dealer phoned a few minutes ago and suggested nine a.m. tomorrow. Would that work for you?"

Jessica picked up her daybook and checked. "Nine a.m. will be fine but I must be back here by eleven. Can you pick up Mrs. Sparks and me at eight-thirty for the drive to the dealer?"

"Certainly, Mrs. Blakerly. I will have my car outside the door to the offices at eight-thirty. I have some pictures and technical data in this file if you wish to look at it."

"Please leave it on my desk and I will look at it this evening. Thank you, Thomas!"

Thomas stood up, smiling. "Just doing our jobs, Mrs. Blakerly. See you in the morning." He walked out of the office and Jessica smiled. *'The old twerp has a wandering eye, oh well I don't mind, kind of makes a woman feel good to have a man eye her curves'.*

When they walked in, the dealer had two SUVs each from Lincoln and Ford sitting in the showroom, each set in blue and red. The manager of the fleet department was there along with the salesman to host them. After the introductions, Jessica stood beside Mrs. Sparks and looked at the vehicles. They walked around and looked at them from the rear. Jessica whispered to her partner, "I don't like the Lincoln red, it is so dark it looks like maroon. Of the four vehicles, I like the look of Ford's red." They climbed into the red Ford and were amazed by the sunroof, mass of controls, leather seats, and the spaciousness. Finally, Jessica started the engine and they listened. The engine was so quiet they could hardly hear it. "Let's go and look at the Lincoln and see what it may have that the Fort is missing." It was a repeat performance in the Lincoln. They found it to be somewhat larger but didn't feel it was any better.

Jessica started the engine and they found it to be slightly noisier, probably because it had a larger horsepower engine. They held a discussion in the Lincoln and Jessica finally said, "I want to find out what the pricing is before I decide."

They got out and closed the doors before walking to Thomas. "Did you get a price on each of these cars?"

Thomas opened his file and pulled out a sheet of paper. All four cars were listed with their features and at the bottom was a fleet price. Surprisingly, there was very little difference. They went back and looked carefully at the Ford before going to check the Lincoln. Standing off to one side, Jessica told Mrs. Sparks, "I think the Lincoln is a slightly better vehicle but I much prefer the red color of the Ford. A little secret of mine is that I don't think Casper would be comfortable driving my car if it were a Lincoln so I intend to buy the Ford."

"You are a wise woman, Jessica. Your husband is very intelligent, always works hard, and is a good boss but he is also down to earth. In his mind, he still thinks he is a farm boy. Which he is, just not a typical farm boy like there were when he was a kid growing up."

Jessica smiled. "Thank you." She turned and walked to Thomas. "I have decided to take the red Expedition. Will the dealer send an invoice?"

"Yes, he will and the car will be delivered by us tomorrow. Please allow me a few minutes to talk to them about the deal." Thomas walked to the fleet salesman. "Mrs. Blakerly has decided to take the red Ford Expedition, please hang on to the blue one until Casper returns from the business trip he is currently on. He is scheduled to return on Friday."

Chapter 24

Jessica carried her son and cuddled him on the trip to the Expedition and Jeffery's nanny trailed behind carrying his food and water and the mother's briefcase. The Expedition was already equipped with a car seat for him to ride in. His mother fastened the belts and settled him. The good Irish nanny, named Shirley Shrapnel, sat behind Jessica where she could keep an eye on the baby. Shirley was a quiet lady of fifty-some years who did her job excellently, read her books, wrote letters to relatives, and never interfered. Wherever little Jeffery was, Shirley was near. On a Saturday, the two ladies had left Jeffery in the care of his father while they went shopping for a sturdy, large-wheeled, and safety approved stroller with which Shirley insisted on using to expose the baby to fresh air and the sun every day. On rainy days, she pushed the stroller around the plant with her determined pace. The plant workers were accustomed to seeing the stern-faced nanny and were always careful when she was going past. Jeffery was nicknamed 'the boss' by the workers in reference to his future.

They drove into the farmyard and Casper's pickup was gone from the garage. Jessica smiled, so her husband was home, and had gone out to the field. She didn't put the new Expedition in the garage but parked close to the house. She planned to ask Casper to please put the SUV in the garage for her. It had taken a couple of days for Jessica to adapt to the large vehicle and now she felt very safe driving it. Even more important, she felt safe taking Jeffery along.

Shirley took the baby to the bathroom for his daily bath and change of clothes while Jessica began cooking dinner. The door opened and Casper had arrived. He grinned at her. "Nice looking car out there."

Without turning, she commented, "After dinner, you can take it for a drive." Casper came and put his arms around her and hugged her tight before he went to find the baby. It was several minutes before he came back with Jeffery in his arms. One tiny hand was pinching Casper's nose as he cooed and teased the baby. Casper could always get what passed for smiles and giggles from him. Jeffery was three months and a week old and growing fast.

On Monday, Casper got his new blue Expedition and started driving it to work each day. Jessica didn't comment on the fact he still drove his old Ford F150 after he got back to the farm.

Jessica walked into his office and informed him, "Jeffery and I are going to drive to Newton for Christmas and stay for a week. When Jeff asked, I told him his father was going to be with us." With her back straight, she walked back to her desk.

Casper walked out and told Mrs. Sparks the news. She smiled and held up her calendar with the holiday already marked in it. Casper shook his head and muttered, "Women, they are always plotting together and taking advantage."

Jessica gave the keys to her ten-year-old car to Shirley and told her to drive home to spend Christmas with her sister and family. Casper drove mother and son to the dairy farm to spend Christmas with the Hornsbee's who knew their grandson was coming. Elizabeth Hornsbee came running to the car as soon as it was stopped. She paced impatiently while Jessica got Jeffery out of his car seat. Granma reached for him. Jessica turned sideways, "He hasn't seen you for over three months mother, it might be best to give him a few minutes."

Jeffery's little head was swiveling as he looked at all the strangers and sucked on a thumb. When Casper came around the car, Jeffery saw him, stuck out one arm, and leaned toward him. Casper took the baby and cuddled him. It only took a few minutes for the baby to orient himself but to Elizabeth, it seemed like a lifetime. She reached for him and he slowly appraised her, finally she took him and instantly began cooing and patting his back. He seemed to enjoy it but his eyes stayed on his father. A few minutes later, when his face began to wrinkle up, Gramma quickly handed him over to his mother. He snuggled up to her and grabbed a hank of hair in one fist as he looked over her shoulder at Dad. Jessica slowly turned so Jeffery got to look the Hornsbee's over again. Casper unloaded the suitcases and stroller from the car and set them on the porch. Karl and Trace lugged them upstairs to the bedroom set aside for the Blakerly's.

The porch was open-air with a roof and a waist-high picketed fence style wall along the outside to keep children from falling off. There were picnic tables, a Bar-B-Q, and many chairs. The men were wearing warm coats and sat down in chairs and started catching up. When the men went inside Jessica came carrying the baby. Karl told her, "It is so nice to have you here with your family and my grandson is almost four months old, you kept us waiting for a long time."

"Sorry about that, Dad. We had to finish the grain harvest, sell steers, and run Casper's business. I was aching to visit you, but we were very busy. Did you have a look at my Christmas present?" She laughed at the look on his face. "The car, Dad. It is a Ford Expedition that Casper bought and gave to me. How do you like the color?"

Karl gazed at the car for a minute. "It is a very nice red, Jess. Later, I will go and have a look at the inside."

Gramma came and took over the baby. She looked at her husband. "Tell them what we did last night."

Karl laughed. "I hope you won't mind, Jess but we emailed all the local Hornsbee's and told them you were coming with the baby today and they were welcome to stop by."

The Blakerly's had a great holiday. They walked every day, pushing Jeffery in his sturdy stroller with him sitting looking back at his mom, or whoever was pushing. He took an instant liking to Teresa, who was the wife of Trace. She could hold him whenever she felt like it. Jessica told the family about Portugal and what they had seen, and Casper described the European plant they now had producing machinery to sell. He also described his last trip and tour of Europe to visit machinery dealers. Every day, cars and trucks drove into the yard with Hornsbee's, all of whom wanted to hold Jeffery and sometimes he complied and often he refused. Christmas Day was jam-packed with Hornsbee's and when they finally left, the action slowed as many Hornsbee's needed to return to work. The day before they were scheduled to go home, Jessica and Casper went for a walk while Jeffery was having an afternoon nap. She held his hand and told him, "You have gone and gotten me pregnant again."

Casper grabbed her and she got a huge hug. "When will the baby arrive?"

"I haven't been to the doctor yet but the baby will arrive very near to Jeffery's first birthday. I think it will be a month after Jeffery turns one. I will phone for an appointment when we get home."

"Such good news, Jess, such very good news, two children in our house, and we can watch them grow up, learn to farm, and go to university. Oh, we are so lucky, Jessica."

"All you say it true, Casper, but there is one thing I believe you should do. I would prefer to raise my children in a new modern house that you have built for me."

Casper laughed. "A great idea. I will look for an architect to design and build for us."

The drive home went smoothly with Jeffery sleeping soundly in his car seat until the red Expedition pulled into the garage and parked. Shirley was home and came immediately to take charge of the baby who was happy to see her and snuggled close. Casper unloaded the car and, after closing the doors, announced, "The blue Expedition sitting over there is certainly the best-looking vehicle made today."

Jessica laughed, swatted his shoulder, picked up a suitcase, and walked to the house. They were home, in two more days, a new calendar year would begin, and they both had many projects to look after. The farm felt like an old, friendly horse, happy to be ridden, while Davenport Machinery was growing and expanding like a mess of mushrooms growing on a large manure pile. Just deciding which project to do next required hard decisions and overriding everything was fitting projects into the yearly budget. Casper wasn't prepared for his company to go into debt so everything was being done with money previously put in the bank account. Jessica hadn't traveled since July because of the baby and now another was on the way. She sighed and thought, *'Well I should be able to get away a few times in the next six months.'* Being married to Casper, she had come to understand why the farm was so important to him, he could go there to the peace and quiet, and for a short time forget the big decisions waiting to be made and get away from all the employees. Clearing his head was what he was doing.

A new Davenport manufacturing plant, very similar to Plant Number II in Iowa, had commenced construction in Austria. It was scheduled to be up and running by April turning out new machines built in Europe. She wanted to travel there for the official opening. When it was producing, the building of a similar plant would start in Brazil to serve several South American countries. After that, there were plans for a plant in the province of Ontario to serve Canada, and already people were in Asia evaluating the safest and most dependable places there. The company now owned large blocks of land in Brazil and Ontario for the plants and after a decision was made for Asia, a land site would be purchased.

Jeffery had developed a habit of sleeping later in the morning so Jessica told Shirley, "I will ride to the office with Casper and when you and Jeffery are ready you can drive to the plant in my car." She gave Shirley a set of car keys and wrote a note to herself to ask Mrs. Sparks to phone the Ford dealer and order two more sets of keys.

When Jessica arrived in her office, there were several stacks of paper to be handled and a handwritten memo from Vice President of Marketing Tom Greig requesting a meeting to discuss the annual Davenport catalogue. She dialed her phone. "Good morning, Tom, this is Jessica. You want to set up a meeting?"

"Yes, Jessica. I want to get it started sooner than normal, could you meet with us?"

"Certainly, Tom, would tomorrow at two o'clock work for you?"

"Thank you, Jessica. We will come to your office at two."

She started on the paper piles, some of which she handled, and most of the paper she sent on to one of the company employees. When she went home that evening, the piles had disappeared. Jeffery and Shirley were in the backseat.

During the meeting the next day, they discussed how best to cover the various countries and languages where Davenport's machinery was being sold. They decided on using the English version in the USA, Canada, England, and Australia with the only difference being on the front cover where they would state Australian Edition or one of the other three country names. Portugal, Austria, and Germany all had different languages and in the end, they decided the company had to put out catalogues in those languages as well. The staff would be put to work on photography and writing the English language version and good competent translators had to be found to produce versions in the other languages. Jessica and Casper were asked to produce an overview of Davenport describing what the company did and where it had plants. Previous editions had included the selling price of each machine. Now, that was much more difficult with exchange rates changing between the countries they were selling in. The question was left open so Jessica could figure out the answers.

The second week in January, Casper came to talk to her. "Dean Everly phoned and we have set up the late March meeting with the graduating Mechanical Engineers for March 29th. Will you be able to go with me?"

Jessica checked her meeting book and wrote in the date. "I enjoyed your little party with the grads last year and would like to go again."

"Thanks honey. Doing these things is much better when you are there with me." Casper walked away and told Mrs. Sparks to make all the arrangements. This year, they would hold the lunch and the tour in the new plant.

In the last week of January, Casper and Jessica flew to Europe to tour the plants and dealers. They left on Sunday morning and returned Thursday evening. While Casper put his Ford Expedition away, Jessica walked up the stairs and went to see her son. As she stood there looking at him calmly sleeping, she was amazed at how large he was becoming. She was sure he had grown while she was away. Shirley laughed at her. Jessica came down the stairs, taking off her coat as Casper walked into the kitchen. "How is Jeffery?"

"I am sure he has grown while we were away. Shirley thinks I have gone insane, but he sure looks larger to me."

Casper took the briefcases to his office. They had both processed paper on the long flight back across the North Atlantic and now everything could wait for morning.

In February, Casper and Ned flew to Brazil to meet with the company's two men who were looking for a plant site. They were taking along the same Black and Black lawyer who had helped them in Portugal and Austria. The first morning, the men showed them road maps and photographs of three sites they believed were usable. In the afternoon, they worked on the contract and agreements for the plant to exist and operate in Brazil. They were written in English and the men had several problems. First were tax clauses which were very loosely worded. They rewrote those in straightforward language and left no loose ends. Doing so filled the afternoon. Next day, they tackled the safety rules and rewrote them to conform to the way other Davenport plants operated. They specified hardhats, coveralls, and steel-toed boots comparable to the other plants. The Brazilian government wanted to appoint safety supervisors, a union foreman, and stated the number of Brazilian citizens that had to be hired and put in the plant. These requirements caused Casper to become angry. They worked and argued over the rewriting of this section. When they were done, it clearly stated employees would be paid fair and competitive wages based on what other companies in Brazil were doing. All employees would follow the safety rules, wear safety clothing, and very specifically stated that there would be no union employees, no union representatives, no government supervisors of any kind, and Davenport would have total freedom to hire and/or fire whoever the company wished as employees. By the time they finished, most of the agreements had been rewritten and it had taken three days. At the end of the meetings, the lawyer agreed to stay to attend meetings with the Brazilian government representatives. Casper told the three men that if Brazil did not accept the fair and honest agreements by the end of next week, Davenport would not build the plant and would put its planned South American operation in a different country. This message was to be given at the very first meeting and frequently re-stated whenever a government representative questioned it.

They copied the rewritten documents so Casper would have

copies to take home. Ned phoned the airline and reserved seats for the two of them. One good thing about flying to South America, there was very little in time changes so jetlag was not a problem.

Two days after Casper returned, Mrs. Sparks came to his office. "Casper, the Brazilian Ambassador to the United States of America is holding on the phone to talk to you."

Casper was surprised and it showed. He opened a drawer and removed a pile of paper. "Please put the ambassador on the line, Mrs. Sparks."

When the phone rang, Casper picked it up. "Hello, Mr. Ambassador, what a nice surprise."

"Thank you, Casper, it has been some time since we talked, and I understand you have been very busy on projects around the world."

"What you say is true, Ambassador, although I have many very good people to assist me. You haven't met my wife who has been with me for almost one and a half years now. You have always said you wanted to visit our plant here in Iowa and if you were to come now, my wife would be very happy to meet you."

"A very good idea, Casper. Unfortunately, I find myself busy with a few problems, which of course is an Ambassador's point for existing. Any chance you will visit Washington in the near future?"

"We would love to visit Washington but unfortunately we have always run our operations with a minimum number of people which is fine when we are not expanding. For the near future, everyone at Davenport is working extra hours and hopefully, it will slow down next year.

"Ah yes, Casper, you have reminded me. I received a message from my president asking basically why Davenport was demanding so many special treatments in the agreements to build a plant in San Paulo and he instructed me to contact you with the question."

"Mr. Ambassador, our company operates plants in the United States, Canada, Portugal, and Austria. Soon, we would like to have a plant in South America and in Asia. All our plants run under the same set of rules on labor practices, safety, healthcare, supervision, pension plans, the moving and storage of materials, and producing the finest machines we are capable of building. Davenport is not asking for anything special from Brazil, just the right to operate a plant in Brazil, should we build it, on the same terms we do in other countries. Our people who are in Brazil have been told to co-operate fully with the government and its representatives but very simply, if Davenport does not receive the right to operate such a plant on the same basis as our existing plants, we will leave Brazil and find another place to build a new plant."

"Well, Casper, you certainly stated the company's position clearly and in forcible language. I will communicate your position to our president as quickly as is possible."

"Thank you, Mr. Ambassador, please allow me to add, Davenport is not asking for special treatment, rather the same treatment we are receiving in other countries. Our products must be capable of competing worldwide in construction, forestry, agriculture, mining, and everywhere else they may be needed. Forgive me for talking like a blunt and direct businessman, I am not a diplomat, and would never long survive if I became one."

The Ambassador laughed. "I will transmit your statement in more sedate language to my government. In the years I have known you, Casper, you have never changed and if I may be so bold, do not change. You are a beacon of light in the dark of night. One more item, Casper. I shall try to find the time to travel to Iowa and eat dinner with your wife. Good day."

"Please come to Iowa sooner rather than later. Goodbye, Ambassador." Casper hung up the phone and pulled out his handkerchief to wipe off his brow. He found he was also feeling very warm. After a few minutes, he walked to Jessica's office and sat down. He told her as well as he could manage everything the two men had discussed.

Chapter 25

The week Casper and Jessica went to Ambrose University for the talk with the mechanical engineers who were that year's grads, followed with a Davenport plant tour, construction got underway on the new house they were building at the farm. They had met with the architect in January to discuss what they wanted to build and every time they talked, the house got bigger. Very soon, there would be four of them and the question was how many more babies would be born? So, the second floor would have a large suite for the parents plus five more bedrooms and baths for children and visitors. The nanny needed space to live so a small suite with a bedroom, living room, bath, and kitchen was added. The two Blakerly's would share a large business office with space for an assistant. They settled on a three-vehicle attached garage. On a farm, the center of life was the kitchen, so it was large with a mudroom for work clothes with a small bath. A large dining room with an attached living room would be needed for birthday parties and entertaining with a large bedroom for visitors and additional baths. An open-air porch similar to what the Hornsbee's had would go on three sides of the house. At the second meeting, Jessica suddenly realized they would need someone to clean and cook for the family so a small apartment was added above the garage. It was designed for a husband and wife team. In the end, the house design was much larger than they had envisioned but Casper never objected when Jessica made the point. Casper made arrangements with Hiram Weinstein to borrow Ralph Shaw to supervise the construction, knowing he would be traveling and busy with Davenport's expansions.

When crop seeding started in April, Casper managed to take

off several days to help seed soy and then corn. Jessica, Jeffery, and Shirley the nanny went to the office every morning, sometimes together and on other days, Shirley came when Jeffery was up and ready.

At the end of June, Ned and Casper were going to Austria for the startup of the new plant and Jessica declined. She was seven months pregnant and she told Casper, "With the baby we are expecting, I will have to stay home." He laughed and hugged his wife, kissed her and his son, and drove off to the airport in Chicago. Jessica and Shirley packed the Expedition and loaded Jeffery into his car seat and took off to Newton to visit the family. With help from the woman, Jeffery walked around, strengthening his legs and gaining a sense of balance and showing off in front of his grandparents. Jessica was taking an extra day away from the plant to make a four-day weekend.

* * *

By the end of July, the new house was being painted inside and out. In a few days, it would be ready for the Blakerly's to move in. Casper drove Jessica to furniture stores to look at what she wanted. First was their large master bedroom. They wanted a king-size bed, table and chairs, two upholstered lounge chairs, reading lamps, and surprisingly a separate room was available to hang clothes and store shirts, ties, socks, shoes, and all the dresses and other items a woman would have. Jessica ordered furnishings for the master bedroom, two children's bedrooms, and went with Shirley to purchase furniture for her nanny suite. Lastly, they bought what they wanted for the new kitchen and then Jessica announced everything else would have to wait until after she gave birth to the new baby which was due any day now. Elizabeth came from the family dairy farm to be with Jessica and help with the new baby.

Jessica was in the hospital for four days while Casper had the new furniture installed and ready for use. It was another boy, a few ounces heavier than Jeffery had been. Although now experienced, Casper was once again a proud and happy father walking around the hospital room with the baby in his arms. His name was Karl Adrian Blakerly. The baby was two days old when Casper brought Jeffery and his nanny to the hospital to see his mom and brother. The baby was sleeping and Jeffery looked at the object in bed with his mom for a long time before his one hand came out slowly and touched Karl on the arm. Karl didn't wake up but Jeffery pulled his hand back quickly before he looked up at his mom. "Good boy, Jeffery, This is your new brother and in a few days he will come home to live with us."

Casper had the house as ready as he could with Jessica's new furniture installed. He had stocked up the cupboards, deep freeze, and refrigerator with food and as near as he could tell, the house was ready to welcome his wife and second son home. When she was ready, they would have to furnish the rest of the house, particularly the dining and living rooms which echoed dully as he walked across them. Jessica wanted an open-air porch and now she had one running along three sides, leaving only the north side where the three garage doors were. There was still much work to be completed and he would hire service people to shape up the yard, sow grass, and plant trees.

Jessica came home, handed the baby to Grandma Elizabeth, and played with Jeffery who had missed his mom. She planned to have more days away from the office this first month to spend with Jeffery as he adjusted to having a baby brother in the house and having to share his parents. He was walking quite well now and toddled around the house so much that someone needed to keep track of him almost constantly and was now saying momma to Jessica. They bought a large wheeled pram, as Shirley called it, in which Jeffery could ride and go for his airing every day around the farmyard. As the days went by, he more and more would demand to be out walking, often helping to push the pram. When Jeffery was put down for his afternoon sleep, Shirley would put baby Karl in the stroller and walk him back and forth around the long three-sided porch. One Saturday afternoon, Jessica commented to her husband, "Our nanny seems bound to make our sons into Daniel Boones with all these airings of hers."

* * *

Davenport had signed acceptable agreements with the Brazilian government and with the Austrian plant up and running, Casper decided to go ahead and build in San Paulo, starting in the fall. He told his company officers that when the South American plant was in operation, Davenport would postpone building any more plants to allow the company to settle in and make sure all the various parts of the operation were functioning as well as possible. In actuality, the break lasted for two years before Davenport built an assembly plant in Canada and then moved across the Pacific Ocean to build a manufacturing plant in Australia.

The morning of Casper's fortieth birthday, Jessica had lunch all planned. They had been married for eight years and both sons were doing well in school. Both boys had inherited their father's mechanical abilities and focused on their projects just as he had. Shirley was still keeping an eye on the boys, getting them on the school bus in the morning with their lunches, and standing at the farm gate like a Sargent Major waiting for their return from school. Jessica rode to work with her husband and left the Expedition so Shirley could go to the school and pick up the boys at eleven. It was a strange fact in their family, all four of them were born in the early fall of the year. Standing up, she walked to Casper's office. "Mr. Blakerly, I want to eat a cheeseburger for lunch and I expect you to drive me to Ma's Restaurant."

Casper glanced at his watch. "It is only nine-thirty?"

"You are being warned, Mr. Blakerly, so you don't go wandering off somewhere. If we leave around eleven-thirty, we should be alright. I am busy so will expect you to come and get me out of my office."

Casper smiled. "You best tell Mrs. Sparks to remind me." Jessica smiled and walked away.

They parked right in front of the main door and Jessica held her breath. She could see the red Expedition parked over in the far corner, but Casper didn't notice it. He held the door for her and they walked in. After a few steps, Casper grumped, "There are people sitting in my favorite place."

Jessica grabbed his arm and gave it a little jerk. In her toughest voice, she told him, "Why don't we go over there and tell them we are going to sit with them?"

Casper stared at her. "We can't intrude on strangers." Jessica laughed right at him.

"If you take a good look, you will see they aren't strangers, they are people you know very well." Casper took another look and smiled.

"Those are my kids over there with their nanny!"

"It is your fortieth birthday, you dumb old farmer, and your boys are waiting to have lunch with you." Casper stared at his wife for a minute before laughing. She grabbed his arm and led him to the table. They were greeted by two youthful voices yelling, "Happy birthday, Dad," mixed with giggles and laughter. The two boys came out to get hugs and Casper let the youngest slide into the booth and he got in to sit between his sons. As was usual, Shirley was taking pictures to keep up to date the historical albums she was building for each boy. It was a happy hour with everyone ordering the same cheeseburgers as Casper did and being allowed to drink root beer. Little Karl put down his cheeseburger and asked his dad, "My dad lived forty years, how many years has me lived?"

A smiling Casper rubbed Karl's head and told him, "You just celebrated your sixth birthday three weeks ago and your brother had his seventh birthday." Most of the conversation was between Dad and sons and it went on until Shirley cleared her throat and pointed at her watch.

On the drive back to the plant, Casper was happy. He always got a big lift from being with his sons. As he parked, he asked, "I didn't get a birthday gift from my wife?"

"You will, Casper. In fact, you will get to make a choice between a stale wiener made into a hotdog or your wife buck-naked in bed waiting for you."

Casper looked at her with a sober face. "A long time since I had an old stale, green, moldy wiener well cooked." Jessica slapped his arm before they got out of the car.

* * *

Winter arrived earlier than normal with several falls of snow and it turned cold. In the middle of October, it was hard to understand why they were suffering through weather which would normally occur in January. Casper and Ned Ambrose were arranging a trip to the Davenport Machinery plant located in Brisbane, Australia. Brisbane was the capital of Queensland and located on the eastern side of the country. The company had picked that city as being best for their operations, supplies they needed could be purchased locally, there was a large workforce in the area, and shipping to markets in other countries by the ocean would be easy. Brisbane had a well-equipped harbor and was one of the major business hubs in all of Australia. Jessica had been thinking about the trip for several days and decided it was time to try her idea on Casper. She walked into his office and sat in a most comfortable chair across the desk for where he was working. "Casper, I have something I wish to discuss with you." Casper had been watching Jessica since she came through the door. He nodded and waited. "You are planning a trip to Brisbane in early December and I wish to propose the two boys, I, and Shirley should accompany you."

Casper slowly leaned back in his chair with his eyes fixed on his wife as he considered her suggestion. The longer he considered the idea, the more convinced he became that it would be a great thing to do. The only flaw he came up with was the boys missing school. If they could agree on a compromise with the teachers, the trip would be good for the whole family and come to think of it they had never gone on a holiday. "Jess, it seems to me such a trip would be very good for all members of our family except for missing classes. You should go and discuss this idea with the school."

"We can reduce the amount of time the boys miss by delaying your trip for a week and staying in Australia over the Christmas season. What is your reaction to that idea?"

"Very good, Jess. I suggest you talk to the school before Ned and I start messing with the travel schedule."

"I will call the school and ask for an appointment for tomorrow. Thanks, husband, for being so considerate." She stood up and walked back to her office. Five days later, everything was arranged with the addition of Ron Smith being added so he could check on the Australian plant's financial department. The Blakerly's would fly to Hawaii and stay overnight before catching a plane to Brisbane. Ned and Ron would take a direct flight a day behind them.

There were six weeks to prepare and Jessica started right away on passports for the boys, medicals, international travel shots, and travel health insurance. Shirley had a passport and did need to take a few shots. It was winter in Iowa and would be summer in Australia so the ladies planned the clothing accordingly. They were taking a minimum of clothing with them and would buy whatever was necessary. Mrs. Sparks took care of hotel reservations, a rental car in Brisbane, and got them Australian currency for their time as tourists. Casper always carried a substantial amount of United States currency in his pockets when traveling.

The company lawyer, Wilford Black, started worrying after he learned of the trip and came to meet with Casper. Jessica was invited to join them. Wilford had a list of items that were of concern to him; the most serious was the whole family traveling together. He explained, "Very bluntly, members of the family should not all travel together. If there is an accident and all four Blakerly's are killed, we will have a major mess on our hands. Who would inherit your assets? Who would own and run this company and I might add, who would run the farm?"

Casper's face went blank. He had never considered such things. He sat staring at Wilford. Jessica asked, "What do you propose we should do, Wilford?"

"I do not want to spoil your family holiday but to start with, you and your husband should travel on separate planes. Secondly, it would be best if Jeffery traveled with you and Shirley. On a separate plane, Casper could take Karl with him. You could switch the boys, which would do no harm. The important point is to prevent an accident from eliminating the whole family."

Jessica studied Wilford for a moment. "Are all the estate planning, wills, etc. up to date?"

"Yes, they are, and they are reviewed once per year to be sure. Both you and Casper have sat in on those meetings."

She nodded. "I do not like what you are proposing, Wilford. Still, I can understand the necessity; this is part of the price we must pay for our business success. Casper and I will discuss the arrangements and let you know what we plan to do."

"Thank you, Jessica." He looked at Casper. "Do you have any

questions, Casper?" He got a negative head shake. "I will take my briefcase and go back to the office. Please phone me if any questions arise."

The office stayed quiet for several minutes and she waited. Finally, Casper told her, "I can understand the logic of what Wilford told us but I don't like it. Being successful will make it hard for the Blakerly's to remain one happy family."

"I do not agree, Casper. Having been successful, we must take certain precautions. In the larger picture, it is a small inconvenience to ensure the future of our children and we are going to have fun. If you agree, I will get Mrs. Sparks to make the changes. My only suggestion is you have Jeffery travel with you, Karl is younger and may need his nanny to comfort him."

Casper smiled and nodded. "Please do that, Jess." Jessica came and kissed his cheek before she left to make the changes.

* * *

Jessica, her son Karl, and Shirley flew out of Chicago on Saturday morning, heading to Honolulu where they would stay overnight. Strapped into her plane seat, Jessica could still feel the tight hug Casper had given her when she kissed him at the departure gate. She had gotten down on one knee so her eyes were on the same level as Jeffery's and told him to take good care of his father before she kissed his cheek. She received a hug from her son. The holiday was scheduled so the two boys would miss the last week of classes before Christmas and they were doing it with permission from the school. Karl surprised his mother as he calmly settled into his seat and started to page through an airline magazine describing how the airplane was built and how it worked. Shirley was helping him with the reading and explained what many of the words meant. In her briefcase, Jessica had reports for the meetings to be held at the Australian plant but very deliberately she had left the rest of the company behind her. She was on holiday with her family and she fully intended to enjoy everything they did. She leaned her head on the seat back and gradually relaxed and an hour after departure, she was sleeping. Shirley warned Karl not to disturb his mother; the conversation didn't register with Jessica.

Karl was anxious to see the ocean so they walked from the hotel to a nearby beach. His mother rolled up the pant legs on her slacks and they walked in the water along the oceanfront. Several times, Karl dipped his hands in the water and sipped. Each time, he looked up at his mother and told her, "Ocean water not good to drink." Back at the hotel, they dialed the phone for the farm and talked to Casper and Jeffery. Karl described the ocean to them. In the hotel dining room, they ordered a seafood platter with shrimp, scallops, raw oysters, large prawns, several kinds of fish meat, and other items they couldn't identify, along with several dipping sauces, and warm cheese toast. Everyone ordered root beer to drink. Karl was hesitant but gradually tried most of the items. He would watch his mother take a shrimp to dip in a red sauce before chewing it happily and then try it. As he went along, he liked the shrimp, scallops, and prawns. Wouldn't try the oysters and ate some of the fish. They laughed and ate and most importantly had a happy time. By their normal time, it became late before they rolled into bed for the night.

Sunday morning, they boarded the flight to Brisbane and would arrive in the afternoon. Casper and his group were flying out of Chicago and were in the air when Jessica departed Honolulu with her companions. When the plane approached Brisbane Airport, the third-largest in Australia, Jessica could see it was a large city spread out along both sides of Brisbane River, some nine miles from the ocean. The downtown area with high-rise buildings was off to her left. At customs, Karl kept waving his passport at the men until finally one of the customs agents took the book, looked at it carefully and compared Karl's face to the picture before stamping it and handing it back. The reserved limo was waiting and loaded their luggage for the trip to the hotel. There was a suite ready for Jessica's five-member party, although two of them would be arriving later in the evening.

Davenport's Australian operation was built on high ground well above the Brisbane River because there had been very destructive floods in the past; the latest in 1974 had been a major disaster for the city. As always, Casper was wary of exposing the company to any unnecessary dangers. For two days, Jessica attended meetings at the Davenport plant before deciding she had done everything needful and told Casper she was now on holiday. Casper stuck to the meetings for one more day before joining his family. Brisbane was a large city built on a low-lying floodplain along the river which presented a flood risk but on the other hand, it was often referred to as a hilly city because of numerous places where the ground rose several hundred meters above the river, mainly due to the Herbert Taylor range of mountains.

On the first day, while Casper and Jessica were at the Davenport plant for meetings, Shirley and the boys walked along the streets and in and out of stores, getting familiar with the local area. Lunchtime came, and Karl pointed at a sign which showed hamburgers. After eating, they toured the Museum of Brisbane, viewing many interesting displays and gathered a stack of tourism pamphlets describing all the many sites available to visitors. After walking the halls, they took the elevator up the adjoining tower where they looked out over the city, buildings, and the busy river with boats that were of great interest. The boys were becoming tired, so Shirley took them back to the hotel.

Jeffery was enthralled after reading about Brisbane's high-speed ferry service along the river. His mother suggested it was a trip his dad would like to go on and he should discuss what time would be best. When Casper arrived at the hotel after a day of meetings, Jeffery was ready for him. Jessica ordered dinner for the group from room service while Jeffery explained to his dad all about the ferry service. The fourth day was agreed on to go for a ferry ride. Since Jeffery had planned the fourth day's activities, Jessica said Karl should pick what to do on the third day. Karl shuffled through the pamphlets until he found the one describing the Australia Zoo and showed pictures of the animals to his mom. It was quickly agreed they would drive to the zoo the next day.

Jessica drove and Shirley held the road map and guided her. The zoo was located at Beerwah on the Sunshine Coast and was operated by Steve and Terri Irwin, who had taken over from his parents. The focus of the boys was on seeing the animals but the zoo had many other activities, such as medical clinics to treat injured birds and animals, projects to help endangered species recover, film-making for promotion and education, and live animal displays with the staff. The tour started with looking at the birds and the boys counted six different types of parrots. Karl was fascinated by the Andean condor, wedge-tailed eagle, and the peregrine falcon. They rode on the safari shuttle which hauled tourists around the zoo and were lucky enough to arrive for the elephant feeding. Jeffery was asked to hand food to one of the elephants. At the walk-through enclosures, they got to feed the kangaroos, wallabies, and koalas. They found the platypus to be weird, the crocodiles scary, and were amazed to learn a kangaroo could leap almost thirty feet across the ground and had great swimming talents. A sign over the koala said it was normal for them to sleep close to twenty hours each day. At the wombat cage, the sign told them wombats were related to koalas. When they toured the reptiles, the boys counted seven different types of pythons, spent a long time studying the crocodiles, alligators, and watched the many different kinds of snakes. On the drive back to the hotel, both boys went to sleep in the backseat, tired out from all the running and excitement.

The next morning, Casper drove the car to the University of

Queensland located on Sir William Macgregor Drive and they boarded a CityCat Ferry for a round trip ride along the river to Northshore Hamilton. The boat was a catamaran named Indooroopilly to honor the Brisbane Broncos rugby team. The name was after an Aboriginal name for part of the river. There were twenty-five stopping places on the route and this boat would stop at most of them. The boat was well maintained with a crew of three. On a beautiful day, they chose to sit on the front deck where they could watch the river, the boat traffic, and see the city sights go by. The boys once again had their cameras out, taking pictures of everything and Shirley was alert for pictures of the family. They all wore wide-brimmed straw hats to protect their heads from the warm summer sun. The traveler host informed Jessica the river was commonly called the 'great brown snake'. After watching her boys for several days, Jessica told her husband, "Your boys are usually as quiet as you are but have you noticed on this trip they are always laughing, pointing, and discussing what they like and don't like?"

Casper smiled at her. "Yes, I noticed, and it has to be one of the best things we have ever done for them. I plan to talk to the concierge at the hotel and ask him where the finest place would be to go for Christmas dinner."

"You do that, husband. At home we always have roast turkey and I will be interested to hear what he tells you."

After the research and discussions, it was the boys who decided. They weren't interested in a fancy restaurant and argued for Japanese food. One of the brochures the concierge had given to Casper described its facilities and the quality food it served. So, for Christmas, they would be Japanese. They sat at a round table with a revolving food tray in the center. Jessica ordered items which the waiters set on the tray and everyone had access to the food by rotating it. Each of them received a glass dish with several types of sauces to select from. Their mom knew both boys liked shrimp, large prawns, scallops, and well-cooked fish. She ordered these things along with rice and ice water before turning to Shirley and Casper to ask what they might like in addition. They were over two hours eating, the adults using chopsticks, which the boys tried before going back to forks.

When they returned to the hotel suite, everyone received a Christmas present to open after which they played gin rummy. Two days later, Casper and Jeffery boarded a direct flight to the United States and the next morning Karl, Shirley, and Jessica followed them.

Chapter 26

The trip to Australia had been an eye-opener for all of them. The boys had come home with a wider understanding of the world. In Brisbane, they had observed people like themselves but with a different way of living and working and the animals had been a fantastic experience. Their parents noticed the changes in them and recognized the value of them going on trips. From then on, at least once each year, the family went somewhere, and the boys were quick to read and research to prepare each time. Davenport Machinery was steadily growing, shipping more machines each year, and always working on something new to introduce. Casper slowly backed away from the load of running the company on a daily basis and installed Ned Ambrose as General Manager to take over much of what he had done for years. He wanted more time to work on developing new machines Davenport could build and sell around the world and he wanted more free time to spend working at the farm.

When Fred Aitchison informed them it was time for him to retire after many years managing farm operations, Casper went on the hunt for a replacement. It proved to be hard to find someone who knew both grain farming and the cattle raising businesses. Casper interviewed several men and it was over half a year before he found a suitable candidate and convinced him to move to the farm. Rollin McPherson, an ex-marine, had grown up and worked on a similar farm where his father was the manager of operations. He had agreed to come to the farm to have a look and meet the people, including the Blakerly's and their sons, and was scheduled to arrive on Thursday afternoon. The old shop was gone and replaced by a large building with wide high doors that allowed any of the farm machines to go in. Fred and Casper were in the shop checking one of the combines over and getting it tuned up for harvest when Rollin drove his Ford pickup into the yard. One thing for sure, he was driving the right make of truck to impress Casper. Rollin was a couple of inches shorter than Casper but strongly built, with wavy blond hair and the brightest blue eyes you will ever see. His face was a rugged brown color and his hands scared and tanned. No movie star but seemed like a good steady man and he was about the same age as Casper. Casper introduced Rollin to Fred, and they talked. Finally, Casper phoned the house and invited Jessica to come and meet the man. When she walked in, he immediately took off the straw Stetson he was wearing. Casper introduced them.

"Mighty pleased to meet you, Mrs. Blakerly, I am from a ranch over at Greeley, Nebraska, a fair drive from here."

"Welcome to this old farm of ours Rollin. The Blakerly's have been living here for four generations now. How do you like that Ford F150 pickup you are driving?"

Rollin laughed. "The best of all the trucks I have driven over the years, doesn't give me much in the way of problems, except it likes to eat up gasoline."

They chatted for a few minutes before Jessica returned to the house and the men went back to discussing the grain and cattle operations. The boys came off the school bus and went to see what the men were doing. They were twelve and eleven now and Jeffery was starting to sprout in growth. In a few more years, he would catch up to his father. Rollin stayed until Saturday and lived in the original house where he seemed to be comfortable and before he left, he had agreed to take the job. Said he would drive back to Greeley and pack his personal property and return in a few days. Fred was looking forward to retirement but agreed to stay until the grain harvest was completed, giving Rollin time to fit in.

Both of the boys were doing well at school and making very good grades. For most of a year, Casper had been bringing up the subject of finding a high-quality boarding school for the boys to take their high school years. Now, he raised it again and they went around all the reasons it would be a good thing to do and they would be better positioned to attend university. In a couple of years, Jeffery would be ready to start high school. That night, they agreed to check out where boarding schools were located and look at their academic records. The three men wrote out letters and sent them off to several schools. It would be some time before they received replies.

Jeffery was driving his dad's old pickup now, also running a tractor during spring grain seeding, and driving a combine to help with the harvest. Karl's legs were still too short, so he kept busy with the dog, helping herd cattle. All these things were fine but they watched closely to make sure both boys were keeping up on their studies.

Both boys had traveled to Canada, Brazil, Portugal, and Austria after the trip to Australia. Together, the family had toured France, Germany, and the British Isles. In that regard, they were far ahead of their schoolmates and had learned many things about the world. The trips opened up their minds and gave them knowledge only a small percentage of the population had.

With Casper spending more time in the farm shop with Ralph Shaw and others working on new machines for Davenport to build and sell, Jessica found she was needed at Davenport's office more and more. Never did she complain because Casper was happy and it forced her to hire people to help and to organize procedures so the business was running on time and was efficient. Davenport's accounting and financials were all done on a computer system connected to all the plants on the operating system. Manufacturing, purchasing, marketing, and personnel were computerized and tied in with the accounting system. She had to admit, they went through a few glitches and a learning period until everything was working correctly, including a new computer system department, which was responsible for fixing and updating the operating system. Clock time was a major annoyance. When Brisbane was starting their workday, Vienna was shutting down for the night. To keep the plants all efficient, the head office in Iowa had a night crew to take calls and information and record orders for machine parts and whatever came up. It took a while, but Davenport's people figured out how to make it work.

They had a happy, hard-working life and were being successful with the companies and operations. Both boys were away from home in a boarding school and harvest was in full swing when they received the biggest shock you could imagine. Jessica was chairing a meeting of the senior management when Mrs. Sparks walked into the room and interrupted the meeting. The first thing Jessica noticed was her wet eyes. "Is there something you need, Mrs. Sparks?"

She dabbed her eyes with a tissue. "There are two men from the farm here to talk to you."

Jessica's instinct told her it had to be about Casper. She stared at Mrs. Sparks for a moment before standing and walking out of the room. Standing there was Rollin and Ralph. The first thing she noticed was they both had their hats in their hands. She couldn't wait. "What has happened, is it Casper?"

Rollin nodded. "Mrs. Blakerly, we found Casper in his combine. He got it shut down but, ma'am, he had died. We got him out and phoned for an ambulance."

Jessica, tough old Managing Director of Davenport Machinery Inc., who handled most of the tough decisions just sat in a chair and cried. Her husband of fifteen years was gone. Finally, she stood and asked Rollin to drive her to the hospital. By the time they got there, she had herself under control, her eyes were red and still watering, but she was walking upright. *'If it is all true'*, she told herself, *'I must think first of the boys'*.

Back at the office, Jessica asked Ned Ambrose if he would drive her to Chicago early the next morning to pick up the boys. She phoned Wilford Black and told him what had happened as best they knew and he assured her he would take care of the proper procedures. At Jessica's suggestion, Mrs. Sparks went home. She had worked for Casper for over twenty years and was distraught with grief. Finally, Jessica told Ned she was going home. Many employees watched her walk to the Ford Expedition and drive away.

She talked with Shirley and that helped her. Afterwards, Jessica walked around the house and everywhere her eyes looked, she saw Casper. Telling herself to get out of the house, she put on blue jeans and drove the F150 over to the shop. When Jessica entered the shop, all work ceased. She found herself with eight people to face up to and shook hands with them before commenting, "Casper was so proud of you fellas and loved being here with you. Please do me a favor and take the rest of the day off and go home." Rollin sat in the F150 while she drove out to see the place where Casper had left her. The combine was sitting there.

Rollin explained, "We left it sitting here in case the police want to come and have a look." Jessica didn't enter the combine; she walked around it, looking to see the last sights Casper might have seen. She stood beside the machine staring across the field of uncut soybeans, seeing what Casper had been driving toward. As she looked, tears started running down her cheeks until she couldn't see anymore; finally, she wiped her eyes and face dry, straightened her shoulders, and walked to the F150. "Where is the other combine working, Rollin?"

"I moved it to the Anderson place to start combining soy." Jessica started the truck and drove back through the yard and along the road over to the Harold Anderson farm, her eyes staring straight ahead at the road. On the way, they met one of the semis bringing a load of beans home. When they arrived, the combine was dumping into the other semi.

Jessica turned off the truck and asked, "Alright with you if I go for a ride in the combine?" Rollin nodded and she climbed out and walked to the machine. The driver saw her coming and had the door open for her. Tom Ford was an older hand now who had been working for Casper before she got married. As she entered the machine, Tom doffed his hat. Jessica nodded and smiled. "Alright with you if I ride for a while?"

"Yes, ma'am, you come with me for as long as you wish. You want to drive?"

"No, Tom, just want to listen to the machine and have time to think." The machine finished unloading and Tom went back to cutting soybeans. Jessica watched the reel on the straight cut header pull the soybean plants across the cutting head for several minutes before starting to talk. "You know, Tom, everything Casper got involved with he did a first-class job and he built operations all over the world. Today we are manufacturing machines which five years ago, we hadn't even thought of. He didn't like all the traveling he had to do but also knew it was necessary and when we started taking our sons with us, he made time to sightsee. Always, he would say he was doing it for their benefit, but he was always right in the middle of whatever they wanted to do. Sure did make the traveling much easier. Our two boys got an education on things very few people have even heard of and Casper always made sure they understood. Why it was there, how it worked, and they explored whether it was beneficial or not. Those boys had the privilege of talking to employees and residents everywhere we went. Casper worked hard, loved those boys of his, and there were very few people around as intelligent as him. All that said, when you boiled it right down, what he loved most was the farm, operating the machines, getting dirty, and skinning his knuckles. He was always happiest when he could slip away and spend time with you fellas. When he came to the house, I always growled at him to get out of his dusty, dirty clothes and have a bath. You know, Tom, city folks will never understand farming, but there is something about listening to the machines, breathing the dust, getting dirty and greasy, putting your hands in the soil, or riding a horse to move the cattle, roping and branding, and watching them grow. Even when you have worked a long day and are tired, there is always a sense of accomplishment and by damn we farmers are feeding the world."

Tom stared at her. "That is a mighty fine speech, ma'am; makes a man like me feel good."

"Thank you, Tom. Got to get this hard time out of my system and the best way is to talk; at least sometimes. Tomorrow, I have to go to Chicago to bring the boys home and it isn't going to be easy. When I leave tomorrow on the trip, my head must be high to give my boys the strength to stand up to what is going to be a terrible surprise for them. It has been good of you to let me clear out my system but now the night is coming, and I have to phone home and tell my parents what has happened. Next time you dump, I will catch a ride home with Rollin."

"Sure thing ma'am. My pleasure having you spend time with me. You come any day you feel like doing it."

Rollin drove her home and Jessica went straight to the phone and dialed. Her dad answered. "Hornsbee Dairy."

"Good evening, Dad. How are you and Mom doing?"

"We are doing just fine, Jess, milking cows, combining, and bringing in the cattle feed for winter. How is that little operation of yours doing?"

"Got some sad news for you, Dad… Casper was out combing

this morning and the men found him dead. Somehow, he got the combine stopped and turned off but now I have lost my husband." Saying that caused her eyes to get wet again.

"Oh my God, that is terrible news." Jessica could hear the sobs. After a minute, in a halting voice, he said, "Here's your mom, you talk to her."

Elizabeth's voice was strong. "What has happened, Jess?" Jessica gave her a rundown of the day and asked if she could come to help Shirley with the boys until the funeral.

* * *

Ned arrived at the farm in the morning and drove the Expedition along Highway 88 with Shirley in the passenger seat and Jessica sitting behind them. The women were quiet so Ned just drove. One way, the trip would be close to one hundred and thirty miles and just before nine a.m., they parked outside the school building where the office was located. Jessica had been there several times to check on her sons and the receptionist recognized her. Jessica explained and told her she needed to take the boys home for the funeral and repeated the story for the dean. The school people left the three visitors sitting in the dean's office while they found the boys and got them from their classes. By the time they got to the office, the boys knew something had happened. Jessica was standing facing the door and both boys rushed to her and she hugged them close. She told them what had happened, and Jeffery started crying. Shirley handed him a tissue. The youngest, Karl, stared at his mother, blinking his eyes but he didn't cry. Inside, Jessica knew Karl was the one most like his father. He was strong, determined, never backed away from a fight, and wasn't far behind Casper in intelligence. She kept an arm around him and rested her head on top of his, thinking about all the times he had come home bruised and banged up, because he wouldn't give in to demands from his schoolmates. When challenged, he always went straight ahead. She had never checked to find out how the other boys came out of each fracas. Casper had advised her to stay out of things unless he asked for help. Karl never asked. The boys changed their clothes and Jessica sat in the backseat with them on the trip home and when they asked, she answered the questions.

When they arrived in the farmyard, Elizabeth's car was sitting near the door and she was on the porch waiting. Grandma couldn't wait, she came down the steps and hurried to the Expedition and grabbed Jeffery, who was the first one out. She hugged him as tight as she could and his eyes got wet again. When Karl came around the car, she held out an arm for him and pulled him close. Jessica watched Grandma walk to the house with the boys before turning to Ned. "Thank you for taking the time to drive me."

"Is there anything else I can do for you? If something comes up, you let me know. Have you given thought to how to fit the employees in? Most of them have known Casper for a lot of years."

"Thank you, Ned, for mentioning these things and frankly I haven't gotten past worrying about the boys. I did ask Wilford Black to start on the arrangements for the funeral and will call him today. Tell all the managers that I will come to the office tomorrow and we can talk about what should be done." She was quiet for several minutes. "I am young, Ned, and have no experience with these affairs. Please apologize to everyone if I have not done what I should have."

"Nothing for you to worry about, Jessica. I will talk to the people and they will be waiting for you tomorrow." Jessica watched as Ned drove out of the farmyard.

Shirley and Jessica leaned against the car and talked. Jessica told her, "Please suggest anything you want to me, for the first time I have a funeral to arrange and have no idea what to do."

"Certainly, Jess. It might be we should make some lunch, the boys might be starting to feel starved."

Jessica smiled. "Very good, Shirley. Do we have the makings for sandwiches?" Shirley nodded and together they walked to the house.

While Shirley put lunch together, Jessica phoned Wilford and he asked for permission to come to the farm. They sat around the kitchen table eating ham sandwiches and drinking coffee. The boys put Bess in the truck box and took Grandma in the pickup to check on the grain harvest and Jessica met with Wilford. Shirley cleaned up the kitchen and started thinking about dinner.

Wilford warned Jessica there would be a large number of people at the funeral. She asked him to arrange to use the DeWitt community hall on the coming Saturday. Pallbearers would be three men from Davenport Machinery and three from Blakerly Farms. The family's minister had agreed and arranged for the church choir to sing. The church ladies would serve lunch in the church hall after the funeral and so it went until they had discussed all Wilford's items.

When the two Ford Expeditions arrived at two p.m., the lawn and sidewalks around the hall were full of people. A large truck from Davenport Machinery was unloading a stack of wooden chairs with a crew of men setting them out in rows. Jessica left the vehicle with a son on each arm and as she walked toward the hall, she stopped many times to speak to people, shake hands, and thank them for coming. Suddenly, she was face to face with Joe and Phillis from the Deli. She asked, "You couldn't get inside?" Joe nodded. "You were good friends of Casper and me, please come with us and we will seat you." Her parents sitting behind her made room for them. The funeral was delayed until everyone had found a place and the minister led them along the aisle to the front. Jeffery was on the aisle, Jessica, Karl, Shirley, Elizabeth and Karl Hornsbee next, followed by Teresa and Trace Hornsbee and then

Joe and Phillis Truman. The leaders of the farm and the machinery company were in the row across the aisle from the family. The hall was packed with people and many more were outside. Jessica had no idea how many were there. The service flowed smoothly with the only speaker called up being Lockley Simpson who related a history of Casper and mentioned that he, his wife Shannon, Joe and Phillis Truman had all ridden the school bus together starting in grade one and been friends ever since. When the minister started to ask if anyone else wished to speak, on impulse Jessica stood up. He came and escorted her to the microphone. She stood there with her head high. "Please forgive me for getting up. Frankly, I was on my feet before I could think. I wish to thank every one of you for coming today to honor my husband. I have no idea how many are here but it must be five hundred or more and you are all welcome. Our minister and the choir have conducted a superb service and there are all those friends and neighbors who worked hard making today's arrangements. My husband was highly intelligent, in fact in a genius category, and came out of university at a very young age with a PhD in mechanical engineering. He worked long, hard, hours and never complained as he built his business and, from watching him over the years, he loved the farm. He would help seed and harvest and it cleared his head, relaxed him, so he could go back to Davenport and put in more long days. In recent years, he traveled around the world on business many times and took our boys with him. Together, they went everywhere to museums, sight-seeing, universities, and a long list of other places. He loved it and often as I watched, he seemed to be younger than our two sons and they deserve credit for tolerating their parents. Today we will bury Casper beside his parents and grandparents and great grandparents, may he rest well. Thank you all for being so tolerant and also for all the phone messages, cards, and flowers. Remember the church ladies have worked hard preparing lunch for you so please come to the church."

Jessica walked back to her seat and the minister finished the service. They buried Casper beside his parents and four grandparents and went to the church and spent two hours wandering through the crowd talking to people. The sons stuck to Jessica through it all. Finally, they went back to the farm. Jessica's brother and his wife left immediately to drive back to the dairy farm to help with the milking.

Sunday morning, the boys drove their grandpa out to see the herd of purebred Black Angus cattle and then watched the grain harvest. Jessica talked to their lawyer and arranged for a meeting to read the will on Monday morning. She wanted her sons to be present for the reading and then they could go back to school. She would work with the lawyers to revise the ownership of Mid-West Holdings and Blakerly Farms Inc. and start preparing the required tax filings and all the other items she knew would pop up.

After breakfast Monday morning, Jessica's parents, Karl and Elizabeth, left to drive home. The lawyers arrived and the meeting in Jessica's home office got underway. Around the conference table were six people. On one side, sitting together were Jessica, Jeffery, and Karl Blakerly and across from them, three lawyers, Wilford Black, and two younger lawyers as assistants. Wilford looked around and started. "This meeting is to read the last will and testament of Casper Edward Blakerly. For clarification, both Casper and Jessica Marie Blakerly's wills are up to date and have always been reviewed once per year. Mrs. Blakerly knows what every document says and has complete understanding but should Jeffery and/ or Karl have questions as we proceed, these files are here so we can answer with clarity and precision. Please feel free to question any answer I give you and we will clarify the reason it is as stated. For your information, gentlemen, your parents met with our firm every February to review and make sure all these documents are in accordance with any changes in laws, regulations, or decisions made by the federal and state governments or on their behalf by the courts. The will of Jessica Marie Blakerly will not be read today unless she so instructs and also when we read the will of Casper Edward Blakerly, there is not definitive information on cash which can be discussed afterwards."

Wilford looked at them and asked, "Any questions?" No one spoke so he opened a file containing Casper's will and began. He read out aloud the head of the will giving all pertinent data on Casper and then moved to the body of the will. "I, Casper Edward Blakerly, being of sound mind and competent, do declare that all my assets of any and all kinds are left totally to my wife, Jessica Marie Blakerly, for her total use and control with the exceptions as follows; Jeffery Edward Blakerly and Karl Adrian Blakerly, my sons, are each individually to receive from my estate twenty percent of the issued shares of Mid-West Holdings, and twenty percent each of the shares of Blakerly Farms Inc., and a Trust fund containing ten million dollars, of which one half will become the property of each of my sons when he reaches an age of twenty-one years. The bank accounts are to be set up within two months from the time of my death and administered by Jessica Marie Blakerly and Wilford Black in accordance with the attached trust document. The shares left to my sons shall be voted as directed by Jessica Marie Blakerly at all times except when the subject owner is gainfully employed working for the companies and are subject to the attached document which restricts sales to anyone not a member of the Blakerly family. In addition, I wish to leave fifty thousand dollars to Shirley Shepard, nanny to my sons and a great help to my wife; fifty thousand dollars to our church in DeWitt to be used for maintenance and upgrading of the building; and lastly fifty thousand dollars to the School of Mechanical Engineering at Ambrose University in Davenport, Iowa."

The meeting went on for two more hours with the two boys asking questions and their mother noticed that most of the questions came from Karl. She told herself, '*Karl is going to be a handful for me in the coming years. And what about Jeffery? He is so quiet, does well at school, and I hope he will be a stabilizing factor in the future.'* Jessica asked Wilford, "We have two Expeditions which are now three years old. Will it be okay if the boys take Casper's car to the boarding school so they can come home when they want to?"

Wilford rubbed his head. "What is the ownership of Casper's car?"

"It is registered to Blakerly Farms Inc."

"I see no reason why they can't drive it and it can stay registered to the farm. Do you both have valid driver's licenses?" Both boys nodded.

Jessica suggested, "Let's adjourn this meeting and go to the kitchen where Shirley will have lunch ready for us. When are you boys going to return to school?"

Karl replied, "It is time we got back in classes so if it is okay with you, Mother, we should take off after lunch." Jessica smiled at them and led the way to the kitchen.

* * *

The boys left in the Expedition and Jessica went into a meeting with the lawyers to discuss all the things waiting to be done to clean up the reporting and satisfy the bureaucrats in Washington and Des Moines. The lawyers had made a list and one by one, they started working through them. Jessica worked with them on some of the items, but others needed input from the V.P. Finance or one of the other officers. The office door opened, and Mrs. Sparks walked in with a bundle of paper. Jessica spent thirty minutes going through the documents with her and signing her name. When Mrs. Sparks packed up to leave, Jessica told her she would be at the office in the morning. It was seven o'clock when the lawyers left and Jessica felt tired, glad the day was over.

Chapter 27

A few days after returning to Davenport's office, the staff realized Jessica was arriving before six a.m. and often staying until nine p.m. They soon figured out what it was all about; Jessica was still doing her old job and had taken on Casper's duties as well. This couldn't keep on, what the company needed was delegation, and Jessica needed time to think, do corporate planning, circulate around, visit the overseas plants, and the staff needed to see her out in their workplaces. Mrs. Sparks marched into General Manager Ned Ambrose's office and glared at him. He almost laughed seeing her standing there with her hands on her hips and her eyes looking angry.

"Is there something you need, Mrs. Sparks?"

"You're damn right there is. Since Casper died on us, Jessica is working far and away too many hours trying to do everything the two of them did. Something must be done about it, someone needs to talk to her, and you as General Manager are the most logical one to do it."

Ned leaned back and in a soft voice suggested, "Please sit down, Mrs. Sparks and tell me about this issue."

She sat across the desk from Ned. "Since the day Casper died, Jessica has added his duties to her own. She is working fourteen or more hours each day. If this keeps on, she will become sick, have a nervous breakdown or something even worse will happen. She owns this company and needs to be sitting at the top with time to think and plan, travel to all the plants, look at the work being done on new machine design, getting around talking to the employees, and all the other things that pop up. I have been worrying myself sick about her. You are a long-time employee and I have noticed you are the one she always goes to when special situations occur. I want you to go to her and discuss this issue, tell her all the employees are worried about her, and suggest what she can do to shuffle the workload onto other people."

"You work close to her, Mrs. Sparks, and you see what is happening. Frankly she hasn't been in my office since before Casper died and I feel ashamed for not noticing. Please stay here, I want to phone Ron and ask him to come here to meet with us." Ned phoned and within ten minutes Ron Smith walked into the office. "Please sit down, Ron. Mrs. Sparks and I have something to discuss with you."

Together, they related the story to him and Ned asked if he would sit on a two-person committee to find a solution. "Of course I will, you know we all work long hours and for sure I didn't realize Jessica was overdoing it. Mrs. Sparks, can you outline for us the different types of things Jessica is being burdened with?" The conversation went back and forth for the next hour and by then; both men had a good feel for the situation.

"You go back to work now, Mrs. Sparks, and thank you for coming to see me today. Ron and I will work out a plan and come to suggest it to Jessica." The men watched her walk away. Ned commented, "She is the most competent lady I have ever worked with and I have often wondered how she learned all the things she knows." They laughed together and got serious.

* * *

Jessica arrived for work at five-fifty a.m. and found the two men sitting outside her office. She smiled. "My, it is good to see both of you, please come into my office." She plunked an overstuffed briefcase on her desk and sat down. "I assume you gentlemen are here because you have a problem, please tell me what it

371

is."

Ned laughed in his quiet, friendly way. "You are correct, Jessica, there is a problem."

She smiled again. "Thank you, Ned, are you going to describe it to me?"

"The fact is, there is a large problem which has all the staff worried sick and very frankly you are the problem."

"Ned, I don't understand." Her face showed surprise and the voice hardened. "Please explain to me what problem I am responsible for."

"Jessica, everyone in the organization likes, respects, and admires you and have ever since you came here as a summer student. The problem is you are working too hard, too many long days, and everyone is worried you will make yourself sick. We want to suggest that you delegate a large part of what you are looking after and become what you are—the owner and corporate head of the company. Arrange things so you have time to think, to plan, to travel to the overseas plants, and enjoy your life. Circulate around and, I don't know, maybe stomp into Ron's office and tell him his numbers are wrong or come to my office and kick my butt because we aren't turning out the machines fast enough. The employees want to see you and say hello and they certainly want to see that you are healthy and happy."

The silence lasted for several minutes as Jessica stared at Ned, her face grim, and considered. The two men waited, both wondering how she would react. Finally, she slapped the top of her desk with the flat of her hand, startling both of them. Sitting up straight, she told them, "Thank you, gentlemen. You have certainly surprised me and I sat here reviewing everything you said and my conclusion is you are right. Frankly, I have been working hard, too hard, but it was because when I am working my mind doesn't get lonely for Casper. We had a great marriage and I am still head over heels in love with him; someday, we will be together again. In the meantime, I do own this company, and have to make sure it is properly run, which doesn't mean I have to do everything. So, bring on your recommendation for how we should reorganize and be fast about it, I need to drive to Chicago to have dinner with my sons." They all laughed at her last comment.

Ned smiled. "Thank you, Jessica, for taking our intrusion in goodwill. We will work out a plan with the other executives and when ready present it to you for your comments."

Jessica frowned and the men waited. "Very good, you gentlemen carry on, but please remember Casper's philosophy that everyone is here to produce and sell machines. If you should forget that fact, I will be disappointed and angry."

"We will do our best, Jessica. Please don't wait on us, you must slow down and become what you are, a business owner who is a total owner, and please delegate. Take time to be a mother." The two men stood up and excused themselves.

Jessica leaned back in her office chair to think, her mind was full of what she had heard and ideas started coming to her. She would wait for the plan the executives brought to her, study it and hopefully find it was a good one. When Davenport had a plan put together, she would insist on Black & Black sitting in a meeting with her and her two sons to make sure it was workable and the two boys understood what was going on. She was still lost in thought when Mrs. Sparks arrived to begin the day. As ideas came to her, she added them to a list she was making on a legal pad on the desk. An hour later, she phoned Wilford Black. "Good morning, Wilford, it is Jessica calling."

"Good to be talking to you, how are things going for you today, Jessica?"

"Very well, Wilford. I want an update on where your firm is on revising the corporate documents."

"The lawyers are very close; my guess is a couple more days and the rewrites will be ready for reading and discussion."

"Glad to hear, Wilford. I have asked the executives at Davenport to bring me an outline of how we should shuffle responsibilities around. I have been working long days doing what both I and Casper were doing and frankly it is too much. When I have Davenport's suggested plan and you have the corporate documents ready, I want to have a Saturday meeting when my sons can attend. I believe it will be beneficial in the long run for them to be aware of what we are doing and the reasons for doing it."

"Sounds logical to me Jessica; as soon as we are prepared, I will contact you and you can schedule the meeting."

"Thank you, Wilford. Have a good day. Goodbye."

* * *

Jessica sat in her chair and looked around. She found the desk heaped high with contracts, agreements, and papers. She stared at them for several minutes before she opened her briefcase and cleaned it out. It was all paper she had cleared last evening after going home. Picking up the pile of paper, she walked to Mrs. Sparks' desk and set the pile down. Sat in one of the chairs and looked at Mrs. Sparks, who was eying her. Jessica pointed at the paper pile. "These are agreements I went through last night and signed. Please send them on." The silence went on for a few minutes. "We need to install a new system around here to route the paper to other people. I met with Ned and Ron early this morning and they are going to bring me their ideas on how we should accomplish that. In the meantime, please send the paper on my desk and incoming paper to whoever you think is the best person to handle it. I have decided it is not my job to handle all these agreements, etc. After all, I am the owner of this operation, and there are more important things for me to handle."

"A very wise decision on your part Jessica, very wise indeed."

Jessica looked at her before speaking. "I knew what I was doing was not right. It was simply a way for me to hide from thinking about Casper. Now, I am leaving to drive to DeWitt to sit beside Casper and tell him how his sons are doing, what is new at Davenport, and how the harvest turned out. Maybe I will discuss this reorganization with him. In any case, I will be back and you just go ahead and run things the way you think best. If you upset anyone, just tell them they can complain to me when I return." Jessica stood up and walked to the elevator.

*   *   *

Mrs. Sparks went into action with determination. First, she delivered the agreements left on her desk. Next, she sorted the incoming paper and made separate piles for whoever she thought would be the best person to handle it. She spent an hour sorting the paper from Jessica's desk into the new piles. When she was done, she sat to rest for a minute, drank a glass of cold water, and screwed up her courage. The first pile she took was for Ned. He was a tough old blister and she was starting with him because he was the one most people would complain to. She marched into his office and set the paper pile in the incoming mail basket before stepping back, prepared for an argument.

Ned had watched her arrival. His eyes looked at her, switched to the pile of paper, and came back. "It appears to me, Mrs. Sparks, that you are starting a one-person reorganization of the company."

With her head high, she replied, "Jessica informed me she didn't want this paper coming to her and I should send it wherever I thought was best."

"Certainly, Mrs. Sparks, and would I be correct to assume similar piles will be going to others?"

"You would be correct; the others are next on my list." A slight smile showed on her face. "Jessica told me to do this and anyone who didn't appreciate it could complain to her."

Ned laughed quietly. "There will be no complaint from me, please carry on."

Mrs. Sparks stared at Ned for a moment and commented, "Thank you, Ned, you are a gentleman." She turned and walked away. By noon, she had all the paper piles distributed and no one growled at her. Giving a thought to what she had done, Mrs. Sparks decided Ned had passed the word to help ease her way.

* * *

Jessica didn't return to the plant later in the day. After a long, one-sided conversation with Casper, she stopped for lunch at Big Joe's Deli, before going to the farm. She put her dog named Bess in the F150 cab and drove out to observe the harvest. It wasn't long until Rollin arrived and came to talk to her. She asked, "You got time to come with me to look at the cattle?" He nodded and got in the truck. Bess was a large dog but she moved over and made room for him. The cows were on pasture over west at the Arson section and Jessica drove there. Rollin opened the gate and she drove in. At a slow speed, they drove through the herd. Jessica asked, "How many of these cows do we have?"

"There are six hundred and fifty-four cows including last year's heifers in here grazing. As soon as harvest is finished, we will truck this bunch over to the Anderson place for the winter. Lots of grass in the pastures over there and rows of this summer's hay bales. It is a dandy place for cattle to spend the winter with lots of water and good trees for wind shelter. In the spring, it provides an easy place to calf out the cows. At the home place, we have a hundred and forty-two yearling steers fattening up to be sold. The other animals we have are last spring's heifers and we have one hundred and forty-five of them freshly weaned and learning to graze to survive."

Jessica was driving downhill and kept going until she stopped near the river. "The river has more water than it did last fall."

"Summer wasn't as dry this year."

"Rollin, that reminds me, you fellas were talking about drilling two water wells on the north side of this section and it has never been done. You got any comments on that?"

"We have eleven hundred and fifty-five acres of grass which should be enough for a couple more years. There are two things we need to improve our cattle operation. The first is those two wells, which would make this much safer and more reliable graze for the cattle. If a dry year comes along, it could save our hides. Also, we could use them to provide irrigation to improve the quality and amount of range grass. Secondly, we need several new, young, registered pure-blood Black Angus bulls to keep our herd improving."

Jessica laughed and turned to look at Rollin. "You find a well driller and get a quote from him and get a list of bull sales. Come to think about it, I haven't been to a bull sale for several years so I will try to go with you and the men." She laughed at the thought of going to a bull sale. "Hell, no one will know you or me and they will be wondering where we came from. It should be fun. It is late afternoon so time for us to get home; I will drive you to your truck and drop you off. Thanks for coming along with me and I appreciate all your comments."

* * *

Two weeks later, the meeting to discuss the reorganization was scheduled for Saturday and the Blakerly boys came home on Friday. Shirley was busy cooking Friday night dinner when they arrived. Jeffery and Karl donned their farm clothes and the four of them sat at the kitchen table to eat dinner. Their mother asked what they wanted to do for Christmas which was just over a month away. It was Karl who answered. "Mom, we have done a lot of traveling the last few years and I would be happy to just stay home and maybe spend a couple of days visiting the Hornsbee's."

Mom's head turned to look at Jeffery. "What about you, Jeff, what would you like to do?'

"Karl's suggestion sounds good to me."

"Okay then, gentlemen, we will do what has been suggested which leaves one other decision. Your grandmother has been after me to bring you to their farm for Christmas. What should I tell her?"

Jeffery was quick to reply. "For me, I would like to stay right here. You could tell Grandma we will drive up there the day after Christmas." Karl nodded.

"You two men have put me in a fight; your grandma is not going to be happy and will come up with all kinds of arguments." Jessica laughed. "Don't worry I will work it out with her. Now it is time for both of you to report to Shirley and me on your grades and anything else we should know that has occurred at school."

Both boys laughed and Jeffery started talking. The reports were good, marks wouldn't be available until after Christmas, and he described playing tennis and told the ladies that Karl was playing football and taking boxing and karate.

When the kitchen grew quiet, Karl announced, "Mom, your son didn't tell you he has a girlfriend now."

Shirley was shocked and Jessica struggled to remain calm. Finally, she looked at Jeffery. "May I ask how you met this young lady?"

"At the tennis courts and I have played against her twice. She is the daughter of one of the teachers. We went to a movie last weekend."

"I see and would you say she is a well-behaved young lady?"

"Seems to me she is, although her tennis game is very weak. She is quiet and seems nice. Says she is doing well at school but I don't think she is a top grade student." Jessica didn't ask anything more but her mind was working and when she could get Karl away from his brother, she would question him.

The meeting was held in the farm office at the house on Saturday and sent the lawyers back to their office with numerous changes and questions to answer. It was clear to everyone that Jessica's main concern was how she could pass the business on to her sons in the most tax effective way and she wanted a report on the various suggestions. She told the lawyers to find a practical, down to earth expert to advise them. The restructuring of the management was relatively simple by comparison.

After the Saturday meeting was over, Karl and Jessica went for an evening walk around the farmyard. In the course of the conversation, Jessica asked, "Have you met Jeffery's new lady friend?"

"Didn't really meet her. I watched part of one of the tennis matches. Not the best looking girl around but you should see her hit a serve. Her chest flips around all over the place and her hind quarters have a nice shake."

"How nice, Karl, please tell me, is she a lady?"

"Cannot say about that, does seem to me that Jeffery is going to end up doing more than hitting a tennis ball." Their walk became quiet as they continue on and Karl knew he had put a scare into his mother.

"Karl, I sure wish your father was still with us; he could sit you boys down and have a discussion about birth control."

Karl looked at her with surprise. "The first month we were at the school, they put us through a lecture on girls and talked all about birth control. Jeffery knows what to do to protect them if it comes to that. You have businesses to worry about besides what your son's girlfriend might allow."

Jessica stopped walking and looked at her son. "Thank you, Karl. You are a good son. You know I have always heard how fathers worry about their daughters and now I find it is just as hard for a mother raising sons on her own."

* * *

Jessica drove into the farmyard at four o'clock and saw Rollin standing talking with two of the men. She stopped her Ford Expedition and got out to talk to them. "Hello fellas, how has your day been?"

"The water well driller moved in his drilling rig yesterday and they are putting the first well down right now."

"That is great news Rollin, can we drive over and have a look?"

"Certainly, do you want to change your clothes before we go?

Jessica thought for a minute, "I'll be okay dressed like this; I am not planning on getting out of the truck."

As the truck rolled down the county road Rollin smiled and pushed his Stetson up at a higher angle. He handed Jessica a Sales Brochure describing a cattle sale sponsored by the Iowa Herford Breeders Association to be held in Des Moines, Iowa in February. As she looked at it he explained. "A friend of mine sent this sale brochure to me for a sale of Angus cattle. It has quite a number of purebred Black Angus bulls listed. I have been phoning around and getting good recommendations on the quality of the bulls. We were considering going and hopefully buying a couple of bulls."

Jessica was looking at Rollin and asked, "Have you marked a bull in here that you like?"

"Yes ma'am, in fact I have marked six bulls that were recommended to me."

"Are they registered as purebreds?"

"Yes they are. They are a mixture of two and three year olds and all are guaranteed to have produced offspring."

Jessica laughed, "Sounds good to me; are all three of you planning to go?"

"It is a three day sale and the bulls on our list may come up in different rings so we need to be able to split up. Tentatively planning on driving to Des Moines on the Tuesday and coming home on Friday."

Jessica was still smiling, "You got room for me to go along with you?"

"Certainly, we would be pleased to have you accompany us. We are planning on staying in a motel; do you want a suite in one of the hotels?"

"Hell no, I grew up on a dairy farm just a few miles out of Des Moines and have gotten dirty many times. Get me a room wherever you plan to stay; only thing is I will need a desk or large table to work on. Our farm is a member of the Association, why don't you phone them and request brochures so we can all have one. When you get them give me one to look over."

* * *

Davenport was reorganized and Jessica liked the new arrangement. She now had time to spend on the financial reports, check on the operations, and think. She and Ned flew south in early December to Sao Paulo, Brazil, to check on the operation. The main language of Brazil was Portuguese with English in the large urban centers. Sao Paulo was chosen because the language was the same

381

as in Lisbon, which helped with the supervision. Sao Paulo had the lowest production costs of all Davenport's plants which enabled the staff to export to nearby countries at low prices, causing the production numbers to steadily rise. Establishing new dealers was difficult because of language differences but Davenport was working on it with Thomas Westbury transferred to San Paulo from Iowa to guide the purchasing and marketing. Jessica invited Thomas and his family to the hotel for dinner and as near as she could determine, the family had settled in very well. Thomas divided his time between training purchasing staff and flying around South America with the marketing people to set up dealers.

The boys would be arriving home for Christmas and Jessica's biggest task remained working with the lawyers on the sorting out the ownership structure to minimize the tax problems and ensure the boys could maintain family ownership of the companies. School was out for two weeks and the boys caught up to their mother hard at work in the farm office. They stood in the doorway for several minutes, watching her write red ink notes in a document she was studying. When she leaned back in the office chair, Karl closed the door to alert her to their arrival. Her head turned to see who was coming and she leaped out of the chair. "What a surprise, I wasn't expecting you until tomorrow!" Jessica hurried over and grabbed both boys in one hug. "Come and sit down and tell me all the news." They were happy together and the two boys turned the tables on their mother, asking her questions about the companies, it was a deliberate act meant to keep her from questioning them about their social lives. Jessica soon realized what they were doing and didn't try to divert them.

A knock on the door stopped the conversation as Shirley walked in. "Wanted to inquire what the Blakerly's would like for dinner."

The silence lasted until Karl said, "What say we four go to the

Big Joe's to eat?"

Jessica looked at the office clock. "Big Joe's it is and we best get going. Shirley, we ladies better wear jackets, it is cool out there today." A light snow was falling and the ground was covered as they drove north to DeWitt. Jeffery asked his mother how the cattle were doing. "The cattle herd is in good shape. We are planning on going to a bull sale in February and purchasing up to six new ones to join the herd. Tomorrow, we can drive out to have a look." They walked into the Joe's Deli and Joe Truman was standing behind the counter.

Joe looked up and his face split with a wide smile. "Phillis, come and see what has arrived, darned if it isn't those Blakerly boys and they have two good looking girls with them."

Phillis hurried in from the kitchen and laughed. "My goodness, look at this, Joe! These boys have sprouted until I swear they are as tall as old Casper. Look at the muscle, why I dare say Karl could go out for football and knock all the players down. Jeffery, I heard tell you are a tennis player, are you winning?"

"Yes, Mrs. Truman, I do win from time to time and it is fun. To tell you the truth, the tennis coach warned me my coordination is not good enough to become a pro so I just play for fun and exercise. Karl now is doing well on the football team and he is a mean old cuss who scares the devil out of the opposition."

Everybody laughed before Joe asked, "Now, boys, tell me where you found these two good looking girls."

"They were standing on a street corner; we stopped to pick them up and came here to feed them. They haven't told us what their names are."

"Jeffery, you are the comedian in the Blakerly family." He smiled. "Jessica, you pick out the table you like and sit down. I will be there in a minute with menus." There were people eating at three tables and Jessica knew them all. She stopped to talk at each table before following the boys to where they had chosen to sit. The boys ordered cheeseburgers and fries with cokes. Jessica ordered a shrimp salad and water and Shirley asked for the same.

Chapter 28

The Blakerly's had always been early-risers and the boys were out in their farm clothes when only the farm dog was around. It was still dark, although the east was turning pinkish white. They backed the farm F150 out of the shop, filled the gas tank, and were washing the windows when Rollin McPherson walked across the yard. "Good morning, boys. Nice to have you back on the farm."

Jeffery stuck out his hand to shake. "Good to see you, Rollin. May I wish you a great Christmas? We will be around here for two weeks until school starts again."

Rollin smiled. "You fellas figuring on going somewhere?"

Karl grinned. "We were asking about the cattle and Mom got tired of us and said take the truck and go look. It would be good if you have time to come with us over to the Anderson place."

"Sure, I can do that." Rollin put the truck tailgate down and Bess, the large collie dog, leaped into the box. Rollin noticed Bess wasn't as agile as usual and thought, *'Guess Bess in getting up there in years.'* The three men climbed into the pickup.

Jessica was watching the boys from an office window and saw Rollin arrive and now they were going out to check on the cattle. That decision made her happy and she went back to studying the proposed changes in the corporate documents. Several times, she swore softly to herself about the dumb lawyers.

The boys spent the whole day touring the farm, talking to the hired men, and sneaking lunch at Big Joe's Deli. They came in tired and hurriedly showered for dinner. Jessica was equally tired from all the document reading. The three of them, along with Shirley, sat in the large farm kitchen to eat dinner and their talking was slow and general while eating. Shirley cleared the table and went to cut the apple pie she had baked. Jessica sat back in her chair and told the boys, "Both of you fellas are grown up now and it is time you both dug in to learn all you need to know about the family operations. After careful consideration, I want to propose the following. Jeffery, tomorrow you set up a meeting with Ned Ambrose and inform him you want a summer job starting after your university courses have ended next spring. Now, mind you, none of the fancy stuff. I want you to work with the men building machines, solving problems, helping to develop new products, and whatever else Ned says you are to do. You will learn every person's name, how to do each man's job, you will be happy and pleasant, and remember you will be the junior member of the staff so there will be no smartassery. If they tease you or pull stunts on you, do not be upset, don't yell, cry, or whatever you men like to do. By the end of the summer, I expect you to have learned the basics of producing our finest quality machines. Shirley will provide you with lunches. Is there anything you do not understand?"

Jeffery's face showed his surprise. "Not at the moment, Mother, but please remember as the summer goes by there may be many things I want to ask about."

"Certainly, Jeffery, you ask me, but please understand you must ask the men and foreman first. Let them teach you." Jeffery nodded.

Jessica's head turned so she was looking straight at Karl. "Son, tomorrow I want you to talk to Rollin McPherson and ask him to hire you on for the summer. You will receive the same rate of pay as the hired men and be expected to put in the same hours they do. You already know how to drive the machines but find out why things are being done in certain ways. What is best for growing top quality grain, cattle breeding, delivering the spring calves, feeding, how to avoid over grazing causing the grass to be damaged. Discuss the haying operations with the men and learn how to determine the proper time to cut hay. You heard my instructions to your brother and you will behave the same way. You will be the junior employee and behave accordingly. Every morning, you will receive your lunch before going to work. Again, if you have questions, ask the men first before you come to me. Now please eat your apple pie."

* * *

December 26th, they loaded the Expedition with their suitcases to go to Newton and the dairy farm. Shirley would drive the car Jessica had given her as she traveled to visit her sister and family. Karl did the driving with his brother sitting in front with him while Jessica listened to their talking from the backseat. When they arrived in the dairy farmyard, Gramma Hornsbee was waiting. As she stood up, Jessica noticed her movements weren't smooth and quick like they had always been: her mother was no longer young. The second thing Jessica noticed was instead of Gramma swinging the boys in bear hugs, they swung her as she laughed and scolded them while the dress skirt swirled out behind her. It made Jessica feel sad when she noticed her mother's hair was mostly white. Jessica sat thinking, *'Damn, I have been so involved in running our businesses I failed to pay attention to my mother and she has grown old on me.'* Jessica opened the back door of the Expedition, exited, and as she walked around the vehicle her mother was watching for her. She smiled and asked, "How is my daughter doing?"

"Just fine, Mother, and it is so good to see you. Did you have a good Christmas?"

"Oh yes, we did and ate dinner over at Trace and Teresa's house. Their three kids had a good time and we watched them open their gifts. Here comes your dad." Karl was coming from the shop wiping his hands on an oily rag.

He stuffed the rag into a back pocket before hugging his daughter. Before they could talk, the boys came from the house after lugging the suitcases upstairs and took over with their granddad. To Jessica, her father still looked the same although she suddenly realized her parents were both well into their sixties. Hell, it is over eighteen years since I married Casper and soon I will be thirty-nine. These were sobering thoughts and she needed to get over them. Jessica watched the three men walk into the shop and went to the house to join her mother. They stayed for three days; the boys played with their cousins and toured the farm. The last evening, Jessica took everyone out for dinner, a group of ten, and they all enjoyed the gathering.

* * *

In late January, Jessica flew to Brisbane along with two company auditors who would check the Australian plant's year-end numbers. Ned Ambrose was booked on the same flight the following day. Jessica was very aware of Davenport's security and didn't allow the officers to travel together. Brisbane was hot during Australia's summer and Jessica spent as little time outdoors as possible as she stuck to her schedule of visiting each operation twice per year. Only the plants in Australia and Brazil gave her a problem when visiting during the local summers as a result of being in the southern hemisphere. On this trip, she would fly from Brisbane to Sao Paulo, Brazil and after her meetings fly north to Iowa. She had flown north to Brandon, Manitoba in Canada in early January. After this trip, she would be left with two plants in Europe to visit in February.

* * *

Tuesday afternoon Rollin drove away from the farm in his four door Ford F250 with two farm hands and Jessica traveling with him on the 180 miles. They wanted to arrive in Des Moines early enough to go and have a look at the six animals they had selected. Jessica sat behind Rollin looking at the crops as they passed and listened to the three men discussing the sale and the attributes of the six bulls they liked. Rollin and Don Tapper argued with each other and once in a while Tom, sitting beside her, chirped into the conversation. Jessica was paying attention to the conversations figuring she was expanding her knowledge of cattle.

They checked in to the motel and left just after three in the afternoon to go to the fair grounds and look at the animals. Jessica was wearing blue jeans and her riding boots and because of the cool wind blowing had on a sheep skin lined leather jacket which had been Casper's. It was a little on the large size for her. All four were wearing well used black wide brimmed Stetsons. Separately, each of them filled out the registering and bidding forms and received their copy of the pamphlet listing details of all the animals in the sale and a bidding card with large numbers. Rollin and Jessica paired up to view the animals starting with number one and Don and Tom would start on the sixth bull. Their plan was to compare notes during the evening. For three hours Rollin and Jessica looked, listened to comments, evaluated the bulls, and checked all the comments made in the pamphlet. Separately they rated each animal on its desirability as an addition to the farms cattle herd.

It was just after seven o'clock when they sat down in an IHOP restaurant to have dinner. After they ordered dinner they started comparing notes on the six bulls. Jessica suggested, "Rollin you are the boss on the farm so you tell us your ratings and we will argue with you. If you could only buy one bull which one would it be?"

Rollin laughed and said, "One of the six bulls is three years old and I must admit I am in favor of the two-year-olds, so I have a bias. After careful consideration if I could only buy one of the bulls it would be Number Two. He seems to be slightly larger than the others and according to the sale catalog currently weighs just over 1700 pounds. Another year or two and he will be around 1800 pounds. He is well muscled with only a small hump on his neck. Also I like the way he walks which is with determination and as reported his cows have calved with ease and their young have had high growth and carcass traits. His eyes are clear and he looks at you with no fear."

Jessica laughed softly, "You sound like you did your homework. What do you think Don?

"Got to admit I liked Number Two but first I would buy Number Five. This bull has all the right traits plus a wider stance and a larger sack diameter."

Realizing Don was finished, she looked at Tom as asked, "What is your opinion, Tom?"

"I liked both of them and to me the simple answer is to buy both of them and our herd of Angus cows will be happy."

Rollin laughed. "Good idea, Tom. Maybe we should think about what prices we are prepared to pay. In the catalog it says that at the sale last year the two and three year old bulls sold for an average price of $2415 with the highest going at $3160. This sale the prices may be up or down and it seems to me we should write down the selling prices and from that figure out what the trend is."

They talked about the other three bulls on their list and agreed all five were good animals to add to the herd. Rollin decided he would bid on Number One, Jessica on Number Two and Five, Tom on Number Three, and Don on Number Four. Tom and Jessica would sit together and Rollin and Don would sit together at a reasonable space away so they would not appear to be from the same ranch.

It was eight thirty when Jessica got back to her room and dialed the phone to call her brother Trace. Teresa answered the phone. "Hornsbee Dairy Farm, this is Teresa."

"Hi Teresa, this is Jessica calling. How are you?"

"Just fine, Jess, and must say I will be happy to see spring arrive."

"We all will, could I speak to Trace for a minute?"

Teresa handed the phone over to Trace and he said, "Good of you to call us Jess."

"I wanted to let you know that I am in Des Moines to attend the Iowa Herford Breeders Sale to buy bulls for the farm. If you have a little spare time come and sit with me tomorrow."

"Good idea, Jess. I haven't been to a sale for a couple of years. See you in the afternoon. I may bring Teresa and dad if he wants to get away from the farm."

* * *

The sale started at nine a.m. on Thursday and all four of them were in seats when the auctioneers arrived. The first bull they were interested in was listed to sell at one thirty so they would spend the morning getting into the rhythm of the sale and record the prices being paid. Also they needed to fit into the rapid fire way the auctioneers talked when selling. The important information needed to be sorted out from all the hype the auctioneers used to keep buyers interested. After the first hour, Jessica was on top of the lingo and felt she understood what was being said. She and Tom were both writing the selling prices alongside each bulls listing in the catalog. The auctioneer finished selling a bull at twenty minutes after twelve noon and announced the sale would stop for one hour. Jessica handed Tom a fifty dollar bill and asked, "Tom, please go and buy lunch for us and I would like a cheeseburger and a bottle of water."

"Quite a large crowd here now so it may be a few minutes before I come back."

Jessica smiled, "Whatever it takes, while you are gone I am going to add up all these selling prices and see what the buyers are paying." Six bulls had been sold and she added up the prices paid on her calculator and averaged it out. On average the price of $2470 was slightly higher than last year's total sale average. One bull had drawn a sale price of $2925 which was lower than last year's high of $3160. She sat there thinking and decided if the first bull up after the lunch break was as good as they thought Rollin might have to go higher to win. She put her calculator away and stood up to stretch her legs. She turned in a circle to look at the crowd and yes there were more people here than earlier.

She spotted Tom coming toward her with his hands bull of food. He had to excuse his way down the seating row. Tom handed her a cheeseburger and her water. "Thank you Tom, I think I am feeling more hunger than I thought."

Tom smiled and replied, "Well we have put in a lot of hurried hours since we left the farm. Eat up and you will be ready for the next bull which Rollin is going to try to get." Rollin and Don were sitting two rows lower than where Tom was and they were right in front of the Auctioneer. They were about twenty feet to the right of Tom. At 1:25, one of the morning auctioneers stood up at the selling mike and turned on the speaker system. He let it warm up and then picked up the mike. "Hello, everyone, can you all hear me?" A number of people yelled back and the auctioneer smiled. "The sale this morning went well and the bulls drew good prices. This afternoon, my father is going to start the bull sale. He is a good auctioneer with a lot of years of experience so listen close and laugh when he slips one of his jokes into the selling routine. Come on up here, Dad, and take over this mic."

A white-haired elderly man walked out and looked around. "Now, folks, first thing is to not believe everything my sons says. If he had been better behaved I'd still have my head of brown hair." Many in the crowd laughed and the auctioneer smiled. It is time to get back to selling. This next bull in number seven in the sale catalog and was raised by K7 Herefords over near Ottumwa Iowa. They have been putting bulls into this sale for a long time and they are always real good animals. The bull is being walked around right out in front of me and you have all seem him. A fine looking animal and so let's get the bidding started. How about $2500 for starters, anyone want to bid $2500, it would be a steal. No bidders so how about $2300, any bidders out there? He looked all around and then dropped his price to $2000 and hands went up. Looks to me like there are three bidders out there, so we will just have to move ahead to break up this log jam of bids. Now I am asking 2100. A hand went up and he gloated, got another bid so you fellas better start thinking or this bull will be sold at a steal price. Anyone at $2200 anywhere? He worked at it and soon had a bid. Jessica watched and felt that there were two bidders completing and Rollin wasn't one of them. The auctioneer kept working and got the bid up to $2500. He struggled and soon was asking for $2550. Jessica saw Rollin raise his bid card. The auctioneer celebrated, "A new bidder at $2550. How about $2600 anywhere and he got a bid. He switched his eyes to look at Rollin and stated that was a good bid and did anyone want to raise it to $2650. He asked for $2700 and worked at trying to get another bid. Finally he sighed and said looks like bids are drying up so I say going once. He looked around and raised his arm again. Rollin held up his bid card and the auctioneer smiled. Have a bid of $2700. Anyone want to raise the bid and win this top notch bull to keep his herd strong? He chattered on for a few minutes and finally got a bid of $2730. He asked, are there any more bidders out there? Rollin raised his card. The auctioneer grinned. Got a bid of $2750 and raised his arm. Going once. He looked around and finally announced. Sold for $2750 to the fella straight out in front of me with card number 194.

The sale went ahead and Jessica and Tom kept writing down the selling prices and paid attention to the sales lingo and what was going on around them. Jessica's brother Trace and his wife arrived and sat down beside her. They chatted between bull sales and caught up on family news.

It was three fifteen when Jessica's bull Number 2 came up for sale and she was paying strict attention. The first bid was at $2300 and slowed after passing $2600. Jessica held up her card at $2700. The auctioneer smiled. A new bidder and listen up gentlemen, the bidder is a lady. Jessica could tell there were two men both bidding against her. She kept bidding and got the bull for $3025. The auctioneer grinned and said loudly, "Thank you, ma'am, for buying this fine looking bull."

On Thursday they bought the other three bulls they wanted and Rollin arranged for a trucker to haul the five bulls to the farm. Friday morning Jessica and Tom went to the office with the sales sheets and paid the total bill with a check for $13,725.00. When the cattle hauler pulled out of the Fair Grounds, Rollin was right behind him with his F250 and passengers.

On the way home, Rollin announced he was going to sell one of the older bulls in the herd immediately before the breeding season began and let the five new bulls pick up their share of the cow herd.

* * *

Besides visiting the plants to talk to the employees and discuss business, she spent most of her time on financials, purchasing of large orders, the farm, and the family's investment trust where she was deeply involved in strategy. Her involvement had made a substantial increase in the annual income and she watched closely for security, particularly in the stock portfolios assets. She developed a strong liking for dividends and DRIPs. There were two large changes in her lifestyle; she now had time to take holidays and a tutor to teach her Portuguese. After several months of lessons and being yelled at by the tutor, she was able to read and converse in the new language and was rapidly improving.

Easter was coming and Jessica kept phoning her father until finally he and mother agreed to accompany her and the boys to Florida for a holiday. Her father was still complaining the trip would cost too much and be a waste of money and she had been tempted to tell him what her assets were worth. She smiled softly. Casper had always told her not to talk about their worth which had reached almost two billion dollars and still grew rapidly year over year. Her sons also knew not to talk about money or assets. Now, she was driving to Chicago to convince her sons taking their grandparents on a holiday was a good idea. It was Saturday, Shirley was traveling with her, and they planned to stay overnight at a hotel near the boarding school.

Mrs. Sparks flew to Europe with Jessica on a plant tour and they were gone for ten days in February, starting at Lisbon for business and sightseeing before doing the same in Vienna, Austria. They took pictures of everything, looked at historical old buildings, toured museums and art galleries, brought home piles of tourist brochures, and tried all the different foods. Both were happy when the airplane landed in Chicago and they anticipated the drive home. Leaving the customs area of the airport, Mrs. Sparks was quick to see two tall Blakerly men standing at the railing waiting on them. She stopped and waited for Jessica. "I do believe there is a committee here to greet you."

Jessica looked around and laughed as she spotted her sons hurrying around the end of the railing. The boys took possession of the suitcases after receiving hugs from their mother. Jeffery asked, "Do you ladies have time to eat dinner with us and stay overnight?" Mrs. Sparks phoned her husband and told him she was back in Chicago and after a meeting tonight, they planned to drive home in the morning. During the dinner meeting, Jessica informed her sons that the Lisbon plant was running at capacity and planning had to get underway on building a second plant. She discussed with them the several approaches which might solve the problem and informed them she planned to ask Ned Ambrose to appoint her sons as members of the committee. The boys had never told her, still she knew from talking to the principal, they were both taking Portuguese classes. Nothing was said and she smiled to herself. There just might be more Casper in her boys than she had expected.

Bit by bit, the year-end financials were coming to her for study and the two-year revision of the Davenport Machinery catalogue was underway. Once again, it would be in full color. She settled herself in at the office to study the paper coming to her. While meeting with Ron Smith, VP of Financial, she asked him to store up money in the company's Portuguese bank account to pay for a new plant.

*   *   *

Jessica Marie Hornsbee had put together a formidable team of executives at Davenport Machinery Inc. and she kept her fingers on the details of production and finances and chaired the management meetings. She knew the names of all the managers everywhere in the operations and many of the production staff. Blakerly Farms was a large operation now with many acres of grain, hay, and pastureland and hundreds of head of purebred Black Angus cattle. She knew all the people by their first names and spent time out on both the grain and cattle operations. Every year, she drove tractor to help seed crops, pulled a hay baler, drove a grain truck, and combined during harvest. When she was home, she rode every week with Rollin McPherson to check the cattle, particularly when the cows were calving. Despite all her wealth, she still preferred Big Joe's Deli for food. Since she and her sons had buried her husband, all the great places they had gone to eat and celebrate had lost their appeal to her and she rarely went to any of them except for occasions when she was entertaining members of the family. She was in her forties now and her oldest son, Jeffery, would graduate from university this coming spring with his mechanical engineering degree. Jessica's face lit up with a smile as she recalled the twentieth birthday last fall when Jeffery had come home to celebrate. She remembered standing in the open house doorway watching a beautiful young woman coming toward her, lugging her own suitcase. As always, Shirley was out to greet the boys and they grabbed her and swung her around in a circle. Karl had exited the backseat and introduced the two women and Shirley hugged the girl as she welcomed her. Jessica stood frozen, holding the house door open, feeling overcome by the surprise she felt at Jeffery bringing a girl home with no forewarning, not even a hint. Karl got to her first and whispered, "Close your mouth, Mother; she is a very nice lady." Karl laughed and walked on past her. The words woke Jessica up and she had a few seconds to orient herself. Stepping out onto the veranda, the screen door closed behind her as she came out to greet the guest. "Hi, my name is Jessica Blakerly, welcome to our farm."

Jeffery took over saying, "Mother, meet Angelina Valoshin who is studying mechanical engineering in my class at university."

"What a lovely name you have, Angelina. I have always liked it. Please leave your suitcase here and the men can take it up to your room. Let's go to the kitchen and get ourselves something warm to drink." The two ladies disappeared inside the house and Jeffery laughed softly to himself as he picked up Angelina's suitcase and took it up the stairs to one of the guestrooms. It was a damp, blustery early winter weekend for celebrating Jeffery's twentieth. The two boys took Angelina out in a F150 to tour the farm, look at the cattle, machinery, and all the buildings. Saturday night, Jessica took everyone out for Italian food at a restaurant she and Casper had favored and Sunday afternoon, the three students drove back to university. Since that birthday weekend, every time Jeffery came home to visit, Angelina came with him, the only exception being at Christmas when she was clerking in her father's pharmacy during the holiday rush. Jessica now accepted that there would be a wedding coming and it pleased her. On the other hand, Karl, foxy little devil he was, gave no hint of what he was doing. She knew nothing of his activities but suspected he was out among the ladies gaining experience in ways she wouldn't approve of.

Jessica shook her head to clear her thoughts and told herself, *'I have at least twenty years and maybe thirty ahead of me and the new generation is nearly ready to take over, and rightly so. Over the next two or three years, I must see that they are making the decisions. Okay, that has been decided and I will back off but by damn I am going to remain as Chairman of the Board of Directors and those two young twerps had better give me grandchildren to spoil.'*

* * *

Both of her sons graduated as mechanical engineers and placed high in the list of grades. The biggest surprise was that the youngest, Karl Adrian Blakerly, rated the highest marks of the two. Jessica didn't comment on this fact but secretly credited it to Jeffery Edward always having a girlfriend to eat into his study time. She knew she might be totally wrong since she had no idea what Karl was doing in the social scene and he wasn't one to talk. If he had girlfriends while being a student, he never told her and his brother remained silent. They were not only very close in age but were also each other's best friends. She watched closely as her two sons worked through apprenticeship in both farming and the manufacturing, trading off each year, until both were well prepared in the basics. After three years of training, her sons informed her they were going to enroll at Ambrose University to obtain MBA degrees. Jessica's sons were twenty-three years old and Jeffery and his long-time girlfriend decided to get married in the coming August before classes opened at Ambrose. Jessica immediately sat her two sons down for a meeting to discuss housing for them in the future. Both sons told her they wanted to live on the farm. Well, that simplified locations. Jessica asked, "How large a house do you want?"

Jeffery replied, "I don't think we need houses as large as this one you live in. Angelina and I want to have children but probably two would be enough. Seems to me the house should have four bedrooms and a couple of bathrooms. A large kitchen which is where most farm families put in time to eat and talk."

Jessica turned her head and asked Karl, "What do you think about Jeffery's suggestion?"

"Sound okay to me. I think there should be an office where we can keep track of the paper coming our way. There should be a full basement under the house and a two car garage. It would be wise to put a mudroom on to help keep the kitchen clean."

Jessica was writing down what the boys were saying. "Okay, I will phone our architect and have him sketch out suggestions for us to look at. You men better think about this so you are ready. Jeffery, it might be wise for you to get input from Angelina. You don't want to forget that your wives will spend most of their lives in the house so they should have things the way they like. Which reminds me, Karl, when are you going to bring a lady home to meet your mother?"

"I have no idea, Mother. I work all the time and it is Jeffery who has time to circulate around." All three of them laughed.

* * *

It was only a week later when a letter arrived addressed to Karl Blakerly. Jessica noticed there was a lady's name and address on the envelope. She set her son's letter aside on the kitchen table. Karl arrived home from the Davenport plant at 5:15 and found the letter as soon as he walked into the kitchen. His face reddened somewhat as he picked up the letter and slipped it into one of his pockets. Karl hurried off to his bedroom to change his clothes and sat on the bed to look at the letter. When he opened the envelope, there was a handwritten letter and a picture of a young woman with a small youngster. He starred at the picture of his former girlfriend, amazed at how good looking she was. He and Jackeline had been very serious about each other and now, looking at her picture, he felt all the old feelings coming back. They had gotten into a heated argument about something, he couldn't really remember what it was, and broke up just before he finished his Mechanical Engineering courses and left the university. Often, he had thought about Jackeline in the time since but had never gotten up his courage to approach her about making up. His eyes moved to look at the little boy in the picture and immediately assumed that Jackeline was married and this was her son. He felt a terrible pain through his whole body at the thought. Finally, he laid the picture down and opened the letter written in pencil on lined school paper.

Dear Karl: Today I ran into Angelina at the grocery store and we talked. She mentioned she and Jeffery were going to be married in August. I am so happy for her. My only regret is that it is not you and I getting married. She told me you were living at the farm and as far as she knew, you didn't have any girlfriends. Hearing the news caused my heart to almost burst with hope that you and I might heal our wounds and be reunited. In the picture I am enclosing there is a little boy, just coming toward his third birthday.

400

If you look closely at him, you will realize he looks much like his father. If you could stand being near me again, we would welcome you to little Karl's third birthday on December 18th here at my parents' home. He often asks why he does not have a father like all the other children living around him. I hope all is well with you and you are healthy. Best wishes from Jackeline.

Karl put the letter down and picked up the picture. He stood up and walked to the dresser and picked up his magnifying glass and studied the little boy carefully. The boy was stocky and sturdy looking just like Karl was and his little face seemed familiar. He switched his eyes to look at himself in the dresser mirror. Well, there were some twenty years' difference in age but he saw similarities. Yes, it could very well be the boy was his son. Returning to the bed, he sat and reread the letter. In his mind, he saw two main themes, one that Jackeline wanted to get back together with him and secondly that she was concerned about their son. Karl put the letter and picture back in the envelope and went downstairs. He said hello to the ladies as he passed through the kitchen and went to find Jeffery. The Ford F150 that Jeffery drove was parked near the shop and he headed that way. When he opened the door and walked into the shop Jeffery was there talking to two of the men.

Jeffery must have read something from Karl's face because he turned to the two men and said, "You fellas might as well go on home and I will see you in the morning." One of the men patted Jeffery on the shoulder and the other greeted Karl.

"Good to see you, fellas, I hope old Jeffery is not being too hard to get along with." Everyone laughed and the two men left the shop. Karl pulled the letter out of his pocket and handed it to his brother. "Got this letter today, please read it and tell me what you think."

Jeffery read the letter and his eyes moved to look at his brother. His mouth opened and no words came out. He walked over

401

to hold the picture under the work light at the bench and studied it for several minutes. He opened the letter again and read it out loud, watching Karl as he recited the words. There seemed to be much more meaning in the words hearing them out loud. "Brother, this letter says to me that Jackeline is still in love with you and by damn the little fella sure does look like he is related to you. Now, the big question is, what do you want to do about this?"

"We had an argument and for three years I haven't been able to forget her. I want to phone her and find out when I can drive up there to talk to them."

Jeffery pointed. "There's a phone right over there, go and phone her. You want me to leave you here by yourself?"

Karl laughed nervously. "No, you stay in case my courage fails me." Karl picked up the phone and dialed. The phone rang three times before it was answered.

"Good afternoon, this is the Winter home."

"Jackeline, this is Karl calling. I got your letter."

"Oh, Karl, I am so happy you phoned. I have come close to phoning you many times and each time I welched out."

"I didn't know you were going to have a baby when we had our argument."

Jackeline laughed. "I didn't know either and when I found out I was pregnant, you were gone and I was all confused. I wanted to phone you but didn't have the courage to do so. You have been a father for almost three years now."

"Can I come to see you and our son?"

"Yes, oh yes, come whenever you want to. Tomorrow would be great or any day when you can leave the farm."

"I will leave in the morning and be there by noon…" Jeffery eased himself out the door and quietly closed it. He wasn't needed and he didn't want to be prying into his brother's business.

Jeffery walked into the house and greeted the two ladies before going into the bathroom and washing up. He came out and sat down at his usual place at the table. Shirley looked at him and asked, "Where did you leave your brother?"

"He is out in the shop, should be along in a few minutes."

The food for dinner was on the kitchen table and Jeffery, Jessica, and Shirley were all seated waiting for Karl. When he arrived, he looked happy. His mother was amazed and decided to rebuke him by saying, "Our food is getting cold while we wait on you to arrive, Karl. Come and sit down."

"Sorry about being late, Grandma. You should have gone ahead and started eating." Karl was pulling out his chair from the table when what he had said registered on his mother. Jessica set down her fork and stared at Karl, who was grinning at her. She turned her head to look at Jeffery and he was smiling.

Jeffery spoke right up. "We have been worrying about you the past two or three years. You seemed to be slipping. Guess being a grandma is hard on a woman."

Jessica glared at her sons. "What is this foolishness you boys are spouting on about?" She banged the table with her hand. "Of course I want to be a grandma, but what kind of foolish joke are you two men trying to pull on me?"

Jeffery was laughing softly and that riled his mother. She glared at him for a moment and then turned her head to look at Karl. He was also laughing. As she watched, Karl put his hand in a pocket and pulled out an envelope which he held out to her. Jessica stared at his hand for a second before reaching out and taking the envelope from him. The two boys and Shirley watched as she pulled the letter out of the envelope and a picture fell to her dinner plate. Jessica leaned over and studied the photo before saying, "He is a good looking little boy."

Karl laughed and announced, "His name is Karl and he is your grandson." The shock she felt showed on her face. Her eyes enlarged as she stared at Karl who continued, "He will be three years old on December 18th."

The two boys could see their mother was in shock. Her face grew pale and she sputtered, trying to talk. "Grandson…Why didn't you tell…Oh my, this is wonderful news. I have a grandson. Karl, why didn't you tell me?"

"I didn't know, Mother, until this letter arrived today. Please take the time to read the letter, afterward you will understand. Read it out loud so all of us can hear what Jackeline is saying." She read the letter out loud twice and everyone listened. Karl commented, "Jackeline is saying two things; she would still like to get married and secondly she wants Karl to have his father." Jessica jumped to her feet and paced around the kitchen. She stopped to hug Karl and kissed his cheek, and kept walking. Her arms were waving.

"A grandson, I have a grandson. Karl, we must get in the Expedition and drive up there to see him. What does he need that we can get for him? Oh, this is so exciting, all these years I have waited. It would be so wonderful if Casper were still alive; he would be even more excited than I am. When can we go, Karl? I can be free in the morning."

Karl was looking at his brother and he frowned. Jeffery knew what he was worried about so he spoke up. "Seems to me Karl should phone Jackeline and discuss the arrangements and how many people she thinks would be appropriate."

Jessica suddenly realized she was being intrusive in Karl's affairs. This was his family and she had no right to be interfering, but it was so exciting, she had dreamed of the time when grandchildren would arrive and now the first one was here. "Of course you are right, Jeffery. I apologize for jumping into your affairs, Karl."

"Don't apologize, Mother, you have made me very happy. I was afraid you might not want to acknowledge the little fella. I will phone Jackeline this evening and see how she feels about us coming." All the talking had allowed the food to cool off so Shirley bustled around reheating it in the microwave. The room was mostly quiet while they ate dinner. When everyone had finished, Karl asked, "Before I go to phone Jackeline, please tell me who you would like to have on this trip with me."

Jessica waved her arm around in a circle of the table. "I would like for all four of us to go, if your lady objects, try to get permission for me to go with you. I so badly want to see and hold my grandson. This is the start of a whole new generation of the family."

Karl checked the time on his watch and it was just after seven o'clock. "Thank you, Mother, I will go to the office and phone Jackeline again." They all watched as he walked away before starting to talk again.

* * *

The Ford Expedition had four people in it, along with suitcases when it left the farm at eight a.m. Rollin McPherson had been briefed by the boys and Davenport had received a phone call from Jessica. They had reservations at the hotel Jackeline had recommended and she knew they expected to be there before noon. As usual, Mrs. Sparks had handled making the reservation and telling the hotel what arrangements were necessary. This was an important day for Jessica and Mrs. Sparks wanted everything to be the very best.

Jeffery drove with Karl riding in the passenger seat while Jessica and Shirley rode in the second seat and were chatting gaily. When the Blakerly's arrived at the hotel, a porter stepped out to take over the Ford Expedition and luggage and told them to go into

405

the hotel. It was a large reception area but Karl's eyes found Jackeline as soon as she stood up from where she was seated. He went right to her and swung her in a circle as he hugged her and started the introductions. "Jackeline say hello to my mother, Mrs. Jessica Blakerly." The two ladies shook hands and hugged. "This other lady is Shirley Shrapnel, who is responsible for keeping us boys on track." The ladies shook hands. "This old coyote you know, Jeffery Blakerly."

"Hi Jeffery, Angelina tells me she is going to marry you and make you toe the line." Jeffery grinned and grabbed her for a hug.

Karl looked at his mother and winked one eye before turning to Jackeline and grabbing her hand. He knelt on his right knee and looked up at her, "Jackeline, will you marry me?"

Jackeline's face turned beat red and she stammered for a second before asking, "Why do you want to marry me?"

"Because I love you and have for four years and secondly because you are the mother of my son."

Her face was returning to normal. "Thank you, Karl. I would be pleased to marry you. You might wish to have a Paternity Test done to insure you are little Karl's father. I can guarantee you are, but I want you to be happy." Karl jumped to his feet and kissed her along with a big hug. When he let her go, all the others took turns congratulating her. Jackeline looked at Jessica and told her, "I know you are anxious to see your grandson but he is sleeping right now and normally will sleep until around two p.m. I thought we might have a bite to eat here before we go to the house."

Shirley went to the desk to check on the reservation while the rest went into the dining room. It was an exciting day for everyone, and nobody wanted very much to eat. They were putting in time until they could go to Jackeline Winter's home to meet Karl Blakerly, Junior.

Chapter 29

Jackeline's mother was the only person in the house when they arrived, and introductions were made. Mrs. Winter was a quiet, pleasant woman who looked like an older sister of Jackeline's and Jessica felt sure the two women could wear each other clothing. There might be a trace of grey in Mrs. Winters brown hair and otherwise, there was very little difference between the two women. Mrs. Winter's first name was Lois and she insisted the visitors use her first name. A large coffeepot was boiling on the stove and it smelled good. Everyone accepted a cup of coffee and there was cream and sugar on the kitchen table. The kitchen was small compared to the ones in the farmhouses; nevertheless, everyone found a seat around the table. The kitchen clock was showing 1:52 when Lois spoke to Jessica. "Would you care to accompany me to check on Karl Junior?"

Jessica came out of her chair immediately and the two women walked down the hallway. Jackeline was holding one of Karl's large hands. In a soft voice, she said, "My mother loves little Karl dearly, it will be difficult for her to see him move away."

Karl nodded his head. "New houses are being built for Jeff and me and your parents will be welcome to visit whenever they wish. There is lots of room out on the farm for everyone. I am sure you will be missing your parents and we will try to visit often."

"Thank you, Karl. I can hear little Karl greeting his grandmother and hopefully getting to know her." They waited and time seemed to drag by slowly before they heard the women coming along the hall. Karl leaned over and took his shoes off and was standing up when little Karl arrived. Jackeline walked over and took Karl Junior in her arms and received a hug around her neck before the little head turned to look at everyone.

Father Karl had seated himself crossed-legged on the kitchen floor and he had his son's favorite red truck on the floor in front of him. Little Karl looked down at the large man sitting on the floor, then back at the three people sitting at the table, before his head came back and he reached out one arm, telling his mother, "Truck."

Jackeline leaned down and set her son on the floor so he could walk to the truck. After studying the large man, he slowly walked two steps to the truck and pushed it as his mother settled on the floor beside him. His dad was smiling and after a few minutes, Little Karl crawled closer and pushed the truck into one of his dad's large feet. Dad grabbed the foot saying ouch as he laughed. A moment later, the truck hit the foot again and the game was under-way. A few minutes later, Jackeline moved over and sat right up beside Karl. This changed the game and their son looked at them for a minute before the truck rammed the foot again. Little Karl was unhappy with his mother sitting close to the large man and he stood up and forced his way between them. His mother smiled and slowly moved away until there was room enough for their son to sit between them and drive the truck. When he looked up at her, she pointed to herself and said, "Mommy." She pointed at Karl and said, "Daddy."

Little Karl turned his head and looked at the stranger who was his dad. Then, he pointed at the red truck and said, "Truck." Everyone laughed and clapped, and the little boy did the same.

Jessica was entranced as she sat and watched her grandson slowly become acquainted with his father. The little tyke was steady on his feet and he could talk, although so far he had mainly talked about trucks. A half hour or so later, Karl Junior pushed on his father's chest until the large man slowly lay down on his back. Karl Junior sat down on his father's right hip and looked at his mother. She smiled at him, giving him courage, and slowly he went back until he was lying across his dad. His little hand came up and one finger pointed at the light in the center of the ceiling. "Light, Mommy, look light."

Jackeline moved close to the father and lay down on her back. She pointed up, "Yes, Karl it is the kitchen light, very nice." They could hear sounds coming from the stove and Jackeline knew her mother was preparing food for her son. She asked, "Are you ready for lunch, Karl?"

Little Karl patted his stomach and sat up. He stood up and walked across the kitchen to his chair. His mother followed him and put a bib on him and tied it behind his neck before lifting him into the chair. She made space at the table beside Karl's chair and moved the highchair up to the table. Jackeline filled his little cup with milk and handed it to him. He stuck the spout in his mouth and had a drink. When he set it down, it fell on its side and his mother set the cup up on its bottom. Lois came with his bowl which had a mixture of potatoes, small pieces of beef, and chopped up carrots. Little Karl ignored the plastic baby spoon and picked up a piece of carrot and popped it into his mouth. As he chewed, he looked at his mother on the left side and then his father on the other. Another piece of carrot went into his mouth and as he chewed he picked up another and held it out toward his dad. Karl leaned down with an open mouth and accepted the donation. He made an act out of chewing the carrot and smiled at his son. All the adults were smiling. When the eating was over, Lois came with a washcloth and cleaned Little Karl's face and hands and Jackeline removed the bib which now needed to visit the washing machine.

The family and guests moved to the living room. Karl and Jackeline sat together on a love-seat while the grandmothers were together on a sofa. Little Karl was playing on the rug and they watched as Grandmother Lois picked up a children's book and showed it to her grandson. He immediately walked to the sofa and climbed up to sit between the two grandmothers. The book had hard covers and was quite large with many pictures and print in large letters. Lois handed the book to Jessica who opened it and began to read. Little Karl occupied himself pointing at the pictures as he listened. After listening for a few minutes, Karl turned to Jackeline and suggested, "We need to go to a jewelery store and buy rings for you. Do you know a good one?"

She smiled at him. "Well, Angelina told me where they purchased her rings, so we could go there."

Karl looked at his watch. "It is four o'clock, could we go right now?"

"Don't see why not, are you going to ask Jeffery to come with us?"

"Certainly, just watch. Jeff, we want to go and look at rings for Jackeline, will you come with us?"

He nodded and stood up. "Expect these three ladies can look after Mr. Blakerly without my help." He headed for the door with Karl and Jackeline following. They waved goodbye and went out to the Expedition. In the store, Jeffery led them right to the part of the counter that had the upscale rings. The clerk who had sold rings to Jeffery recognized him and hurried to serve him in whatever he wanted. It wasn't every day that people who could afford the more expensive items came in and he was hopeful. Two hours later, they left the store with Jackeline wearing a large engagement ring and Karl had the wedding ring in the case in his suit coat pocket. The two men had smiled at each other when Jackeline protested that the cost of the rings was too high and they should choose something else. Jeffery had told Karl what the rings he bought had cost and Karl had more than enough cash in his pocket. When the clerk asked how he was going to pay, Karl reached into a pants pocket and his hand came out with a large wad of money and he peeled off thousand dollar bills until he had covered the price. They admired the engagement ring while they waited for the change.

Next morning, the happy couple along with the two grand-mothers went to talk to the minister at their church. In this instance, Jackeline was firm in her opinion. She wanted a small wedding with just the two families in attendance. Jessica knew her relatives would be disappointed but this wasn't their affair. If Karl and Jackeline wanted a small wedding, it was just fine with her. The wedding was set for the middle of June, which gave them a month to get ready and more important, to have the construction company get Karl's new house completed. Jessica promised herself she would demand it be ready, painted, and furnished even if they had to work two shifts each day. The landscaping could get done during the summer. Also Jeffery's house must be done before his wedding scheduled to be held in August.

Jessica paced back and forth around the long porch which circled her house, thinking about the future. When the summer was over her immediate family would have grown to seven and maybe in time those youngsters would grow it to ten. Now that would be a real good number. Finally she sat down in a wicker chair with soft cushions from where she could look out across the farmyard and see what the construction company was doing. The past few weeks had been very busy and slowly her eyes closed and she slept. A few minutes later, Shirley Shrapnel came with a lightweight quilt and placed it over Jessica. That was the first time she had ever known Jessica to relax during the day and not worry about business.

About the Author

Arthur C. Eastly

Arthur C. Eastly, a third-generation Albertan, grew up listening to frontier stories of the west told by his grandparents and great uncles who came from Iowa and Dakota Territory in 1901 to homestead and establish farms. He loves to relate stories of the early days of the west—stories of self-reliance, determination and the courage to overcome danger and hardship, to survive; and occasionally prosper.

Other Books by the Author
(In order of publication)

Black Arrow: A Western Novel in

the Best Tradition

Willow Flower: A Black Arrow Novel

Bamford Luck: A Modern Western Novel

in Idaho

Lady Prodigy: A Contemporary

Black Arrow Novel

Palardy: One Woman's Real Estate Success

Big Creek Ranch: A Bob Bamford Story

Savage Wolf: Western Ranchers Settling
1860s Colorado

AND NOW:

DAVENPORT MACHINERY

**Using Intelligence, Grit, and Hard Work to
Build an Empire**